By Ken Goddard from
Tom Doherty Associates

Prey
Wildfire
Balefire
Cheater

CHEATER

◆

KEN GODDARD

TOR®

A TOM DOHERTY ASSOCIATES BOOK
NEW YORK

CHEATER

Cover art by Donato

A Tor Book
Published by Tom Doherty Associates, Inc.
175 Fifth Avenue
New York, NY 10010

Tor Books on the World Wide Web:
http://www.tor.com

Tor® is a registered trademark of Tom Doherty Associates, Inc.

ISBN: 0-812-55388-8
Library of Congress Card Catalog Number: 95-53923

First edition: May 1996
First mass market edition: August 1997

Printed in the United States of America

0 9 8 7 6 5 4 3 2 1

This book is dedicated to the memory of
San Bernardino County Sheriff's Lieutenant Al Stewart and
DEA Technical Agent Henry Klein.

ACKNOWLEDGMENTS

My sincere thanks to Bob and Linda, who were kind enough to lend me their basement so that I could spend the evenings and weekends dreaming up assorted acts of violence and mayhem instead of sitting in a hotel room and brooding about temporary duty assignments to Washington, DC; and to Ed Breslin, who has an eye for wayward plots, and a truly nice touch with the editorial pen.

A CAUTIONARY NOTE

As far as I am aware, the appointed delegates to the World Trade Organization, CITES, and the related Non-Government Organizations of CITES have never come together in Washington, DC, for the purpose of planning so much as a simple meal, much less the economic downfall of member nations. There has never been, to my knowledge, an environmental group named *Terre-Mère Vert*, or a CIA covert operation entitled Mother Earth Green. And I have no idea how the field operatives and lab staff of the CIA's Science and Technology Division actually go about their daily routines, mostly because the management is understandably reluctant to allow a fiction writer to poke around in their crime lab benches and closets. Accordingly, the plot, the characters, and the interrelated conspiracies within this book are simply the product of my occasionally warped imagination, and a useful stage upon which I can release my demented burglar.

However, lest my readers become a little too complacent in the safety and security of their darkened living rooms and bedrooms: the crawl space scenes are most assuredly real.

"For nothing can seem foul to those that win."

—WILLIAM SHAKESPEARE (1564–1616)
KING HENRY, IN *KING HENRY IV*,
PT. 1, ACT 5, SCENE 1

"If he who breaks the law is not punished,
he who obeys it is cheated."

—THOMAS SZASZ
THE SECOND SIN, "PUNISHMENT" (1973)

Excerpts from the Field Notebook of Fairfax County Police Detective Henry Culver

INTERPOL:

France:

Lt. Col. Charles L'Que   Delegate to WTO/CITES Meeting

Germany:

Lt. Col. Karl Kostermann   Delegate to WTO/CITES Meeting

U.S. GOVERNMENT:

Central Intelligence Agency:

<u>Director's Office:</u>

Samuel Nokes   Deputy Director

<u>Directorate of Operations:</u>

Associate Director's Office:

Elliott Parkinson   Associate Director ("Topcastle")

Covert Collection Division:

[*Operation Mother Earth Green*]:

J. Winston Weatherby   Special Assistant ("Forecastle")

Alberto Paz	Senior Field Operative ("Rudder")
Marcus Grey	Field Operative ("Ballast")
Jane Doe	Field Operative ("Figurehead")
Bok Hämmarchov	Contract Agent ("Cutlass")
John Doe	Contract Agent ("Digger")

Covert Action Division:

| John Kregg | Field Operative |

Directorate of Science and Technology:

Associate Director's Office:

| Arthur Traynor | Associate Director |

Electronics Laboratory:

| R.C. Cohen | Electronics Specialist |

STATE OF VIRGINIA:

Courts:

| Harold Mauser | Judge |

FAIRFAX COUNTY, VIRGINIA:

Police Department:

Technical Services Bureau:

Crime Laboratory Division:

Theodore Gauss	Crime Lab Director
Henry Culver	Criminalist/Police Officer
Steve Balloch	ID Technician

Emergency Operations Center (EOC):

Sally Henderson   Dispatcher

Criminal Investigations Bureau:

Major Crimes Division (MC):

Jack Bullar   Captain/Commander, MC
Morris Markham Craven   Lieutenant/Dep.
                         Commander, MC
John Russelli   Detective-Sergeant,
                         Burglary Unit
Al Stewart   Detective-Sergeant,
                         Homicide Unit
Bradford Carpenter   Detective, Homicide Unit

Patrol Bureau:

Fair Oaks Station (District 8):

Mike Donahugh   Captain/Station Commander
Pete Christey   Lieutenant/Watch
                         Commander
Jack Hattabaugh   Patrol Sergeant
Tess Beasley   Patrol Officer
Billy Joe Moorestead   Patrol Officer
Vinny Delacroix   Patrol Officer
Mike Quinzio   CSI Officer

Office of the Chief:

Internal Affairs Division (IA):

Harold Mays   Captain/Commander, IA

District Attorney's Office:

Mike Toledano   Deputy District Attorney

Coroner's Office:

Jim Waldrip   Pathologist

Mental Health Services:

Dr. Benjamin Scholtz   Psychologist

FRIENDS AND FAMILY:

Sharon Russelli	Wife of John Russelli
Michelle Russelli	Daughter of John Russelli
Martine Russelli	Daughter of John Russelli
Paul Radlick	Defense Attorney
Doreen Radlick	Wife of Paul Radlick

BURGLARS AND SNITCHES:

Molly Hunsacker	Burglar
Bobby Morgan	Burglar
Otis Lawnhart	Burglar
Pogo Waters	Snitch

VICTIMS:

Karl Kostermann	Burglary/Homicide Victim
Ingrid Kostermann	Burglary/Homicide Victim
Kostermann children	Burglary/Homicide Victims
Kathy Harmon	Burglary Victim
Lisa	Niece of Kathy Harmon
Teresa Hardy	Burglary Victim
Nichole L'Que	Burglary Victim
Michel L'Que	Burglary/Assault Victim

Chapter One

Saturday, November 28, 1845 hours

He came in through the crawl space. Slowly and methodically pulling himself through the cool, humid, musty, and ever-confining darkness. Grasping at the rough concrete footings with his callused bare hands. Scraping his chest against the supporting crossbeams and his back along the rough-textured rubble. Brushing his face against the low, cobweb-covered drainpipes. Pausing every few feet to listen.

And smiling—a thin, distant, and chilling smile—all the way.

Something moved in the darkness behind his head, making a faint rustling sound as it cautiously sought a better view of the intruder, but he ignored it. He knew all the creatures that inhabited the dark crevices under houses; knew them intimately. He also knew that in this place, at this time of the night, he was the predator to be feared. The creature to be avoided at all costs.

The crawl space in this particular house was more confining than most. So narrow in some spots that he had to turn his head sideways and empty his lungs to work himself under one of the thick, splintery, and dusty beams. So dark and disorienting in others that it took him almost a half hour to find the wires and the entry point he had chosen.

Then he started to work.

He used a tiny, battery-powered circular saw, adjusting the depth of the thin, exposed blade to three-quarters of an inch, and then timing his cuts through the partially rotted plywood flooring to coincide with the periodic concealing noises of the nearby heat pump. He paused frequently to let the blade cool, using his bare fingertips to judge the remaining distances.

He could have used the small penlight in his jacket pocket; but in his perverse way of thinking, that would have been cheating. And he didn't want to cheat.

Not on this one.

The work was cold, difficult, and demanding, and yet he savored every claustrophobic moment; glorifying in the almost-hallucinatory feeling of being trapped beneath a huge, all-encompassing mass. A sensation that seemed to intensify every echoing noise and magnify every movement of his body.

He paused for a moment to take in a few deep breaths, feeling his expanding chest muscles press up against one of the rough support beams, and then immediately went back to work. He was only vaguely aware of the fine sawdust particles striking against his face, and the condensation of warm breath against the back of his hands, as he continued to cut through the laminated wood barrier with the whirring blade.

He paused again, halfway through, to install the pair of thick, carefully oiled brass hinges and a latch, using another miniaturized power tool to drill the holes and then drive the stubby screws. Then he went back to his task with a single-mindedness that was characteristic of everything he had ever done in his life.

Fifty-two minutes, two batteries, and one blade change later, he completed the last of the four cuts. Sliding his bracing knees out of the way and then inching himself sideways, he allowed the hinged, twenty-four-by-thirty-inch piece of mildewed plywood to fall free. The resulting trapdoor swung noiselessly back and forth, with the tip of the latch mechanism just barely brushing against the rough dirt floor.

Then he reached for the terribly sharp razor knife.

The tantalizing part, from his viewpoint, was that he didn't have to enter the house this way. There were many other—and far easier—methods that he could have used that would never be detected, such as picking the front door locks with his spring steel tools, or tapping the latch on the sliding glass door, or carefully removing one of the heavy aluminum storm windows out of the wall.

There were many other ways, but he didn't want to take the easy, undetectable path on this one.

He wanted the effect.

The thin razor edge made three smooth, easy cuts through the thick padding, allowing the loose foam sheet to drop noiselessly against the hinged plywood. Three more cuts at a slightly inward angle, and then he allowed the carpet flap to slowly drop down against the padded trapdoor.

The crawl space was immediately filled with a faint, diffuse light that forced him to blink until his irises readjusted to the new semidarkness. Then, ever so cautiously, he raised his head until his pale blue eyes were just barely visible above the floor line.

Nothing.

Moving quickly now, he levered himself up through the relatively large hole and hurried over to a small plastic box mounted on the wall opposite the front door. It took him less than two minutes, using a fine-tipped screwdriver and a pair of needle-nose pliers, to temporarily disable the alarm.

He paused for a brief moment to check his watch. Then, gliding the soles of his shoes over the carpet surface, he began moving toward the stairs.

He was upstairs, in the master bedroom closet, moving the dial slowly and waiting for the incredibly sensitive acoustical device he had designed and built himself to detect the spring release of the final tumbler pin through a half inch of tempered steel, when a loud "DING!" jarred at his nerves.

He located the source of the noise on top of a small cabinet in the adjoining den. It appeared to be an extremely complicated version of a fax machine, complete with a monitor display screen that read:

GOOD EVENING, HERR KOSTERMANN
ARE YOU PREPARED TO RECEIVE?

He started to turn away, to go back to the potentially far more interesting floor safe in the master bedroom closet, when the machine emitted another loud, demanding "DING!" which, in turn, caused a dog in the downstairs garage to start barking . . . which was quickly followed by the higher-pitched yapping of several smaller dogs.

The barking and yapping slowly died out, but then started up again immediately when the machine emitted yet another loud, penetrating "DING!"

Grimacing in irritation, he located the thin operations manual in a plastic sleeve attached to the side of the machine, took a small red-lensed penlight out of his jacket pocket, and began to read. When he got to the part on "suggestions for selecting and changing your personal password," he quickly thumbed through the manual, and then smiled when he got to the back inside page. There were four very similar hand-printed character sequences, three of which had been lined out.

Shaking his head in amusement, he quickly pressed the "Y" and enter keys. The monitor responded with:

PLEASE ENTER YOUR PERSONAL PASSWORD

Referring to the back inside page of the manual, he carefully typed in:

SCHWARZ##WALD

It took the machine almost a full minute to churn out the first page, the noise of which set the dogs into another extended period of barking. Intrigued by the format and header information, and the possible implications of why a resident of Fairfax County, Virginia, might be in possession of a fax machine equipped with a scrambling/descrambling device, he waited patiently for the next four pages to drop into the receiving box. Then he sat down to read.

The barking and yapping continued.

Fourteen minutes later, he selected a baseball bat from what appeared to be the room of a ten-year-old boy, went downstairs, and proceeded to silence all of the dogs with the exception of one quick-reflexed pup that managed to avoid the full impact of the killing blow and then stay conscious long enough to crawl back into the recesses of a large, heavy-gage wire cage where it couldn't be easily reached.

He was in the process of dealing with that last tenacious pup, setting the stage in a manner that appealed to his warped and malicious sense of humor, when he heard the car doors slam in the driveway.

Pausing only a brief moment to retrieve the blood-splattered fax pages from the garage floor, he moved quickly back into the carpeted den; hurried around to the darkened corner behind the L-shaped couch and a large potted plant; lowered himself down through the trapdoor into the crawl space; carefully pushed the carpet, the padding, and the hinged plywood back into place; and finally secured the latch.

Then, having effectively concealed himself from all but the sharpest of prying eyes, he dropped his head back down onto the rough-textured ground and lay still in the cold, quiet, cobwebby darkness.

Like a trapdoor spider, waiting with inhuman patience for its unwitting prey to arrive.

Chapter Two

Sunday, November 29, 2030 hours

Henry Culver stood in front of the opened trunk of the un-marked police unit and stared across the yard at the darkened front porch of the seemingly abandoned Kostermann residence.

He was trying to reassure himself that a growing sense of gloom and foreboding was nothing more than a normal human reaction to the late hour, the dense surrounding fog, and the chilling night air. But he also fairly certain that most "normal human beings" wouldn't have considered a late-night visit to an especially bloody and gruesome homicide scene as being an especially cheerful way to spend a winter Sunday evening.

It occurred to the Fairfax County police criminalist to wonder, briefly, what it would be like to be a normal person again.

"Are you sure this is something we *really* need to be doing tonight?" Culver asked his longtime friend and fellow law enforcement officer as he reached into the trunk for his crime scene kit.

"I *told* that goddamned pin-headed Craven something like this was going to happen if we didn't put this guy away," Detective John Russelli muttered to the world at large, seemingly ignoring the question as his dark eyes glistened with barely controlled rage and frustration.

"Russelli, it's not your fault. You tried—"

Russelli shook his head. "No, it *is* my fault. You can't expect a moron like that goddamned Craven to understand something as simple as a progressive sociopath. Everybody knew the guy was going to graduate from animals to people some day. I'm the one who should've realized the miserable little fuck would probably go after kids next." The hulking detective was breathing heavily, the cold air turning his breath into huge billowing clouds as he reached into the trunk for his canvas kit bag and a heavy-duty flashlight.

Oh yeah, that's right. The kids. Culver nodded in sudden understanding as he closed the trunk and followed Russelli up to the porch, trying to recall the details of the initial scene report. *How old had the Kostermann girls been? Twelve, fourteen? About the same age as Michelle and Martine. Christ, Russelli, no wonder you're acting like a caged mother grizzly tonight.*

It wasn't at all unusual for people who knew John Russelli to compare him to any number of fear-inspiring creatures. Possessing the thickly muscled physique of a middle-aged Bigfoot, the sensitivity of a professional embalmer, and the general demeanor of a foraging crocodile, most suspects, citizens, and even a goodly number of his fellow cops tended to give Russelli a wide berth whenever possible. In point of fact, the oversize detective was widely regarded as being precisely the type of intensely focused and unforgiving police investigator who would have likely taken a baton to every single individual—cop, suspect, *and* amateur video photographer alike—at the Rodney King scene.

Given that description, it wasn't surprising at all to learn that Detective John Russelli's known weak spots could be counted on four fingers of one hand. They were, in rough order of influence: his two ever-conniving young daughters, his amazingly gentle and understanding wife, and any particular batch of their homemade chocolate chip cookies. And God help the poor misbegotten soul who made so much as a suspicious move in the direction of any one of them.

Culver stood back as Russelli stuck the flashlight under his left arm, fumbled for the keys, drew back the internal dead bolt, and then broke the seal on the door.

The smell hit both of them immediately. The unmistakable aroma of an aged homicide scene: essence of drying blood, evaporating urine, and exposed intestinal contents intermixed with that indefinably sweet emanation of dead human flesh.

Instantly recognizing and then ignoring the all-too-familiar scent, the two investigators used their flashlights to illuminate the pristine living room. Culver reached over to flip on the switches for the living room lights, to no effect.

"Was the power off when you guys got here?" Culver asked. He hadn't been part of the initial response team.

"Yeah, it was. Looked like somebody screwed around with the main panel," Russelli said, seemingly indifferent to the gloomy darkness as he swept the beam of his flashlight across the door and window frames—one of which was boarded up with a piece of three-quarter-inch plywood. "Never could figure out how to get the lights back on. Finally had to bring in the generators and floodlights."

Culver watched the methodical sweep of Russelli's flashlight beam for a few moments.

"So what are you looking for?" he finally asked.

"Place of entry. We're still trying to figure out how the bastard got in."

"Not the window?" Culver asked, flashing his own beam against the thick piece of plywood that had been woodscrewed into the window frame.

Russelli shook his head. "Nah, that was us. First officer at the scene."

"So who made the call?"

"Some guy Kostermann worked with at the German Embassy who got worried when he didn't respond properly to the receipt of some kind of sensitive fax. Said he drove out to the house to see what was wrong, and then called for help when he spotted the blood through the window."

"Some kind of *sensitive* fax?"

"That's what he said."

"So what's that make Kostermann?" Culver asked after a moment.

"Interpol."

"Ah," Culver responded noncommittally. And then: "Do we know if that's relevant?"

"Not so far."

The beam of Culver's flashlight flickered momentarily into the adjacent family room, where dried blood covered a goodly portion of the light-colored carpeting, and then came back to the window frames and the front door lock.

"I thought our freak's M.O. was popping sliding glass doors or picking door locks."

"That's what we've been assuming until we found this one." Russelli shrugged. "Best guess is that this place turned out to be a harder nut to crack. The sliding glass doors and windows all dead-bolt from the inside, and the front door lock's some kind of Swiss import. Locksmith we called in claims it's damn near impossible to pick without a crowbar."

"So why not take a pass on this one and go after another house?"

"Beats the hell out of me," Russelli admitted.

"But you're *sure* this is our boy's work?" Culver asked skeptically as he moved his flashlight beam back into the family room.

"You want to see the pictures of the dogs?"

"No, that's okay." Culver nodded his head in acknowledgment. "Gauss gave me the general rundown. What about the alarm system?"

"State-of-the-art electronics, which is why we wanted you to come out and take a look. Thought you might have some idea how this bastard managed to get in without—"

They both heard it at the same time: the faint rustling sound of movement.

Instantly, the two flashlight beams flicked off.

The two Fairfax County police investigators stood silently in the middle of the living room, holding their duty revolvers out and ready as they listened intently for another—

The second rustling sound was louder, which made it easier to focus in on the direction.

"In the garage," Russelli whispered, turning his flashlight back on and then holding it out and away from his body as he directed the beam toward the opposite wall.

They went in fast, in three lunging strides, Russelli tearing the door loose from its hinges with a savage shoulder and forearm blow. Then they were inside the garage, positioned back to back, the beams of their flashlights and the barrels of their pistols sweeping in tight unison as their widened eyes and tensed fingers sought a target.

Terrified by the sudden noise, the bloodied pup scrambled noisily back into the depths of the heavy wire cage, whimpering with fear.

The pup's eyes glowed a bright green as both flashlight

beams immediately intersected, revealing bloodied fur around the pup's head, and tiny bared fangs.

"Where'd he come from?" Culver whispered, continuing to sweep the garage with his flashlight, just in case, while Russelli knelt down by the cage door.

"I don't know. I never saw him when we were in here before," Russelli replied. He was down on his knees, trying to retrieve the pup, but his arms weren't long enough, and the terrified young animal backed farther into the cage alternatingly snarling and whimpering in fear. Russelli started to lift the cage up, to slide the pup forward where he could be reached, but Culver put a restraining hand on his arm.

"Why don't we leave him in there for a while," the criminalist suggested. "There's still some water in the bowl. And if we pull him out now, he'll just get in the way. We can finish the search first, and then pick him up afterward. He's survived this long, a few more minutes shouldn't matter."

Russelli hesitated and Culver suddenly smiled, aware that he was one of a very few people in the PD who knew that John Russelli had a fifth weak spot in his otherwise feral heart. "And besides," he added, "you can always use another dog."

"Yeah, that's just what I need," Russelli growled as he staggered back up to a standing position, the stiffness and fatigue evident in his slow movements.

Back in the family room, Culver was examining the large bloodstain in the middle of the carpet in front of the couch. The stain had expanded well beyond the taped outline of a large sprawled figure.

"This where they found Kostermann?" he asked.

"Uh-huh."

"Throat cut?" It wasn't really a question. They could both see the concentrated pooling of dried blood that had spread out evenly from the neck area of the taped outline.

"Yeah. Probably right to left."

The injured pup started barking plaintively in the garage, but both investigators ignored it. "Looks like he got caught from behind," Culver observed, briefly flicking his flashlight beam into the space behind the couch and to the right of a large potted plant, and then back to the seemingly clean carpet surrounding the large dried bloodstain. Then he stopped to consider something for a few moments before he looked up at Russelli.

"The wife and kids were hit upstairs, right?"

"Yeah," Russelli replied in a cold and decidedly unpleasant tone of voice.

"I think I'm going to try some luminol around here, see if we can figure out which way our friend went. Give ourselves something to go on."

A few minutes later, while Russelli methodically searched the adjacent kitchen and living room and the puppy continued to bark and whine in an increasingly desperate and forlorn manner, Culver put on thin plastic gloves and a small dust mask. Then, after aiming the beam of his flashlight across the taped body outline, he began to spray a fine mist of the revealing luminol solution over the seemingly unstained carpet. Finally, he turned off his flashlight.

The expanse of carpet suddenly began to glow with the faint luminescence of dozens of partial and fragmented shoe prints, most of which were barely visible against the diffused and flickering light coming into the family room from Russelli's flashlight.

Culver moved over to the potted plant, turning his back to the empty corner behind the couch, and squatted down as he tried to figure out the directions of the partial prints.

"Hey, Russelli," he called out, "how about shutting off your flashlight for a couple of minutes?"

"Yeah, sure," the deep voice rumbled from the living room. A moment later, the entire room went dark. "How's that?"

Culver looked around in satisfaction at the brightly glowing expanse of partial shoe prints.

"Perfect."

"I'm going to go check on that damned dog," the deep voice rumbled again from the darkness. "Let me know if you need some help."

"Okay, will do."

The partial shoe prints faded out under the glare of the diffuse light as Russelli used his flashlight to get to the garage door. Then the door slammed shut amid a sudden burst of excited barking, and the prints glowed once again in the darkened room.

Culver started to stand up, to get a better view of the directional patterns, when he saw something out of the corner of his left eye.

Turning around, he realized that there was a blood spray pattern on the back of the couch that spread out onto the floor to his left. Reflexively, Culver went through the motions in his head.

Right to left. Left-handed cut. Probably swung the knife around to his left and . . .

Then he saw it. The splatter pattern on the floor. Or to be more precise, the two distinct splatter patterns—the streaked blood droplets clearly going in two different directions—that, for some strange reason, were separated by a thin, straight invisible line.

"What the—" he started to say, when the silence was suddenly torn by a jarringly *loud* crash, a scream of agony, and a sharp, high-pitched, animalistic shriek that ended almost as soon as it had begun.

Rushing to the shattered doorway with gun and flashlight in both hands, Henry Culver burst into the garage to find Detective John Russelli rolling on the floor in agony, his massive hands clutched tightly around his lower right leg.

Chapter Three

At exactly one-fifteen that following morning, Elliott Parkinson, associate director of Operations for the Central Intelligence Agency, was jarred awake by the phone on his nightstand.

"Hello?" he mumbled, resting the handset on his pillow.

"Parkinson?"

The familiar tone of the unfamiliar voice caused Elliott Parkinson's eyes to blink partially open.

"Who is this?" he rasped, coming up to a partial sitting position in the queen-size bed.

"You can call me Digger," the strangely nongendered voice giggled.

It took Parkinson a few moments to realize that, as far as he could remember, he had never heard of—much less met—anyone with the name or code name of "Digger."

"You dialed the wrong number," he mumbled, yawning sleepily.

"That's interesting. I really didn't think there would be more than one Elliott Parkinson working for the CIA."

Parkinson blinked and brought his head up off the pillow.

"How did you get this number?" he demanded. He was extremely irritated by the intrusion, not to mention the implied breach of security; but at the same time, he was equally interested in hanging up so that he could go back to sleep. It had been a long and frustrating day, and the last thing he needed was some office clown—

"I got it from Herr Kostermann."

That response brought Parkinson wide-awake, and he reflexively punched the START RECORD button on the ADX secured receiver console on his nightstand. His assistant, J. Winston Weathersby, had given him a briefing on the murder of Lt. Col. Karl Kostermann—Parkinson glanced at the glowing numerals on the console—less than three hours ago.

"I don't know who or what you are talking about," the associate director responded as he slowly pulled the covers away and sat up in the bed with his bare feet on the carpeted floor, ignoring the chill in the room as his suddenly energized mind began to churn.

"Karl Kostermann. K-A-R-L. Interpol officer. Federal Republic of Germany. Are you *sure* you don't recognize the name?" the voice chided. "I find that very strange, Mr. Parkinson, because he certainly knew a *great* deal about you."

"I doubt very seriously that this Interpol officer, whoever he may be, would have given you my home number," Parkinson said calmly, noting the caller's past tense usage of the word.

"Then how do you *think* I got it," the whispery voice asked.

There was a long pause before Parkinson spoke again.

"And just what, precisely, did Mr. Kostermann tell you?" he asked carefully, making no effort to conceal the displeased tone in his voice.

"Oh, he really didn't *tell* me much of anything," the voice responded in a silky purr, causing a sudden cold chill to run down Parkinson's spine.

"Listen to me," the assistant director whispered menacingly as a light on the sophisticated recording device began to blink steadily, indicating that the point of origin of the call had been located and recorded, "whoever you are, *whatever* you are, I would strongly suggest that you destroy any records you have of this number. Because if you *ever* call it again, I will—"

"—be delighted to hear from me, I'm sure," the chillingly androgynous voice interrupted.

"I'm going to hang up now," Parkinson said matter-of-factly. "And then I'm going to call the police and have you arrested."

"Before you do that, would you mind answering two questions?"

"What did you have in mind?" Parkinson asked, curious in spite of himself.

"First, do you have any idea why over three hundred delegates from the World Trade Organization, CITES, *and* Interpol would travel all the way to Washington, DC, just to meet with a bunch of privately sponsored environmental groups?"

Parkinson blinked in surprise, but managed to maintain a calm outward demeanor. "No, I don't," he said evenly. "Good night, Mr. Digger." He started to reach over with his free hand to disconnect the call.

"Do you think Colonel L'Que might know?"

Elliott Parkinson's hand froze in place.

"What did you say?" he whispered hoarsely.

"I was just wondering if the name of Lieutenant Colonel Charles L'Que meant anything to you at all."

Moving his hand slowly downward, Elliott Parkinson first pressed the STOP button on the phone recorder, and then a second button labeled REVERSE/ERASE.

"Keep talking, Mr. Digger," he said, the tone of his voice turning deadly cold. "You now have my full and undivided attention."

Chapter Four

SIX WEEKS LATER: Saturday, January 9

Alberto Paz, a veteran field operative of the Central Intelligence Agency, possessed a swarthy appearance, a solid muscular frame, a cold indifference to mayhem, and a well-earned reputation as a merciless, back-alley survivor.

He also knew better than to allow his emotions to override his innate sense of caution.

But Alberto Paz was angry at being stood up, and impatient to report in, so he entered the front door of his rented house in an uncharacteristically hurried and incautious manner. He paused only to slide the dead bolt back into place, and to make a cursory inspection of his alarm system, before placing the laptop computer next to his living room chair and then going immediately over to the telephone in his den.

The Digger situation was going out of control. He was certain of that now. Which meant that they—or more likely, *he*—would have to do something about it, and do it quickly.

And he also knew, with absolute certainty, what that something ought to be.

"God damn it, Parkinson, what the hell were you thinking about, bringing a sick little bastard like that into MEG, especially at the last goddamned minute?" Paz muttered to himself as he punched the memorized number with a quick, smooth motion of his scarred hand. His dark, Mediterranean features were set in an irritated frown as he waited for somebody at the other end of the line to pick up the phone.

The trouble was, they were running out of time.

In four weeks, on Saturday, February 6, the standing committees from the World Trade Organization, CITES (the Convention on International Trade in Endangered Species) and Interpol would come together for a historic meeting in Washington, DC.

At this meeting, delegates from the independent NGOs—powerful and influential Non-Government Organizations of CITES such as the World Wildlife Fund, and Greenpeace, and *Terre-Mère Vert*—would present their case for something unprecedented in the history of the United Nations: the implementation of widespread economic sanctions against nations accused of violating or simply ignoring international wildlife and environmental laws.

Sanctions which—if actually implemented by every signatory country of the World Trade Organization and CITES, and enforced with the technical assistance of Interpol—were capable of bringing even the most highly developed nations to their economic knees.

And in four weeks, the elements of a CIA covert operation that had been over ten years in the making, an operation that CIA Associate Director Elliott Parkinson had set into motion as a young and aggressive field operative back in 1985, would finally bear its poison fruit.

Mother Earth Green, or MEG—as Parkinson's wildly imaginative and incredibly daring operation was known among the chosen few—represented a grasp of international power on a scale that had the potential to dwarf every industrial and social revolution in recorded history. But it would all hinge on timing, and access, and precisely accurate information on the primary and fallback positions that each of the hundred-odd delegates would bring to these high-charged meetings. Information that would allow Parkinson's surrogates in his now extremely powerful and supposedly European-wide NGO group to detect strategies, manipulate votes, and implement a series of programs that would put the United States—through the sure hands of CIA Associate Director Elliott Parkinson, and with the unsuspecting assistance of Interpol—back into the international driver's seat for decades to come.

And now all that information was about to be theirs for the taking . . . if they could just manage to keep their incredibly talented—albeit maliciously perverse—new asset and the furious Fairfax County police investigators separate from each other for at least four more weeks.

A whole goddamned month, Paz thought gloomily, knowing full well that every additional day would bring the police that much closer to their illegal operation; and worse, at a time when the MEG team operatives were supposed to be directing their full attention to the complex and extremely risky details of the intelligence-gathering process.

Digger's timing couldn't possibly have been worse.

As Alberto Paz and virtually every one of the presumably

small group (no one other than Elliott Parkinson himself knew the actual number) of trusted MEG operatives had feared, a major element of Mother Earth Green was about to come apart at the worst possible moment . . . which meant that *somebody* was going to have to make a decision, and make it fast, before things got irretrievably worse.

Paz wasn't worried about his likely role in the cleanup process. He'd taken part in many such assignments during his twenty-four years with the Agency, and had never once felt any sense of remorse or regret. What he *was* concerned about was the mind-numbing scope of Parkinson's operation, and the closely related issues of security and control. Too many people were aware of the most sensitive details now, and it would only take one careless comment, or a momentary loss of nerve, to—

The phone clicked in his ear. The voice was calm and unhurried.

"Seven-one-five-five."

"This is Rudder," Paz said, growling into the mouthpiece. "Give me Topcastle."

There was a momentary pause as practiced fingers quickly attacked a keyboard, then:

"Hold on, Rudder."

A calm, cool, and reassuring voice. *Good. About time we got some professionalism into this deal.* Paz nodded appreciatively as he stared at his reflection in the darkened window glass opposite the door.

The line clicked twice, and then cleared, leaving a barely discernible high-pitched humming in the background as Elliott Parkinson calmly picked up the phone in his office.

"Yes?"

"He didn't show," Alberto Paz said without preamble.

"What happened?"

"I waited an hour," Paz began to explain, relaxing a little now that he had a protected line. "No show, no delivery, no call-off."

"What about L'Que?"

There was an edge to Parkinson's voice, and Paz picked up on it immediately.

Christ, he thought, *you don't know what's going on either.*

"I've got three people camped out on the perimeter right now," Paz said. "The colonel came home early, an hour ahead of his normal routine. Parked his car inside the garage, went inside, turned on lights, and started moving around upstairs. His wife and son showed up about forty-five minutes later. There's movement in the house, and no indication of any unusual activity. If Digger's still inside, they don't seem to know about it yet."

"They wouldn't know in any case, unless he wanted them to," Parkinson responded calmly, bringing his vocal cords back into control. "Not even someone like L'Que. Digger is quite good at this sort of thing. That's one of the reasons we brought him on board."

"You want my opinion, he's also one sick little bastard," Paz growled, "and if we're not careful, his mental problems are going to get every one of us into some deep shit." When Parkinson didn't respond, Paz continued: "I've said this before, and I'll say it again: it was a mistake to bring a guy like that into the operation. Too many loose wires. He's not worth the risk."

"At this point, precisely accurate information on Lieutenant Colonel L'Que is worth almost any risk," Elliott Parkinson corrected. "It is absolutely essential that we know what L'Que is doing here, and why he was suddenly attached to the French delegation."

No, it's absolutely essential that you *know,* Paz thought to himself. *No one else seems to care about L'Que, so why should you?*

"We all understand that L'Que is a priority issue, but . . ."

"What about Hämmarchov?" Parkinson interrupted, his voice cold, hard, and demanding.

"Nothing to report. Nobody's seen him since last Wednesday."

"What about his apartment?"

"We've checked the interior four times so far. A few paperbacks in the bedroom, some dirty clothes in the hamper, and a couple beers in the refrigerator. No sign that anything's been moved in between checks."

"Any indicators?"

"Nothing specific. Just a gut feeling that he might be out of the game."

"Are you suggesting that Digger put him down?"

"Hämmarchov? Christ no." Paz shook his head, amazed and dismayed by Parkinson's seeming inability to fully understand the problem. "Digger might take one of his other baby-sitters by surprise, but that fucking Cossack'd eat him for breakfast, raw."

"Then we're looking at the possibility that Hämmarchov may have gone rogue . . . along with Digger?"

"That's one possibility, yes. He's been known to walk away from a contract if the money's right," Paz reminded.

"I thought we offered him quite generous terms."

"Yeah, so did I."

There was a deep sigh at the other end of the line, which immediately suggested to Alberto Paz's street-tuned senses that some other part of the operation—something that he wasn't privy to—was also starting to come apart.

Christ, Paz thought. *What now?*

"We knew Digger was unpredictable; that was a given from the very start," Parkinson said after a long moment.

Paz snorted in amusement. "Yeah, no shit."

"But his access techniques and monitoring talents are exceptional, and the initial information he provided us on L'Que may turn out to be pivotal to the entire operation. I would hate to bring him in, or to . . . terminate our relationship, without being absolutely certain."

Paz mumbled something noncommittal.

"So how do you see the situation, overall?" the CIA associate director pressed.

"I don't know," Paz admitted. "Digger could show up tomorrow, ready to work; or he could be sucking dirt under

Hämmarchov's boot right now. Too many unknowns. Probably depends on the police as much as anything else. Which reminds me, do we have anything more on their progress?"

"I'm led to believe that they're starting to close in on a primary suspect," Parkinson replied evenly.

"You mean Digger?"

"Yes."

"What about the time factor?"

"The latest estimate gives us a ninety percent confidence level on seventy-two hours. Fifty-fifty on forty-eight."

"For Christ's sake!" Paz exploded.

"Yes, exactly," Parkinson acknowledged. "Under anything resembling normal circumstances, the police probably *wouldn't* have made the connections as quickly as they have; but the, uh, nature of the Kostermann scene seems to have focused their efforts," the CIA associate director added without a discernible trace of irony in his voice.

"Cutting the throats of a resident Interpol officer and his family, and beating their pets to death with a baseball bat tends to do that," Paz muttered, making no effort to restrain his sarcasm. And then, when he failed to get a rise out of Parkinson, he added: "So we're going to have to bring him in anyway, regardless."

It wasn't a question. Just a statement of the obvious.

"Either that, or bring him back under control immediately," the CIA associate director agreed.

"Do you really care which way it goes?"

Parkinson hesitated.

"Yes, I do care. I want him in if at all possible."

"Well, don't get your hopes up too high," Paz warned. "What about Culver?"

"Who?"

"Henry Culver. Used to be one of our tech-ops. Works for the Fairfax County PD now, in their crime lab. Sci-Tech suggested that we might want to keep an eye on him."

"Why is Sci-Tech making any suggestions whatsoever about this operation?" Parkinson demanded.

"They're not. I just . . ."

"We've discussed this before," Parkinson said in a chilling voice. "MEG is a strictly classified, need-to-know operation. Neither Arthur Traynor or any members of his Sci-Tech Directorate are to be involved in any conceivable manner with MEG, period."

"I understand, but this was backdoor info only. No connections to MEG. I checked to make sure."

"All right," Parkinson said, apparently mollified. "What did they say, exactly?"

"This Henry Culver guy is supposed to be a real hotshot on scenes and surveillance. Traynor's aware that we have some assets working the DC metro area. The word is, he was concerned that Culver might pick up on one of our patterns, start nosing around, and get the agency into trouble. I got the impression that Culver's probably maintained contacts with some of the Sci-Tech staff over the past few years."

"We don't need that kind of interference. Especially not now," Parkinson said, his voice betraying a new level of tension as he made a quick note on a brand-new memo pad. "This Culver—you said he works in the Fairfax County crime lab now?"

"Yeah, right. Mostly dope and crime scenes. Some electronics stuff."

"Was he at the Kostermann scene?"

"I don't know for sure, but I'm fairly certain that he wasn't part of the initial call-out team."

"Then he shouldn't be a problem."

"So far, maybe not," Alberto Paz agreed. "But an investigator with Culver's background could be brought into the picture at any time, especially if Digger keeps on committing those goddamned burglaries of his," he added pointedly.

"We've gone over this issue many times, Alberto. Everyone except you seems to agree that a series of burglaries, if properly spaced in time and distance throughout the county, would provide an excellent diversion."

"Except when it's our guy who keeps on getting diverted," the CIA operative said, the disgust evident in his voice.

"We can hardly consider ourselves responsible for the Kostermann incident. That occurred what, six weeks ago? Well before our watch."

"Actually, that was pretty much the beginning of our watch, as far as Digger is concerned," Paz reminded. "Which is precisely why . . ."

"We will deal with Digger's extracurricular activities later, after the WTO meetings are concluded," Parkinson said firmly. "In the meantime, I'll make some inquiries regarding this Culver fellow. Perhaps we can find someone he used to work with, someone who might encourage him to lie low for a while."

"I already looked into that," Paz said evenly. "His file isn't available in personnel, but . . ."

"What do you mean, his file isn't available?" Parkinson demanded. "Everyone's files are available."

"Not if an AD slaps a restriction cover on the damned thing," Paz reminded.

"Which AD?"

"I didn't want to dig that deep, but there was enough information in the basic data file to make a good guess. Culver worked primarily in the European Theater on one of the MOSS teams. His immediate supervisor was . . ."

"Traynor."

"Bingo," Paz nodded.

There was a five-second pause while the Operations AD considered this new bit of information. Then:

"Do you have any recommendations?"

Parkinson—who had some very specific ideas about who the next director of the Central Intelligence Agency ought to be—asked the question with forced calm as his cold, bureaucratic mind continued to sort through several unnerving possibilities; the least disconcerting of which was that one of his arch rivals just might be making an early move.

"Yes."

"Other than the obvious?"

"No."

"We are completely committed to the final stages of this operation, Alberto," Parkinson said firmly. "And the time factor is even more critical now that L'Que seems to be involved. At this point, I'm afraid that Digger would be an extremely difficult and expensive asset to replace."

"That's right. Either way you look at it, he could be very expensive," Alberto Paz said, watching his darkened mirror image nod in agreement.

Another pause, this one almost twice as long. Then Elliott Parkinson made his decision.

"All right, bring him in. You've got two days. If you can't accomplish the job within that time frame, then take him out. You have clearance. In the meantime, I'll have Forecastle make contact with Culver. See if we can arrange for his cooperation."

"What about Hämmarchov?"

"Contract replacements at this late date are completely out of the question, so try to salvage him if you can. But in any case, keep things tight. And don't forget," the CIA associate director reminded, "we are going to require deniability on every aspect of the operation from this point on. *Absolute* deniability."

"I understand," Paz grunted, staring at his own cold, emotionless face as the line clicked dead. Then his eyes flickered as something in the mirror caught his attention—something that didn't look right.

Movement?

He was up out of the chair and starting to come around, the heavy 9mm Sig/Sauer P226 semiautomatic pistol already half out of its shoulder holster, when all of the lights in the house suddenly went out.

A nonprofessional might have remained in place for the half second or so necessary to work through the logic: all of the alarm lights—including the reset alert—had been burning green when he came in, implying that none of perimeter beams or interior motion detectors had been tripped. Ergo, there couldn't be anyone in the house other than himself.

Being the professional that he was, Alberto Paz considered all of that while twisting and rolling across the floor of the den, coming up against the familiar doorway with the Sig/Sauer aimed in the general direction of the living room in a double-handed, arms-extended, point-fire position.

Not couldn't be, he reminded himself as he searched the almost-complete darkness for any sign of shadowy movement. *Shouldn't be. Major difference.*

Moving as quietly as possible, Paz came up into a standing position alongside the doorframe, breathing slowly with his mouth open as he listened patiently for a telltale creak of a door, or window, or floorboard.

It was happening now, much earlier than he'd expected, but that was okay. He had been concerned about the time it would take to track at least one of them down. But that wasn't a concern anymore because one of them was here, and one was all he needed. With one, it would be easy to find the others.

In a vague, distant portion of his brain, he hoped that it wasn't Hämmarchov.

It wasn't a question of fear. As always, the abrupt onset of action had brought on relaxed and almost-serene anticipation. As a veteran CIA operative, Alberto Paz had spent the better part of a long career dealing with hired or twisted assets who needed to be brought back under control in one way or another. And besides, here—in his own house—he had an overwhelming advantage. Among other things, he knew exactly where all of the loose floorboards were located.

It was not a question of fear. It was more a matter of regret over the waste of professional talent.

If it's Hämmarchov, he's not here to talk, Paz reminded himself as he started to move forward around the door frame. *Go for the kill-shots immediately. Fourteen in the magazine. Neighbors in close on both sides. Make it quick. One in the heart, one in the head, then . . .*

The reading lamp—located less than fifteen feet away, next to the reclining chair in the living room—came on with a sudden surge of electrical current. The unexpected glare shocked and blinded him for a brief moment. Blinking frantically, he started to twist away, to escape the silhouetting light.

But then he saw it and he couldn't help himself.

Oh shit.

Crouched there, exposed and openmouthed, with the deadly Sig/Sauer pistol still held out in the combat grip, he stared at what he could only think of as an absolutely absurd sight: a black, rectangular hole right in the middle of his living room floor.

"Hi, Alberto, how's it going?"

He reacted to the soft, familiar voice by freezing in place.

"Hello, Digger, you're late," Alberto Paz said, forcing the words out slow and easy. The voice had come from behind. Probably the kitchen door entry to the den, but he couldn't tell. All he knew for sure was that he was backlit, and every other area in the house—other than the chair and the area of the living room floor illuminated by the shielded reading lamp—was dark.

"Put it down on the floor."

He knew there wasn't much hope for a turn and shoot, because he'd only be able to guess at the direction, and that wouldn't be enough. At the most, he might get off two or three rounds. *Have to be awfully goddamned lucky,* he thought morosely.

For some reason that he couldn't quite define, he didn't feel lucky on this one at all.

"Mine's a twelve-gage, Alberto," the familiar voice said softly. "Number four mags. Put it down, now. Use your left hand."

No inflection of anger or fear—or any emotion at all, for that matter—in the eerie, androgynous-sounding vocal tones. Nothing obvious to work with.

The key, Paz told himself, was to *think,* and not let his mind go numb.

Slowly grasping the front slide with his left hand, Paz drew his trigger finger and then his whole right hand away from the weapon in a slow, deliberate motion; and then sank down on one knee and gently placed the pistol down on the living room carpet.

"Now stand up."

The veteran field operative did so, maintaining his slow, deliberate body movements that said "yes, see how cooperative I'm being?"

"Did you bring . . . ?" he started to ask, but the disembodied voice interrupted.

"Now kick it into the hole."

"Bad idea, it might go off," Paz tried, making the effort out of reflex more than anything else. It gave him more time to think.

"A Sig? I don't think so. Do it now, Alberto, and don't be difficult."

"Coming from you, that's almost funny," Paz commented easily, feeling a numbing sense of emptiness in his stomach as he watched the weapon drop out of sight.

Jesus Christ, a trapdoor. The devious little bastard cut a fucking trapdoor in the middle of my living room floor.

"Now go sit in the chair."

Alberto Paz let out an audible sigh as he sank into the familiar chair. He didn't even bother to look in the direction of the voice now. The lamp had been moved slightly so that it sat directly between the chair and the doorway to the den. The glary bulb illuminated the right side of his face.

Very nice, he thought morosely. *You're a lot better than I expected, pal. A whole lot better.*

For reasons he didn't care to dwell on, Alberto Paz now realized that he would have much preferred to have Hämmarchov, the cold, professional, and absolutely ruthless killer, standing there in the darkness with the shotgun. He could *understand*—and deal with—a man like Hämmarchov.

"Are we ready to talk now?"

"Certainly, Alberto," the silky, echoing voice responded. "What shall we talk about?"

"I was thinking that maybe I should give you a key to the place. Save you a lot of trouble the next time you want to stop by for a visit."

"But that wouldn't be any fun."

"No, I guess not," Pax nodded, his eyes drawn to the black rectangle in front of his feet, watching the flap door swing gently back and forth. *

Jesus Christ, he even hinged the damn thing.

Paz shook his head in mute wonder.

"You were supposed to bring me the package on L'Que tonight, Digger. What happened?"

"Oh, I decided to bring it here instead." *

Paz tried not to let the relief show in his face.

"So what was wrong with the drop point we gave you?" he inquired, cautiously feeling his way now. He was trying to remember if Digger had ever seen the backup derringer he carried in his left boot.

"I decided that we need to renegotiate my contract."

Alberto Paz's eyes flared.

"What the hell do you think you are, a free agent?"

"That's funny, Alberto," the whispery voice said with absolutely no change of inflection.

Then why the fuck don't you laugh, like a normal human being, so I know whether to go hard or easy? Alberto Paz knew that he would have to decide one way or the other very soon. The thing was, once he started, he'd have to be consistent—one of the guiding principles of the verbal judo techniques that operatives were trained to use when things went to shit.

"What about Hämmarchov?" he tried.

"You already asked that question."

"What are you talking about?"

"On the telephone. You said 'what about Hämmarchov?' " Then, after a pause: "What did they say, Alberto?"

"What, about Hämmarchov? They . . ."

"No, not about him." The androgynous voice giggled. "About me." .

Oh shit. Go hard, now!

"Topcastle wants to talk with you, Digger," Paz said firmly. "He thinks you're out of control."

"He's right, you know," the silky voice responded, and this time there was a discernible change of inflection.

"What?"

"You were my control, and now I'm out. Good-bye, Alberto."

"No, wait!"

The sound that echoed out of the hollow darkness of the den was more like an extended *Thhhhh-Thunk!* than a gunshot, and the resulting impact was even more unexpected.

Too stunned to react to the sudden, sharp, and numbing pain, Alberto Paz stared down in disbelief at the brightly feathered end of the long, pencillike projectile that was sticking out of his neck.

Dart gun? He blinked in confusion. *What the . . . oh Christ, it's working fast.*

His right hand had started down toward the small backup weapon in his boot, but the impact-driven hydraulic pressure of the dart had already sent the paralyzing drug flooding into his rapidly pulsing bloodstream, turning his powerful arm and leg muscles into tingling chunks of numb and unresponsive tissue.

He fell forward onto the floor, immobile and mute, but still fully alert and aware. He could see, and hear and think, but he couldn't move—not even his eyelids. Thus it took him several moments to understand what was happening when the room began to slowly rotate from top to bottom.

It got bad when he realized that he was being wrapped—his arms and legs, and in fact his entire body—with what seemed to be an endless supply of nylon strapping tape, but that wasn't the worst part.

The worst part came a horribly long five minutes later,

when—limp and helpless, but nonetheless completely aware of his surroundings—Alberto Paz found himself being dragged slowly across the carpet to the trapdoor in his living room floor, and then down into the narrow, dark, and cobwebby crawl space.

Alone in his darkened executive office that was illuminated by a single expensive Stiffel desk lamp, Elliott Parkinson was making notes in the margins of a recent intelligence estimate when his special assistant, J. Winston Weathersby—a young man of distinctive Ivy League pretensions—knocked gently at the doorway.

Parkinson looked up.

"You wanted to see me?"

"Yes, I have an assignment for you."

"I understand Paz called in?" Weathersby probed, instinctively adding the precisely appropriate degree of deference to his query as he placed himself in one of the chairs in front of Parkinson's expansive desk.

Parkinson nodded, silently acknowledging his youthful assistant's networking talents.

"Did he obtain the information we needed on L'Que?"

Parkinson shook his head slowly, considering how much he would reveal to his talkative assistant, very much aware that networking contacts usually worked both ways. "No, he didn't show."

"I knew it. I knew that crazy bastard was going to go sideways on us," Weathersby said with a degree of self-satisfaction that he immediately regretted when he saw the look on Parkinson's face. "Uh, what are we going to do?" he asked hesitantly, immediately shifting back into his obsequious role.

"Alberto is making arrangements to rectify the situation."

"I hope you reminded him to be careful," the special assistant said. "That Digger is a real case."

Parkinson sighed.

"You still don't understand, do you?"

"Understand what?" The young man looked perplexed.

"Alberto Paz is an operative, certainly; but in the context of MEG, he is much more correctly viewed as an asset. Digger, too, for all of his useful talents, is nothing more than an asset. And as you know, by definition, assets are always expendable."

"But . . . ." the youthful special assistant started to protest, but Parkinson shook his head.

"Winston, if you want to make a place for yourself in this Agency," the CIA associate director for Operations warned in his characteristically cold, matter-of-fact voice, "or anywhere else in the Government for that matter, you need to understand something: policies, findings and authorities are what count. Individuals are nothing more than tools—resources to be utilized to their fullest capacity, and then discarded when no longer useful."

"But Digger . . ."

Parkinson held up a manicured hand.

"I want Digger brought back under control because he has very specific talents that can help us meet our objectives. But no matter what happens, you must remember he and Paz are resources to be used. Nothing more."

"Just a couple of expendable assets, right?" The youthful special assistant grinned knowingly.

For the first time that evening, Elliott Parkinson allowed his lips to form a slight smile. "Yes, exactly."

Two hours and fifteen minutes later, Digger stepped out of his Agency-rented apartment for the last time, balancing a box of books in one arm as he pulled the door shut.

Once again, he smiled his cold distant smile as the sharp click of the oiled lock signaled the end of his previous career, and the beginning of another which he expected to be far more lucrative.

Humming to himself, he turned . . . and then froze in place, his pale blue eyes blinking in shock as he found himself staring into the barrel of a sawed-off twelve-gage shotgun held in the rock-steady hand of a partially crippled Fairfax County police detective named John Russelli, whose cold, unforgiving gaze offered a chilling mirror image of his own.

Chapter Five

Friday, January 29

Henry Culver felt a chilling numbness at the back of his neck, and his stomach starting to twist in revulsion. But even so, he found himself unable to take his eyes away from the unimaginably macabre yet horribly fascinating scene.

Jesus, he thought to himself, *what if Russelli hadn't spotted the bastard?*

It was uncharacteristic of Culver to react in that manner, for the simple reason that the men and women who spent their professional careers picking through the blood-soaked evidence of mankind's inherent disregard for his fellow *sapiens* were not, by nature, the most sensitive of souls.

Needing clarity of mind to reconstruct the unthinkable, crime scene investigators quickly developed a callous indifference to scenes that would likely send a normal, civilized person staggering for the nearest toilet; knowing full well, of course, that the unacceptable alternative was to end up hunched over one of those ever-practical ceramic bowls that really should have been dusted for fingerprints first.

But every now and then, and in spite of their mental blinders, CSI officers like Culver find themselves face-to-face with a scene so bizarre, so perverse, that they can't help but be emotionally jarred.

In this particular situation, Henry Culver simply couldn't believe his eyes.

You're right, Russelli, you screwed up, Culver thought to

himself. *You should have shot him when you had the chance.*

Fascinated and repulsed, he continued to sit in the witness chair and watch silently as the defendant—a thin, wiry, light brown–haired individual in his mid-thirties who sat at the defense table less than twenty feet away—continued to slowly turn the pages in the thick ringed binder with an unimaginably serene and distracted expression on his gentle and vulnerable-appearing face. Looking for all the world like any other thirty-five-year-old male who just happened to be rummaging through an old family picture album, peacefully reliving cherished memories of his childhood.

Culver tried to imagine the aberrant mind-set necessary to make such an incredible transition, and then gave up because the whole thing was completely beyond his comprehension.

The problem was, Henry Culver knew *exactly* what kind of photographic enlargements were mounted in that ring binder. They were, to put it mildly, the furthest things imaginable from family snapshots; and in fact, were some of the most gruesomely violent, cruel, and nauseating crime scene photographs that Culver had ever seen in his entire law enforcement career. And having worked over 150 homicide and suicide scenes, along with their accompanying autopsies, during the past ten years, Culver figured that probably meant something.

Means I'm getting to be an expert on goddamned freaks, he decided morosely, continuing to stare at the incredible scene before his eyes until the defendant—seeming to sense that he was being watched—suddenly brought his head up.

For a brief moment, Digger's widened pale blue eyes stared straight up at Henry Culver, the distracted serenity replaced by an oddly familiar expression that, to Culver, vaguely resembled surprise. Then he blinked, as if suddenly aware of his surroundings, and his eyes seemed to ice over. He gave Culver a long, cold look, and then returned his attention to the photographs.

Henry Culver's eyebrows furrowed in concentration as he

stared down at the wispy light brown hair, trying to remember what it was about that brief, furtive expression that seemed so familiar.

Shyness?

Culver shook his head. No, definitely not shyness. Not with eyes like that.

Something like embarrassment, maybe?

Culver continued to let the hauntingly familiar expression that had momentarily filled Digger's empty pale blue eyes drift around in the back of his mind, absolutely certain that he had seen it before, but—

Then, suddenly, the deep, numbing chill spread down his spine as it hit him.

Oh Christ.

Culver shut his eyes and took in a deep breath, fighting against an almost-physical sense of nausea, as the answer crystallized in his mind with terrible clarity.

Those kids—the ones that Jack Hattabaugh and I caught reading porno magazines in the alley behind that 7-Eleven.

Jesus . . .

"Officer Culver?" The deep, amplified voice broke through Culver's dazed thoughts.

"Huh, I'm sorry?" Culver blinked as he turned his head to stare at the black-robed judge sitting next to him on the dais.

"You do realize that this is a preliminary hearing on the evidence in this case, and that you are still under oath from this morning's session?" the judge asked patiently.

"Yes, I do," Culver hurriedly agreed, embarrassed by the realization that everyone in the courtroom had been staring at him. *No, not quite everyone,* he corrected himself, observing that the defendant—whoever the hell he was, because nobody at the PD or the prosecutor's office or even the FBI had been able to get him identified yet—had returned to his perverse fascination with the crime scene photographs.

No wonder Radlick's going to waive a jury trial, Culver thought, momentarily shaken again as he watched the defendant moistening his thin lips with the tip of his tongue as he appeared to focus his attention on an especially memorable scene. *If a group of jurors ever saw that . . .*

"I'm sorry, Your Honor, I lost my train of thought for a moment," he added apologetically.

"That's quite all right." The black-robed circuit court judge nodded sympathetically, having been witness from his high-perched vantage point to the same distracting scene. "Mr. Toledano, would you like to continue with your witness?"

"Just a few more questions, Your Honor." The prosecuting attorney nodded. "Now then, Officer Culver, before we discuss your examination of evidence on this case, let me ask you something. Aside from the pair of Reebok tennis shoes that you've already described, did you find anything else at the defendant's residence that you thought might be relevant . . ."

"Objection, Your Honor!" Defense Attorney Paul Radlick rose to his feet.

"Sustained. Would you care to rephrase your question, Mr. Toledano?" Judge Mauser asked.

"Uh, yes. Officer Culver, did you find any animals in the defendant's residence?"

"Objection!"

"Overruled. I'm going to allow the prosecution to pursue this line of questioning," Mauser said pointedly.

"Yes, I did," Culver answered.

"Please describe what you found," Toledano said, flashing a victorious smile.

"I found eleven cats and three dogs in the defendant's basement freezer."

"All dead, I take it?" Toledano said, still smiling.

"Your Honor!" Radlick protested, but to no avail.

"Yes, all dead," Culver nodded.

"Did you happen to notice how these animals had died?" Toledano asked.

"Your Honor," Radlick interrupted in an exasperated tone of voice, "the witness is *not* an expert on veterinary pathology."

"I'm going to allow the witness to testify as to what he actually saw," Mauser ruled after a moment of contemplation. "Proceed."

"Their throats were cut open, in every case," Culver said quietly. "I also observed what appeared to be dried blood around the ear and nose areas, and what appeared to be impact wounds across the upper surface of the heads. There was also some evidence of, uh, sexual assault . . ."

Judge Harold Mauser's eyebrows went skyward as he turned his head slowly in the direction of the defense table.

"Your Honor, that's . . ."

"Overruled. Would you please repeat that last statement, Officer Culver," Mauser said quietly as he stared contemplatively at the half-smiling defendant.

"There was evidence of sexual assault—that is, mutilation of sexual organs—on some of the animals," Culver explained. "But Mr. Radlick is correct, Your Honor, I can't testify as to the actual cause of death." Culver observed the defense attorney out of the corner of his eye, nodding his head in apparent satisfaction.

"Yes, of course. Thank you." Judge Mauser sighed, closing his eyes for a moment. "You may continue, Mr. Toledano."

"And in regard to the related burglary crime scenes that we are discussing here, did you find other small animals—pets of the victims—in similar conditions at those homes?" Toledano asked.

"Yes, I did."

"Objection!"

"Overruled."

"In every instance?"

"No."

"But in every instance where the related burglary victims in this case had pets, were those pets later found dead somewhere near the scenes or found to be missing?"

"Yes, they were," Culver nodded.

"And as to the eleven cats and three dogs that you found

in the defendant's freezer, were you able to confirm that all of those animals belonged to victims of the burglaries in this case?"

"Yes, we did," Culver nodded again, watching Radlick sit mute at the defense table.

"And now then, getting back to the blowup photographs and plaster casts of shoe impressions that you have before you on the twelve burglary cases, Officer Culver," Toledano went on. "Not including the homicide scene. Did you reach a conclusion as to the origin of those impressions?"

"Yes."

"Would you tell the court your opinion?"

"I determined that all of the shoe print impressions that you've described were made by either the left or the right shoe in exhibit number forty-seven," Culver said evenly.

"Specifically, this pair of Reebok tennis shoes that you found at the defendant's apartment?" Toledano asked, holding up a pair of marked tennis shoes for confirmation.

"That Detective Russelli found at the apartment, yes."

"Did you see Detective Russelli find these shoes?"

Culver thought for a moment, and then said: "No, but I was in the immediate area when he found them."

"And what about the shoe print found outside the residence of Mr. and Mrs. Kostermann and their three children?"

This time there was a detectable edge to Toledano's voice. He had spent several hours with Culver and the other police investigators, going over the crime scene photos in nauseating detail.

"That was made by the left shoe that you're holding in your hands," Culver said matter-of-factly.

Much to Culver's surprise, his last answer seemed to catch the attention of the defendant, who looked up sharply from his photo album to stare directly at Culver with his empty pale blue eyes, seemingly puzzled.

"Officer Culver," Toledano sighed, ready to ask the final, all-important question. "Is there any doubt in your mind, any doubt whatsoever, as to accuracy of your identifications in this case?"

"No," Culver shook his head slowly. "None at all."

"Thank you, Officer Culver," Toledano said. "Oh yes, one more thing. Isn't it true that about six weeks before the defendant's arrest at his apartment, Detective Russelli received a serious injury during a search of the Kostermann residence?"

"Yes, it is."

"Since Detective Russelli isn't available at the moment, can you describe that injury to the court?" Toledano asked.

Culver paused a moment, scanning the courtroom as he waited to see if Radlick was going to object, noting as he did so that the huge, gray-haired man was in the courtroom again. He had a closely trimmed gray beard and Slavic facial features, and aside from the intelligent look in his wide-spaced eyes, had the appearance of a retired heavyweight boxer. He was sitting in the same seat in the far left rear corner of the courtroom. Culver continued when the defense counsel remained mute in his chair.

"The evening after the initial investigation at the Kostermann home, Detective John Russelli and I went to the residence to conduct a follow-up search. In doing so, we discovered a live animal in the garage, a small German shepherd puppy. No one had reported seeing it earlier, and it had dried blood smeared all over its head, so we assumed it had been unconscious during the initial crime scene search. It had food and water, so we decided to leave it there until after we finished our follow-up search. Detective Russelli got back to the cage before I did," Culver recited in a calm, flat voice.

"And?" Toledano encouraged.

"As it turned out, the cage was wired—booby-trapped. In trying to remove the pup, John—Detective Russelli—was struck in the lower leg by a length of heavy metal pipe that had been rigged with a series of industrial springs and a release mechanism to swing across the floor at about ankle level, something like a mouse trap turned on its side."

"And the puppy?"

"The puppy was crushed by the trap. It died," Culver said in a tight voice, momentarily glancing over at the defendant, who seemed intent on ignoring the entire discussion in favor of the ring binder, before returning his attention to Toledano.

"Thank you, Officer Culver," Toledano nodded in apparent satisfaction before turning to face the judge. "I have no further questions."

Okay, here we go, Culver thought, straightening himself up in the witness chair as he watched Paul Radlick step around behind his distracted client and pick up a display board that had two high-contrast black-and-white enlargements—one of a shoe sole and the other of a plaster cast of a shoe impression—mounted side by side with several numbered lines drawn to matching points.

"Officer Culver, you just testified that you were able to match a pair of tennis shoes that you—excuse me, that Detective Russelli—found in my client's closet against a shoe impression in the dirt outside the Kostermann residence. Is that also correct?"

"Not exactly—no." Culver shook his head.

"Oh?"

"May I explain?"

"Yes, certainly," Radlick nodded, staring at Culver thoughtfully.

"The match that I made was actually between the shoe and a plaster *cast* of that shoe impression which was made at the scene," Culver explained.

"Did you make that plaster cast?"

"No, I did not." Culver shook his head.

"Do you know who did?"

"My knowledge would be based upon the records of the investigation, and identifying marks which are etched into the top surface of the cast."

"And what do the records indicate?" Radlick asked.

"That the cast was made by Criminalist Theodore Gauss."

"Do the markings on the cast confirm that?"

"Yes, they do."

"How do you know that?"

"I recognize the initials of Criminalist Gauss, and his manner of marking a cast."

"I take it that Mr. Gauss is employed with the Fairfax County Crime Laboratory also?"

"Yes, he is."

"And you and he often worked crimes scenes together. Is that correct?"

"Yes, that's correct."

"But you didn't actually see Criminalist Gauss make this plaster cast, did you?"

"No, I wasn't there at that time," Culver said.

"So your testimony regarding the shoe print match is based on evidence collected by another person, is that correct?"

"Two people, actually, not counting Detective Russelli," Culver said.

"Two people?" Radlick asked, a puzzled expression crossing his face.

"I was able to confirm the match of the defendant's tennis shoes to the cast by also comparing a *photograph* of the shoe print impression taken at the scene by Mike Quinzio, one of our uniformed crime scene investigation officers. That photograph was taken *before* the cast was made," Culver explained patiently.

"Are you certain of that?"

"Absolutely certain."

"And how can you be so sure of that?"

"Because the process of making a plaster cast of a shoe print impression in dirt invariably destroys that impression mark," Culver replied.

Radlick was silent for a few moments, staring at the confirming photographs and contact sheet, and seeming to reconsider something carefully for a few moments before he finally spoke again.

"Officer Culver, when you searched my client's residence, did you have your CSI kit with you?"

"Yes, I did."

"I assume that as a forensic scientist and an experienced crime scene investigator, you carry a lot of equipment in that case—flashlights, tweezers, cameras, and the like. Is that correct?"

"Yes."

"Would there have been enough room in that carrying case for a pair of shoes? Say a pair of size twelve Reebok tennis shoes?"

Culver shook his head. "No, there wouldn't."

"And what about Detective Russelli? Did he have some sort of carrying case with him also at the search of my client's bedroom?"

"Yes, he did."

"The same kind of case?"

"No, just an athletic bag made out of heavy canvas."

"So I assume that Detective Russelli's collection of crime scene search equipment is nowhere near as extensive as your own?"

"That's right, just basic search gear—flashlight, rope, tape."

"And was there enough room in *his* carrying case for a pair of Reebok tennis shoes?"

"Yes, I'm sure there would have been," Culver nodded slowly.

Plenty of room, Culver thought, *because that was exactly how we carried them back to the lab. So what? Come on, Radlick, what the hell are you . . .*

"Officer Culver, other than yourself, didn't all of the people you mentioned who located and collected evidence on this case—Criminalist Gauss, CSI Officer Quinzio, and Detective Russelli—subsequently receive promotions as a result of their work?"

"Objection!" Toledano leaped to his feet. "That is completely irrelevant . . ."

"Sustained," Judge Mauser growled, favoring Radlick with a glare that clearly suggested he ought to know better.

"So what you're telling the court, Officer Culver," Radlick went on, unfazed, "is that in *your* opinion, there is *no* possibility that the shoe print found outside the Kostermann home was made by *any* other pair of Reebok tennis shoes except the pair that are in this courtroom right now—the ones marked exhibit forty-seven. Is that correct?"

Culver noticed that the defendant had abandoned his ring binder and was now favoring him with a pale, malevolent glare.

"That's correct, Mr. Radlick," Culver nodded, noticing that Judge Mauser was now leaning over toward the witness box and listening carefully, "no question whatso . . ."

"YOU CHEATED!"

The high-pitched scream came from behind Radlick, who turned just in time to see his client start to heave the heavy metal water pitcher from the defense table at Culver. However, the extended hand of one of the lunging bailiffs managed to deflect the throw at the last minute, causing the heavy water pitcher to richocet instead off the left temple of Judge Harold Mauser.

In the excitement that followed, no one paid any attention to the huge, heavyset man seated in the far back row as he stood up and walked out of the courtroom with a satisfied smile on his broad Slavic face.

On the third floor of the Fairfax County Judicial Center, at the far end of the main hallway, an elderly woman hurriedly fumbled through her purse for a quarter, made a quick casual check of her surroundings, and then reached for the phone.

Dialing a long-memorized number, she continued to look around casually until a familiar gruff voice came on the line.

"This is Figurehead," she said in a gentle, grandmotherly voice that didn't quite mask an underlying edge of case-hardened steel. "Connect me with Topcastle, right away, please."

Chapter Six

Associate Director Elliott Parkinson replaced the telephone handset into its plastic receiver and then stared down at the immaculate felt blotter on his expansive desk as he mentally worked his way through the details one last time, just to be sure.

Then he looked up at his anxious special assistant. "The Fairfax County Mental Health Ward," he said calmly. "They'll be transporting him within the hour."

J. Winston Weathersby shook his head slowly in mute amazement.

"I thought I was doing well to get an early hearing date, but if Paz managed to rig that courtroom scene all on his own, then he's an absolute genius," he finally said, seemingly not the least bit concerned that all of the exceedingly complex and dangerous arrangements he had made during the past three weeks were now completely irrelevant, because Digger would no longer be in the custody of the Fairfax County Sheriff's Department. "Compared to the County Jail, the Ward will be a piece of cake."

"Alberto can be a very effective operative at times, but he lacks a sense of the overall picture," Parkinson contradicted. "A truly competent operative would never have allowed an asset like Digger to go out of control in the first place."

"Amen to that," Weathersby whispered, silently grateful that he was not going to end up being a primary accessory to a jailbreak after all.

"Furthermore, he should have spotted that police surveillance and contacted us immediately when Digger was arrested. Waiting six days to report in was inexcusable."

"I agree, but you know Paz. And besides, he did get the operation up and running again, without Digger's help," Weathersby argued.

"The next time he checks in, I want a full report on his activities during the past twenty days. A computer message saying they are back in business is not a report. Tell him that," Parkinson ordered.

The special assistant reached for his ever-present notebook.

"Oh, and one more thing. Allowing Hämmarchov to be seen in public, and associated with Digger in any manner whatsoever, is a mistake that will cease immediately."

"Hämmarchov is out in public?" J. Winston Weathersby cringed visibly.

"According to Figurehead, he was in the courtroom again this morning. The same seat."

Parkinson's special assistant blinked. "That's absolutely incredible," he whispered. "What's he doing, challenging us?"

Parkinson shrugged indifferently. "We'll deal with Hämmarchov's insolence later. Right now, we have to concentrate on resolving the L'Que issue."

"Are you sure Digger's worth all of this risk? I mean we've got all kinds of techs around here who could make that kind of entry, no sweat. A guy like R.C., he'd be in and out of L'Que's place in a half hour, max."

"But as I'm sure you recall, Mr. Cohen reports directly to Arthur Traynor," Parkinson reminded. "As I've told you many times before, I don't want Traynor to have anything to do with MEG."

"Then why not let Paz handle it himself?" the special assistant argued. "According to the last report, he's got nine functional teams out on the street right now. Let him pick the best one and work it through the warehouse with Marcus."

Parkinson shook his head. "That would be too obvious for someone like L'Que. The last thing we need right now is for him to get suspicious and start making arrangements to change the meeting sites."

"But . . ."

"We have eight days to resolve the L'Que situation," Parkinson said flatly. "And to do that, we need aggressive action, not caution."

"But . . ." Weathersby tried one last time.

"I want Digger put back on L'Que, as soon as possible," Parkinson said firmly. "Get him for me, now."

In the basement cafeteria of the new Fairfax County Judicial Center, forty-five minutes after a tight-jawed but still dazed Judge Mauser declared the trial in recess, Henry Culver was sitting at a far corner table, contemplatively sipping at a cup of lukewarm coffee when he looked up to see Paul Radlick blocking his view of the doorway.

"Greetings, Counselor, take a load off," Culver smiled, gesturing with his head at one of the empty chairs.

"Thanks," Radlick nodded, dropping his heavy briefcase down next to the square, wooden table as he sat down and stretched his legs out with a grateful sigh. "God, that feels good," he whispered as he leaned back in the chair and stretched lazily.

"Way I see it," Culver commented, giving Paul Radlick's strained belt a meaningful glance, "you want to keep on whipping my ass at racquetball, you're either going to have to divorce Doreen, or dynamite your kitchen."

"I guess that's what happens when you get married," the diminutive attorney nodded as he patted his noticeably bulging waistline and then ran his fingers through his thinning scalp. "Soon as you stop chasing women, you start growing a gut and your hair falls out."

"Mother Nature's way of saying congratulations." Culver grinned. "And you love every minute of it. Admit it."

"That I do," Radlick nodded agreeably. "You and Tess ought to try it. Might put a little meat on that scrawny carcass of yours."

"I don't know"—Culver shrugged, easily deflecting the almost-ritual question—"unless one of us learned to cook, we'd both probably end up starving to death. Why do you think we spend so much time conning meals out of you and Russelli?"

Paul Radlick chuckled and then brought his head up suddenly. "Hey, before I forget to ask, tell me something. Where was Craven when you guys took my client down? He's listed in the reports as the raid supervisor, but nobody mentioned his name, and I never could work it into a legitimate question."

"In his cruiser with a reporter, about a hundred yards down the street, maintaining the command post," Culver replied sarcastically.

"Good old Craven, always was a chicken shit when it came to risking his own ass." Radlick nodded, pleased to learn that his suspicions had been justified.

"So tell me, good buddy, do we still have a hearing? Or should I ask, do you still have a client?"

"Personally, I think I've got pretty good grounds for a mistrial on the basis of judicial prejudice, if Mauser doesn't have the crazy bastard hanged first," Radlick said, shaking his head. "Anyway, I managed to get a one-week continuance while they give my boy a mandatory psych workup."

"Mauser order it?"

"Yeah," Radlick nodded. "Probably wants to give himself a little time to cool off, just to make sure he doesn't go over the bench and strangle the guy."

"Or enough time for the swelling to go down," Culver suggested. "You see that knot on his head?"

Radlick nodded.

"You know, Mauser'd be doing the whole county a big favor if he did string that sorry bastard up," Culver said half-seriously.

"What are you doing, Henry, starting to go right-wing on me?" Radlick asked, staring at the man he'd known as a childhood friend, partner on patrol, and finally as a quasi adversary during the past five years. "I hear tell that you're seriously considering a transfer back out to the field."

"You do know that he did it, don't you?" Culver asked, ignoring the question; his voice soft and serious.

"Yeah, I do," Radlick nodded. "That's part of the problem."

"Only part? So what else is bothering you?" Culver asked, wary and cautious because he and Radlick had a very clear understanding on this sort of thing. Neither of them wanted to put the other in a position of saying something that might violate their respective occupational ground rules.

"Henry, there's something I want to ask you, off the record."

"Yeah, what's that?"

"When you and Russelli searched his apartment, did you see any kind of portable computer? Laptop, notebook, anything like that?"

"No."

"You sure?"

Culver smiled. "Yeah, of course I'm sure. If we'd found one, we'd have taken it to the lab and opened it up, just to see what the bastard was doing with it."

"How about any other computer stuff. You know, like disks, or manuals, or any of that kind of shit?"

Culver blinked and then settled back into his chair, lost in thought for a few moments as he worked himself mentally through the scene. Then he shook his head.

"No, nothing like that at all. Why?"

Radlick hesitated for a long moment and then shook his head. "Never mind, it's probably not important. Just my goddamned client driving me out of my skull."

"I see," Culver smiled. "All this nice-guy defense work must be starting to get to you."

Radlick sighed. "You really want to know what's bothering me, read this," he said, handing Culver a folded piece of paper. "My client requested—or to be more accurate, demanded—that I give that to you personally. Said he'd get out a call to the press and get it to you that way if I didn't."

Culver unfolded the note, scanned it quickly, read it through a second time much slower, and then looked up at Radlick.

"You read this thing?"

Radlick nodded his head. "Yeah, of course I read it."

"He really thinks Russelli and I scammed him?"

"That's right."

"Why us? Why not Quinzio or Gauss too?" Culver asked, a perplexed expression forming on his face. "I mean, Quinzio was the one who found and protected the footprints out at the Kostermann house, and Gauss put the whole case together when he started checking all the hit-and-run cases on animals. And that was a hell of an idea, too. Probably never would have tagged your little buddy if it hadn't been for that German shepherd he ran over near his apartment the week before."

"You still believe it, don't you, Henry?" Radlick asked in a soft voice.

"What's that?"

"The thing you always used to tell me—that you forensic types have to be absolutely straight because you're the check on the system?"

"Yeah, of course I still believe it." Culver nodded his head slowly, his eyes focused on his longtime friend. "What's the problem?"

"Apart from everything else, and I do mean everything else," Radlick emphasized, "my client is adamant that he wasn't wearing those shoes the night that the Kostermanns were killed. For reasons I don't care to discuss right now, I think I believe him. But the trouble is, you just testified that you made an absolutely positive, no-questions match of those shoes to Quinzio's photo and Gauss's cast. If I believe that, too, then I've got to go with the idea that Quinzio and Gauss worked together to fake those footprints at the scene . . ."

"Which they couldn't possibly do unless they had the shoes, which they didn't because Russelli and I didn't find those shoes until several weeks later," Culver pointed out.

"Exactly," Radlick nodded.

"And even if they'd had the opportunity," Culver went on, "you and I and everybody else in the department knows that Gauss and Quinzio can't stand each other. What do you figure the chances are of those two patching things up for a few days, just so they can conspire to fake evidence on a major case that they know every defense expert in the county's going to be looking at?"

"I'm not arguing with you, Henry," Radlick said softly.

"I know—just as I know the chance for it happening is just about zero," Culver went on, answering his own question. "Especially when you consider that Quinzio came on the scene first and shot the overall photos—which even you could tell were taken before the investigation started," Culver reminded his ex-cop friend. "And then he gets pulled off to handle an emergency hit-and-run before Gauss and the lab team ever get to the scene. Jesus, Paul, you read the CSI reports. Quinzio and Gauss never even saw each other out there that night."

"Exactly the way I read it," Radlick nodded, facing Culver squarely and asking the question with his eyes.

Culver's eyebrows furrowed in momentary confusion, but then he smiled as the implication hit home. "Uh-uh, buddy, nobody's worth it. Not even your client. You know that."

"You guys wanted him bad," Radlick pressed. "Especially Russelli. After he got out of the hospital, every time he came around the courthouse, hunting this guy down was all he could talk about."

"Sure we did," Culver nodded. "We wanted him about as bad as you could ever want somebody. You saw the photos. If you were still on the job, you'd have been out there gunning for the guy, too. Besides, the Kostermann girls were just about the same age as Russelli's daughters. Hell, he couldn't even stay in the morgue to finish watching the autopsies. How did you expect him to feel?"

"Probably about the way he felt after he got forcibly transferred out of homicide," Radlick commented.

"Come on, he earned those stripes," Culver retorted unconvincingly, knowing that the nerve and tendon damage to Russelli's leg had been the primary reason for the overly aggressive detective's "promotion" to the vacant burglary sergeant slot.

"And the thing was," Culver went on when Radlick remained silent, "you could see the guy was progressing. Those obscene phone calls to the burg victims, before and after they got hit. And the way he went after their pets, like he hated animals. Every scene we went to was more violent than the one before. I mean, you knew it was just a matter of time until he went after people. You could see it coming. Everybody could; especially Russelli. The Kostermanns just happened to be the unlucky ones."

Radlick sighed. "I know, I know."

"Listen, Paul, don't let this 'cheating' crap get to you," Culver said, holding up the note. "The guy's a loony-tune who gets off on gory pictures and likes to mess with animals. What the hell do you expect him to tell you—'I did it, I'm nuts, put me away?' Hell, he probably doesn't even remember wearing shoes that night. And don't forget about the blood we dug out of the soles of those Reeboks."

"Which the lab couldn't type because it was all mixed together," Radlick reminded.

"But they did get positive reactions for dog, cat, and human with the antisera screening," Culver countered. "Give them time and they'll get it all separated."

For a long moment, Radlick remained silent; the expression on his face seeming to suggest that he was being torn between several conflicting emotions.

"Listen, Henry, don't read this guy wrong," he finally said, leaning forward to face Culver. "He's not just a nutcase running wild. The guy's a real manipulator, and he's got it together a hell of a lot more than everybody thinks."

"Oh really, how's that?"

Radlick hesitated, took in and then released a deep breath, and then spoke softly. "Look, before you guys found him, I think he was about ready to stop doing the burgs himself. He knew you were getting close because he watched you guys working some of the scenes. He even remembers seeing you in particular."

"He hung around the scenes afterward?" Culver asked incredulously.

"I don't know; I didn't ask." Radlick shrugged. "But anyway, the important thing is that I think he was setting up some kind of system to do everything remote, to cut down his risks. And don't ask me what kind of system it was, because I don't know that, either. He wouldn't tell me."

"Why not? You're his attorney, aren't you?"

"How the hell am I supposed to know why not?" Radlick almost snarled. "He won't even tell me his name, for Christ's sake!"

"Which reminds me," Culver said, "what's with this 'Digger' business anyway?"

Radlick shrugged. "Beats the shit out of me." He hesitated once again, and then: "But I'll tell you something I do know, and that is, the guy really levels out when you start talking electronics and computers. He even talked me into buying a couple of the damn things for my office and home. Spends half our conference time helping me install the programs, and program the modem, and telling me how I can automate my office, handle twice as many cases and make twice as much money with half the people," he said, watching Culver's eyes carefully.

"He's interested in money?" Culver asked, jarred by the unexpected bit of information.

Radlick nodded. "Better believe it. As far as I can tell, about the only things he does care about are money, computers, and that goddamned photo album—which, I might add, is just about enough to make even a defense attorney puke."

"No wonder the guy doesn't trust you." Culver smiled. "You just can't talk his language."

"Listen, Henry, the guy's a perverse freak, no doubt about it," Radlick went on, ignoring Culver's irrepressible humor. "But I'm telling you, he isn't crazy—or at least not in the sense that matters. He's intelligent, analytical, methodical, and cold as a goddamned ice cube. And he can function out in the world just like anybody else when he wants to—I know that for a fact!"

Then, seemingly disturbed by the idea that he'd gone much too far, Radlick settled back in his chair.

"I talked to Scholtz, too," Culver said quietly, referring to the Fairfax County Police Department's residential psychiatrist.

"He tell you his theories on adaptive personalities?"

"About how the guy supposedly makes up all these different people to deal with his problems? The mental chameleon bit? Yeah, sure," Culver said, unable to keep from smiling. "Sounds about right. I always thought the guy acted more like a lizard than a human being, anyway."

"And the fixation part—did Scholtz tell you about that, too?" Radlick went on, ignoring his friend's easy banter.

"One set of problems becomes overwhelming, so the corresponding personality takes over, becomes dominant . . ."

". . . until the problem is resolved," Radlick finished.

Culver shrugged. "Sounds like typical shrink bullshit, you ask me. Scholtz is one hell of a smart dude, and he's probably the only one around here with the brainpower to figure that guy out; but it's like he said—we all do the same thing, to varying degrees. Your client just gets more intense about it than most. So what?"

"So I think he's got his sights fixed on you and Russelli. He seems to think that you two are his major problems in life right now, and I don't like that."

Culver smiled. "I wouldn't be too crazy about it either if I really thought you were going to get him off. But I don't think that's going to happen, because we've got the bastard nailed down tight. You're going to do your job, give him the best defense you can, and then we all get to watch Toledano put him away. So what's the problem?"

"But what if Toledano doesn't put him away?"

"Is that what's bothering you? You really are afraid that you're going to break one of us down and force Mauser to cut him loose?" Culver asked, cocking his head as a curiously amused expression spread across his face.

"Henry," Radlick said seriously, "pay attention for Christ's sake. That note happens to be a death threat from a guy who's perfectly capable of carrying it out, even from a jail cell."

"Okay, so it's a death threat. So what? Cops get them all the time. As I recall, you even picked one up a few years back, remember?"

"But we're not cops," Radlick emphasized. "You and I were only out on the street for three years before you transferred to the lab and I passed the bar. I'm a lawyer and you're a scientist, dammit!" Radlick hammered his fist on the table in emphasis.

"Yeah, I know, don't remind me." Culver grinned. "But by the time we get this trial back on track, I just might be a cop again—assuming I can remember what I'm supposed to do in one of those new cruisers. Even got honest-to-God computers in them now. You know that? Good thing you didn't stay with the program," Culver said. "You'd have had to learn all about those bits and bytes anyway."

"You'd be out of your mind to go back out on the street. You know that, don't you?" Radlick demanded. "Hell, everybody knows you deserved the crime lab director's job. The only reason Gauss got it was because he hit it big on this case."

"Being a lab director is nothing but a bunch of paperwork. Probably would have driven me nuts anyway, not being able to go out and play at the scenes."

Radlick nodded. "Exactly. You get along with Gauss okay, even if he is an asshole. Long as you do all the supervisory and paperwork crap, you know he'll let you get out to work the crime scenes every now and then. Why risk your butt on patrol?"

"Great idea," Culver snorted sarcastically. "That way I can go out to the crime scenes where it's safe, spend my time poking into puppy dog cages with a pole to see if some prick rigged a guillotine to the door."

"Yeah, okay. You've got a right to be bitter."

"Me? What about Russelli? You want to be the one who tells him he's going to have to retire?"

"Come on, Henry, you and I both know that Kostermann trap was rigged low on purpose. He wasn't trying to kill a cop . . . then," Radlick added pointedly.

"Yeah, just kids, puppies, and kittens. Nice guy, your client," Culver said, nodding his head as he stared silently at the tabletop for a moment. "Speaking of which, where is he now?"

Radlick glanced at his watch. "Probably still in the holding cell. They're going to transport him out to the Ward this afternoon."

"Good," Culver grunted. "Hope they find him a nice deep hole. You going along for the ride?"

Radlick shook his head. "I'm supposed to meet with him next Thursday, day before the trial, talk with his doctors, see if I need to work up some kind of insanity plea."

"I'm glad you've got the stomach for that sort of thing. Personally, I'd rather work floaters for a living."

"I'll tell you what, the guy's a hell of a lot easier to deal with than you and Russelli," Radlick retorted. "At least he listens."

Culver smiled. "Hey, buddy, I appreciate the advice, I really do. But just do us one favor, okay?"

"What's that?" Radlick asked suspiciously.

"If you ever do manage to spring that asshole loose, try to give Russelli and me a little advance warning," Culver said, looking down at the note once more and sighing before wadding it up, tossing it back on the table, and then patting his friend on the shoulder as he got up to leave. "All things considered, we just might need it."

The transport van carrying Digger—who was chained to a metal bench and otherwise secured behind a thick metal mesh screen that kept prisoners isolated from the two uniformed Fairfax County deputy sheriffs in the front cab—was less than a mile from the receiving door of the County Ward when its right rear tire began to vibrate.

The deputy in the front passenger seat noticed it first and started to say something to the driver when he realized that a late model BMW had pulled up even with the van on their right side and its driver was waving frantically.

Well trained, professional, and suspicious by nature, the deputy noted the closely cropped gray hair and beard, wide-set eyes and tough Slavic-looking features of the BMW driver; and accordingly let his right hand slide down to the butt of his .357 revolver.

But the combination of the vibrating tire, the brightly polished chrome of the new BMW, and the frantic waving of the driver provided the right imagery, so he cautiously rolled his window partway down instead.

"You are starting to lose your right rear tire!" the driver of the BMW yelled out.

The guard waved a thank-you and then rolled the window back up before turning to his driver. "Looks like we're getting a flat. Better pull over."

"Yeah, I can feel it. Just what we need on a Friday afternoon," the uniformed van driver grunted in irritation as he checked his mirror to confirm that the BMW had dropped back to pass on the left before he steered the heavy van over to the far side of the road and began breaking to a stop. As he did so, the cautiously alert guard reached for the radio mike, intent on calling for a cruiser to provide security backup.

At that moment, a solid metal project struck the driver's side door of the van with a solid THUNK!

Before either of the deputies could react, the armored tip of a Mark III Gas Dart punched through the multilayered doorframe and began to hiss loudly as it filled the interior of the van with a colorless, odorless gas.

Twenty minutes later, a huge Fairfax County deputy sheriff with a closely cropped gray beard, wide-set eyes, and distinctive Slavic features brought the marked transport van to a slow, cautious stop in front of the receiving door. Then he got out and solemnly delivered John Doe Thirty-three, a.k.a. Digger, into the waiting confines of the Fairfax County Mental Health Ward.

Chapter Seven

Thursday, February 4, 0535 hours

If you ever do manage to spring that asshole loose, try to give Russelli and me a little advance warning. All things considered, we just might need it.

Six days after his client had been booked for the additional charge of felonious assault in Judge Harold Mauser's courtroom, Henry Culver's bantering comment was still echoing in Paul Radlick's sleep-starved mind as he tried to concentrate on the voice at the other end of the line.

He understood the words, and he understood their meaning. What he couldn't understand was how it possibly could have happened.

"What do you *mean* you don't know? Who the hell's in charge out there?" Radlick demanded when the apologetic voice finally seemed to be running out of excuses.

"Oh Jesus, he got out," Radlick whispered to himself, staring out his blackened den window at the cold, dark, and drizzly February morning, as the security chief tried to explain how one of the patients in the Fairfax County Mental Health Ward had apparently gotten out of his locked room in the middle of the night, knocked the attendant unconscious, used the attendant's keys, several pairs of scissors, and—as best they could tell—several willing volunteers to enter all of the other rooms and cut the ID bands off of the other 297 patients in the North Wing, then remove the name tags from the doors and then set the file room on fire.

The fire alarms had brought the rest of the graveyard shift running, but they'd been too late to save the files. As it was, it took everything they had just to get their mostly tranquilized patients back into a locked room—any room—before things *really* got out of hand.

Everybody was under control, the security chief explained, but now they had a problem because they were trying to figure out who was who by matching confused patients back to fragments of checklists that had survived the flames. It wasn't easy because the graveyard medical staff rarely dealt with any of the patients face-to-face, and it didn't help that about half of the residents didn't know who they were either, or simply didn't care.

None of which made any sense to Radlick at all.

But in trying to match people with fragmented records, the security chief continued, the Ward staff had come across a partially burned clipboard that listed John Doe Thirty-three, a.k.a. Digger, as being scheduled for an evaluation session with his attorney on Thursday afternoon, which was why they had called Radlick.

"Listen," Radlick interrupted when the security chief paused for breath, "what about the head count?"

"Uh, what about it?"

Paul Radlick fought to maintain control of his own sanity. "Jesus," he whispered in a voice almost overcome by rage and fear, "didn't you guys check to make sure that nobody got out?"

"Well, yeah, more or less, but . . . uh, just a second, I'll be right back."

Jesus, how could they not *know?* Radlick fumed, his mind numb with apprehension as he found himself staring at a note on his desk. A note reminding him to ask Henry Culver the question that had been nagging at him from the moment that he'd finished reading the crime scene investigation reports.

Where's Digger's computer?

It was a very simple question; but the all-too-likely answer, and the recurring image of another note being crumpled in Henry Culver's hand was starting to make Radlick physically ill.

That and the fact that the article he'd read the week before about the two deputy sheriffs who had rolled their transport van into a ditch was now taking on an even more ominous significance. The coroner's report had indicated that both men died from smoke inhalation and burns, but Radlick hadn't been able to relax until he confirmed by phone that Digger had been delivered to the Ward before the accident.

He'd felt better then, but now . . .

The security chief was back on the phone two minutes later, breathing heavily but anxious to let Radlick know that something had finally gone right. "It's okay," he said, "they're all here. Eight hundred and sixty-three on the nose. Nobody got loose."

"Thank God for that," Radlick whispered fervently. "What about Digger? Did you actually see him?"

"Well, uh . . . no, not exactly."

"What do you *mean,* not exactly?"

"Well see, we . . . uh, still don't know what he looks like."

"Goddamnit, I already *told* you . . . he's about five-eight, with thin light brown hair and *pale fucking blue eyes!*" Radlick almost screamed into the mouthpiece.

"Yeah, I know, but you gotta understand," the security chief pleaded, "we're running this place at maximum capacity. We've got 810 beds, and fifty-three cots, and every one of them's filled. I mean there must be at least a couple dozen guys in this place that could fit that description."

"What about the doctors? Don't any of *them* know what he looks like?"

"Well, yeah, you'd think so. What we got going right now is two of the residents checking their personal notes to see if they can figure it all out; but see, we've got a pretty good-sized rotating staff coming through this place. I guess it's the only way they can keep people working here . . . so anyway, what I'm saying, I guess it's not unusual for one patient to be seen by five or six different shrinks."

"Christ, doesn't *anybody* stay on the job out there?"

"Not if they can help it. Kind of a depressing place to work, you want to know the truth. I mean last month . . ."

"Absolutely fucking incredible."

"Yeah, I can't argue with you there." The security chief sighed. "The thing is, though, we know you're not scheduled to be out here until this afternoon, but the doctors were kinda hoping you'd come out here early and take a look, help us get everybody sorted out," he added wistfully.

"Now?"

"Well, you know, it's not like there's somebody missing or anything. And we're all gonna look like a bunch of jerks if we don't get this all straightened out pretty quick. So they thought maybe if you could get here sometime this morning, before we have to file a report with the county . . ." The security chief let his voice drift off in hopeful anticipation.

Radlick glanced over at the illuminated dial of the clock on his desk. It was 5:48.

"Yeah, all right. I'll be there before eight," Radlick whispered as he hung up the phone. He sat there in the darkness for a few moments, closing his eyes and sighing deeply as he massaged his neck.

"Paul?"

Deep in thought, the sudden unexpected sound of the voice in the darkened room jarred at his nerves.

"Is everything all right?" his wife asked, barely visible as a silhouette in the doorway of his den.

"Just some problems with one of my clients," Radlick

said, reluctant to let someone like John Doe Thirty-three intrude into his family life. He tried to tell himself that it was probably just a holdover from being a cop; that he really should have gotten over being paranoid by now.

"You might as well go back upstairs to bed," he said with far more lightheartedness than he felt. "I'm going to make myself some coffee and read the paper."

"Fine by me." Doreen Radlick yawned agreeably, her blond hair flickering in the dim light from the clock as she turned away and disappeared back into the darkness. He listened to the faint swishing sounds made by her slippers on the hardwood floor until they were replaced by the creak of the carpeted stairs, and then silence.

Turning back to stare at the self-illuminating telephone on his desk, Paul Radlick's eyes focused on the hand-printed name HENRY just barely visible next to the first of twenty autodial buttons. Without really thinking about it, he reached for the handset again, punched the button, and got a busy signal.

"Jesus, Henry, who the hell are you talking to this time of the morning?" he whispered to himself.

Radlick stared at the blank screen of the laptop computer on his desk—the one that his client had talked him into buying for his home—and rested one of his chilled hands against the armored plastic case in an attempt to absorb some of the faint radiating warmth as he tried redial and got the same busy tone.

Deciding to play with his new computer while he waited for Henry Culver to get off the line, Radlick turned it on, listened to the hard drive churn through the boot-up process, watched the C> symbol appear on the color screen, and then tried to figure out what he could do with the thing for the next couple of minutes.

He finally decided to format a disk, remembering that the salesman had advised him to keep a stock of formatted floppies on hand. Secretly pleased with his newfound knowledge,

Radlick inserted a brand-new disk into the drive slot, typed in the word FORMAT, and then hit the enter key again.

WARNING! THE DATA IN DRIVE C: WILL BE DE-
STROYED. DO YOU WANT TO CONTINUE THE
FORMAT (Y/N)?

Worried and distracted, Paul Radlick blinked at the sight of the unfamiliar message. He didn't remember seeing that warning before when he'd formatted the other floppy disks. Then he shrugged, deciding why the hell not? There wasn't any data on that floppy disk anyway.

He hit the "Y" key, and then started to redial Henry Culver's number again, ignoring the fact that his computer had begun to churn busily.

Then he blinked as he suddenly realized that he didn't know what he was going to say.

Hi, Henry. Yeah, I know you're working swings, and it's six in the morning and you've probably only had a couple hours of sleep. I just thought I'd wake you up to let you know that Digger might have tried to escape this evening.

But the head count's right, so he probably didn't. Thing is, I won't know for sure until I go out to the Ward and check for myself because it seems like the stupid bastards out there can't tell one crazy asshole from another unless they have their names tattooed on their foreheads. Nothing to worry about, Henry. Go back to sleep.

Shit!

Shaking his head in irritation, Radlick returned the handset to the receiver, stood up, and headed for the kitchen, completely oblivious to the fact that his computer was still busily reformatting its entire hard drive memory back to zero.

CIA Associate Director for Operations Elliott Parkinson looked up from his desk as J. Winston Weathersby stood hesitantly at the door to his office.

"Well?" Parkinson said coldly, infuriated by the fact that it had been six days since he'd ordered Digger extracted from the County Ward. Six days, and it was only last night that they'd finally been able to get a plan set into motion.

"It wasn't him," the special assistant said in a hoarse whisper, the strain of working virtually nonstop during the past seventy-two hours evident in his voice.

"What do you *mean* it wasn't him?" Parkinson demanded.

"The subject in the Ward, North Wing, Room 242. The one they have logged in as John Doe Thirty-three," Weathersby tried to explain, leaning against the doorway out of pure exhaustion. "We were all set to pull him out. Had the smoke screen all set. Everybody's ID band cut off, all the doors opened, and a fire started in the file room. Even had the subject drugged and ready to go. Turns out he's got light blue eyes, light brown hair, and he's about the right height; but he sure as hell isn't Digger. Good thing I went along or we'd have had a real mess on our hands."

Parkinson blinked as the full implication of J. Winston Weathersby's words hit home.

"Then where the hell *is* he?"

"We don't know."

"And Paz?"

The special assistant shook his head. "I've got a twenty-four-hour surveillance in place, and we've been through his house twice now; but so far, nothing. All we know is that he's transmitting, and apparently back in business; but we have no idea where he's at."

"Did you order him to call in?"

"Twice. Still no response."

"The meetings are scheduled to begin Saturday evening. That's two days from now," Parkinson reminded unnecessarily.

"But we've got more than ninety-five percent of the installations in place," Weathersby protested. "Including the French Ambassador and two of his chief deputies. So maybe we don't need L'Que all that bad anymore," he added hopefully, but Parkinson shook his head.

"Lieutenant Colonel Charles L'Que is a dangerous man. When I walk in to that first meeting with the French, I've *got* to know what they're up to."

Weathersby shrugged. "R.C.'s still available."

"We've already discussed that. I will not give Traynor that kind of advantage."

"Then we need to find Digger immediately."

Something seemed to snap behind Parkinson's eyes, and he looked as though he was about come up over his desk and throttle his young assistant. But before he could get up from his chair, Weathersby came forward hesitantly and dropped a thick file folder on his desk.

"And if that's the case," he continued, "maybe all we need to do is bait a trap."

For about five minutes, the only sound in the plush office was that of Elliott Parkinson flipping rapidly through a marked-up copy of a court transcript with the relevant portions circled in red. Finally, he looked up.

"Do you really believe Digger wants them that badly?"

"The way I read that transcript," the exhausted special assistant said with forced confidence, "right about now, our friend Digger would probably do just about anything to get his hands on a couple of cops named Russelli and Culver."

Parkinson thought about that for a moment, and then nodded his head in agreement. "All right, we'll give him Culver. I want you . . ."

At that moment, the intercom line on Parkinson's phone began to beep.

"Yes?"

"Communications," a hollow-sounding voice replied. "We just received a message from Paz. I think you'd better get down here, right away."

"Hello? What? Speak up, can't hear you," Henry Culver said in a low whisper, oblivious of the fact that he had started to shiver uncontrollably as he tried to concentrate on the voice at the other end of the line. A voice that for some absurd reason sounded like a muted alarm clock at some distant corner of his darkened bedroom.

"Who is it?" the motionless form huddled under the thick down comforter next to Culver's back demanded sleepily.

"Don't know . . . won't say anything. Just keeps humming," Culver mumbled. He rolled his head back on his shoulders, giving in to a deep yawn.

"Hang up," the muffled voice suggested.

Suddenly, the likely source of the steady humming sound registered in Culver's fatigue-drugged mind. He realized that he was sitting on the edge of his bed in his undershorts, holding a telephone up to his ear and damn near freezing to death.

Busy signal. Oh shit.

Culver sighed deeply, his chin almost resting on his chest. "I must have been talking to somebody."

"You don't know?" Tess Beasley's distinctive mop of curly, reddish blond hair and one half-closed eye appeared from under the comforter.

"Uh-uh."

"Then hang up and get back in bed. It's starting to get cold in here."

"Probably a call-out," Culver said, ignoring the logical suggestion as his finger reflexively punched a number on the lighted dial that he had memorized a long time ago.

"Henry, for Pete's sake . . ."

"Police Dispatch." The voice was clear, crisp, professional, and feminine, not to mention very familiar.

"This is Culver. Uh, was I just talking to you?"

"What? Who is—Henry? Is that you?"

Crisp, professional, and definitely familiar. Culver smiled. "Hi, Sally."

"What are you doing up? Aren't you supposed to be asleep?"

"I don't know." Culver yawned. "Woke up and found myself sitting up in bed listening to a busy signal. Thought it might have been a call-out, so . . ."

". . . you called me to see if you'd been talking in your sleep again," Dispatcher Sally Henderson finished, her crisp and clear telephone demeanor giving way to a decidedly unprofessional sigh.

"Uh-huh."

"Henry," the voice said gently, "you don't work in the lab anymore, remember? They took your name off the call-out list last Monday."

"Oh yeah, that's right." Culver nodded, feeling relief and vague disappointment all at the same time.

That's right, I'm a cruiser jockey now. No more call-outs. Why can't I remember that?

"Henry, are you still there?"

"Uh-huh?"

"Unplug the phone and go back to bed," Dispatcher Sally Henderson advised before another ringing line demanded her attention. "Gotta go. Good night."

"Uhmm, yeah, good idea." Culver nodded sleepily. He reached down next to the nightstand to disconnect the telephone line and noticed the notepad and pen lying on the carpeted floor.

Groaning audibly, Culver leaned forward, picked up the pad, and held it next to the illuminated dial of the telephone. It contained mostly illegible scribbling, but he was able to make out the words "Harvard Crimson," a one, a four, two zeros, and the capital letters "LC."

Harvard Crimson. Fourteen hundred hours. Library of Congress.

Oh shit, not again.

Shaking his head in irritation, Culver snapped the telephone line out from the wall jack and then quickly slid his chilled body back into the alluring warmth of the comforter.

"What's a good idea?" Tess Beasley shivered as Culver snuggled up against her bare back and brought his hand gently up against one of her firm breasts.

"Attack your body," he mumbled against the back of her neck.

"Uhmm, sounds nice, but you already did that. Who was it?"

"Sally." This time, his voice was more of a sigh.

"No, I mean who called you?"

"Dunno. Wrong number, salesman, pervert, somebody." Culver's words seemed to drift away in the darkness.

"You get obscene phone calls at six o'clock in the morning?" Tess Beasley whispered.

"Yeah, 'xactly what it was," he whispered softly.

Tess Beasley snuggled herself back in tighter against Henry Culver's chest and midsection, and then waited agreeably for the gentle, callused hand to begin its slow caressing motion. Instead, she felt the muscles in his hand slowly relax.

Turning her head back to rest against Culver's neck, she whispered in his ear. "Hey, I thought you were going to attack."

Silence, and then a long sighing snore.

Sighing to herself, Tess Beasley wrapped her fingers in through the loosened fingers of Culver's warming hand, pulled it in tight against her midsection, and then allowed her mind to drift away into a secure and easy unconsciousness.

Chapter Eight

Thursday, 0645 hours

Sitting at his kitchen table while he waited for the coffeepot to stop perking, Paul Radlick let the phone ring twelve times before finally giving up in disgust.

"Jesus Christ, Henry," he muttered to himself as he walked over to the cupboard and found his coffee cup, "you were just on the phone five minutes ago. What the hell are you *doing* over there?"

Having no way of knowing that Henry Culver was now sound asleep next to his unplugged bedroom phone, Radlick punched the redial button one more time, waited another dozen rings, and then shoved the phone away in disgust. Then he picked up the letters and the addressed envelopes that he had anguished over the previous evening.

Somebody had scammed his client. He knew that now, even if he couldn't prove it. The question was, who?

You may not believe it, Henry, and you may not even care, Radlick thought as he slowly went through the motions of folding the letters, sealing the envelopes, and licking the stamps, *but it happened. And if it wasn't you and Russelli, then who the hell was it?*

He set the sealed envelopes down on the table next to the one he'd received in the mail yesterday—the one that contained a cashier's check for seventy-five thousand dollars with the hand-printed notation "Attorney's Fee—Digger"— and stared at them both for a few moments.

He was tempted to throw both the envelopes *and* the check into the trash and just simply not worry about it anymore; let the system deal with John Doe Thirty-three. It was very tempting, because Paul Radlick knew—in spite of his legal training to do his job and fight for his client—that the last thing his client needed was more legal help. What he *needed* was to be put away somewhere, preferably in a place where he could never hurt anyone ever again.

Agonized by the knowledge that a little more work on his part might actually get his demented client released, Radlick continued to stare at the envelopes, wondering for perhaps the hundredth time who the hell would shell out an anonymous seventy-five thousand to help a freak like Digger.

Then, shaking his head in resignation, he picked up the sealed envelopes and walked out into his garage. There, he thumbed a button that sent the heavy garage door noisily clanking upward, pulled a large blue plastic poncho over his head, and walked out into the cold, drizzling darkness to get his newspaper.

Paul Radlick was halfway up the long asphalt driveway before he realized that the expected moonlight was being blocked by the clouds. The only available light was at his back—a diffuse beam coming from the ceiling fixture in the kitchen, just barely visible through the exterior dining room window. The bulb in the front entry door lamp had burned out several days ago, and he hadn't gotten around to replacing it yet.

There was enough light from the kitchen to throw a strangely billowing weak shadow out in front of his feet, as Radlick continued toward the distant mailbox, trying to remember what shifts Henry Culver and John Russelli were on now.

Regardless of the security chief's vaguely reassuring comments, Radlick had already decided that he was going to stop by the homes of both Culver and Russelli before he drove out to the Ward. He'd pound on their doors until somebody answered, and then make sure they were aware that Digger might be loose.

Just in case.

Distracted by the eerie pattern of rain falling through the bare tree branches in the darkness, Radlick almost missed the diffused flickering sweep of another outstretched shadow that quickly passed from left to right across the driveway from behind his legs, and then immediately disappeared into the blackened grass and trees.

It was the remnants of his street-honed survival instincts, more than anything else, that caused Paul Radlick to stop for a moment in blinking confusion.

Then he twisted around sharply—a move that sent a chilling rush of adrenaline through his spine—as he brought his hands up in a defensive stance. He immediately felt ridiculous because there was nothing there.

Embarrassed and irritated with himself, Radlick hurried out to the end of the driveway, put the letters in the mailbox, and pulled up the metal flag. He was about to reach for the paper when a discordant image started to nudge at his subconscious and he brought his head up sharply.

Clearly visible in the glary light from the empty dining room window, the driveway was empty—just a glistening sheet of water-covered asphalt that swerved to the left into the black mouth of the garage illuminated by a single toothlike rectangle of light that was the doorway into the kitchen.

As Paul Radlick stood there in the rain, blinking his eyes and staring, he suddenly realized that gray-black mouth of the garage reminded him of the blank computer screen in his office.

Then, suddenly, he remembered something else.

The fact that he'd worked on the computer for several hours the previous evening before finally giving up in frustration, turning it off, and going up to bed.

He looked down at his watch. Six-thirty. Seven and a half hours ago. So why the hell was it still warm?

And more to the point, why should the fact that his computer was warm or cold bother him anyway? Just because Digger couldn't find his . . .

Paul Radlick's head came up sharply, his eyes widening in shock.

The horrible possibility of what the source of that flickering shadow *might* have been sent numbing chills surging through Radlick's arms and legs as he lunged forward, desperately trying to get traction on the slippery asphalt as he slipped and scrabbled toward his house.

No!

Pulling himself through the illuminated doorway in a mindless fury that was almost overwhelmed by an equivalent sense of dread, Paul Radlick's police-trained eyes swept from left to right, through the empty kitchen, across the open walkway to the family room, and farther across to the open dining room.

No movement.

Nothing.

Shaking away the rationalizations that tried to flood his mind, and completely unaware that his right hand had formed itself into a rigid claw, Radlick moved slowly and purposefully forward. He passed through the kitchen and family room, watching and listening for the slightest movement, until he finally stood at the doorway of his den.

He tensed as he threw the light switch, shielding his eyes for a moment to protect his vision before he brought his hands back up to ward off . . . what?

No movement. Nothing.

He turned his head slowly, scanning every corner, every possible hiding place.

And still saw nothing. The room was still and empty, the way he'd left it only minutes earlier.

Feeling every sensory organ in his body almost tremble with anticipation, he walked forward to stand in front of his desk, his back to the closet. Then he reached out to touch the computer again.

The tough cream-colored plastic case was still warm.

What does that mean? Radlick fumed. *Is there some sort of motor inside that stays running, even after you shut the damned thing off? Dammit, Henry, why aren't you around when I need you?*

Slowly shaking his head in frustration, Paul Radlick tried to walk himself through the events of the previous evening; using his body movements to try to recall exactly what he'd done.

Reached out, shut it off, he remembered, reaching forward to brush his hand against the cool plastic switch.

Got up, picked up the box of disks, turned around, put them in the closet, he nodded silently as he turned around and motioned with his hands toward the closed closet door.

Turned around, shut off the den light, and walked out to the kitchen. He started forward, confident now of his memory.

And left the closet door open.

Paul Radlick stopped dead still, and then slowly turned

back around to stare at the securely shut closet door, feeling a sensation of chilling numbness that felt like someone had just poured ice water down the back of his neck.

Left it open. Radlick nodded silently as he continued to stare at the darkly stained wood door. Doreen was already upstairs in bed. *Absolutely left it open.*

It wasn't a conscious decision. One moment, Radlick was simply standing there; the next he was lunging forward, his left hand reaching for the door handle and ripping it open as his right came up in the instinctive claw that drove upward into the throat of . . .

Nothing.

He blinked, staring into the closet that was half-filled with shelves of papers, and computer disks and everything else that Radlick *expected* to be there. Everything except an elusive excuse for a human being who called himself Digger.

It was at that moment that the draft of cold air hit him and he looked down.

A trapdoor in the carpeted floor of the closet—a door that would have remained invisible to the casual eye, had it not been propped open with a small stick—stared up at Radlick like the dark slit in the eye of an unimaginably huge and terrible beast.

It was only then that Radlick, stunned and shocked by disbelief, noticed the mud.

There wasn't much of it. Only small chunks, rectangular in shape, that seemed to form a trail from the partially opened trapdoor, across the carpeted floor of his den, to his desk, back to the door . . .

"Oh God, no," he whispered.

. . . across the polished wood floor of the living room . . .

"No!"

. . . to the stairs.

Chapter Nine

Thursday, 1319 hours

At 1:19 P.M. on that still-cold and drizzly winter day in Fairfax County, Virginia, Molly Hunsacker drove her van up the long driveway of an isolated, single-family residence on Fairfax Station Road. At the top of the driveway, she came to a slow, gentle stop. Then she reached for her console-mounted car phone and dialed a recently memorized phone number.

Moments later, at precisely 1:22 P.M., she stepped down out of her van, walked up to the door, and entered the weather-beaten, two-story, Colonial-styled house the way she almost always entered a house.

Which was to say that Molly Hunsacker—or, as she was more commonly known by the Fairfax County Police Department, Molly-the-Hun—rang the doorbell, waited a few moments for a very unlikely answer, reached down into her canvas kit bag with her thickly muscled arms, and then proceeded to rip the doorknob lock apart with a four-foot-long, twenty-three-pound plumber's wrench.

The entry took all of twelve seconds, door to door.

It was, even for a residential burglar of Molly-the-Hun's far-ranging reputation, an eye-opening performance; and one that would have certainly opened the eyes of Henry Culver, had the tall, slender, thirty-nine-year-old police officer happened to drive past that particular Fairfax Station address while on an essentially random patrol of his assigned area.

But Henry Culver wasn't in a position to spot Molly Hunsacker at work on this cold and dreary Thursday afternoon for two simple reasons.

First of all, he wasn't due to go on shift until three o'clock that afternoon.

And two, he was already on his way to a covert meeting with an individual whose professional goals and ambitions were very closely related to Molly-the-Hun's activities on Fairfax Station Road, although they were far more menacing in nature.

The DC Metro Rail System, with its five lines linking the Northern Virginia and Eastern Maryland suburbs to the central hub of Washington, District of Columbia, held several advantages over its New York City counterpart. Among other things, it was smaller, cleaner, quieter, and much safer to ride.

But in spite of the hundreds of millions of taxpayer dollars that had been poured into the swampy soil that supported the nation's capital, the trains still didn't run on time.

The Orange Line train that was supposed to depart from Vienna, Virginia, at precisely 1300 hours en route to the distant end point of New Carrollton, Maryland, had been nine minutes late leaving the station, which meant that Henry Culver wasn't going to make his two o'clock appointment unless he ran.

Eighteen stops and fifty-one minutes later, Culver got off the train at the underground Capitol South Station at First and D streets, Southeast, and headed directly for the exit gates. He gained an extra fifty seconds, a moderate amount of self-esteem, and some badly needed exercise by jogging up the slowly moving steps of the tunnel-encased stairway.

Ten minutes later, Henry Culver entered the Old Library of Congress Building through the ground level public entrance. Once past the uniformed security check, he ignored a familiar black-and-white photo display of DC night life; made a series of left and right turns, and then used a small circular key to enter and operate a tiny elevator that more closely resembled a janitor's closet and rode like a Model T.

After dropping a good thirty or so feet while the ancient hoist made a determined effort to rattle itself apart, Henry

Culver gratefully stepped out into a narrow and dimly lit corridor. About fifty feet and two sharp right turns later, he stopped in front of an unmarked door and knocked.

The door was opened by a young man of slender build with clear blue eyes, carefully trimmed hair, and a superbly tailored three-piece gray suit. He stood there in the doorway for a few moments, staring with visible distaste at Culver's blue jeans, red-and-black flannel shirt, down jacket, and hiking boots before finally glancing down at his watch and then motioning for him to enter.

Henry Culver didn't move.

"Excuse me, I must have the wrong floor," Culver said evenly, staring at the unfamiliar face.

Christ, wasn't it Traynor who called? Culver thought as he tried to remember even a fragment of the early morning phone call that he wouldn't have remembered at all if it hadn't been for his scribbled notes.

"It's all right, come inside," the young man urged, searching both sides of the corridor with his flickering eyes as he motioned at Culver with a neatly manicured hand.

"I'm sorry, I must have made a wrong turn at the corridor," Culver said.

Don't panic. Give him five more seconds. One thousand and one. One thousand and two. . . .

The young man continued to stare at Culver, his eyebrows furrowed with confusion. "What's the matter with you?" he demanded, and then suddenly understood. "That's right, you want it by the numbers, don't you? All right. Virginia Tech . . ." He hesitated, visibly wincing at the word. ". . . Gobblers. There, is that better?"

"Much," Culver said as he stopped counting and stepped in quickly through the narrow doorway.

The interior of the artfully concealed room offered an unlikely contrast to the decrepit elevator and the gloomy access corridor. It was bright and spacious and tastefully decorated. At a small bar in the corner, a fancy-looking coffee machine bubbled quietly on the countertop, filling the room with the deliciously warm and fragrant aroma of an expensive roasted brew. But even more interesting to Culver was the inconspicuous code-locked door and flush-to-the-wall mirror behind the bar, suggesting the presence of adjoining rooms possibly even more tastefully decorated.

Or even more sinister and deceiving. Culver smiled as his trained eyes took in the familiar surroundings. Given all of the other distractions, the noise-dampening acoustics and the ultrahigh-pitched "white noise" being generated within the thick walls were hardly noticeable at all.

"You're late," J. Winston Weathersby said gruffly as he carefully sat in a period chair, crossed his hands and ankles, and favored Culver with a stern glare.

"Maybe you folks could find an easier place to meet next time," Culver suggested, ignoring the young man's comment as he tossed his jacket on the couch and settled comfortably in an overstuffed chairs. "Like on the roof of the White House."

"How and where we meet is not your concern," Weathersby replied stiffly.

"That's a matter of opinion. Where's Traynor?"

"You said you'd be here at two," Weathersby said, ignoring his question. "In the future, it may be very important for you to be on time."

"You're lucky I can write in my sleep, or I wouldn't be here at all," Culver said, staring directly into the young man's deceptively clear blue eyes. "I repeat, where's Traynor?"

"I have a tape for you to listen to. I assume you're capable of recognizing Arthur Traynor's voice?"

"I think so," Culver nodded, and then listened carefully as the man activated a cassette player on the lamp table.

"Hello, Henry," the familiar gruff voice spoke. "Sorry to do this to you, but we have a substantive problem on our hands and we can really use your help. The person I'm referring you to—the, uh, young man you are talking with right now—is currently operating under the cover name of Forecastle. He is about five-foot-seven, with blue eyes, short blond hair, and what you might classify as a rosy complexion. He also has two dark moles about a centimeter apart on the back of his right hand."

Culver watched the young man casually expose the back of his hand, noting the presence of the two moles as he considered the fact that Traynor despised the word *substantive* because he considered it a prissy bureaucratic affectation. He was also fairly certain that he had never heard Traynor include complexion as a part of a subject's description.

Okay, Traynor, Culver smiled to himself. *I think I understand.*

"As a personal favor to me," Traynor's voice continued to echo across the small room, "please try to help him *if you can.* Apart from everything else, the issue may be very important indeed."

Culver remained silent as the young man reached across the table and hit the rewind button.

"So am I also supposed to call you 'Forecastle,' or do you have a real name?" Culver inquired.

" 'Forecastle' will suffice for the time being," J. Winston Weathersby replied in what Culver decided was his customary, self-important voice. "I am due at an extremely important meeting in exactly forty-five minutes, so we'll need to hurry," he added as he picked up a thin manila folder.

"I'm listening."

"The director isn't happy," the meticulously attired young man began in an understated but authoritative voice.

"The director?" Culver's eyebrows rose in amusement.

"Yes, that's right, *the* director." Weathersby seemed about ready to add a stinging retort, but then apparently changed his mind. "We may have a problem developing with one of our operations. It involves some Fairfax County locals, within your jurisdiction."

Culver waited for the pompous young bureaucrat to continue, and then finally said: "Yes, so?"

"We'd like for you to be on call during the next few weeks,

available for some crime scene work—if it becomes necessary."

"Yours or theirs?"

"I beg your pardon?"

"I was just wondering who might be committing the crime," Culver said, irritated that he had allowed himself to get caught up in all of this nonsense.

"Traynor mentioned that you had an interesting sense of humor," Weathersby said, forcing his lips into a reluctant smile as he went on. "In addition to the scene work—which, I can assure you, is directly related to an urgent matter of national security—we would also like you to arrange for a transfer to another position within the police department, where you would have a little more flexibility in assisting us, should it become necessary." The CIA special assistant broadened his smile encouragingly.

"*Us* meaning you and Traynor?"

"No, 'us' meaning me and . . . just me."

"So Traynor's not involved in this project?"

"No. As the tape indicated, you were a referral."

"And exactly what position within the PD are *you* talking about?" Culver asked, watching the young man's eyes carefully.

"There are several possibilities," J. Winston Weathersby replied as he diverted his gaze over to the bubbling coffeepot. "Robbery or Homicide investigator might be the most, ah, useful. Or, I suppose, you could always transfer back to your previous position in the crime lab."

"Apparently we both have a sense of humor."

"I'm led to believe that several months ago, you told Traynor that you had an excellent chance to be assigned to a Major Crimes Unit *if* you spent some time in Patrol," Weathersby reminded. "Presumably that was why you were given the authorization to make the move."

"And I take it that you're new to all of this."

"Why do you say that?"

"What I was *given,* by Traynor, was continued access to

the Agency's electronics lab, with no strings attached. You people don't authorize *anything* I do, for the simple reason that I don't work for you anymore."

"Actually, I understand that's just a technicality," Weathersby said, favoring his casually attired guest with a confidently superior glare.

"No. Actually it's more like a federal law," Culver contradicted. "The rules are very clear on that point. This is the home field, and you guys don't get to play on it."

"I believe that the overriding principles of *posse comitatus . . .*"

". . . have absolutely nothing to do with anything that we are talking about," Culver finished. "Read the law. Or better yet, go talk to one of your lawyers. I can work for Fairfax County, or I can work for the CIA, but not both. At least, not at the same time."

"But . . ."

"But nothing. The answer is no," Culver said firmly. "I'm not interested."

"Traynor also mentioned that you might be difficult."

"Not difficult." Culver shook his head slowly. "Just careful. When I left the Agency, Traynor arranged it so that I could continue to have access to some of his high-tech toys. The people I work for like that, so in exchange, I stay in touch. On occasion; when I can, I try to be helpful. But that's all, nothing more."

"You could be much more helpful if you were back in the lab," Weathersby suggested.

"Which one, yours or ours?" Culver smiled, taking some pleasure in baiting the irritatingly precise young man who looked like he'd been born in a three-piece suit.

Probably never owned a pair of jeans in his life, Culver thought. *Wonder what he used to do before going to work for Traynor. Probably sat in some fancy, air-conditioned office, brushing flecks of dust off his desk in between drafting memos for his boss that would end up causing some poor soul in some remote part of the world a lot of grief. Looks the type.*

Plenty of brains, but no guts, and not a trace of a conscience. Christ, they ought to just get it over with and start making them out of robots.

"The PD. Don't be difficult," Weathersby said testily.

"I've already explained all of that to Traynor." Culver sighed in exasperation as he stood up and reached for his jacket. "The situation in the lab changed. I requested a transfer to patrol for a number of reasons, most of them personal. I think I've got a decent chance at a detective slot in Major Crimes, and I'm going to take it if it's offered—but *not* because I want to get involved in any more of your little games."

"You do realize that we could be much more insistent, don't you?" Weathersby asked calmly.

Culver stopped, turned back around, and then stared down at the cold, unfeeling eyes of the young man in the neatly tailored, three-piece dark gray suit.

"I'm very much aware that you and your associates could make my life extremely difficult," Culver replied in a slow, careful manner.

"That's right, we could."

"I'm also very much aware that something like that can work both ways."

"Oh really, how so?" Weathersby asked, momentarily taken back by the implied threat.

"Traynor spent a lot of money on my education," Culver said, continuing to speak slowly and carefully, knowing with absolute certainty that the room was wired. He was pretty sure he even knew who had wired it. A minimum of four microphones and two pinholes that he had spotted, and probably several others that he hadn't. A typical R.C. Cohen job—pure class. "I was a good student, and I've got a good memory. That's probably why Traynor gave me the emeritus rating. The Agency would win, eventually, but it would get messy."

"Of course we would win! What did you think . . . ?" J. Winston Weathersby started to exclaim when Culver interrupted.

"I said the Agency would win, eventually. Not you."

Weathersby blinked in stunned disbelief, his cheeks blushing crimson with barely suppressed rage. It took several moments before he was finally able to bring himself back under control.

"I sincerely hope that none of that was meant as a threat," he said indignantly.

"Me too." Culver nodded in agreement, fixing his gaze on Weathersby's clear blue eyes until the young CIA special assistant finally turned away.

"Yes, well, as you said, we would win in any case—but I was only referring to political pressure," he added, waving his hand casually as if to dismiss the thought of anything more drastic or messy as absurd. His eyes, however, suggested nothing of the sort. "I'm sure that if we put our minds to it, arrangements could be made that would be a little more, shall we say, official? Perhaps with your chief of police?"

He's really trying, Culver thought, realizing that the young CIA bureaucrat, for all his efforts to appear friendly and congenial, was probably little more than a cold, calculating, and ultimately indifferent expediter of misery and misfortune. Specific laws and individual people wouldn't matter to him in the least.

Christ, where do they get guys like that?

"Personally, I think the chief would tell you, eyeball-to-eyeball, exactly what you could do with your 'arrangements'; but yeah, you might be able to pull it off," Culver acknowledged as he put on his jacket. "Thing is, though, you'd need my cooperation to make it work and keep it clean."

"And you don't think that you could be that . . . cooperative?"

"Not a chance." Culver shook his head as he turned his back to the man and walked over to the door.

"Why not?"

"Simple." Culver turned his head back and smiled as pleasantly as he could at the cold, deadly eyes as he pulled the heavy door open. "No matter how official you guys make it, and no matter how many higher-ups give the final okay, it all still comes down to one thing."

"And what's that?" the furious young bureaucrat demanded.

"You'd be cheating."

Elliott Parkinson was sitting in an upright chair in a darkened room behind the flush-to-the-wall bar mirror when the door behind him clicked open. A heavyset man with a full red beard entered the darkened room, glanced through the one-way mirror to confirm that Culver and Weathersby had departed, and then turned on the lights.

Parkinson didn't even bother to turn around.

"Now do you understand?" Dr. Arthur Traynor, associate director of the CIA's Science and Technology Directorate inquired as he sat down in the chair across from Parkinson, tossed a half-inch-thick summary file stamped "TOP SECRET—OPS" on the center coffee table, and then solemnly contemplated his associate director counterpart for CIA Operations, and chief rival for the soon-to-be-open director's job.

Traynor's Sci-Tech staff, who were predominantly specialists in wire-tapping, electronics, communications, computers, and such, were charged with the task of providing close technical support to the CIA operatives in the field; these being genuine, federal government employees who ran authorized missions under the direction of people like Parkinson. In theory, the Operations and Sci-Tech directorates worked in close harmony with each other, and with their sister Intelligence Division, to the benefit of the Agency as a whole. In practice, the political battles fought within the walls of the CIA's Langley Headquarters Building over turf, access, and funding were as bloodthirsty and vicious as anything ever seen or heard within the Washington, DC, Beltway. So it was of no great surprise that Dr. Arthur Traynor and Mr. Elliott Parkinson, a.k.a. Topcastle, thoroughly despised and distrusted each other.

The fact that Parkinson had just been ordered by the deputy director of the CIA to provide Traynor with a status summary of operation MEG had done little to improve their relationship over the past four and a half hours.

"You have him listed in the reference directory as a potentially useful asset. I question your judgment on that," Parkinson said quietly.

"Henry has a great deal of potential," Traynor contradicted. "He may even come back to us someday, once he's outgrown some of his idealism."

"Did you ever send him out on field assignments?" Parkinson asked.

Traynor hesitated for a moment, then said: "Henry was primarily a field operative when he worked for us."

"Then he should have gotten that sort of thing out of his system a long time ago."

"Some of us try to maintain the illusion that a better world is possible if we try to work together." And then, when Parkinson failed to respond, the Sci-Tech AD added quietly:

"Elliott, let me try this one more time. You're on the wrong track. First of all, an associate director shouldn't be running field operations, period, much less this one. And you, in particular, should not be running this operation in any case."

"Are you questioning my competence?" Parkinson bristled.

"No, just your common sense." Arthur Traynor sighed. "Elliott, what I'm saying is that you don't deal well with people. By your own admission, you don't give a damn about your employees, and they know it."

"I'll have you know that my deputy and my special assistant both . . ."

"Your deputy has submitted five separate requests to be transferred back to the field, and Weathersby's a fawning idiot—you saw that for yourself a few minutes ago," Traynor interrupted. "Elliott, listen to me. You can't run an operation when your own people don't trust you, even if your planning is flawless. And in this case, it's not."

Parkinson started to spit out a scathing reply, but Traynor put up a restraining hand.

"Elliott, I read the file. I read it very carefully. And aside from everything else that stands between us, I have to tell you that based upon what little information you placed in that file, I truly believe your operation is critically flawed. Creating and manipulating an international environmental group for the purpose of directing economic sanctions toward uncooperative nations is an incredibly dangerous concept. If word were to leak out that the Agency was involved in such a conspiracy, we would be terribly damaged. For your own good, and the good of the Agency—not to mention our standing in the international community—I urge you to terminate it immediately . . . and to forget about this idea of using Henry Culver and the Fairfax County Police Department to try to protect this sociopath asset of yours. Digger may be talented in a technical sense; but in my experience, someone that unstable is never worth the risk. And you don't want to add Henry to your problems," Traynor added. "He can't help you, even if he wants to."

"MEG is my operation, and I'm the one who decides *when* or *if* to terminate it," Parkinson snapped.

"Yes, I understand that." Traynor nodded in solemn agreement.

"I want his file."

"I beg your pardon?"

"Culver. I want his file. It was supposed to be transferred to Operations immediately. The director signed off on it. You saw the memo."

Traynor nodded silently.

"And I would remind you that the director doesn't share your opinion on this operation. In point of fact, he is very much in agreement that my objectives in this operation are of critical importance to the Agency."

"I'm not questioning the value of your objectives," Traynor said. "Just your methods . . . and your selection of resources."

"Fine, then we'll leave it at that," Parkinson nodded, his voice shifting into a more neutral tone that made Traynor immediately alert. "One last thing. The director's memo ordered Sci-Tech to provide technical support on this operation as needed."

"You're requesting our support?" Traynor blinked in surprise.

"You've disagreed with several of our projects in the past, but Sci-Tech has always been supportive," the Operations AD reminded.

"And as long as you have a sign-off from the director, we will continue to be supportive." Traynor shrugged. "What's the situation?"

"One of our operatives is missing. I need a search team," Parkinson said with almost visible reluctance. "I was hoping to use Culver, but . . ."

"Who, exactly, is missing?" Traynor asked as he reached into his coat pocket for his notebook.

Parkinson hesitated before speaking. "Alberto Paz."

Traynor's head came up with a start. "Isn't he your controller on Digger?"

"Yes."

Jesus H. Christ, Traynor thought to himself as he began to take notes, using his personal cryptic codes.

"How long?"

"We're not certain."

"What do you *mean* you're not certain?" Traynor looked up from his notes. "When was your last contact?"

"We're not sure."

"What?"

"We've been getting reports from Paz on a daily basis for quite some time now—over six months," Parkinson explained. "We—"

"What is today, operationally?" Traynor interrupted.

"One hundred and ninety-four. Anyway, we—"

"And how do you receive the reports?" Traynor interrupted again as he continued to scribble seemingly random blocks of numbers and letters.

"We use a firewall-protected electronic bulletin board—triple-coded access with periodic replacements. Paz uses a notebook computer with an internal modem and a 5Y Cyberchip. Your techs provided the equipment," Parkinson added. "He's been averaging about a hundred words a day in block phrases—status, time-tales, standard stuff. He's an early riser, so he usually transmits between 6:00 and 8:00 A.M."

Traynor nodded as he continued to write in his notebook.

"As you know," Parkinson went on reluctantly, "we've had several problems on this operation, and then the one major setback."

"You consider one of your operatives getting arrested for murder a setback?"

Parkinson hesitated, but didn't rise to the bait.

"We're not completely certain that Digger was actually involved in that incident," he said with forced restraint. "At least one of the detectives may have been running a personal vendetta, and it appears that some of the evidence was tainted. But anyway," he went on hurriedly, "in spite of all of that, we had every indication that Paz was able to get the operation back on track without Digger. Aside from a few missed reports, everything seemed to be back to normal, until this morning."

"What happened?" Traynor whispered. He could feel his arms starting to tingle.

"This morning, he used the same code."

This time it was Traynor's turn to blink while Elliott Parkinson forced himself to continue.

"We sent back a request for a repeat, indicating that we had a receiving problem at our end. The reply came back about three minutes later, using the identical code."

"When you say identical . . . ?"

"Paz is scheduled to switch access codes on the twenty-second of each month," Parkinson said reluctantly. "As far as I'm aware, this is the first time he's ever missed a changeover."

Traynor could feel his chest muscles start to tighten. "Digger," he whispered, staring straight into Elliott Parkinson's eyes. "Is he still in custody?"

The associate director of Operations hesitated for a moment, and then shook his head.

"Jesus Christ," Traynor rasped in horror, "you lost him."

Chapter Ten

Thursday, 1522 hours

It was obvious to Culver that the dog had tried to put up a fight.

The evidence was all there: the torn curtain, the overturned chair and the smashed lamp just inside the front door, the elbow-level gouges in the plasterboard wall, the smears of dried blood all across the living room floor.

And most telling of all: the little piece of cloth.

Culver smiled, remembering how the girl had slid the soggy piece of blue denim fabric off the dog's left incisor; and then had to leave it on the counter for him to pick up later, because the severely injured and barely conscious German shepherd had made it perfectly clear—with a couple of deep-throated growls—that he had no intention of allowing Culver to get within touching distance of any member of the household. The definition of which, as Culver quickly discovered, apparently included a small, weasellike animal that they called, for some undetermined reason, Spanky.

Gotta be close to a hundred pounds, not counting the cast-iron skull, Culver thought, watching the incredibly limber little animal scamper fearlessly beneath the shepherd's fearsome set of open jaws to grab and pull at the dish towel the eleven-year-old girl was using to clean and inspect the dog's injuries.

Which was going to be a problem, Culver decided, because it was fairly obvious that the young girl and her aunt weren't going to be able to lift the dog by themselves.

Wonderful, he thought. *Hope the hell Tess can get her hands on that stretcher.*

The girl was sitting on the floor of the kitchen with the massive head of the coal black German shepherd in her lap, gently swabbing at the swollen area around the dog's left eye and ear with the moistened dishcloth. She'd stopped crying a few minutes after Culver had arrived, but her shoulders quivered every now and then, and her cheeks were still marked with long tear streaks.

"You were right, he was bleeding," the girl said in a choked whisper.

"That's okay, it really doesn't look too bad," Culver said reassuringly, hoping he was right. Even half-conscious, the protective shepherd had its intimidation routine down pat. Especially the deep-throated growl part.

"Will they be here pretty soon?" the girl asked.

"In just a couple of minutes, hon."

Means the blood in the living room is probably from the dog. Culver shrugged disappointedly, watching the dishcloth darken as it continued to absorb the dark, semiliquid blood. Aside from the value of the blood smears as evidence, there was one possible version of the break-in that had been very appealing to Culver on a purely emotional level. The one that would have had him making cheerful inquiries to the local hospital emergency rooms.

Too bad, he thought to himself. *Had to have been one hell of a shock for her to have walked in on something like that.*

Culver smiled momentarily, visualizing the residential burglar coming in fast through the broken door, only to find a fiercely protective, hundred-pound nightmare with fangs waiting on the other side.

It was a nice thought, but the nightmare had been dealt

with all too effectively, Culver reminded himself. Probably with ice-cold nerves and reflexes to match.

Sorry, Bear. He shook his head sadly. *Better luck next time.*

"Lisa," Culver said softly, startling the girl and causing her head to jerk up—which, in turn, caused the dog to bare his teeth and growl once again.

"What?" she whispered in a shaky voice.

"You aren't afraid of me, are you?"

"No, why?" the girl replied in what Culver interpreted to be a decidedly uncertain tone.

"I'm pretty sure Bear thinks you're afraid of me," Culver explained. "And if he thinks that, he's not going to let me help put him in the car."

"Oh. Well, I guess maybe I am a little bit afraid of your gun," the girl admitted as she continued to stroke the dog's head, her eyes flickering over to the .357 Smith & Wesson revolver securely holstered to Culver's right hip.

"Don't be." Culver smiled reassuringly. "It's not meant to scare or harm people like you."

"But it *is* meant to kill people though, isn't it?" she said with a frankness that startled Culver.

"I suppose it is," Culver said after a moment. "But listen," he went on, choosing his words with care, "would it help if I told you that I've never had to shoot my gun at *anyone* as long as I've been a police officer, and that I have no intention of *ever* shooting anybody if I can possibly avoid it?"

"You're a policeman and you've never shot anybody?" the girl asked, expressing both disbelief and confusion.

Culver shook his head firmly. "Not even once."

The girl seemed to think about that for a few moments.

"I guess I really wouldn't care too much if you shot the person who hurt Bear," she finally said.

"Can't say I blame you for feeling that way. Looks like you two are really good friends."

The girl nodded solemnly. "We are. My mom and I gave him to my Aunt Kathy for Christmas when he was a little puppy. Aunt Kathy's letting me help train him. I'm staying here with her while my mom's in the hospital. Oh, and I guess Spanky's helping, too," she added, scratching the head of the small mammal who had curled himself up against the thick neck of the shepherd.

"And Spanky is?"

"Oh, he's a ferret. The good kind."

"The good kind? You mean there's good and bad ferrets?" Culver asked, smiling.

"I guess." The girl shrugged. "Most of them aren't very affectionate. I mean, they're real playful, and they *really* like to dig a lot—especially him, and they're not afraid of anything. But usually they just don't care about people—you know, like a dog does. Usually, all they want to do is run away and look at everything."

"And Spanky's different, I take it?"

"Sort of. He likes to run away too, but he always comes back. And he likes to be held, and he and Bear really like each other a lot."

"So I see," Culver said, observing the limber ferret twist around beneath the lethal jaws of the shepherd as he and the dog continued to eye each other warily.

The young girl was silent for a moment, then she said, "I'm sorry about . . . I mean, I guess I thought all policemen—you know, had to kill people," she went on hesitantly, still stroking the dog's long nose and ears. "I mean that's all you ever see them doing on TV."

"I know, but that's TV, not real life. Or at least not real life around here," Culver added thoughtfully. "Fairfax County is a pretty safe place to live. There aren't too many criminals around here stupid enough to carry guns when they commit crimes. So unless there's real serious trouble, we try very hard not to shoot our guns. It's too dangerous to everybody else in the area, including ourselves."

"I'm glad to hear that," a shaky voice behind Culver spoke up.

Culver turned his head in time to see Kathy Harmon come

into the kitchen with her hands full of string-tied manila envelopes.

"I'm, uh, trying to explain a few things about police work to Lisa and Bear here," Culver said, barely remembering his manners—not to mention departmental policy—in time to stand up in the presence of the reporting party.

Kathy Harmon was a strikingly attractive woman in her thirties, apparently unmarried, with dark brown hair and absolutely beautiful green eyes. She had already made it perfectly clear that she was not at all happy about having a uniformed police officer in her house.

"Another police car just pulled into the driveway," she said, laying the envelopes out across the kitchen counter and then quickly kneeling down beside her niece and the sprawled shepherd. "Do you think he's all right?" she asked in a whispery voice as she stroked the dog's head and extended ears.

"He looks stable, but he definitely needs to be examined," Culver said, as he heard the car door slam shut outside, and then hurried footsteps coming up to the front door. "Okay, Lisa," he turned to the young girl, "as soon as Officer Beasley gets in here, we'll see if we can get Bear up and walking on his own."

A few minutes later, it was obvious to everyone in the kitchen that Bear was not going to be able to make it out to the driveway under his own steam.

"He *is* hurt, isn't he," the girl whispered, the tears reappearing on her cheeks as she and Culver and Canine Officer Tess Beasley watched the woozy shepherd sink its head back down into her lap, where he exchanged a halfhearted lick with the irrepressible ferret.

"Don't worry, Lisa, the vets'll have him all fixed up in no time," Tess Beasley smiled reassuringly, gesturing with her head for Culver to bring his end of the small animal stretcher in closer. "Okay, here's what we'll do," she went on. "Lisa, you take my hand and bring it over to Bear. That's right, let him sniff it.

"Okay, good dog, you smell Sasha, don't you?" Beasley said soothingly. "Now we'll rub his ears and his throat . . . that's right, Bear, it's okay. Now you take his front legs and I'll take the back ones, and we'll roll him over just like this," Beasley whispered in her almost-hypnotic voice as they gently turned the limp and unprotesting animal over onto the stretcher.

". . . and now you cover his head with that towel, so he can only see you. That's right. Now pet him and talk to him real easy-like while Officer Culver and I lift him up and take him out to the wagon."

Two minutes later, much to Culver's relief, the dog and the girl were in the back of the Canine Unit station wagon, and on their way to Pender Veterinary Clinic in the protective and soothing company of Tess Beasley.

"I guess she's really good with kids and animals, isn't she," Kathy Harmon said, her voice betraying an uneasy nervousness as they both watched the blue-and-gray station wagon maneuver down the long driveway.

Culver smiled and nodded in agreement. "Yeah, she's got the touch. Oh, and you don't need to worry about either of them for a while," he added. "Tess will stay out at the vet's with Lisa until you can get there."

Looking relieved, Kathy Harmon stroked the wiggling ferret one last time before reaching down and gently dropping it to the floor. "Then maybe we'd better hurry up and finish your report."

"Sure. I take it you found the receipts?" Culver said, glancing over at the manila envelopes.

"Most of them," Kathy Harmon nodded. "The TV, the stereo, and the VCR."

Suddenly her head came up, her eyes flashing with anger that had been repressed much too long. "It took me almost six months to save up enough to buy that VCR," she said in a raspy, whispery voice. "But you know what? if I'd known they wanted it that bad, I'd have given it to them. So why did they have to hurt Bear?" she demanded, her voice catching as the pain and the frustration threatened to overcome the anger. Culver could see the tears starting to well up in her eyes.

You cannot, repeat, cannot allow yourself to get emotionally involved in an investigation. It doesn't help and it doesn't work, Culver reminded himself for what was probably the hundredth time in his career, understanding that it was impossible not to react to the frustration, pain, fear, and heartbreak in an endless stream of victims; but knowing also that the long-term payoff for that kind of involvement was something that no law enforcement officer could afford.

And this is only a minor res burg. Outside of the dog, nobody got cut or hit or raped or shot. Culver sighed inwardly. *So why the hell am I gunning so hard for a Homicide detective's slot? Gotta be some kind of masochist.*

"You can't let criminals manipulate you, and take over your life," Culver said quietly. "We're going to try very hard . . ."

"But it isn't going to do any good, is it?" Kathy Harmon demanded. "Why don't you tell me the truth? Some *bastard,*" she emphasized the word, "broke into my house, almost killed my dog, and you—the Fairfax County Police Department—can't do anything about it, can you?"

"Do you really want to know the truth?" Culver asked quietly, easily ignoring the anger that he knew—from long experience—wasn't really directed at him personally as he looked up from his notebook.

"What do you *mean,* do I really want to know?" Kathy Harmon said, her striking facial features suddenly masked with confusion. "Of course I want to know. Why do you think . . . ? Oh." Her voice suddenly dropped down into a whisper as realization dawned. "I see." She nodded her head, her eyes glowering furiously. "You people have a standard spiel for this kind of thing, don't you?" she demanded, the words coming out accusing and bitter.

Culver shrugged. "I suppose we do, in a way. But the thing is, I could put out a call to our crime scene investigation unit, and they'd be by in a little while to dust your home for fingerprints while I record the serial numbers on these receipts and write my report. Later this afternoon, I'll turn the list over to the burg detectives, and if everything goes well, they might be able to get the serial numbers and the fingerprints into our computers by this evening, so that maybe by tomorrow morning—if we're really lucky—we just might end up with the name of the suspect.

"All of which could mean that you would have your property back by tomorrow evening," Culver finished, somehow maintaining a serious and professional expression even as he gave in to temptation and stared into her eyes for a brief moment.

"But in reality I won't, will I?" Kathy Harmon said in a raspy whisper, her voice no longer accusatory, just resigned.

Culver shook his head sympathetically. "I am going to record the serial numbers in my report, and the detectives will run the numbers through our computer, and they may come by sometime tomorrow afternoon to ask some more questions. But to be perfectly honest? No, you probably won't get your property back. Not by tomorrow evening, certainly, because even if we did find it, we'd have to process it all for prints and then probably hold it for trial. But more likely, not ever."

"But I . . ."

"Let me make sure I have this right," Culver said, raising his hand to gently interrupt while rechecking his notes. "You and Lisa left your house at about seven this morning. You dropped her off at school and then got to the university at about half past seven. You lectured until eleven. I'm sorry, I forgot to ask—you're a professor of what?"

"Biology."

"Biology professor," Culver mumbled, nodding his head as he filled in the blank space in the report form. "So after your lectures," he went on, "you came home for lunch, didn't notice anything wrong—including the doorknob—and left the house again at about twelve-fifty. At two-fifteen, the university announced an early closing because of the storm, so you immediately went back to the school, picked up Lisa, and returned home about three o'clock or thereabouts, whereupon you discovered the break-in. Correct?"

"That's right." Kathy Harmon nodded her head slowly.

Culver looked at his watch. "It's 3:35 now, so they've had about two hours at the outside. By now, the TV, the stereo, the VCR and your new movies have almost certainly exchanged hands at least once for probably no more than twenty percent of the value on these receipts," Culver said, gesturing at the crumpled pieces of paper. "Probably more like fifteen percent for the TV."

"Fifteen . . . twenty percent?" Kathy Harmon whispered in shocked disbelief.

"These people don't spend a lot of time bargaining. In fact, there's a good chance that it was all prearranged. These days, most of the burglars—especially the pros—get orders for specific items, for a predetermined price, from their fence. That's the character who buys from burglars and sells to bargain hunters who really don't want to know why they're getting a bargain. So probably what happened was that your burglar picked up a shopping list for electronic equipment this morning and went out to fill it."

"By breaking into my home and trying to kill Bear?"

The frustrated anger was starting to return, but it was clear to Culver that the threatening image of some intruder—a stranger—rummaging through her house was equally unsettling.

"Yours and several others," Culver said absentmindedly, aware that the entire situation was creating an uneasy feeling in the back of his mind as he started to record the serial numbers of the TV, stereo, and disc player in his notebook. "Fairfax County's kind of a happy hunting ground for burglars. Lots of well-paid bureaucrats, lobbyists, embassy staffers who aren't at home a lot."

"But why this house?" Kathy Harmon persisted. "As you said, there have to be a lot of people around here with all kinds of expensive stereo equipment who *don't* own a dog. And besides, it couldn't have been a big surprise that Bear was here. He starts barking the minute he hears a footstep on the porch."

"It is unusual for them to pick a house with a dog barking inside," Culver admitted. *Not only unusual, but pretty goddamn stupid,* he added to himself. "If it helps any, this is the third residential burglary report I've taken in this neighborhood this week."

"If it helps?! You—the police know what they're doing, but you don't stop it?" she exclaimed, incredulous.

"We *try* to stop it," Culver corrected, looking up from his notebook, "but it's not that easy. With the courts the way they are, to really put a burglar out of business, we almost have to catch him in the act. But that's hard to do because there's several thousand homes in the Fair Oaks patrol district alone, and at the most, there's only seven or eight of us in each district out on patrol on any one shift.

"And even then," he added with a shrug, "we spend a lot of time out of the cruisers taking reports."

"Is that what we're paying our taxes for, so the police can drive around in their cars and write reports?" Kathy Harmon demanded sarcastically.

"Well, as a matter of fact, yes, that's about it." Culver shrugged. "If we don't get the information recorded, then the whole system goes under."

"So what do you expect *us* to do—go out and buy our own guns? Take a correspondence course on vigilantism?"

"Some people do, but it rarely works out the way they expect," Culver said. "If you're willing to take the time to become proficient with a firearm, and to understand the inherent dangers—to yourself, to Lisa, and your neighbors—fine. Otherwise, I wouldn't recommend the gun. I think you're doing the right thing with Bear."

"In other words, just sit back and wait to see if I'm going to be a victim . . . again."

"Or give us some help by providing all the information you

can for our reports. We may not ever locate your property, but the more evidence we accumulate . . ."

"Okay, you want evidence," Kathy Harmon interrupted. "What about fingerprints? You said you could call out your crime scene person." She stopped when she saw that Culver was shaking his head, a patient expression fixed on his face. "Well why the hell not?" she demanded hotly.

"Gloves. There are glove marks on your front doorknob, or what's left of it. Same kind of marks on the TV stand and stereo cabinet."

"What the hell's a glove mark?"

"Bare fingers leave nice identifiable fingerprints on a smooth or oily surface. Gloves leave streaks that we can't match to anything. From what I can see, it's pretty obvious that your burglar wore gloves. The pros usually do."

"Oh shit," Kathy Harmon muttered in frustration, leaning her head back closing her eyes for a moment.

Seemingly responding to his owner's emotional shift, the ferret scurried over to the side of Kathy Harmon's foot and then began to climb up the leg of her jeans. She picked the small mammal up and began stroking its head.

"If you want," Culver tried to explain patiently, "I will put in a call for the CSI unit in our area right now. But he's busy working a residential burg for some big shot diplomat from Mexico right now, so it'd probably be at least another hour before he got here."

"An hour?"

"Or I could go pull my gear out of the trunk and do it myself," Culver suggested. "I'm not supposed to, but it'd be all right as long as I don't get another call. What I'd do is go all through your house, dusting shelves and counters and toilets and any other smooth surface that your burglar might have handled, just on the off chance that something was picked up or touched bare-handed. And in doing so, I'd end up spreading a lot of very messy fingerprint powder all over the house that'll take you at least a couple of days to clean up."

"Officer Culver," Kathy Harmon said, deliberately emphasizing the word "Officer" as she spoke with determined self-control, "I don't think I'm making myself understood. I don't care about things getting messy. This whole damn place is already a mess!" She gestured with her free hand at her dismantled living room and then across to the dried blood in the entryway. "And I really don't care that I lost a bunch of electronic junk either. What I *do* care about is that you find the bastard who broke into my house and hurt my dog, because I don't want him coming back!" She was holding the ferret close to her neck now, her eyes starting to fill with tears.

"Ms. Harmon," Culver said soothingly, "I don't think you have to worry about your burglar coming back. They rarely do. Your house was almost certainly selected because you didn't have a dead bolt on your doors. And assuming that you take the necessary precautions now, they'll just go looking for some other unsuspecting victim who will be a much easier target."

"You're sure of that?"

"Positive."

"And you're certain about the fingerprints?"

"As I said, I can get my gear out of the cruiser and dust your home for prints myself, right now. I'm perfectly willing to do so. And if I do, I'll probably end up collecting at least a couple dozen latent prints, which I'd take back to the station along with elimination fingerprints from you and Lisa. Oh, and by the way, that's going to be messy too," he added. "The ink we use tends to seep under fingernails. Takes a couple of days to wash out completely."

Unable to help herself, Kathy Harmon glanced down at her short, unpolished, but clean fingernails, and then around at her admittedly untidy home.

"So after all that," Culver went on, "if the computer's up, and there's a terminal available, and I didn't get pulled back out to handle another call in my area, I might be able to get all the latent and elimination prints entered into the system before I go off duty this evening, at about one in the morning. That being the case, by tomorrow morning, we'll almost certainly discover that most—or in this case, more likely all—of the identifiable prints either belong to you, or Lisa, or one of your friends."

"Oh." It was a brief, subdued, and telling comment, suggesting that Kathy Harmon had learned far more about the realities of police work in the last few minutes than she ever really wanted to know.

"The trouble is," Culver added, "by the time I do all that, somebody will have long since plugged your VCR into a stereo system that will never see the light of day, as far as serial numbers are concerned."

"I suppose you really can't go around asking to see serial numbers on everybody's stereo, can you?" Kathy Harmon said ruefully.

"I'm afraid not. We look if we get the chance, but that doesn't happen too often. People who buy things from fences don't usually invite the police into their house to snoop around their property. To tell you the truth, we have enough trouble getting some of the victims to let us work in their homes."

"I can understand that." And then after a moment: "And you're sure—about the gloves, I mean?"

Culver looked into Kathy Harmon's still-watery eyes, nodded silently, and then went back to his notebook and the receipts. For the next three minutes, the only audible sounds in the room were those of Culver's pen.

"Officer," Kathy Harmon said softly.

"Yes?" Culver's head came up.

"I . . . I'm sorry if I sound . . . ungracious. I know it wasn't your fault we were burglarized, and it was very kind of you and the other officer to help with Bear. I . . . I usually live alone out here, and I guess I'm not comfortable with the idea of calling in the police to help solve my problems." She took a deep breath, as if relieved to have gotten that out, and then added in a very businesslike manner: "Please call me Kathy. Ms. Harmon makes me feel . . . old."

Culver smiled. "My name's Henry and no apologies are

necessary. That's what we're here for. And besides, I'd have been just as upset as you were, if it had been my house or dog. Which reminds me," he added, reaching down into his briefcase and pulling out a small eyedropper bottle and a bag full of cotton swabs, "I want to collect some of that blood from your living room floor, just in case Bear managed to get close enough to do some damage."

Kathy Harmon followed Culver out to the entryway of her home and then watched as the uniformed officer bent down and began working on the dried blood with a damp wooden swab.

"You do a lot of that, don't you?" she said finally.

"What's that?"

"Collecting evidence. I thought only the people in the crime lab did that sort of thing."

"They do, and I did," Culver replied, looking up as he transferred a lightly bloodstained swab into a small manila envelope. "I used to work in our crime lab before I went back into patrol."

"Oh, so that's why you knew all about the fingerprints."

Culver nodded. "Sure. Latent prints, blood, hair, dope, bullets, doorknobs—all that stuff. That's what crime scene investigation is all about. Collect everything you can get your hands on, because you won't know what means something and what doesn't until after you get everything back to the lab. And by then, once you start analyzing things, it's usually too late. Great job for a scientist who likes to rummage through garbage cans and also happens to be a mind-reader."

"I'm sorry. I guess I didn't understand." Kathy Harmon shook her head in confusion. "You used to be a scientist in a crime lab? Like a police chemist?"

"A criminalist. Same thing."

"And now you're a cop—er, a policeman? I'm sorry, it's none of my business, but why . . . ?"

"Why am I back on patrol? It's a long story, and kind of complicated." Culver smiled, shrugging as he closed up his notebook and reached down to pick up his heavy, top-hinged patrol briefcase. "And I'm afraid that if I tried to explain it all right now, the sergeant would come looking for me. So maybe . . ."

"It really is none of my business," Kathy Harmon repeated firmly. "And I appreciate your taking the time to be so patient with me, considering everything else going on out there—although actually, I suppose it is our time, isn't it," she said as she walked Culver to the door. "I mean, we *are* paying you to be out there watching our homes, aren't we?" she added with far more frustration than sarcasm in her voice now.

"That's right." Culver said, and then hesitated as the pack set radio on his hip beeped twice. He pulled the radio out of its belt holder, brought it up to his mouth, and keyed the transmit switch.

"Eight-Forty-Charlie, go."

"Eight-Forty-Charlie, you've got a missing juvenile call holding on Colchester. Do you have an ETA?"

Culver looked at his watch and noted the time.

"I've got a couple more minutes here, then I'm clear," he replied.

"Ten-four," the dispatcher acknowledged.

"Eight-Forty-Charlie, is that what they call you?" Kathy Harmon asked as she wrote the number down on a piece of paper.

"My call sign," Culver said as he opened the front door and stepped out onto the porch, wincing against dropping air temperature.

"Call sign? You mean like a CB handle?"

"Something like that."

"That's horrible, using numbers instead of names. It makes you sound like robots."

"Yes, I suppose it does." Culver nodded absentmindedly as he gestured with his flashlight at the ravaged front doorknob. He was already thinking about the juvenile call. "Listen, when you get back from Pender, you should call a locksmith immediately and have him put something a little more sturdy on this door. Otherwise, I'm liable to be back here tomorrow filling out another report. I'd strongly recommend a dead bolt on both doors, front and back."

"Which will be something else I can't afford, thanks to that creep," Kathy Harmon muttered with unrestrained bitterness.

"Actually, in a way, you were probably lucky the way it all worked out. She usually isn't violent—at least not against people."

It took a moment for Culver's words to register.

"She? You mean . . . you think a woman broke into my house? A woman you *know* broke into my house?" Kathy Harmon exclaimed incredulously, staring wide-eyed at Culver.

"That's right." Culver nodded as he reached into his patrol briefcase, pulled out a screwdriver, and quickly removed the mounting screws on the door lock mechanism, completely unaware of the distant vehicle that had pulled off the narrow tree-lined main road so that it had a line-of-sight view of Kathy Harmon's front door. Moments later, he held up the twisted piece of metal that had once been Kathy Harmon's doorknob.

"As I said, you were lucky."

Chapter Eleven

Thursday, 1545 hours

Increasingly alert for any sign of a surveillance, Digger spotted the Fairfax County police cruiser and the two distant figures the moment he came around the next-to-last high-rising curve in the rain-slickened, undivided two-lane country road.

Startled, because the time factors were all wrong, he reacted immediately by swerving the ten-year-old pickup truck over to the side of the road and coming to a quick stop.

He tried to tell himself that it wasn't her, that someone other than Sea Glass—a close neighbor perhaps?—had discovered the break-in and called the police. But she didn't have any close neighbors. And even at a distance, the red shirt and blue jeans were distinctive.

No, it had to be her.

The only logical explanation that Digger could come up with was that she'd left work early, probably because of the storm the radio was warning everyone about, discovered her ransacked house, and then made the call.

He looked at his watch again and realized how close a thing it had been. Much too close. But then he thought of something else, too.

What if it isn't Culver?

Jarred by the sudden realization that six days of work might have been wasted by a single casual impulse, Digger quickly set the hand brake, reached for his binocular case, and then brought the expensive glasses up to his eyes.

The marked blue-and-gray cruiser was parked at the top of the long access road to the Harmon house. He ignored the vehicle, and the red shirt, and centered the view field on the taller of the two figures. He readjusted the focus, and then breathed an audible sigh of relief.

It was Henry Culver. No question about it.

Using Paul Radlick's computer and his Commonwealth Attorney's privileges, Digger had been able to tap directly into the Fairfax County's widely interconnected data management system. And once he was in the tightly protected legal subsystem, breaking the codes that allowed access into the county's personnel files had been a trivial exercise. As a result, he now knew a great deal about a very interesting police officer named Henry Lucas Culver.

To give himself a chance to relax as much as anything else, he ran through some of those details in his head once again.

Culver, Henry Lucas. Thirty-nine. Five-eleven. One-seventy-five. Neatly trimmed grayish brown curly hair. Single. Aggressive, and apparently hardworking. He was secretly amused that someone who had actually been described by his supervisor as "thick-headed and persistent at the scenes—a 'digger' who refuses to give up" would turn out to be so predictable.

Digger smiled at that memory as he continued to watch his intended victim with focused intensity.

"She must have caught you just as you came on shift, Henry," he whispered as he shifted the binoculars over to the far less interesting of the two figures.

But here, too, he already knew the relevant details by heart.

Kathy Harmon. Female White. Thirty-three. About five-six, with shoulder-length dark hair and a full, firm figure beneath her ever-present blue denim jeans and long-sleeved red sweater. Her face truly set her apart. The full lips especially. They curved intriguingly at either corner, providing an almost-irresistible focus of attention before opening into a wide dimpled smile beneath those intense, green eyes. In a certain light, they looked as though they were made of light crystalline jade.

In effect, she was an absolutely radiant backcountry woman, from the windblown strands of her dark, silky hair under the red-and-white umbrella, down to the bushy-tailed, wet animal that appeared to be battling fierce, invisible demons around her calf-high rubber boots. Digger had become so intrigued by the potential of her alluring beauty that he'd even given her a special code name.

"Hello, Sea Glass," he whispered. "Do you like what I brought you?"

As Digger watched, the serious expression on Kathy Harmon's water-streaked face broke into a very fleeting grin—apparently in response to something Culver said as he got back into the cruiser and shut the door. At that moment, he understood why men like Culver would be drawn to her. In a terribly warped way, he almost liked her himself.

But then, he really didn't *like* anyone.

"Especially cheaters," he whispered, and then came alert as a sudden flurry of movement drew his attention back to the cruiser. It was the ferret, which had climbed up Kathy Harmon's leg and scrambled in through the open window of the cruiser onto Culver's lap. The uniformed officer cautiously retrieved the squirming muddy animal and handed it back to Harmon, his teeth exposed in a wide grin as he started up the cruiser and waved good-bye.

"Not sure about him yet, are you?" He smiled to himself.

"That's right," he whispered again. "Don't be easy. Do what you always do. Make him think about it."

Then, Digger dropped the binoculars to the seat and reached for the gearshift, ready to accelerate into an immediate U-turn, but Culver made a right turn at the road and disappeared in the opposite direction.

Digger waited for another thirty seconds, just to make sure that Culver didn't turn and come back the other way. Then he brought the binoculars back up once again.

Kathy Harmon had walked down to her mailbox at the bottom of her dirt-and-gravel access road, and was allowing the ferret to play in one of her empty trash cans as she hurriedly sorted through her mail, sheltering herself from the rain under the large red-and-white umbrella. The ferret seemed indifferent to the rain and the increasing chill in the air as it swiped and bit at a tattered length of fabric that had gotten lodged in a crack in one of the splintery rail posts.

It was aggressive *and* independent—not like all the other cats and dogs, who just wanted to be held and petted.

He liked that.

As the temperature continued to drop and the rhythm of the falling raindrops increased, raising small geysers of mud around the energetic ferret, Kathy Harmon seemed to remember that her niece was waiting for her at the vet clinic. But her ferret had no intention of being cooperative.

After several futile attempts at catching the elusive animal, she finally threw up her hands in resignation, and then hurried up the long driveway toward her car.

"That's it," Digger whispered, his pale blue eyes glistening with anticipation, "let it stay out there, all by itself."

Humming cheerfully, he waited until Kathy Harmon made a right-hand turn out of her driveway. Then he released the emergency brake, steered the truck back onto the road, and accelerated in a direct line toward the mailboxes. At the last moment, he jammed the truck into second gear, accelerated into a sharp right-hand turn up the deeply rutted driveway, slammed his foot against the worn brake pedal, and slid the pickup to a sudden, jerky, mud-and-gravel-splattering stop. The showering pattern of mud, gravel, and rocks from the oversize tires just missed the mud-smeared ferret, who leaped high in the air and seemed to vaporize into the surrounding underbrush.

Still humming to himself, Digger leaned out through the side window of the truck, opened his oversize mailbox, and pulled out the four weeks worth of mail that had accumulated in his absence. He spent a couple of minutes sorting, mostly so that he could watch Kathy Harmon's house—to see if any other interesting patterns would develop—but also to see if the ferret would reappear.

After a few moments, he tossed the mail on the seat. He stepped out into the rain, pulled his own long-ago emptied trash cans out of the brush, and put them in the back of the pickup. Then he got back into the cab and accelerated up the long, narrow, and slippery driveway to his house.

This was only the second time he'd approached the house since Hämmarchov had helped him escape from custody six days ago. He was still wary of a surveillance, even though he'd spent the six days sleeping and hiding in the surrounding woods, watching and waiting during the daylight hours, especially for the first sign of a raid team, which never came.

But in spite of his wariness, Digger was in a hurry. Saturday, February 6, was the absolute deadline on the L'Que deal. By Saturday morning, everything had to be in place. It was the most important assignment that he'd been given so far, and there was a lot of money involved—more than he would ever make with his burglaries, no matter how many teams he put on the street—so he had to get back in contact with his teams immediately.

Before Saturday.

Before it was too late.

The frustrating part was that he'd already regained contact once, using Paul Radlick's computer—sneaking into his house, at night, through his carefully constructed trapdoor when Radlick and his wife were asleep and connecting to his hidden computer system through Radlick's modem. He'd been able to set the parameters of the Harmon burglary into place without any trouble. But then Radlick had gotten that 5:30 A.M. phone call, and had come downstairs, and for whatever possible reason, had reformatted his entire hard drive—setting to zero every one of those 540 million bytes, including the critical remote access link to his hidden computer network that had taken him so long to rewrite from memory while he was supposedly "helping" Radlick to program his computer during their client-attorney sessions.

So now he had a choice. He could either start over with Radlick's computer one more time, which meant spending another twenty or thirty hours rewriting thousands of lines of code, or he could take the risk of reentering his hidden domain where his own computers—already programmed to communicate with his teams—were waiting.

All because of a goddamned lawyer who was supposed to be on *his* side!

Yet Digger smiled, remembering Radlick's expression—the look of shock and rage when the attorney had burst into his upstairs bedroom and found his wife already taped. Then came the moment of disbelief when the dart had struck, sending the carefully buffered cobra venom flowing into Radlick's bloodstream, rapidly smothering the nerves that governed the voluntary muscle systems, one after another, until finally only Radlick's eyelids would respond.

He continued to smile as he remembered the look of horror that had appeared on both of their faces when he'd turned on the flashlight and let them see where they were, and what he'd left down there with them.

He'd enjoyed leaving them like that—alive, alert, and absolutely helpless—but he reminded himself that he would have to be much more careful in the future.

He'd already made the nearly fatal mistake of leaving a single piece of telltale evidence in the hard disk of his portable computer. The computer that the police had taken from the trunk of his car without saying anything about it in their reports, which meant they could have had the house, the tunnels, and the sanctuary, with all its hidden treasures, if they'd been smart enough to know where to look.

He wasn't certain that any of them were that smart, but the fact that the house *hadn't* been surrounded by spying cops didn't necessarily mean anything, he reminded himself. They'd cheated before, and they'd probably cheat again if given the chance. And that meant he didn't dare make any more assumptions about being watched. They'd already caught him once, and he knew he'd never get away from them that easily again.

As he stepped around to the tailgate, intent on unloading his supplies quickly in order to get to work, he discovered how Kathy Harmon's ferret had managed to disappear so effectively.

His trash cans.

He found it in the back of the camper shell, rummaging in a grocery bag, its long, mud-splattered tail bushed out excitedly as it tried to claw its way into one of the deliciously scented packages.

He reached in to grab it up by its scrawny neck, and then stood in fascination as the young ferret relaxed, hanging limp in his hand, then yawned deeply, exposing its sharp teeth.

Startled by the unexpected reaction—apparent indifference instead of fear—Digger tried to remember what she called him. Something to do with an old children's show.

"Spanky," he whispered, nodding his head, remembering now. He'd hated that show. Hated it almost as much as the puppy that his parents had given him in an unknowing gesture of overwhelming cruelty. The puppy that wouldn't go near him because even that young, it seemed to understand that there was something terribly wrong about its young master.

Apparently sensing a change in the nature of things, Spanky suddenly twisted around and sank his sharp teeth into his captor's thumb.

"That's it, fight back," Digger whispered, his thin lips twisted into a smile beneath his cold, pale blue eyes as he stared at the trickle of blood streaming down his hand. Outwardly, he hadn't responded to the pain at all.

Then, wrenching the ferret's jaws loose with his free hand, he flipped the squirming animal up in the air and caught it by the tail. In one sharp motion, he swung his hand down, smacking the ferret's head sharply against the side of the truck.

He held the ferret's still-twitching body up at eye level for a moment, watching the leg tremors with amused interest as they gradually subsided. Then he tossed the limp body out into the forest with an indifferent shrug. He had much more important things on his mind.

From a distance, there was nothing especially remarkable about Digger's weather-dulled, two-story wood house on the high, gravel-covered knoll; or the adjoining grassed-over septic field; or the surrounding twenty acres of hardwoods, separated from Kathy Harmon's neighboring twenty acres and her distant house by the one-lane strip of dirt and gravel, to distinguish it from any of the other old houses in the rural neighborhood.

It was just a little hideaway place. The only connections to the outside world were a poorly maintained access road and a pair of sagging utility wires. Hardly the sort of house where a person might expect to find something evil or sinister.

And in point of fact, there was nothing specifically evil or sinister-looking about the house at all. No loose, rattling shutters; no late flickering lights; and certainly nothing to suggest the presence of anything more ominous or sophisticated than a simple telephone.

It was only when you got up close—close enough to smell the rotting boards, to hear the creak of the expanding or contracting wood joints, and to sense the presence of hollowed ground underfoot—that you knew something unspeakably evil and malicious resided there.

It had been that way a long time—certainly as long as Digger could remember, and probably even before he'd been born. He really didn't worry much about the possibility of casual observers, but even so, he had no intention of taking any more unnecessary risks.

Determined that nothing else should be left to chance, he spent almost a half hour with the binoculars, scanning the wooded exterior of his familiar home for any sign of a surveillance or entry.

Finally satisfied that there was nothing to be seen on the outside, he released the hidden door bolt and then entered his home.

The olfactory effect was instantaneous—cedar wood, musty fabric, aging carpet, and machine oil. The same distinctive mix of odors that had been his home for as long as he could remember. Instinctively trusting the heightened senses he had developed through uncounted days and weeks of working in absolute darkness, he allowed himself to relax, confident that he was alone.

But even so, before he did anything else, Digger made a rapid check of his defenses, examining each of the thirty-two detector and alarm circuits that protected his windows and doors.

Then, finally satisfied that he wouldn't be bothered for the next few hours, he went into the bathroom and turned an otherwise nonfunctional water valve to its full clockwise position. The sounds of magnet relay switches snapping into place behind sections of drywall were just barely audible.

Humming to himself in quiet anticipation, Digger checked his vast collection of tools—shovels, hammers, power saws, drills, and the like—and made a visual confirmation that they were all there, carefully cleaned and oiled and ready for use.

In the master bedroom, he stepped into the walk-in closet, gently pulled aside the hanging shirts and jackets, and carefully pulled up on a sparsely filled tie rack attached to a seemingly solid cedar panel that made up one interior sidewall of the narrow bedroom closet. Released from its switch-controlled locks, the panel slid noiselessly up into a concealed slot, revealing a darkened, three-foot-square-by-head-high chamber.

The cool, earth-scented air hit his face, causing him to sigh with pleasure as he reached into the darkness and found the dangling light switch chain. The single bare bulb socket nailed to rough-finished studs above his head, and connected with bare Romex wire, illuminated a wood-framed, thirty-by-thirty-inch hole that seemed to drop endlessly into the earth.

He stepped down onto the second rung of a crude but solid two-by-four stud ladder and pulled the concealed closet door shut. Then, after turning in place on the ladder and carefully bolting the panel shut from the inside, he climbed the rest of the way down the twelve-foot ladder.

At the bottom, he flipped a switch that turned off the incandescent bulb high overhead. Using a powerful five-cell flashlight, he stepped into a long, dark underground passageway that was just barely shoulder wide and head high.

This particular tunnel—the first and most important one, he reminded himself—had taken him an entire summer to construct. It had been a difficult task for a thirteen-year-old boy to take on, but it had provided him with the one thing he wanted more than anything else: the start of an escape from the prying eyes and ears of his ever-repressive, but ultimately stingy, callous, indifferent, and cruel parents.

He still remembered every single day and every single foot of the construction.

Six months of careful digging through the heavy claylike soil.

Six months of pausing at three-foot intervals to install the beam, plastic, plywood, and pipe cross-structures that defined the walls and supported no less than forty-eight inches of overhead dirt, rock, and brick walkway.

Six months of stopping at three in the afternoon, so that he could have all of the dirt and rocks and bricks replaced and smoothed over by the time his parents returned home from work.

The first tunnel had been difficult, and the results crude, but he learned quickly. The next one—a cross-connecting section, providing a remote escape route out to the distant, shedlike garage—had been easier, and the subsequent ones even more so. In the end, when he had finally stopped digging, he had crude tunnels branching out from the root cellar of the house in all directions.

All of that, so that no one would know.

And now that corrugated metal pipe escape tunnels were in place, and both of his parents were dead and properly buried, and the house was finally his, no one would *ever* know.

He used the flashlight to spot and avoid an especially treacherous section of the flooring: a set of three hinged boards designed to collapse open under a minimum load of twenty-five pounds, and concealing a dozen needle-pointed, barbed metal spikes. He hesitated at this trap, brushing his fingers across the concealed slivers of sharpened metal that would first penetrate the thickest boot sole and then hold the ruptured tissues in place like a fishhook, wondering if any of them had any idea how much effort, over the years, he had put into avoiding the suffocating presence of people like themselves.

People who simply didn't count.

The renovation of his childhood catacombs had been a difficult and exhausting job, he remembered as he turned sideways in the confining semidarkness to squeeze past one of the narrow sections, using his flashlight to disarm, step past, and then rearm, one at a time, the series of deviously vicious traps that he had carefully set in place along the narrow and confining tunnel. Digging the new tunnels and laying the pipe had been far more difficult, exhausting, and demanding of his limited resources than he had ever imagined.

That was what really irritated him—the fact that he had worked so hard, and had been so close to pulling it off without detection. Another couple of hours and he would have been out of the town house and gone, in spite of their cheating. The difficulties, delays, and indignities he'd been forced to suffer still churned through his mind. All on account of four men.

Four cops.

Cheaters, all of them.

Or maybe only one, he reminded himself.

But none of that mattered—at least not for the moment—because now, after six days of careful planning and manipulation, without a single detail committed to paper, he was back in business.

He stopped at the midpoint of the tunnel and slid his hand into a narrow, deep hole in the wall to lock the hidden safety switch of an especially cruel trap (the one he'd installed on the opposite side of the narrow right-angled turn). He could feel it start to build up inside of him now—the urge to scream, to fill the dark, branching tunnels with the echoing sounds of his anguish, and frustration, and rage.

But none of that mattered anymore because he was back home now, deep in his sanctuary, hidden from the agency that employed him and the people *he* employed. And known only by a single name.

Digger.

Once the curious nickname of an incredibly complex and

tortured boy who, for lack of affection, had driven himself downward, into the earth, to escape his parents and the oppressions that threatened to smother his fevered soul.

And then, one of several smoldering personalities locked in the mind of a dangerously twisted young adult who had sought to nourish his warped desires, and at the same time to enrich his pockets, only to be trapped by the man—or men—who had been unwilling to play the game fair.

And now, the coded identity of a single-minded, tightly focused, and absolutely relentless man who, after the completion of the L'Que job, would stop at nothing to exact his revenge at the expense of those whom he perceived as his oppressors.

Smiling his cold, heartless smile, he snapped the hidden switch to the lock-back position, took a deep breath, and then filled the dark tunnels with the echoing sound of a vengeful and raging scream.

Associate Director Elliott Parkinson was extremely pleased with himself.

At precisely four-thirty that Thursday afternoon, he poured himself a four-ounce glass of expensive sherry to celebrate what, in his opinion, had been a day highlighted by several tactically brilliant and predominantly successful moves.

First of all, with one possible exception, virtually all of the known meeting sites were now being monitored—electronically, instead of the photo/video surveillance that the director had ordered, but monitored nonetheless. Relevant tapes, of course, would go to his office for review and distribution—which would be basically limited to himself, his special assistant, and the burn bag.

And as far as that exception was concerned, Lt. Col. Charles L'Que's movements were being closely watched pending an entry as soon as they retrieved their ace burglar and electronics surveillance expert.

Which shouldn't take all that long because Digger was out

and available. It was just a question of which lure he went for—the tripled fees or the dangling live bait.

During which time, thanks to what must have seemed like an incredible lapse on Operations's part, Arthur Traynor and his infuriatingly loyal technicians would be neutralized by a massive search for a missing CIA field operative that would probably take days, Parkinson decided, because wherever he was and whatever he was doing, Alberto Paz clearly did not want to be found.

Yes, Parkinson nodded to himself, very nice indeed. Not quite perfect, perhaps, but certainly the best that could be expected under the circumstances.

He was standing at his south-facing window that overlooked the expansive park, gazing out at the snowflakes drifting across bare-limbed trees against a darkening backdrop of gray sky when he heard the tentative knock at his doorway.

"Yes," he said, not bothering to turn around.

"We've got Culver under a full surveillance," J. Winston Weathersby reported from the doorway. "The moment Digger makes a move, he's ours."

"Fine."

The flakes were getting bigger now, clumping together into larger and even more fragile structures as they continued to fall at a visibly increasing rate.

"I'm going home now," the clearly exhausted special assistant said. "Anything else I should do first?"

Parkinson paused for a moment in thoughtful contemplation. "One more thing," he said finally.

"Yes?"

"Tell the surveillance teams to stay back, let Digger have plenty of room. All things considered, I don't think we need to be overly concerned about the welfare of Mr. Henry Culver."

Chapter Twelve

After making a final check of his remote monitors and alarm board, to make certain that he would remain undisturbed, the brooding and somber man who had stolen Digger's computer turned in his chair to face his workbench—actually a small table surrounded on three sides by overhead illuminated county maps of the Washington, D.C., metro area—and reached out to snap on a single wide switch.

One of the two computer monitors on the table glowed into life. He hesitated only a moment before keying in the seven-digit code word and then waited patiently for the computer to boot up the complex programs.

The computer indicated that there was a message waiting, but he ignored it. He had more important things to do on this particular Thursday evening. There would be plenty of time to read messages later.

As he waited, he casually glanced through his penciled notes, making final decisions as to teams and times and places, knowing that he had to be cautious with the two new people. Neither of them had much in the way of experience, so he would have to choose carefully.

There was what looked to be an easy one with a lot of support data in area eight-eleven, on Miller Heights; and a slightly more difficult one on Fox Mill Road, in area eight hundred, he noted, comparing his list of potential sites against the blue-lined Fairfax County Patrol Area map on the wall to his left. The map divided the county into eight primary patrol districts and approximately seventy individual patrol areas, each of which was supposedly covered by a blue-and-gray cruiser twenty-four hours a day.

There were names associated with the sites, most of them foreign, but he wasn't interested in names; he was much more interested in the ease of entry versus the expected pay-off.

Finally, he made his decision.

They weren't supposed to start until tomorrow, but he decided to give the new team the Miller Heights site. The one with the most data. The easy one.

He had also noted and then discounted the fact that the target was close to Henry Culver's assigned patrol area. There wouldn't be any problems with this one, he decided. Culver would be kept busy in his own sector, and the safety margin was at least double what he normally allowed.

As he began to enter data into the preformatted screen blanks, the brooding man allowed himself to be distracted once again with the question that had preoccupied his mind for most of the past several days:

The question of just how long he could afford to play with Henry Culver before he would have to deal with the man who was now his most interesting—and potentially most dangerous—adversary.

Lost in his thoughts, Crime Lab Director Theodore Gauss forgot to notify the warehouse that he had rescheduled the drop-off times.

Chapter Thirteen

Thursday, 1730 hours

Elliott Parkinson was going over a draft of his planned Sunday morning presentation to the Interpol intelligence chiefs meeting when J. Winston Weathersby hurried into his office and then stood there waiting, respectful but anxious, in front of the ornate walnut desk.

"I thought you were going home," Parkinson said, looking up from the triple-spaced draft text.

"I was, but fortunately, I stopped by Communications to see a friend."

"Fortunately?"

The visibly nervous special assistant nodded his head as he dropped a piece of teletype paper onto Parkinson's desk. "Take a look at this."

Parkinson scanned the half dozen lines, then looked back up with a puzzled expression on his face.

"I don't understand."

"It's a garbled signal," Weathersby said as if that explained everything.

"I can see that," Parkinson retorted, "but what . . . ?"

"Digger sent it."

"What?" Elliott Parkinson blinked, his eyes widening in shock. "How do you know that?"

Clearly pleased with himself, Weathersby took another teletype message out of his blazer pocket and handed it over to his boss. "We decided to stop by the cafeteria, to have a cup of coffee before we went out to dinner," he began, smiling as he watch Parkinson's eyes scan down the printed page.

"While we were there," he went on, "Todd mentioned this strange message they'd received a couple of hours ago. Said that it looked like another one of those weird signals from Paz, but they weren't sure because this time the transition codes were completely off. They didn't want to send it up until they had some sort of verification."

Parkinson was nodding his head in complete understanding now, but Weathersby continued anyway, determined that he was going to get full recognition for this one.

"So I asked Todd what kind of signal would we get if Paz hadn't made *any* of the resets on his computer—just sent a message like he didn't know what day of the week it was, or anything like that. So we went down to the lab and tried it, and guess what?"

"Digger." Parkinson smiled patiently as he allowed the

correctly unscrambled message to drop out of his hand onto the polished surface of his executive desk.

"Right. The way I figured it, he must have gotten hold of Paz's computer and he's been trying to communicate with us, only he doesn't know about the transition codes. So I sent him a message explaining how to make the resets, and that's what I got back."

"So he really is back in business." Parkinson nodded with visible relief.

J. Winston Weathersby looked at his watch. "In a little less than three hours, we should have the whole thing locked up—*Including* Lieutenant Colonel Charles L'Que," he added with a self-congratulatory emphasis.

"Absolutely wonderful," Parkinson whispered.

"I, uh, took the liberty of telling Digger to make sure he delivered the L'Que materials tonight, and not to wait until tomorrow."

"Fine, fine." Parkinson nodded absentmindedly. "Good job."

"So what about Paz," Weathersby asked after a few moments of extended silence.

"What about him?" Parkinson blinked, looking up.

"Digger must have taken him out, right?"

"I suppose. Either that or he's gone over with Hämmar-chov. What about it?"

"I was just wondering if you wanted to call off Traynor's people."

The associate director shook his head firmly. "No, absolutely not. If anything, it's even more important that we find them now—Digger especially."

"I'm not sure I understand."

"Think about it. Once Digger completes the L'Que job, his value as an asset will be extremely limited."

"But he becomes one hell of a liability once the police find out he's on the loose." Weathersby nodded, catching on quickly. "Because he'd give us up in a second if they caught him."

"Yes, very good," Parkinson said, genuinely impressed. "Maybe it's time we discussed a new assignment for you, assuming that the, uh, transition works out in our favor."

"I did have something in mind," Weathersby admitted, deciding that this was the appropriate time to put his oar in the water.

"What's that—Operations?" Parkinson asked, favoring his assistant with a calculating smile.

"That would be nice, in time, but you've got several loyal people in Operations who deserve to step up," Weathersby suggested diplomatically. "Actually, I was thinking that the AD slot at Sci-Tech might be a nice move, assuming it was vacant, of course," he added with a sly grin.

"That's a very real possibility," Parkinson said. "I don't anticipate an overwhelming success on the search for Paz."

"You don't think Traynor will give the search a number one priority?"

"Oh, of course he will. On something like this, he'll use everything he's got. You see, I know the way Arthur Traynor thinks. He'll figure that if he can find Paz and Digger before anyone else does, he protects the Agency and gives me an elbow in the ribs at the same time. Knowing Traynor, I fully expect him to be out there working this one himself—which, of course, will only simplify the process of assigning blame."

"So all we need to worry about now," Weathersby said with just a trace of uneasiness, "is Digger, right?"

"There's no need to be overly concerned about Digger," Parkinson said reassuringly. "Aside from his unfortunate, uh, quirks, he's very much the consummate professional."

"But does he understand how important the L'Que job is?" Weathersby pressed, increasingly aware over the last few days that his fate had become tightly linked to that of the Operations AD, who, in the bureaucratic way of things inside the Beltway, could rise or fall in the blink of an eye.

Parkinson nodded. "Digger is very much aware of the importance. He and I worked out the L'Que situation a long time ago. And as it turns out, he and Traynor have a lot more in common than you might think."

"Oh really, how so?" Weathersby's eyebrows furrowed in confusion.

"On something like this," Parkinson explained confidently, "I fully expect both Traynor *and* Digger to be out there doing the important work themselves."

Chapter Fourteen

Thursday, 1925 hours

Otis Lawnhart, the driver of the darkened van, was starting to lose his nerve.

According to the map, there should have been a pair of striped posts about three-quarters of a mile north of the Chain Bridge Road intersection marking the turnoff from Jermantown Road, but the van's odometer had already clicked off eight-tenths of a mile, and there was no sign of the black-and-white markers through the ice-streaked windshield.

"Think we missed them?" Lawnhart asked as he adjusted the speed of the noisy wipers that couldn't quite keep up with the steadily falling splatters of icy rain.

"Couple of black-and-white-striped one-by-sixes, sticking up about five feet out of the ground?" the dark silhouetted figure in the front passenger seat snorted. "Not likely."

They drove on for another tenth of a mile in silence as they stared out into the gloomy, glare-streaked darkness, until Lawnhart couldn't stand it any longer.

"Man, I can't believe we're doing this," he whispered.

"Getting shaky?"

"Yeah, a little," Lawnhart admitted. "Never did anything this heavy before." In fact, the tension had reduced his voice to a raspy whisper that was barely audible over the noise of the van's defroster blowers.

"Don't worry about it." The bearded man shrugged, having an easier time masking his own nervousness. "You know what they say about working out on the edge."

Bobby Morgan never got to explain what he meant by that because they both spotted the pair of striped posts at the same time, at the outer range of the van's headlights.

"Those our markers?" Lawnhart asked, his raspy voice shaky with relief. "Gotta be them, right?"

"Gotta be," Morgan agreed, nodding in the darkness as he quickly checked their map with a pencil flashlight, being careful to shield the narrow beam with his gloved hand. Even so, his neatly combed-back dark hair and trimmed full beard were momentarily visible in the brief glow of diffuse light.

"Yeah, that's it," Morgan said, shutting off the light. "Take a right in front of the poles and then another right just past the nursery."

Lawnhart downshifted into second, prudently electing to use the gears rather than the brakes to slow the heavy van on the slush-slickened narrow road.

Given the van's low clearance and wide wheelbase, he knew they'd belly out for sure if he dropped a tire in one of the water runoff ditches that ran along both sides of the narrow, two-lane road. Some of them were a good eighteen axle-killing inches deep in places.

And that would just about do it, as far as the quasi-professional careers of these two young men were concerned, because it wasn't just a problem of getting stuck. A car or a van in a ditch could expect to have help within a half hour, max; but help from the Fairfax County Police Department, no matter how well intended, was the last thing that these two men wanted on this particular evening.

"How we doing on time?"

The pencil flashlight briefly glowed once more.

"Seven-twenty-eight," Bobby Morgan said.

"Running a little late," Lawnhart whispered anxiously as

he made the turn in front of the marker poles. He pressed down on the gas as the powerful halide lamps lit up another fifty-yard section of glistening, slush-speckled black asphalt lined with hundreds of stark, bare-limbed trees, but then quickly let up when he felt the back wheels start to fishtail in a patch of built-up ice.

"Easy," Morgan cautioned. "We've got plenty of time."

Lawnhart pondered that thought for a moment.

"You don't think it really matters then?"

"What's that?"

"The time. You know, all that crap Molly gave us about not getting behind on the schedule and making sure everything got delivered tonight?"

"Beats the hell out of me." Morgan shrugged as he continued to stare out the front windshield. "Way I see it, Molly's one tough broad, and we've been waiting over a month to get assigned a job, and now we've got one, so we probably ought to do what we're told."

"Yeah, I can't argue that," Lawnhart agreed as he continued to guide the heavy dark van through the icy rainstorm.

Out in front of the van, the vertical pattern of ice-water droplets, falling rapidly through the penetrating length of the headlight beams to merge with the sheet of glistening water coating the dark asphalt, seemed almost hypnotic in their distracting beauty.

But Otis Lawnhart refused to allow himself to be distracted. Having driven these back roads all of his young adult life, he knew the hidden dangers of that reflective surface all too well. Increasingly wary of the treacherous runoff ditches, he found himself unconsciously edging the van closer to the pair of solid yellow lines dividing the narrow, curving road.

"Looks like it's gonna ice up pretty soon," he commented nervously as he eased the van back into the middle of their lane. That was something else they didn't need this evening: a head-on with another car hugging the center line.

"That's okay," Morgan shrugged. "Weather slows us down, it'll slow everybody down. All works out even, long as we stay careful." He stared out through the plummeting streaks of near-ice until he spotted the yellow road sign warning of an approaching sharp curve to the left.

"Miller Heights. Coming up on the right, just past the sign," he said.

"Yeah, got it."

Lawnhart made the turn and they dropped down into a dark, shallow valley interspersed with winding narrow side roads, tall stands of bare trees, and a multitude of expensive, upper-middle-class homes built on half- and three-quarter-acre wooded lots. Like many similar lifestyle-conscious neighborhoods in the area, there were no sidewalks, no streetlights, and the street signs were very small and unobtrusive.

"Okay," Morgan grunted, "last turn coming up."

"Yeah, I see it," Lawnhart nodded. "You ready?"

Crumpling the map and then tossing it to the floor, Bobby Morgan reached into the glove compartment and pulled out a black knit watch cap and a .380 Browning semiautomatic pistol. He pulled the cap down over his long hair, checked the safety on the double-action pistol, and then slipped the small but lethal handgun into his jacket pocket.

"I am now."

Thirty seconds later, at precisely 7:30 P.M. on what had already proved to be a typically cold, windy, rainy, and icy February evening in Fairfax County, Virginia, Otis Lawnhart carefully turned the van into an upward-sloping driveway that was almost completely concealed by thick stands of darkly silhouetted, bare-branched poplar, red oak, and hickory. The driveway led up to an asphalted guest parking area, a three-door garage, and a huge, single-family Dutch Colonial–styled home illuminated only by a single, low-watt porch light and now—briefly—by the headlights of the van.

There were only a few scattered porch lights visible among the widely separated homes in the immediate area. No sign of anyone out working in their open garage. No sounds of children laughing or screaming, or dogs barking. Only the van's engine and the noisy windshield wipers disturbed the

muted roar of icy raindrops falling through the dense, surrounding cover of finely branched bare trees.

"Okay," Morgan whispered, "keep your eyes open."

Lawnhart came to a stop at the end of the driveway, set
the emergency brake, and turned off the engine. Then he
hunched down, watching nervously for any sign of movement in or around the house while his more aggressive partner removed the remote control device—the one that Molly
Hunsacker had given to them several weeks ago—from the
overhead sun visor.

After giving Lawnhart a final nod of reassurance, Bobby
Morgan opened the van door and stepped out into the near-
freezing darkness.

To any casual observer, the device in Morgan's hand
looked exactly like an automatic garage door opener. And,
in fact, it functioned just like one, with one significant difference: instead of being coded for one specific door code,
this particular transmitter was set to scan the entire authorized
range of garage door opener frequencies automatically.

Carefully following the instructions he'd been given by the
infamous Molly, Morgan walked cautiously around to the
side of the garage and briefly looked through the single,
tightly secured storm window.

The two side bays were empty. The middle bay was occupied by some sort of Jeeplike vehicle that definitely was
not the Peugeot that the owners of the house supposedly
used for most of their running around.

Bobby Morgan smiled, secretly relieved that everything
was falling into place. Like his more nervous partner, he had
also been troubled by the uneasy suspicion that the job
sounded almost *too* good.

Considerably more relaxed now, but still alert, Morgan
walked back around through the icy slush to the front door
of the house, knocked loudly, and rang the doorbell, waited
a few seconds, rang the doorbell again, and then walked
back around to the garage doors.

Standing directly in front of the first garage door on the

left, he extended his right hand, pointed the transmitter at the exact center of the door, and then firmly pressed the single wide button with his thumb.

For about fifteen seconds—although it seemed much longer than that to Morgan—a small red light just above the button flickered as the transmitter ran through its preprogrammed range of frequencies. Then, with a series of jarring clanks that seemed impossibly loud in the chilled night air, a single-horsepower motor mounted overhead inside the garage jerked into life and began to drag the hinged segments of the heavy wood door up a pair of galvanized steel rails that curved up against the garage ceiling.

"Well I'll be damned. It worked," Morgan whispered.

The door was only halfway up when Lawnhart accelerated the van forward, turning sharply into the guest parking area off to the right, and then quickly backing into the garage, using only his parking lights for guidance. Morgan used the button mounted outside the kitchen entry door to activate the overhead motor, this time in reverse, as Lawnhart turned off the engine and shut off the parking lights.

For a few eerie moments, the interior of the garage was almost completely dark and quiet. But then the silence was broken as Lawnhart slid the van's side panel door open while Morgan hurriedly unlatched and opened the storm window in the garage wall that faced the street below.

The two men met at the connecting door, and then hesitated, both seemingly reluctant to take that last irrevocable step.

Then, as usual, Morgan took the lead.

"Seven-thirty-three," he said. "We've got forty-two minutes to work. Another forty-five to get clear and make the meet. Got your gloves on?"

"Yeah," Lawnhart acknowledged, feeling his heart pound in his chest as he briefly illuminated his gloved hands and the leather bag of tools with his red-filtered flashlight.

"Then let's do it."

They began in the living room by pulling a new Mitsubishi

integrated TV-stereo-amplifier system away from the wall. Morgan left his partner there to begin pulling wires and cables while he went back to the van, returned with a portable copier, set it down carefully next to the TV, and then went upstairs to make absolutely certain that the house was empty.

Meanwhile, downstairs, Otis Lawnhart had run into a problem. The cable connections were protected by a piece of heavy-duty fiberboard that was attached to the back of the console with sixteen long wood screws that would take a good ten minutes to remove the right way. They didn't have ten minutes to spare, so Lawnhart removed it the wrong way, using a heavy rubber hammer and a pry bar.

He was still busy pulling and sorting out patch cords when Morgan came downstairs with a handful of files and a pair of matched shotguns.

"Place is clear. All kinds of crap in the master bedroom and the kid's room upstairs. You can start copying this stuff when you get the chance," Morgan whispered in the red-tinged darkness as he dropped the files next to the copier, laid the long-barreled weapons on the couch, and then hurried back upstairs, his thick-soled boots clomping loudly on the padded boards.

Two minutes later, Morgan was back with a Macintosh computer under one arm and a printer under the other, the connecting cables and power cords dragging behind him on the floor.

By the time Morgan completed his fifth round-trip from the family room to the upstairs and back—this time staggering under the weight of a cardboard box bulging with several jars of coins, four holstered handguns, and a dozen boxes of assorted ammunition—Otis Lawnhart had finished with the cords and was now stacking the amplifiers, equalizers, tuners, turntables, tape players, CD players, and VCRs into approximate forty-pound piles. After that, he told himself, they'd make the copies. They had plenty of time.

It took four back-bending trips apiece for the men to stack the expensive pieces of electronic gear against the interior sidewall of the garage, and then a fifth to lug the incredibly heavy television monitor out to the waiting open door of the van.

They had just finished shoving the monitor back against the wheel well–mounted spare tire, and were leaning against the side of the van, breathing heavily in the quiet darkness as they gathered their strength for the final stage of loading, when they heard the sound of a car accelerating around a corner at fairly high speed somewhere down the street.

Otis Lawnhart gripped his partner's jacketed arm, silently asking the question.

Morgan shook his head. "Way too early," he whispered.

"Yeah, but maybe I oughta keep an eye on it anyway," Lawnhart suggested nervously. "Just to play it safe."

"Yeah, sure, go ahead," Morgan shrugged. He wasn't really worried. Molly Hunsacker, a.k.a. Molly-the-Hun, the incredibly tough professional burglar who had talked them into this deal, had been emphatic in her assurances that the best part of these operations was the careful planning. Everything was scouted out in advance and scheduled down to the minute. And as far as Molly-the-Hun was aware, there hadn't been a single screwup yet. And the noted Fairfax County bar brawler had emphasized the word "yet" with a meaningful glare that had nearly turned Otis Lockhart's bowels into water.

Groaning audibly, Otis Lawnhart shuffled wearily over to the opened storm window, took one look outside, and then squealed out, "Jesus Christ, it's turning into the driveway!"

The verbal warning wasn't really necessary. The sudden appearance of two headlight beams blasting in through the storm window almost blinded Morgan as Lawnhart dived to the floor and then scrambled toward the now clearly visible side door of the van.

Bobby Morgan, who had always been the leader of the pair, was still frozen in place when the clicking sound of an electronic relay snapping shut over his head provided a focal point for his survival-oriented reflexes.

Without really thinking about it, he lunged up at the ceiling with his right arm fully outstretched, missed, went back up in a desperate second attempt. He groped for the drooping power cord with his gloved fingertips—and missed again, just as the chain-driving motor clanked into life and the garage door behind the van started to move up the curved rails.

The rattling sound of the drive chain seemed to provide the extra incentive that Bobby Morgan needed. Grunting in desperation, he lunged up at the ceiling once more, this time coordinating his frantic movements so that his left hand grabbed at the moving drive chain and then pulled, giving his right hand the extra couple of inches of reach necessary to yank the power cord out of its socket.

The bottom edge of the roll-up door clattered to a stop less than three inches off the garage floor.

For a few terrifying moments, Morgan just stood there and stared at the cord in his hand while his partner seemed to be transfixed by the twin beams of light streaming in through the narrow gap between the partially open garage door and the cement floor.

Then, before either man could say or do anything, the horribly familiar sounds of an electronic relay snapping shut, and a single-horsepower motor clanking into life, jarred at Bobby Morgan's rational thought processes.

"No, it can't," he started to whisper, his eyes still fixed on the prong end of the dangling power cord, when his ears, and then his eyes, as his head snapped around, provided a rational explanation.

"Oh Jesus, no, not the other one," he whimpered as he watched the garage door on the far right side start to go up. Then his eyes focused on the whirling pulley underneath the distant motor, and the drooping power cord.

Morgan was already scrambling up on top of the shiny new Ford Bronco in the middle bay, intent on lunging for the offending power cord, when he realized—just in time—that he was much too late.

As he crouched there on the roof of the Bronco, frozen in place, a low-slung red Mustang accelerated into the right-side garage bay under the still-rising garage door and braked to a stop amid muted sounds of youthful masculine laughter, loud radio music, and high-pitched giggling.

In addition to being disinterested in whatever had caused the left-side door to jam, and oblivious to the presence of an unfamiliar dark van in his parents' garage, the impatiently horny young man also failed to notice the bearded man with desperation in his eyes crouched on the roof of his father's new Bronco.

Instead, in a hurry to consummate his plans for the evening before his parents got home, the young man pulled himself out of the driver's side door, stood up facing the Mustang, stretched lazily, and then bent back down to whisper something to his still-giggling friend. Tightly wrapped in a mild alcoholic fog, the overprivileged youth only realized that something might be wrong when he heard the sound of a pair of size twelve boots hitting the concrete behind his back.

As far as Bobby Morgan was concerned, the kid was history the moment he stood up out of the car. It wasn't a matter of rational thinking, but one of survival, and in Morgan's mind, survival was synonymous with escape at whatever cost.

Morgan had already started to push himself off the roof of the Bronco with his hands when the youth bent back down, so the timing was perfect. He hit the floor with bent knees and was back up when the kid suddenly straightened up and started to turn his head to the left, which put his aquiline nose and orthodontically straightened teeth in perfect alignment with a full body–powered roundhouse left that slammed the back of his head into the solid doorframe of the Mustang.

The girl, as it turned out, was no less intoxicated than her amorous boyfriend, but her survival instincts were far more alert and functional.

Because of the loud music blaring in her ears, she never heard the sound of Bobby Morgan's boots hitting the garage floor, but she thought she saw something in her peripheral vision that caused her to turn her head just in time to see a large, bib overall–clad body standing up behind her boyfriend.

She was opening her mouth to scream when she saw, heard, and then distinctly *felt* the impact of her boyfriend's head against the doorframe of the Mustang. In the span of a single "one-thousand-and-one" count, those well-functioning instincts snapped her mouth shut in mid-scream, threw open the passenger door of the Mustang, and launched her in the direction of the open garage door when the lunging impact of a 170-pound body sent her sprawling face first into the concrete.

In those first few moments, the outcome was actually in doubt, simply because those feminine-oriented survival instincts knew all about the ruinous effect of elbows, knees, fingernails, and teeth on vulnerable portions of the male anatomy. And then, too, Bobby Morgan was handicapped by untold generations of Southern chauvinism that ridiculed the use of a clenched fist on a woman.

As a result, the only thing that saved Morgan's hand, in those first few moments while he was busy trying to protect his genitals, was the fact that the young woman couldn't quite get her teeth through the thick leather of his workman's gloves.

The outcome was actually in doubt during those first few moments only because the young woman truly believed that she was fighting for her life, whereas Bobby Morgan only wanted to get the hell out of there as quickly as they could without being spotted by one of the neighbors. But once Morgan's mind-shocked partner finally got into the act, the odds shifted in favor of two large, desperate, and frightened males against one small, desperate, and terrified female.

After a great deal of thrashing about on the cold concrete floor, Morgan was finally able to get his one gloved hand wrapped around the girl's mouth and his other around her wrists, while his partner tried to pin her equally dangerous knees to the concrete floor.

Twisting her head around, she managed to shift Bobby Morgan's weight forward enough so that she was able to bite down as hard as she could on the fleshy part of his ungloved thumb.

"Jesus Christ, get the . . . augghhh! Get the goddamned tape!" Morgan screamed at Lawnhart as he wrenched his hand loose—smashing his wristwatch in the process—and then spent another thirty or forty seconds scrambling around on the floor, trying to muffle and contain the desperately fighting girl and to protect his increasingly vulnerable groin, until they were finally able to get her secured with about thirty yards of the silvered duct tape.

Gasping for breath and frightened out of their minds, the two men quickly dragged the tightly wrapped young woman over next to the unmoving form of her boyfriend, secured them together with a few more yards of tape to keep her in place for a while, and then hurriedly took stock of their situation.

A few moments later, the lights and radio in the Mustang were turned off, the right-hand garage door was closed, the motorized opener for the left-hand door was plugged back in, and the other two door openers were unplugged.

"Forget the small stuff. We've gotta get out of here, right now! It's almost twenty after eight if their goddamned clock's right," Morgan gasped as they hurriedly began to stack their newly acquired property inside the van.

They were forced to take the time to wrap the more fragile pieces of electronic gear with old blankets and mattress pads, and hindered by an assortment of painful injuries, it was almost ten minutes before they were able to secure the last piece and slam the sliding panel door shut.

"Come on, get that engine started and let's get the hell out of here!" Morgan yelled as he ran over to the kitchen doorway and reached for the garage door button.

Otis Lawnhart had hobbled frantically around to the driver's side door, and was in the driver's seat and reaching for the key when he remembered. "Oh shit, the copier."

Three long minutes later, an exhausted Bobby Morgan punched the button that opened the left-side garage door, threw the tool kit and flashlights into the back of the van, slammed the back door shut, staggered over to the passenger side door, pulled himself in, and gasped: "Get the hell out of here, *now!*"

They were halfway down Jermantown, pushing it too hard on a narrow road that was now almost completely iced up, when the van's right front tire—and then, immediately thereafter, the right rear—hit a long patch of loose slush.

Before Otis Lawnhart could react, the heavily loaded van lost traction and began sliding out of control to the right. He tried to compensate by jerking the steering wheel sharply to the right and then back to the left while jabbing at the accelerator to regain traction, but it was too late.

The van slid out of control toward the right side of the road, and finally came to a jarring, nose-down stop when the right front tire suddenly dropped into a badly eroded section of the runoff ditch and dug the exposed axle deep into the icy, crumbling asphalt.

Chapter Fifteen

Thursday, 2031 hours

After checking his watch on what had turned out to be a cold, rainy and icy Thursday evening, Officer Henry Culver hesitated with the mike in his hand, crossed his fingers, and then radioed in to advise the station that he was clear from the shoplifting call at the Oakton Shopping Center.

Maybe, he thought, *just maybe.*

But he really didn't think so.

Less than fifteen seconds later, while cautiously maneuvering the still-unfamiliar dark and-gray patrol cruiser through the storm-disrupted traffic, and still hoping against the odds to stay warm and dry for at least another hour or so, he received the expected call from the dispatcher. A woman had just reported a vehicle going off into a ditch in front of her house on Jermantown Road.

So much for warm and dry. Culver shrugged as he reached for the mike again.

"Eight-Forty-Charlie, copy. I'm south on one-twenty-three now, just past Hunter Mill. Ten-nine the crossroad?"

"Eight-Forty, be advised, no cross street available at this time," the dispatcher's voice echoed through the cruiser's interior. "Reporting party disconnected. We're attempting a call-back now."

"Ten-four, I'll be at the intersection of one-twenty-three and Jermantown in a couple." Culver sighed, using the side of his gloved index finger to activate the cruiser's roof-mounted emergency lights, sending alternating beams of red and blue light sweeping through the steadily falling pattern of icy rain to help clear traffic ahead.

"SHIT!" Bobby Morgan screamed, reacting as much out of utter frustration as to the pain and the god-awful cold when the precariously angled jack gave way for the second time under the crushing load, shot out from under the van, and then smacked solidly into his shin, sending him tumbling backward into the deep drainage ditch where he landed shoulder first against a large rock.

Horrified, Otis Lawnhart quickly scrambled down into the icy slush after his partner.

"You okay?" Lawnhart whispered, his voice shaky and his hands trembling—from the cold as well as his shattered nerves—as he pulled his groaning and cursing partner up out of the ditch and alongside the disabled van.

"Ughh . . . yeah," Bobby Morgan gasped, his eyes blinking from the sharp, agonizing pain radiating from his leg and shoulder as he held his arm tight against his jacket, which was now completely soaked with frigid ice water. "Get the jack, we gotta—oh Jesus, no."

Otis Lawnhart didn't even have to turn around to know what caused his badly injured partner to suddenly freeze in shock. Dancing bits of red and blue light had suddenly appeared out of the darkness, and were reflecting off the ice-laden trees, the water, and the van from the rotating emergency lights of the police patrol cruiser less than a hundred yards down the road.

"She must have got loose," Morgan whispered, his mind seemingly numbered by the cold, the sudden appearance of the cruiser, and the still throbbing pain in his leg, arm and shoulder as he fumbled for the .380 semiautomatic pistol in his jacket pocket.

"No, wait a minute, she couldn't have gotten loose!" Lawnhart shook his head frantically, panicked by the sight of the pistol and the thought of being shot and killed in this horribly cold and dark place. "Honest to God, I taped her tight. There's no way."

"Then the kid worked himself loose, or maybe the parents came home early. Either way, doesn't make any difference now," Morgan whispered through chattering teeth, his unblinking eyes seemingly fixated by the sweeping pattern of the oncoming lights.

"But . . ." Lawnhart started to plead, and then there wasn't time to say anything more because the whirling red and blue lights were right above them now. The police cruiser braked to a stop on the far side of the road opposite the van, and Otis Lawnhart suddenly found himself standing up and walking toward the marked patrol vehicle in a daze, having no idea what he was going to do or say as he heard his partner drag himself and the jack underneath the van.

"Anybody hurt?" Patrol Officer Henry Culver asked from the driver's seat of the cruiser, resting his right hand on the grip of his holstered revolver as he quickly took inventory of the man coming around the front of the van in the rapidly falling ice-rain.

Hands empty. Soaking wet, filthy dirty, and probably just about done in, Culver thought, making the standard observational checks as he swept the powerful spotlight across the approaching man—causing him to stagger for a moment in the blinding glare—and then across the length of the vehicle, noting the presence of a second man fumbling with a jack underneath the van, before switching it off.

Otis Lawnhart had just started to put his hands up over his head when he suddenly realized that the uniformed officer hadn't said anything at all about being under arrest.

His hands were already at waist level, and he didn't know what else to do with them, so Lawnhart just turned them open and shrugged, blinking through the water dripping down his face and squinting against the strobelike effect of the still-rotating emergency lights that were now at eye level.

What did he say? Something like 'are we hurt?' Was that it? For the life of him, Otis Lawnhart couldn't remember.

"Uh, yeah, we're okay. Just got bounced around a little," he finally managed to get out through his tight vocal cords, hoping his answer made sense.

"Looks like you guys've been having a rough night." Culver smiled sympathetically, gesturing with his head at Otis Lawnhart's thoroughly soaked, dirt- and ice-smeared overalls.

"Oh, uh, yeah, having trouble with the jack. Damned thing keeps slipping." Lawnhart nodded blankly, staring down at his overalls and thinking *Jesus, man, you don't know the half of it,* which, somehow, didn't make any sense at all.

"Hey, listen, are you two going to be okay out here on your own for a few more minutes?" Culver asked as he pulled a lever underneath the cruiser's dash to pop open the trunk, put on his plastic-protected visor hat, and then opened the door of the cruiser and stepped out, sliding the five-cell flashlight out of its door clip.

"What?" Lawnhart shook his head in confusion, his

thought processes distracted by the terrifying image of his partner sprawled underneath the van, aiming that pistol.

"Are you two going to be okay here by yourselves for a little while longer?" Culver repeated, stepping closer to the man to take a quick look at his pupils for any obvious signs of shock. They looked okay. They were both the same size, almost pinpointed against the glaring sweeps of the emergency lights.

The only thing unusual about the man, Culver decided, was the Confederate flag earring in his left ear.

Amazing, he thought to himself. *Even the rednecks are going punk.*

"Huh? Oh, uh . . . yeah, sure, we're doing fine," Lawnhart nodded blankly.

"Got any flares?"

"Uh . . . no. No, we don't," Lawnhart shook his head, remembering the two packs of red flares in the pouch attached to the spare tire cover—right next to the stolen TV monitor and the copier.

"Thought that might be the case." Culver nodded as he walked around to the back of the cruiser, opened up the trunk, pulled out a half dozen long red flares with attached wire legs and handed them to Lawnhart.

"Know how to set up a pattern?"

"Uh, yeah, sure," Otis Lawnhart said, having no idea what the officer was talking about.

"Here, I'll get you started." Culver took one of the flares from Lawnhart, removed the protective end cap, ignited the end with the friction strip, and then carried it about thirty feet up the road from the disabled van where he set it at an upward angle in the middle of the road.

Otis Lawnhart held his breath as the uniformed officer walked back to the cruiser, waiting for him to turn and look inside the van with that goddamned flashlight, knowing that as soon as he did, his partner would open up with his little .380, and then everything would turn to shit. He couldn't tell if the officer was wearing a bulletproof vest under the loose-fitting raincoat, but Lawnhart figured he probably was. And even if he wasn't, he would certainly have called in their license number before he got out of the police car. They always did that on TV.

Imagining the worst, Lawnhart almost broke down in relief when the officer made it back to his cruiser without being shot at.

"Got a couple in a station wagon somewhere up the road," Culver explained as he got back in the cruiser, shut the door, started up the heavy-duty engine, and then looked out the window at Lawnhart. "Same thing happened to them. I'm going to make sure they're okay, maybe get them towed, and then check back on you guys in a little bit. Okay?"

"Uh, yeah, sure." Lawnhart nodded in almost-frantic agreement. "Uh, no hurry. We'll probably be out by the time you get back anyway."

"Hope so. Make sure you keep those flares going," Culver reminded, and then accelerated the light-flashing cruiser up the road.

It took Otis Lawnhart a few long moments, standing there in the icy downpour with his hands full of flares, to truly accept the fact that the cop was gone. But then Culver's words—the ones about returning in a few minutes—came back to him. Tossing the flares into the ditch, he ran back around to the side of the van, screaming for his partner to hurry.

At 9:18 that evening, almost twenty minutes past their scheduled arrival time, Otis Lawnhart pulled the dark van up in front of an isolated garage in northeast Washington, DC, shut off the headlights while leaving the engine running, and then waited for their contact to appear.

They saw movements in the shadows on both sides of the street, but it was at least another five minutes before an almost-bald black male of indeterminate age stepped out of a nearby alley.

"Hey, man, you know better than to show up late to a . . ."

he started to say as he came up to the driver's side window, a 9mm Sig/Sauer semiautomatic pistol held tight against the side of his leg. But then he looked inside and blinked in surprise.

He'd obviously been expecting someone else.

"Who the hell are you?" Marcus Grey demanded as he casually slid the 9mm semiauto back into his coat pocket.

"Uh, Otis and Bobby," Lawnhart said hesitantly, suddenly afraid that they'd gone to the wrong address.

"The new guys? Shit, you weren't supposed to start working until tomorrow," the elderly black man grumbled, staring in through the rolled-down window at the pair of soaking wet and absolutely filthy burglars.

"Yeah, well, the word we got was to pick up this stuff tonight," Bobby Morgan replied, in absolutely no mood to take any crap from some DC nigger fence.

Morgan was shivering cold, in spite of the van's full-blowing heater. His arm and shoulder throbbed, his shin felt as though it was broken from knee to ankle, and he had a headache that wouldn't quit. But more importantly, he had a van load of stolen property that he had to do something with before the police started making car stops on guys driving dark vans.

He'd been trying to think back, to remember if the overhead light on the garage door motor had cut out before he'd jumped on the girl, or if the guy might have turned all the way around before he'd hit him. It was going to make a big difference if one of those kids could make an ID on either of them.

He'd been doing a lot of thinking during the past few minutes about a lot of things, but the one thing he was trying not to think about was the sound of the kid's head hitting against the doorframe of the Mustang; a sound that still reminded him of a green melon being dropped on a concrete sidewalk.

After a lot more grumbling, and a couple of calls on a small portable radio he pulled out of his pocket, Marcus Grey finally agreed to accept the merchandise. He had them drive through a pair of garage doors connected by a narrow concrete tunnel that led into a large open warehouse area. The warehouse seemed to be divided equally by a twelve-foot-high Sheetrock wall running about halfway up to the exposed, red primer–coated metal trusses and sheet metal roof.

There were a half dozen men of widely varying ethnic backgrounds visible on this side of the wall, two of whom were hurrying toward the van with handcarts while a third opened a door in the dividing wall and yelled something unintelligible to someone on the other side.

From their position, Morgan and Lawnhart could see the top of a large truck on the other side of the partial wall, and two dark figures who were standing on opposite ends of the overhead catwalk, keeping deadly-looking assault rifles trained on the front windshield of the van.

It took the two warehouse men less than five minutes to remove the six hundred and some pounds of burglarized property from the van while the elderly black man did the inspecting and kept a running tally of quantity and quality.

Marcus Grey was still adding up the totals, muttering to himself and pausing to consider current market values that he really didn't give a damn about, one way or the other, when one of the unloaders walked up and pointed out an inscription of one of the stolen rifles.

As Morgan and Lawnhart watched nervously, Grey and the warehouse man walked over to one of the overhead lights where they could examine the weapon more closely. Then the balding black man turned and stared curiously at the two men in the van.

After considering the entire situation for another twenty seconds or so, Marcus Grey walked slowly around to the side passenger window of the van and stared at the ravaged face of Bobby Morgan.

"You know the address of the place you hit?"

"Uh, yeah, sure," Otis Lawnhart nodded, rattling it off from his jumbled memory.

Marcus Grey blinked again as he listened to the familiar address being repeated in a nervous West Virginia drawl.

"You boys run into some trouble this evening?" he finally asked in a cold, suspicious voice.

"Some," Morgan acknowledged, impatient to get the hell out of this place as soon as they could, but at the same time, aware of the need to appear calm and relaxed. "We handled it okay. No big deal."

"Hope so," the elderly man nodded solemnly as he hesitated for a few more seconds, and then reached into his pocket and peeled off several high-denomination bills from a thick roll. "You picked up some nice merch. I'm callin' it an even twenty-one hundred, minus two bills penalty for showing up late. Oughta cost you more, 'cause we set these drop times real careful, and you don't wanna be screwing around with the system first time through," the old man emphasized with a gnarled finger.

"Yeah, I know. It won't happen again," Morgan promised, biting back the words that he didn't dare utter in this back-alley DC warehouse.

"Thass good," the old man continued on, "'cause what I'm gonna do is cut you boys a little slack this time, and maybe even slip in a little bonus for them bad-ass forty-fives. Fast movers 'round the District these days. Take all them bad boys you can get," he chuckled, slipping the remainder of the fat roll back into his pocket and then holding the folded bills up to the window. "Way I figure it, your piece 'a the pie comes out t' two grand even. Fair enough?"

"Fine," Morgan agreed, accepting the currency and slipping it into his jacket pocket, making a point of not counting it. He and his partner still had a rep to make in this business. It wouldn't pay in the long run, to seem too greedy right up front.

They had to wait a few more minutes for the warehouse men to finish loading up the truck on the other side of the wall. Finally the diesel rig roared into life and rumbled out of the warehouse. Marcus Grey stared at his wristwatch for another two minutes, giving the truck time to disappear into the bowels of the District, and then nodded his head.

"You boys come back soon, hear?" he smiled as he motioned for the doorkeeper to let the van out through a separate exit.

"Yeah," Bobby Morgan said, smiling contentedly for the first time since that evening, in spite of the pain, "we just might do that".

The couple who had gone off the road at Jermantown turned out to be a panic-stricken mother and daughter who— in coming home from an extended shopping spree at the Fair Oaks Mall—had suddenly found themselves sharing the right-hand lane with an oncoming truck being piloted by an inexperienced young driver who apparently didn't understand that the brakes on a motor vehicle were only designed to bring the *tires* to a sudden stop.

As he quickly discovered, stopping the forward momentum of a two-ton truck that had suddenly turned into a sled on an icy road was another problem entirely.

The unavoidable impact had sent the smaller sedan spinning into one of the infamous Jermantown Road drainage ditches, resulting in a considerable amount of sheet metal damage to the sedan but no significant injuries to either of the badly shaken occupants. It was, in other words, a typical Northern Virginia winter season fender-bender.

The normal policy of the Fairfax County Police Department in these circumstances was to allow the two drivers to sort the whole thing out with their insurance agents, thus saving the department a tremendous amount of essentially useless paperwork. But in this case, the truck driver had left the scene without exchanging the relevant information. That, to Henry Culver's utter dismay, made it hit-and-run.

Which meant a great deal of paperwork.

By the time that Culver got the tow truck out to the scene, finished his incident report, and was ready to clear from the scene, it was nearly 2145 hours; over an hour since he'd stopped to check on the two men with the van in the ditch.

Better get back there and see how those guys are doing, Culver thought as he filed the completed incident report in his carry case. He was reaching across his chest for the safety harness clip when he heard his call number being broadcast over the primary dispatch frequency. He reached for the mike instead and discovered that his supervisor, Patrol Sergeant Jack Hattabaugh, wanted to meet for coffee at a local restaurant.

"Eight-Forty, hold one," Culver spoke into the mike and then leaned his head out the window of his cruiser and yelled to the tow truck driver. "Hey buddy, when you came up Jermantown, did you see a Dodge van off the road on the opposite side, about a quarter mile back?"

The tow truck driver shook his head. "Nope. Road was clear all the way back to Chain Bridge."

"You sure?"

The man in the greasy overalls laughed. "Hell yes, I'm sure. Nights like this, I always keep an eye out for business."

"Okay, thanks." Culver nodded and then brought the mike back up to his mouth. "Looks like I'm clear, Sarge. Be there in a couple."

At 10:03 that evening, Otis Lawnhart turned the dark van into the driveway of the bank that had been specified in their instructions, pulled up next to the automated night service teller, and then rolled down his window.

Lawnhart took the electronically altered Mobil credit card out of his shirt pocket and slid it into the marked slot. The video screen facing Lawnhart flickered for several seconds—much longer than he thought was normal—and then finally flashed a message of the screen:

PLEASE ENTER YOUR PERSONAL CODE
NUMBER

"Two-two-nine-two-two," Bobby Morgan repeated from memory as his partner punched in the numbers.

HOW MUCH DO YOU WISH TO DEPOSIT INTO YOUR ACCOUNT?

"Wish it *was* my account," Lawnhart grumbled. He reached down through the van window and removed a deposit envelope from the supply bay. "Well, what do we put in? The full five hundred?"

Morgan hesitated for a moment.

"I don't know," he finally shook his head. "Wasn't our fault the son-of-a-bitch kid came back early. We take all the risks, damn near get ourselves killed trying to get back on time, and still get docked two hundred bucks for showing up late, even though he thinks we weren't supposed to start until tomorrow. They're gonna be like that, I figure we ought to split the penalty too."

"Yeah, sounds fair to me." Lawnhart shrugged. "So what's that come out to?" he asked, having no head at all for complex math.

"Straight twenty-five percent split, that'd be fifty bucks," Bobby Morgan calculated.

"So I should put in what, four-fifty? What about that three hundred and something in cash you found in the drawer?"

"What about it?"

"Figured maybe we oughta count that in too," Lawnhart said. "Remember what Molly told us. The rules say that everything gets turned in, no matter what, and that it all gets split four ways. Three for us and one for them. And you didn't turn in that .357 and the Rolex watch either," he reminded.

"So how are they going to know what we found?"

"That nigger fence'll probably report in on how much he paid us," Lawnhart suggested.

"Maybe," Morgan agreed. "But the way I figure it, those people at the warehouse and this guy Digger can't be tied in too tight. I mean if they were, why turn his share over to us in the first place?"

"So you figure the most this Digger guy knows is what the fence paid us, and maybe not even that, right?"

"Exactly." Morgan nodded.

"So why don't we play it safe," Lawnhart suggested uneasily. "Give them the full split on the property, eat the fine this time, and keep the cash for ourselves as a bonus?"

"Yeah, sure, what the hell." Morgan shrugged, distracted by the growing concern that he might have actually broken his leg, as his partner leaned out of the window and carefully punched in the appropriate digits before sealing 475 dollars into the preprinted envelope they'd received and sliding it into the appropriate slot.

The screen seemed to flicker in reproach for a few moments before flashing a final message:

THANK YOU
HAVE A NICE DAY

Chapter Sixteen

Thursday, 2210 hours

"You *sure* it was Molly?" Burglary Sergeant John Russelli asked in thoroughly irritated tone of voice.

The question was directed at Henry Culver, but it was fair game for any of the other four uniformed officers clustered around the thick wooden table in the far back corner of Amphora's—a popular Greek-American restaurant located in the geographic center of Fairfax County.

"Stubby little feet, great big wrench, in and out like a goddamned jackrabbit, and nothing but glove marks for prints."

Patrol Sergeant Jack Hattabaugh shrugged. "Sounds like Molly-the-fucking-Hun to me."

Culver nodded in agreement. "If you ignore that business with the dog, she might as well have signed her name on the door." He wrapped his chilled hands around the rough ceramic surface of the dishwasher-abused coffee cup and took a cautious sip at the steaming liquid before looking back up at Russelli. "Figured you'd want to know."

"God-*damn* that miserable little bitch," Russelli muttered darkly as he pulled a pen and notebook out of his jacket pocket.

Russelli, a huge, dark, heavy-shouldered man of indeterminate Italian heritage, was one of those compulsive notetakers who could easily fill a standard department issue blue-lined notebook—all forty-nine thread-bound pages, front and back—in a single day. He'd picked up the habit during his eight years with the Secret Service Presidential Security Detail, and had never been able to kick it. He kept the sequentially numbered and dated field diaries in neatly labeled cardboard boxes, and insisted that all of the investigators in his unit do the same.

A gruff, demanding, and often overbearing supervisor, John Russelli remained well liked and respected by his men anyway, mostly because they knew he'd back them up with the brass, no matter of how badly they screwed up. But in the opinion of the entire unit, the note-taking fetish was not one of his more endearing traits.

After hesitating a moment to cross-check the time references that Henry Culver had provided, Russelli looked up. "You pull the knob?"

Culver nodded. "Got it in the trunk. I'll drop it off at the lab this evening if I can get clear. Why, you think it'll do any good this time?"

Russelli shrugged wearily and shook his head as if to say "How the hell would I know?"

The fatigue from working five overtime shifts in a row, the last three on mobile surveillance, was clearly visible in John

Russelli's sagging shoulders and reddened eyes. Thanks to a last-minute tip from one of Russelli's supposedly more reliable snitches, the entire five man team had just completed a futile six-hour surveillance in the McLean District, trying to nail a very aggressive and elusive burglar named Molly Hunsacker. Unfortunately, however, based upon the CSI evidence that Henry Culver had just provided, it was all too apparent that Molly had been working the opposite end of the county at the time.

This error in judgment, and the fact that Russelli's team had failed to spot a single criminal violation during the surveillance, much less Molly-the-Hun in action, would be one more black mark logged against the new res-burg unit. One more, that is, among many, thanks to Molly and her many cohorts who had been ransacking all seven Fairfax County Patrol Districts with increasing success during the past five months that Russelli's unit had been in operation; a fact that did not go unnoticed by the Central Headquarters brass.

Being a pessimist, Russelli figured he had maybe another month to make a substantial change in his unit's arrest stats before he found himself reassigned to the jail, administering breath tests to drunks. And having wiped more alcohol-laced vomit out of the backseats of patrol cruisers than he cared to think about, Sergeant John Russelli's determination to put a halt to Molly Hunsacker's B&E career had taken on an intensity that now bordered on the obsessive.

As far as Russelli was concerned, Molly-the-Hun was another John Doe Thirty-three in the making, and he carried the memory of Digger with him constantly now, with every painful step.

It was this obsession that had driven John Russelli to trust the word of Pogo Waters—a normally reliable snitch who had either been sadly misinformed about Molly's work schedule, or had decided to start playing games by working both sides of the criminal fence. Nothing new either way. Cops expected that sort of thing from a snitch. But this was the first time that one of the local informants had scammed

Russelli—for the simple reason that they were all scared shitless of him.

Street rumor, cheerfully spread among their contingent of snitches by the other res-burg detectives, had it that Russelli had once strangled a family cat with his bare hands for urinating on one of his favorite sweaters. The story was supposedly true, although Russelli vehemently denied it and had threatened to deball and dismember the first person who even *hinted* at such a thing within hearing range of either one of his sixteen-year-old daughters.

"Just a little cat piss," the detectives would whisper softly to a wide-eyed informant, shaking their heads slowly in shared disbelief. "Just imagine what the crazy son of a bitch would do if anybody actually went sideways on him. Myself, I don't even want to think about it. No sir-ree."

Actually, as far as departmental rumors went, it really wasn't all that unlikely a story. Everybody knew that Sergeant John Russelli disliked whiny animals in general, and despised arrogant cats in particular. That, in addition to his normally brooding and somber nature, gave the story just enough credence to make it absolutely believable.

A radio call pulled two of the uniformed officers away from the table, leaving Russelli, Hattabaugh, Patrol Officer Billy Joe Moorestead, and Culver to enjoy the warmth of the restaurant for a few more minutes.

"So what's the knob look like?" Russelli asked, mostly out of reflex.

"Torn to shit," Culver said. "Couple of half-decent bite marks, but it was one of those brass-coated pot metal jobs. Lock mechanism snapped before the teeth could really dig in, so we don't have much in the way of useful striations. Still, give ol' Balloch a chance to work at it and he just might be able to make a match, assuming that we manage to get our hands on the wrench in time," he added.

"I'll get a warrant for it first thing in the morning," Russelli muttered. "In the meantime, if one of your guys happens to see Molly driving around tonight, I'd appreciate it if you'd take that goddamned wrench and beat her half to death with it."

"Personally, I'd advise shooting her in the knees a couple of times first," Moorestead added. "Last I heard, she was bench-pressing 280 at Gold's, ten reps. No point in making it a fair fight."

"Amen to that." Hattabaugh chuckled, but then the veteran patrol sergeant's gray eyebrows furrowed in confusion. "Hey, Henry, answer me this. Why can't we make her on some of the old test marks? I mean, Jesus, the guys at the lab must have used a couple hundred pounds of lead by now, making test impressions of that wrench."

Culver shook his head. "We taught her too well. Ever since that last bust, when she had to sit in court for two days listening to Balloch and me testify about how we make a tool mark match, she's been running a file across the teeth of that wrench after every job."

"Shit," Hattabaugh muttered.

"Exactly," Russelli growled a nodded agreement.

"So what does that mean, exactly? We can't get her on tool marks?" Hattabaugh asked pointedly.

Culver shook his head. "Not necessarily. Actually, all she's really doing is making it easier for us to nail her to a job once we catch her in the act. Every time she cuts on those teeth, she makes that wrench all the more unique. It ought to be an easy match."

"So all we have to do is catch her with the damn thing *before* she gets back to that file, right?" Moorestead asked.

"Exactly," Culver said.

"But *after* she rips a door that we know about," Patrol Sergeant Hattabaugh added, nodded in understanding. "Which means the res-burg detail would probably like us to be on top of her when she does the job."

"Be nice if somebody was," Russelli muttered gloomily.

"Shit, we gotta do everything for you guys?" Billy Joe Moorestead complained good-naturedly.

"Tell you what," Russelli said, yawning widely and absentmindedly readjusting the shoulder-holstered .357 concealed under his rumpled suit coat as he stood up, "anybody on the squad ties Molly-the-Hun to a door job within the next thirty days, Sharon and I'll spring for steaks and booze. Might even put in a good word to Stewart and his door-kickers for you, too, buddy boy, if you're still that friggin' nuts," he added, gesturing with his head at Culver as he scooped up the check and limped over to the cash register near the door.

The limp didn't go unnoticed by the three uniformed officers, but neither of them said anything as they watched Russelli pay the check and then hobble over to the rest room. Everybody in the department knew that Russelli was living on borrowed time as a cop. The res-burg assignment was simply a delaying tactic by a sympathetic captain, giving the determined but effectively crippled investigator another six months or so for his leg injuries to try to heal so that he could try to pass the physical again.

But nobody, including Russelli himself, believed he had the slightest chance of making it.

"Jesus, Henry, don't tell me you're still gunning for Major Crimes?" Hattabaugh asked disbelievingly as he raised his empty cup to catch the attention of their waitress—a dark-haired and dark-eyed young woman with the stamina of a high school middle linebacker who nodded cheerfully as she hurried by with a trayful of steaming plates. The Fairfax County cops knew how to pick their restaurants.

"Sure, why not?" Culver shrugged, looking over at the veteran field supervisor who had been a willing and understanding advisor during the past few days that Culver had been back on patrol.

"You know how much paper you've got to write on a res-burg, right?" Hattabaugh reminded. "Well, let me tell you something, Major Crimes's a hell of a lot worse."

"It can't be," Culver protested. "Res-burg's nothing but paper."

"Yeah, that's pretty much it," Hattabaugh acknowledged,

"but you got a couple other things in homicide, robbery, and rape that you don't see all that much in the burg detail."

"What's that—handcuffs?"

"Don't let Russelli hear you say that." Hattabaugh chuckled appreciatively but then shook his head and turned serious. "Pressure," he said solemnly. "Pressure like you'll never see out on the street. Pressure that eats at you every hour you're awake, 'cause you can't walk away from it at the end of the shift like you can out here. Pressure," he repeated with emphasis, "and freaks who want to play games with your head."

"Come on, Hattabaugh, what about all the nutcases we deal with out on the street?"

Hattabaugh shook his head firmly. "You're not even in the same ballpark. Listen, hot dog, it's one thing to make 'em on a traffic stop, or run 'em down in a pursuit. Most guys can handle that, no sweat, 'cause all it takes is some technique and a little bit of guts.

"But you try having to live with those bastards," Hattabaugh went on. "Try getting inside their heads and thinking like a freak so you can figure out what they're going to do next so you can stop them before they do it. And you gotta try, 'cause if you don't, there ain't nobody else gonna stop 'em from hurting somebody else."

"Right," Culver said, nodding his head in agreement. "That's exactly it. That's the interesting part."

"Jesus Christ Almighty, Henry," Hattabaugh swore under his breath in deference to the surrounding diners. "I swear to God I don't understand you."

"That's okay, Sarge." Billy Joe Moorestead laughed as Russelli sat back down at the table. "Nobody else on the department does either. Everybody figures he's just a burned-out rocket scientist. Probably harmless."

"No, I mean it," Hattabaugh went on, trying to make his point. "I mean I thought I did. But Jesus, a guy who walks away from—how many years was it, eighteen?"

"Two on the street and then thirteen in the lab." Culver

shrugged, smiling easily at the veteran sergeant whom he had long looked up to as a street-hardened professional, but one with a curiously gentle and caring streak that managed to show up every now and then. Hattabaugh's entire squad had him pegged as an easy touch, just as long as they played him right.

"Okay, and then add those three years you spent in the army crime lab and there's your eighteen. And what were you, a senior criminalist in what I'm told is a first-class, high-tech crime lab?" Hattabaugh went on insistently, barely remembering to keep his voice down. "Right up near the top of the ladder. Degrees up the wazoo. Big bucks—what was it, equivalent to captain's pay, right?"

"Thereabouts."

"And you walked away from it. Just plain-ass walked away from it. And to do what? Go put on a uniform and write traffic tickets?" Hattabaugh shook his head in disbelief.

Culver nodded again, the easy smile resting comfortably on his face. This wasn't the first time that he and Hattabaugh had had this discussion.

"See, the thing is," Hattabaugh explained to Russelli and Moorestead in a slightly calmer voice, "at first, I thought I had this turkey figured out. I mean, I really did. A guy makes a career crossover like that, at his age—what are you now, Culver, forty?"

"Pretty soon."

"Okay, so at thirty-nine, the guy isn't a young Turk, thinking he can clean up the whole damn county single-handed his first year on the job. Am I right?"

Russelli nodded his head in agreement, grateful for the chance to stop thinking about Molly-the-Hun and his rapidly dwindling career as a burg sergeant.

"So," Hattabaugh continued on, "I figure he's gotta be in love with one a' two things."

Here we go, Culver thought, wondering how far the ever-inquisitive Hattabaugh was going to get this time.

"Badge or the gun," the uniformed patrol sergeant persisted. "Lotta cases, it's both; but the thing is," he went on, glaring suspiciously at Culver for a moment before turning back to Russelli, "it didn't fit, 'cause it turns out your old school buddy here doesn't even know how to be badge heavy. Fact is, I gotta get on his ass to make sure he's getting the right word out to some of these street clowns."

"You *are* a little light-handed when it comes to whipping on them crime-loving perpetrators, Henry." Billy Joe Moorestead grinned teasingly.

"And then you know what happens?" Hattabaugh added with a pained expression on his face. "The goddamned brass make the guy a master police officer the first day he's back on the street."

Hattabaugh was one of those sturdy, no-nonsense cops who truly believed in the system. According to the Fairfax County police promotional system, the absolute minimum time for a nonsupervisory patrolman to move up to the rank of master police officer was seven years. It had taken Hattabaugh eight, and then another five before he was finally promoted to sergeant. The Fairfax County Police Crime Lab scientists, on the other hand, were given basic training as police officers, a six-month minimum tour on patrol, and then were quickly transferred to the lab, whereupon they typically lost all interest in rank. But then, too, no one in the lab, to Hattabaugh's knowledge, had ever seriously considered a voluntary transfer *back* into the cruisers.

"Just goes to show what can happen when you're nice to all those perpetrators," Culver said, grinning.

"Listen, Henry," Russelli suggested, getting caught up in the lighthearted exchange in spite of his black mood. He gestured with his head at Culver's brand new light gray uniform shirt. "Maybe if you'd shine that badge once in a while, it'd make the sarge here feel better."

Culver, Moorestead, and Russelli laughed while Hattabaugh continued to glare at them.

"Okay," Hattabaugh growled, moving his head in closer to Russelli after looking around to make sure no one was within earshot. "So it isn't the badge, and it sure as hell isn't the gun, 'cause he never cleans the damn thing. He can't drive worth a shit, so it can't be the big shiny cruiser with the reds and blues. So you tell me, Russelli," the veteran patrol sergeant demanded of the still-grinning burglary investigator. "Just what is it that makes this buddy of yours tick?"

"Beats the hell out of me," Russelli confessed.

"Hattabaugh, I've explained it to you maybe a couple dozen times now, but you just won't accept the straight truth," Culver replied easily, his eyes sparkling with amusement. "Read my lips. I *like* being a police officer. And I want to be a Homicide investigator. Period. No games, no bullshit. I like what I'm doing right now, but I still want a shot at Homicide."

"You really want to work with those freaks, don't you? Make yourself sick in the head?" The thought was almost more than Hattabaugh could stomach.

"But it doesn't have to work that way," Culver said insistently. "You don't have to think like those idiots to deal with them; you just dig around in their environment and look for the pieces."

"The what?" Hattabaugh's graying eyebrows furrowed into a perplexed frown.

"The evidence, Sarge," Culver explained patiently. "It's all there, just like a trail of bread crumbs. All you gotta do is figure it out. Put the pieces together. Sift through all the details until you find the ones that mean something, so you can figure out the pattern. That's the interesting part."

"But you were doing that in the lab," Hattabaugh interrupted. "What's the difference out here?"

"Adrenaline kick, for one thing," Culver admitted. "Working a cruiser's addictive, no doubt about it; but there's more to it than that. I'm not real sure I can explain it, but in the lab all we did was work with the pieces. We typed the blood and matched the bullets and all that sort of stuff, but we'd never get to see the patterns develop like you do when you work the scenes."

"What're you talking about? You worked scenes. I must have seen you at least a couple hundred call-outs," Hattabaugh said. "Homicides, burgs, everything."

"But never to the extent that the Homicide guys did," Culver explained. "They'd go out to follow the leads while we went back to the lab and tried to figure out if all that evidence we collected actually meant anything. It was interesting, but not quite the same thing."

"Not close enough to the edge," Hattabaugh said, his eyes widening as he nodded in sudden understanding. "That's it, isn't it? You can't taste it back there in the lab like you can out in the street. Right?"

Culver shrugged. "Yeah, something like that. When Gauss got promoted to the lab director's job, I was going to end up having to stay in the lab supervising the dope and tox sections, which meant no more playing around at scenes. And let me tell you, after you've seen about ten thousand Baggies of grass, and about that many blood and urine samples, you start thinking that maybe Russelli's paperwork doesn't look too bad after all."

"Oh yeah?" Russelli's eyes lit up, a broad smile spreading across his grizzled face.

"Oh no you don't." Culver shook his head quickly, his eyes taking on a panicked look. "I told you guys, I want a shot at Homicide first. I passed the exam and I'm on the list for the oral. If I can't make it the direct route—well then maybe . . ."

Hattabaugh sighed. "Okay, hotshot, maybe I won't try to pawn you off on this thick-headed wop just yet. I . . . oh, hey, almost forgot," he said, reaching into his pocket, pulling out a folded envelope and handing it over to Culver. "This came in the mail for you. Lieutenant asked me to drop it off."

"What've you got there?" Russelli asked curiously, observing the puzzled expression that spread across Culver's face as he ripped open the envelope and stared silently for a long moment at what appeared to be a crumpled piece of paper.

"Uh . . . I'm not sure," Culver said, blinking in confusion

for a moment, and then handing the paper over to the uniformed patrol sergeant.

"Jesus Christ," Hattabaugh whispered, staring at the letter with a startled and concerned expression on his face as he handed the note to Russelli, "what the hell's that all about?"

Culver briefly explained the circumstances in the courtroom that led up to his receiving the threatening note from Digger via Paul Radlick six days ago.

"That slimy little bastard," Russelli whispered, his eyes glaring dangerously as he studied the note.

"You sure it's the same one?" Hattabaugh asked.

"Yeah, it sure looks like it," Culver said, taking the threatening note back from Russelli and staring at it again, as if searching for something that he couldn't quite remember—something important.

"So why would Radlick send it to you?" Hattabaugh had been a cop too long to have much faith in coincidence.

Culver shrugged. "Guess he must have figured I'd want it back as a souvenir." He was checking the envelope to see if there was any other explanatory message, but there wasn't. "Think I'm going to give Paul a call at home, see what's going on with this thing," he said after a few moments. "Back in a minute."

"See you out there, Henry," Billy Joe Moorestead called out to Culver and then tossed some tip change on the table. "Well, guys, I guess one of us had better get back out on those bricks before Vinny manages to get himself lost again."

Russelli waited until Moorestead and Culver had disappeared around the far side of the restaurant. Then he turned to Hattabaugh, forcing himself to drive the hated images of John Doe Thirty-three out of his mind. He had other more important things to discuss with the veteran patrol sergeant.

"You said you wanted some time to think about it," he said in a deep whispery voice. "So what do you think?"

Hattabaugh shrugged. "Henry's done okay so far. He handles himself fine out on the street. Thinks about what he's doing. Doesn't get careless on the car stops. Calls for backup when he needs it, handles things on his own when he doesn't."

"Yeah, right," Russelli acknowledged, having heard exactly the same thing from the other members of Hattabaugh's uniformed squad. "So what do I tell Stewart?"

"You mean about the transfer?"

"Yeah." Russelli nodded. "You had to call it, would you recommend him?"

Hattabaugh hesitated, and Russelli pounced on him immediately.

"You got a problem, don't you?" he said with quiet intensity. "Come on, Jack, spit it out."

"I don't know." The veteran patrol sergeant shrugged uncomfortably. "I mean, Henry's good people, and he's a good cop. He's inquisitive as hell, he's got all that tech background, he writes one hell of a report, and he really wants that job. But if it really came down to it . . ."

"You don't think he'd shoot, do you?" Russelli pressed, his bloodshot eyes almost glowing.

Hattabaugh paused for a long moment before answering. "No," he finally said quietly, shaking his head. "If it really came down to it, I think he'd probably hesitate and take a bullet before he'd smoke a guy."

Hattabaugh paused again before going on. "The thing is, Henry'll be fine out on the bricks with us. He's careful, and everybody jumps their area to roll on backups anyway. But if he starts running around with all those crazy-ass door-kickers in Homicide . . ."

Russelli nodded his head wearily, grateful for Jack Hattabaugh's cautious words that confirmed his own fears. He started to say something and then noticed that Culver was on his way back to the table.

"Well?" he demanded.

"No answer. His recorder's switched on, so I figure he's probably chasing Doreen around the house and doesn't want to be disturbed. I'll stop by his place this weekend, check it out."

"Hey, you sure you're okay on this note deal?" Hattabaugh asked, staring suspiciously at Culver.

"Huh? Oh yeah, sure," Culver said, smiling easily. "Just stirred up a bunch of memories I'd just as soon forget. No problem."

"Yeah?" Hattabaugh narrowed his eyes skeptically. "Well, personally, I think you've been bullshitting me all evening, but if you wanna go gunning for a job driving yourself crazy dealing with freaks like that all day," Hattabaugh shrugged his heavy shoulders and gave Russelli a meaningful look, "that's your decision."

Culver grinned. "You're all heart, Sarge."

"Yeah, well, in the meantime," Hattabaugh said, shaking his head, "seeing as how it's getting close to my bedtime, you think you and Bobby can keep out of trouble long enough to let a tired old man take it easy the rest of the shift?"

"Come on, Sarge," Culver said, winking as he stuffed the note in his jacket pocket. "How much trouble do you think we can we get into"—he looked at his wristwatch, noting that it was almost ten-thirty in the evening—"in two and a half hours?"

"I don't want to think about it."

"Come on, Jack, look on the bright side," Russelli said in his deep, growling voice as they all got up from the table. "If you can't trust a flipped-out rocket scientist and a good-ole-boy redneck with your career and your pension, then who the hell can you trust?"

Jack Hattabaugh stared at the still-smiling Culver for a few moments, and then said "Just try to be careful out there, Henry. That's all I ask."

Chapter Seventeen

At precisely 11:00 that Thursday evening, according to the computerized log that kept track of such things, the Emergency Operation Center at the headquarters station of the Fairfax County Police Department received a nine-one-one call from a woman with a strong French accent who seemed to be on the verge of complete hysteria.

Although in all fairness, Mrs. Nichole L'Que really wasn't the type of person who normally allowed herself to panic in the face of a crisis.

A career military wife of twenty-two years, Mrs. L'Que had long since learned to cope with the fears, confusions, and uncertainties that were an inevitable part of her husband's profession. And likewise, when her husband received his mysterious emergency transfer to the French Embassy's military attaché post in Washington, DC, she was able to step forward and confront the everyday Northern Virginia hazards of ruptured pipes, fallen trees, overflowing septic tanks, and creosote chimney fires with hardly a blink. The point being that, as far as domestic emergencies were concerned, Mrs. L'Que considered herself perfectly capable of dealing with the worst that life in the Washington, DC suburbs might have to offer.

But all of her worldly experiences notwithstanding, Nichole L'Que had never even considered the possibility that she might come home from an evening at the opera to find her house ransacked, and then discover her son lying on the floor in the far garage bay, securely taped in an obscene manner on top of a young American woman whom he had just started dating the previous week.

That in itself would have been difficult enough for even a woman of Mrs. L'Que's proven stamina to take, but the worst was yet to come.

Because the young woman in question was thrashing around on the garage floor with her eyes widened in shock, the lower portion of her dress darkly stained with blood, and her lungs hoarse from trying to yell through several wrappings of duct tape, it took a few moments for Mrs. L'Que to realize that it was her son who was doing almost all of the bleeding—from the nose, mouth, and both ears—in addition to being unconscious and barely breathing.

That was when she started screaming.

Mrs. L'Que was still screaming and tearing at the sticky strips of duct tape when her husband—a combat veteran of the French Army and the French Secret Service, who had considerable hands-on experience in dealing with violent encounters—exploded through the garage door, took one look at the situation, dragged his wife into the kitchen, punched nine-one-one on the wall phone, placed the handset into her hand, and said in a tightly controlled voice: "The police and the paramedics. Get them here now!"

He grabbed a handful of kitchen towels and ran back into the garage.

Jarred out of her bewildered frenzy by the rage in her husband's voice, and far too shaken to do anything but obey, Mrs. L'Que really did try to be communicative, first with the 911 operator and then with the police dispatcher. But given her traumatized mental state, it was simply too much to ask.

After spending the better part of a minute trying to elicit an intelligible name and address from the hysterical woman who kept shifting back and forth from strongly accented English to rapid French, the EOC dispatcher finally gave up and did precisely what she had been trained to do when she heard the words "police," "blood" and "dying" from a caller on the emergency line.

Cutting Mrs. L'Que off in mid-shriek, the dispatcher used her keyboard to run a cross-index search on the telephone number that was flashing brightly on her computer monitor. Moments later, possessing all information on the L'Que household that she needed, she went to work.

The first thing she did was to check the status of the cruiser assigned to the eight-one-one patrol area. According to the code next to the designation "811C" on her monitor screen, Eight-Eleven-Charlie was temporarily out of his unit, directing traffic for a malfunctioning signal light; a traffic hazard that could easily result in serious injuries or even death in this kind of weather if the Fairfax County drivers were left to their own sense of fair play for too long. Balancing what amounted to almost-certain disaster at the intersection against circumstances as yet unknown on Miller Heights, Eight-Eleven-Charlie had to stay right where he was if at all possible.

Shrugging silently, the dispatcher turned to her overhead-mounted microphone, activated the mike with her foot, ordered all units in the field to stop transmitting immediately, and then began her search for the closest available cruiser.

"EOC to any units in area eight-eleven . . ."

The brooding man who had stolen Digger's computer, and then shortly thereafter had taken over his franchised burglary organization, had been working in the dimly lit room for almost twenty minutes when Mrs. Nichole L'Que made her call on the 911 line.

Crime Lab Director Theodore Gauss was tired, and he needed to sleep. But he had driven out to the rented office anyway, in order to check on the progress of Digger's burglary teams. Tonight was a special night, and he wanted to be available, just in case something went wrong.

He had been concentrating on Morgan and Lawnhart, the new ones, methodically playing back the conversations recorded by the voice-activated transmitter that had been concealed in the dash panel of their van. In doing so, he'd been disappointed—but not really surprised—to learn that the novice burglars had shown up late at their assigned drop point.

It was a bad start, but he'd been willing to shrug that off as a first-time offense. The weather was bad, they were new at the game, and they were not yet accustomed to the demanding time schedules. As far as he was concerned, it was all perfectly understandable, and therefore acceptable.

But his subsequent discovery that the two men had chosen to hold back on their take from the Miller Heights home, was a much more serious matter. The penalty for that infraction, he decided, would have to be far more severe.

He'd been in the process of deciding exactly what that penalty would be when he was distracted by the sudden change of pitch in the normally disciplined voice coming through the police scanner mounted above his head.

It was the familiar voice of the Fairfax County Police EOC dispatcher.

"EOC to any units in area eight-eleven . . ."

Probably the L'Ques, calling in to report their burglary, he thought, briefly glancing over at the wall clock to see how much of the allocated two-hour safety buffer his newest burglary team had really needed. Right on time, he noted. Next time he'd . . .

". . . clear for a priority call in the vicinity of Miller Heights Road, area eight-eleven," the EOC dispatcher continued.

His head jerked back up.

A *priority* call, on a residential burglary?

Then he heard another familiar voice over the radio call out "Eight-Forty-Charlie, I'm clear to roll."

Responding to the dispatcher's request for available units almost simultaneously, Henry Culver and Jack Hattabaugh gave their locations.

"Heading west on Chain Bridge, coming up on Hunter Mill right now," Culver replied.

"South on Highway 50," Hattabaugh came on the air immediately thereafter, "just past the 66 on-ramp."

The dispatcher acknowledged.

"All responding units, be advised we have an unknown situation in progress. Possible burglary or assault with serious injuries of unknown nature. Possibly two victims of unknown age. Also unknown if the suspect is still at the scene or in the area. Address is coming over your monitors now. The informant is a French foreign national, apparently the mother of at least one of the victims, and is extremely upset. Hold one."

The EOC dispatcher punched the "SEND" key on her console, thereby transmitting the relevant information to the two patrol units closest to the scene, as well as to the paramedic-equipped fire station located just off of Jermantown Road, and then turned back to her mike.

"Mrs. L'Que?"

"Yes! Where have you been?! My son . . . my husband!"

"Mrs. L'Que," the dispatcher went on calmly, forcing herself to concentrate on each word that was being screamed into her ear through her headset-mounted earphone, "this is Emergency Control Center of the Fairfax County Police Department. I have police officers and paramedics en route to your house right now, but I need some information. Tell me, who is hurt?"

"My son, he's lying there on the . . ."

The dispatcher interrupted. "What happened to him, and how badly is he hurt?"

"He . . . I don't know. Somebody broke into our house. He's bleeding. His face . . . from his ears and nose. He and his friend, they were taped together. I thought she was bleeding and I didn't see . . ."

"Mrs. L'Que, are the people who broke into your house still there?"

"I . . . WHAT? I . . . I, I don't know. My husband . . . *Charles, what are you doing?!* Oh my God, Officer, my husband, he's a military officer. He has a pistol. He's looking around . . ."

"Mrs. L'Que," the dispatcher broke in hurriedly, "please describe your husband, quickly."

"What? He's . . . he's tall, he has short gray hair . . ."

"What is he wearing? And please, the color of his clothing?"

"He has . . . slacks, gray slacks, and a—a coat and tie. The tie is red—no, maroon. A maroon tie. We were . . ."

"What color is his coat?"

"Uh, I don't—blue. It is navy blue, a—what do you call it? A blazer."

"Did you say that your husband is armed?"

"What? What do you mean, armed? What . . . ?"

"Does he have a gun—a pistol?"

"What? Yes, he has his pistol that he keeps in his car. Why do you . . . ?"

"Is it his service—his military weapon?" the dispatcher pressed.

"What? I guess—I don't know! Why are you asking me all this? What about my son? Why aren't you . . . ?"

"Mrs. L'Que, this is important. We will be looking for the suspects, but we *must* be able to identify your husband. I want you to stay on the line. Don't hang up. Help is on the way right now, but you must stay on the line. I'll be right back."

The dispatcher quickly flipped a switch on her console.

"All units responding to Miller Heights, be advised that one of the victims is a young male with unknown head injuries, bleeding from the ears and nose. Second victim is apparently his girlfriend. No identity or extent of injuries at this time. Also be advised that the victim's father is a French military officer. He is apparently armed with a pistol and is searching for the suspects now. He's wearing a blue blazer, and his name is . . ." she punched program keys swiftly, ". . . Lieutenant Colonel Charles L'Que."

In the dark underground bunker that served as his command and control center, Digger—the demented madman who had risked everything in order to regain access to his computerized burglary system, only to discover that the multileveled programs in his computer would no longer respond to his password—stared up at his wall-mounted speakers in absolute disbelief.

He had been working at a steady pace to re-create the password matrix necessary to reenter his tightly protected programs, dredging up line after line of the complex code out of his memory as the voice of the Fairfax County police dispatcher chattered in the background from his scanner, when something the dispatcher said first caught his attention—and then began to destroy his carefully cultivated world.

In a matter of minutes, he knew beyond all doubt why the password access to his programs no longer functioned; why he could no longer contact his teams of burglars.

First, they'd stolen his portable computer, and used the embedded access codes, and the modem, to change the codes in his underground command and control system.

And then they'd stolen his burglars. The source of power, and his future.

And now—*now*—they'd stolen L'Que.

"You filthy, slimy *cheaters*," he whispered savagely.

For a moment, he felt himself start to lose control, feeling his mind start to expand out into an uncontrolled frenzy of hate, just as when the Kostermanns' dog had tried to protect her pups. He couldn't stand to think about that, because nobody had ever tried to protect him—but then he brought himself back.

"No, not now," he shook his head as he returned to his keyboard, typing furiously now as he sought to re-create the program language key that would give him access to his tools, and his weapons, and his reason for being.

"Goddamn you, Culver," he whispered to himself over and over again as his fingers flashed across the keys. "Goddamn you, goddamn you, goddamn you."

At 11:02 that evening, J. Winston Weathersby, Elliott Parkinson's fawning special assistant, was casually listening to the Fairfax County Police radio calls down in the basement of the Communications Monitoring Section while he continued to work on the project that he now understood meant everything to his future career.

He had already received a startling call from Marcus Grey, advising him that a pair of Digger's rookie agents had shown up at the warehouse with property belonging to a Lieutenant Colonel Charles L'Que. He was still trying to digest that piece of incomprehensible intelligence—along with Grey's subsequent comment that both subjects appeared to have been injured—when he heard the dispatcher signal a priority call for patrol area eight-eleven.

"Sounds like there's something heavy going down in Fairfax County," his Communications technician buddy commented, and then quickly sat up in his console chair. "Hey, eight-eleven, isn't that where L'Que lives?"

"What?" Weathersby exclaimed, quickly coming up out of his chair and hurrying over to his friend's computer console.

There, he found himself staring in horror as the all-too-familiar Miller Heights address came up on the wall-mounted monitor that duplicated the smaller video screens in the Fairfax County Police Department cruisers.

"My God," he whispered, "that's L'Que's house. What's going on out there?"

At that moment, they both heard the familiar "Eight-Forty-Charlie" acknowledgment from a responding cruiser.

The Communications technician quickly reached over to a bookshelf for the Fairfax County Police Manual and flipped through to the radio codes section.

"Henry Culver," he said, looking up from the updated Fairfax County patrol log. "That's his call sign."

"But what's *he* doing out there?" Weathersby demanded, looking stunned and very near panic.

"Sounds to me like he's responding to the scene."

"But he's not supposed to be working that area."

Then J. Winston Weathersby simply stood there in horrified silence as the Fairfax County dispatcher continued, describing the victim's unknown head injuries, and warning the responding officers that the suspects might still be in the area.

"Oh Jesus," he whispered.

The numbing sensation that flooded the young CIA special assistant's nervous system was almost comforting because it gave him the feeling that his entire body—hands, arms, legs, and especially his brain—had suddenly lost all contact with time and space. But he shook it off because he didn't dare lose control now.

"What are you going to do?" the Communications technician asked nervously.

Weathersby was silent for almost a half minute, furiously trying to work himself through problem the way Parkinson had taught him. Finally, taking in a deep steadying breath, he turned to his friend. "Who's on emergency standby for Ops?"

"Kregg, but . . ."

"I need to talk to him, right away."

"But what about Parkinson?" the comm-tech stammered, the look on his face suggesting that his high-climbing friend had lost his mind.

"Can't wait. He's got at least a forty-five-minute response time, and I don't dare brief him on this over one of the comm lines. By the time he gets here, the cops are liable to have those two idiots in custody, and then we're really screwed."

"But . . ."

"No, I can't call him," Weathersby said, shaking his head firmly. "Get me Kregg."

He simply couldn't accept the fact that it was all coming apart. Not at this phase. Not now!

"I hope the hell you know what you're doing," the Communications tech muttered as he reached for the telephone on his desk.

"So do I," the young special assistant whispered, and then turned away to stare in awe at the mind-boggling display of data that was coming in over the Fairfax County dispatch screens.

"Digger, you idiot," he whispered, "what in God's name have you *done?*"

The thing that had Police Crime Lab Director Theodore Gauss so enraged—to the point of being in a near-frenzy—was that he'd been so insistent on this very point.

The critical element for this phase of the operation was the absolute need for low-profile entries. No one was to be hurt; he'd been ruthlessly firm on that in his instructions.

Everything depended upon the police responding to his burglaries in a routine, low-key manner, accepting the occasional loss of property in order to focus their resources on the more serious threats to life and limb. He knew precisely how the police would react to that more serious kind of threat, and he also knew—beyond any doubt whatsoever—that he could not afford to be the focus of that reaction.

Not with Henry Culver still running loose.

Not now.

But then the thought occurred to him. What if the boy dies?

For a brief terrifying moment, Gauss felt himself being caught up in an all-encompassing vortex of panic and confusion as his mind raced through the relevant probabilities, calculating the enormity of the investigative effort that would be turned loose to sweep the county.

They'd be like a pack of hounds at the first scent of blood—they'd never stop until they found something.

He was numbed by the thought, and tempted almost beyond endurance to let himself go and pound his fist into the wall. But he had spent too many hours preparing for just this sort of emergency to allow himself to lose control now.

Moments later, as the numbing sensation ebbed, he knew exactly what to do. Exactly what he had to do.

It all centered on the L'Que boy now.

As best he could tell from the dispatcher's ongoing broadcast to the responding units, there were now at least two people out there who represented an unacceptable risk to his operation. They would have to be dealt with now, before it was too late.

"Idiots," he muttered darkly, his fingers punching savagely at the keyboard as the monitor scrambled to keep up with the human and processor inputs.

```
PRIMARY ACCESS CODE?
     CHEATER
PRIMARY ACCESS ACTIVATED. SUB-CODE?
     TRIP WIRE
TRIP WIRE PROGRAM ACTIVATED. BE ADVISED
THAT THIS PROGRAM WILL ERASE ALL FILES.
DO YOU WISH TO CONTINUE?
     YES
```

Obeying the booby-trapped command by following its preprogrammed orders to the letter, the small stolen computer bypassed a hidden subprogram that—had he, or more importantly, had anyone else typed "NO"—would have immediately erased all of the incriminating files in the 540-megabyte drive. Instead, it set about establishing an electronic link with another very similar computer located approximately five miles away.

```
TRIP WIRE LINK INITIATED.
REQUESTING CONFIRMATION CODE . . .
```

"Come on," he muttered, tapping impatiently on the edge of the keyboard as the computer waited the appropriate number of microseconds and then made another emotionless attempt to complete the link.

```
REQUESTING CONFIRMATION CODE . . .
```

"Come on . . ." he almost snarled as he glared at the screen. The instructions had been very specific. On-call status would last until midnight every night, no matter what, and it was only a little after eleven.

REQUESTING CONFIRMATION CODE . . .

"Goddamn you, Hämmarchov!" he exploded. "Where the hell . . . ?"

HAMMAR

He closed his eyes for a moment as he released a pent-up breath, and then immediately went back to his keyboard.

THIS IS DIGGER. WHERE WERE YOU?
  I DID NOT EXPECT A SIGNAL THIS LATE.
NEVER MIND, WHERE WERE YOU? YOU ARE
SUPPOSED TO BE ON CALL.
  TAKING A PISS

Momentarily enraged by the insolence, Gauss started to type out a scathing rebuke, and then hesitated, remembering that this man was nothing more than a tool. A very expensive and exceedingly dangerous tool, according to Digger's computerized files; but a tool nonetheless . . . and therefore always expendable.

ARE YOU AVAILABLE?
  YES
GOOD. I HAVE A JOB FOR YOU. IMMEDIATE PRI-
ORITY. IS YOUR PRINTER ON?

This time there was a brief hesitation before the answer appeared on the screen.

  YES
TARGET INFORMATION TO FOLLOW. MUST BE
DONE IMMEDIATELY. IMPORTANT TO USE THE

SHOTGUN. SECONDARY TARGETS TO FOLLOW
ALSO. CONFIRMATION IS ESSENTIAL, REPEAT
ESSENTIAL. BE ADVISED THAT POLICE ARE
ALERT AND IN THE AREA.
     BONUS?
YES. STANDARD $10,000 BONUS, PAID UPON
CONFIRMATION.
     DO I TAKE OUT THE COPS IF THEY GET IN
THE WAY?

Gauss hesitated. It wasn't working out quite the way he'd
planned; but then most things didn't work out that way anyway. He shrugged. That was what made the whole thing so
interesting.

ONLY IF ABSOLUTELY NECESSARY. VERY IM-
PORTANT THAT YOU TAKE NO UNNECESSARY
RISKS.
     WHAT ABOUT TOPCASTLE?

Okay, I give up. What about Topcastle? Gauss thought,
having no idea who or what Topcastle was. Shrugging indifferently, he began typing again.

TOPCASTLE IS IRRELEVANT.
     OKAY, YOU ARE THE BOSS.

"That's right, Hämmarchov, whoever you are," he whispered as he quickly terminated the link, "I *am* the boss, and
don't you ever forget it."

After hesitating a moment, he keyed a brief but pointed
message to his still-unresponsive novice team, and then
began scanning his program screens for updates on the others.

Then, finally satisfied that the other burglary teams were
functioning as expected, he stood up from his chair, closed

the briefing book, and then reached for his jacket, considering as he did so the likelihood that he would have to go looking for some more reliable tools in the very near future.

At a little past ten-thirty that Thursday evening, Otis Lawnhart and Bobby Morgan had driven the dark van into the garage of the two-bedroom home that they had been sharing for the past three years and then shut the garage door.

The first thing the men did after they got inside was to put all but two hundred dollars of their first night's earnings into the safe concealed in the floor of the bearded man's bedroom closet. The next thing they did was to crack open the fifth of Jack Daniel's that they'd picked up in DC after leaving the warehouse.

By eleven o'clock that evening, with the fifth of Jack Daniel's well on its way to being a tenth and his new .357 S&W Magnum revolver already lovingly disassembled, cleaned, and oiled, with six hollow-pointed hot loads in the cylinder, Bobby Morgan decided that it was time to set a few things straight.

As far as he was concerned, they could start with the inequity of a two-hundred-dollar fine for a late arrival that wasn't their fault, and the deal on loose cash, and maybe even a little renegotiation on their end of the split.

The way he figured it, twenty-five percent was a hell of a lot of money for somebody to be raking off the top when *they* weren't out there in the goddamned freezing rain and mud, worrying about cops and fighting with flipped-out bitches and getting their legs broken by flying jacks. He'd agreed to the percentages several weeks ago, but the numbers looked a whole lot different now.

"Let's go talk to that damned computer," he growled, pulling himself up out of his chair and scooping up the glistening blue-steeled revolver and the box of high-velocity reloads as he hobbled drunkenly over to his bedroom, his partner staggering close behind.

The small portable computer had been dropped off at their

front door several weeks ago by an unknown messenger. It had an internal modem and very simple instructions, and was devoid of any traceable serial numbers.

According to Molly Hunsacker, who had apparently been working for their unknown benefactor for the past six months, they would obtain instructions for each assigned job through the computer.

Each job would be prescouted to confirm that the residence contained plenty of highly priced and easily fenced merchandise, and to determine the times when the owners would most likely be elsewhere. Occasionally, Molly had warned, there would be things in the home—mostly papers—to be looked for and copied, but that wouldn't be any big deal, they'd both agreed.

Molly Hunsacker had no idea how the individual at the other end of the computer link—who, for some strange reason, called himself Digger—figured out the time schedules. All she knew was that she had made over ninety entries based on this new remote-controlled system, and had never come across a homeowner once. And that was good enough for her, she had said.

Lured in by the potential profits, and more than a little intimidated by a woman known even among her peers as Molly-the-Hun, Morgan and Lawnhart had agreed.

To receive one of these prescouted assignments, all the two young men had to do was turn on the machine, type in a specific five-digit code, and then wait for the computer to display the date, the location, and times, the location of the fence, and even a crude map of their destination.

It was, Molly-the-Hun had emphasized reassuringly, a nice, simple, dependable, and damn near foolproof system. But it was also, she had added pointedly, the only way that any of them would ever communicate with their new boss. The rules were very specific:

There would be no face-to-face meetings.

No letters.

No phone calls.

In effect, there would be no communications at all, except through the faceless, anonymous computer; which had been perfectly fine with Bobby Morgan then, but it wasn't perfectly fine now because what he really wanted right now was a face-to-face chat with the asshole who had screwed up their scheduling and caused him to suffer such pain.

Morgan sat in the desk chair, put the stolen .357 down, turned on the computer, and prepared to type out what he and his partner had decided—in their alcoholic haze—was a much more equitable system for dividing the proceeds of their future efforts.

But instead of a message prompt, directing the user to select from a menu of easily understood options, the computer displayed a simple, three-word message on the small screen:

YOU STUPID BASTARDS

Chapter Eighteen

Thursday, 2305 hours

They were less than a half mile out from the L'Que residence, coming in fast from opposite directions, when Patrol Sergeant Jack Hattabaugh's distinctive gravelly voice demanded Henry Culver's attention.

"Eight-Zero to Eight-Forty, go to tac two."

Forcing himself to stay focused on the glistening surface of the dark and dangerously slick back road, Culver took one gloved hand away from the vibrating steering wheel of his cruiser, switched his radio over to the car-to-car tactical channel, and then brought the palm-sized radio mike up to the side of his mouth.

"Eight-Forty, on tac two."

"Where are you at, Henry?"

"West on Miller from 123, just passing the pond. ETA at the residence about one."

"You copy the advisory on the colonel?"

"Ten-four."

"Okay," Hattabaugh spoke loudly out over the background noise of his sirens, "keep an eye out for him. I'm coming up on Miller Heights from Oakton, with Station Thirty-two medics and a fire unit on my tail."

Culver quickly calculated the distances in his head. "I've got the slow road. You're going to get there first. How do we handle it?"

"Get in position and stay low until we see what we've got," the veteran patrol sergeant directed. "I'll take the front. You cover from the back."

"Copy. Taking the back, low profile," Henry Culver acknowledged.

Coming up to the top of the hill at the end of Miller Road, at a spot where the road widened from two lanes into the unmarked equivalent of three, Culver quickly pulled the cruiser over to the side of the road, released his safety belt, and then hurriedly pulled himself out of his bright yellow raincoat.

The ice-rain was still falling heavily, and he would have liked to stay dry, if at all possible, but Henry Culver had decided that Hattabaugh's warning made a lot of sense.

Better to be cold and wet than a bright yellow target silhouetted in somebody's gunsight, he thought as he threw the raincoat into the backseat, snapped himself back into his safety harness, and sent the cruiser roaring up toward the Miller Heights intersection.

At the top of the hill, he powered his fishtailing cruiser into a barely controlled turn onto Miller Heights, and then slapped at a switch with the palm of his gloved hand to cut off his lights and sirens as he accelerated down the road, sending sprays of icy slush flying from the wide-treaded tires.

"Eight-Zero to Station Thirty-two, you copy the situation?" Hattabaugh called out to the rescue units following in his wake as he made the right-hand turn onto the south end of Miller Heights and sent his marked patrol car roaring down into the dimly lit suburban neighborhood.

"Two injured in the residence, at least one serious, with possible suspects in the area," a feminine voice from the paramedic unit responded over the crackling radio frequency.

"You got it," Hattabaugh acknowledged. "I've got another cruiser coming in from the north. You want to hold back a little bit until we clear the area?"

"Sounds good to us," the feminine voice responded, the tenseness in her voice just barely discernible. "But don't forget, you've got at least one bleeder in there."

"We'll remember. Watch yourselves."

A veteran of more code three runs than he cared to remember, Jack Hattabaugh continued to scan the pathway illuminated by the outreaching twin beams of his headlights, watching for stray bikes, dogs, and possible suspects all at the same time as he accelerated up the windy Miller Heights roadway at almost full power, well ahead of the fire and rescue units, with his red and blue lights sweeping through the bare trees.

Then he grasped the steering wheel tightly with both hands, tapped the brake and accelerator pedals, and sent his police cruiser roaring up the dark tree-lined driveway of the L'Que home, coming to a sliding, brake-screeching stop about halfway up in a position that would leave enough clearance for the larger paramedic and fire units.

"Eight-Zero, ten-ninety-seven on Miller Heights!" Hattabaugh called out his arrival over the air. Then he dropped the mike on the passenger side front seat and reached for the door handle.

Two seconds later, he crouched behind the cruiser's opened door, jacked a round into the chamber of his twelve-gage pump shotgun, and scanned the illuminated area around the opened garage door and the surrounding red-and-blue-streaked darkness.

No colonel.

No movement.

Nothing.

Off to his left, Hattabaugh heard and saw Henry Culver accelerate his darkened cruiser up into the next-door drive-way, bail out of the marked vehicle fast, and then disappear into the dark mass of bare trees and brush separating the two houses.

That's it, Henry. Get your ass back there.

For a long three seconds, Hattabaugh continued to scan the area, searching for shadowy movements that might be a wet dog or a curious neighbor or a homicidal suspect of as yet undetermined description. Then a readily identifiable voice came out over the radio speaker.

"Can't see much of anything back here, Sarge," Henry Culver gasped as he crouched behind the massive trunk of a shoulder-wide red oak, fully exposed to the steadily falling sleet that was starting to soak through his field jacket. "Too many trees in the way."

Culver had his four-inch .357 Magnum revolver clenched tight in his black-gloved right hand, the scrambled portable radio in his left, and he could feel his heart pounding solidly against his vest-protected ribs as he tried to get a better view of the house.

"What's your position?" Hattabaugh queried.

"Ten o'clock to your six. House is at a weird angle."

"Affirmative. Can you see the north side?"

Hattabaugh was frustrated and concerned by the realiza-tion that—because of the orientation of the house relative to the driveway—he and Culver had ended up in the wrong po-sitions for his initial plan to work. He couldn't get to the front door without making a long and dangerously exposed run up the driveway, and Culver couldn't watch for an escape out the back because there were too many concealing trees in close to the house.

"Negative, but I can work my way around to the front, going clockwise. Nobody'll spot me—all the windows are over my head. Nothing but bricks at my level. Looks like you might be in a better position to spot a runner anyway."

Good read, Henry. Hattabaugh nodded in silent appreciation, having already made his decision to ignore his gut feelings and go with the tactical advantage.

"Hey, Jack, what's the situation," the paramedic driver demanded impatiently.

"Hold one." Hattabaugh hesitated another second, and then keyed his mike again. "Okay, Henry, you take the front. Come around the far side to the garage door. I've got the driveway."

"Ten-four."

Jamming the portable radio back into its belt holder and grabbing up his five-cell flashlight out of the door mount, Culver came out around the far dark side of the house on legs numbed as much by adrenaline as by the cold. Forcing himself to ignore the darkened door and windows, he took a half dozen lunging strides across the slush-covered lawn; slipped and fell; and then scrambled toward the brightly lit open garage door—the one on the far left—trusting Hattabaugh to keep his back covered as he threw himself up tight against the right side of the garage doorframe.

Pausing only a moment to catch his breath, he yelled "PO-LICE!", brought his right arm around to cover the garage with the .357, and then exposed just enough of his head to be able to make a quick sweep of the brightly illuminated garage.

He saw the girl to his far right. She was kneeling on the garage floor next to a sprawled body of a young man, holding a kitchen towel tightly against his head with both of her hands. Her head came up sharply at the sound of his voice.

"Here . . . over here, quick, he's hurt!" she called out, her strong but shaky voice a distracting contrast to the wildly disheveled look of her hair and dress.

"Who else is in the house?" Culver demanded, squatting down quickly to place the five-cell flashlight on the concrete floor. He moved closer to the girl and her unconscious boyfriend, his eyes still sweeping the garage, but constantly flickering back to the open doorway leading into the kitchen.

"What? Uh . . . I don't know," the girl responded, blinking her eyes in confusion before turning her attention back to her boyfriend for a moment to adjust the darkly stained towel against his head. Then she looked back up at Culver. "His mom and dad," she rasped hoarsely. "I think she's flipped out, but his dad's . . ."

"Police officer, freeze!" Culver yelled, his voice echoing in the enclosed garage as he swept his extended arms around in a double-handed grip to center the sights of the deadly .357 on the chest of the figure that had suddenly filled the doorway.

It was a very near thing.

The man standing in the doorway between the garage and the kitchen had spent the better part of his adult life hunting down a wide assortment of exceedingly dangerous men, including some of the more prominent terrorists of the decade. Highly skilled in his chosen profession, he would have had no trouble whatsoever in dealing with a far lesser trained police officer like Henry Culver.

But fortunately for Culver, the man standing in the doorway had no intention of killing a cop.

Instead of instinctively dropping backward and triggering three 9-mm rounds into the stomach, chest, and forehead of the dark-jacketed figure that had suddenly appeared at the garage door, the man simply ignored the .357 aimed at his chest, and turned instead to stare at the motionless body lying on the floor of the garage. As he did so, he raised both of his hands, holding the lethal automatic pistol out by the frame—one-handed—in plain sight.

"I am Lieutenant Colonel Charles L'Que. This is my home," the man said in a voice that was disconcertingly calm even as his eyes remained fixed on the sprawled body of his son.

As far as Culver was concerned, the deadly calm voice wasn't the only thing disconcerting about the man who remained fixed in his gunsights.

There was something about his face that seemed so—what was it?—familiar?

Gray slacks and maroon tie. No blue blazer, but he could have taken it off. Spare mags tucked into the left front waistband of his slacks, he noted, searching for the element that had jarred his subconscious—the element that wouldn't let him lower his weapon until he was sure.

Then the man shifted his gaze to stare directly at Culver, and Henry Culver suddenly realized what had set off his mental alarms. Two things actually. The gun first of all, because he hadn't expected a French military officer residing in the United States to be armed with one of the new, readily identifiable nine-millimeter Beretta semiautomatics; but more importantly, the eyes.

Especially the eyes.

From Henry Culver's shaky point of view, there should have been panic, or fear, or anguish, or at the very least *sorrow* in the eyes of the man standing there in the doorway—some sort of emotion to reflect a sense of hurt or loss. But the eyes that had briefly stared into his own didn't look at all like those of a suburb-dwelling father who had come home to find his son unconscious and bleeding on the floor. To Culver, they looked far more like something else.

Something *very* familiar.

Like the eyes of a stone-cold killer.

He'd seen a lot of people like that when he'd worked for Traynor and the CIA. More than he ever wanted to think about again.

"You, the young lady on the floor," Culver called out to the girl, never allowing his gaze or his gunsight to drift away from the figure in the doorway for even a moment. "Can you identify that man?"

"Tha . . . that's Colonel L'Que—Michel's father," the girl said, her voice betraying her failing nerves and a rapidly approaching state of shock.

Culver started to drop the .357, and then hesitated.

"Henry, are you clear?"

Hattabaugh's voice on the radio.

No, not yet. Be careful of this guy.

"Colonel L'Que, please clear your weapon," Culver ordered, taking quick, shallow breaths as he shifted the barrel of the .357 slightly so that it was no longer quite pointing at the man's chest. He could feel his heart again, pounding away against the confining vest that all of a sudden seemed much too thin.

For a moment, it appeared as though the man in the doorway was going to laugh out loud, but then the cold eyes blinked in recognition.

"Henry, *are you clear?*"

Hattabaugh again, this time more insistent.

In a series of easy, fluid movements that were almost too quick for Culver to follow, Lt. Col. Charles L'Que thumbed the magazine release button on his weapon, dropping the heavy cartridge-filled magazine into his hand; jacked the chambered round out onto the concrete floor; locked the slide back; and then slid the handgun into the back waistband of his slacks.

"Have you checked the inside of your house?" Culver asked, breathing easily again and trying not to let his hands shake as he reached down to his belt for his radio.

"Yes." L'Que nodded almost indifferently.

"Is there any one else in the house?"

"Only my wife."

"The suspects . . . ?"

"They are gone."

"When?"

L'Que shrugged.

"Henry . . . !"

Culver immediately brought the radio up to his mouth.

"The house is clear. Station Thirty-two, get in here right now! Victim is a young male, lying on the garage floor, middle bay. I can see bleeding from the nose, mouth, and ears."

"On our way," the paramedic driver acknowledged as Culver continued to hold the radio against the side of his mouth.

"Jack, I've got Colonel L'Que with me in the garage," Culver went on quickly, wondering if his heart rate was ever going to return to normal as he knelt down beside the girl and helped hold one of the towels against the young man's head. "His wife's in the house. Suspects are ten-eight, but may still be in the area. Better get somebody out on a perimeter check."

Moments later, the two paramedics had taken the place of Culver and the blood-splattered young woman, and were hurriedly working to stabilize the L'Que boy in preparation for a code three run to Oakton Hospital. As they did so, the three blue-uniformed men in the follow-up fire units quickly checked the girl and Mrs. L'Que for signs of shock prior to loading them into the fire chief's truck for a hurried but less urgent run to the hospital. The truck had just cleared the driveway when Hattabaugh and another officer reported in an all clear on a sweep of the first and second quadrants.

Culver responded by notifying the dispatcher that the immediate scene area seemed to be secure, advising the rest of the responding backup cruisers to drop down to a code two status. Then he turned to find himself staring at the blank face of Lt. Col. Charles L'Que, whose gaze remained fixed on the rapid, coordinated movements of the two paramedics.

"Your son's receiving the best treatment he could possibly get, Colonel," Culver said, reflexively shifting to his PR training as he watched the somber scene on the garage floor, waiting impatiently for Hattabaugh and the other scout cars to finish the perimeter sweep so he could relax and begin thinking about the crime scene search. "These people are highly trained, and they're in direct contact with a first-rate shock trauma team standing by at the hospital. They'll . . ."

"You should wear a badge on the outside of your jacket when you enter a doorway like that, Officer," L'Que interrupted in a dulled and raspy whisper.

Startled by the cold, emotionless inflections in the man's voice, Culver looked down and discovered that he'd forgotten to transfer his badge from the outside of his raincoat to his field jacket.

"That's why we wear . . ." he started to say, and then he remembered.

Hat's back in the car. Shit.

Culver realized then that when he had stepped out in front of the opened garage door, he had appeared as a dark figure wearing a black jacket with a gun in his hand.

At first Culver was embarrassed that the professional soldier had noticed the serious procedural error—a rookie-type mistake that would have earned him a loud and stinging rebuke from Hattabaugh, had the veteran patrol supervisor been there at the scene.

But then he remembered how L'Que had been standing when he'd first spotted him standing there in the doorway. Coming up *out* of a crouch, his extended hands separating as he dropped the aim point of the semiautomatic pistol in his hand away, toward the floor.

Christ, he had me cold, Culver thought, numbed and shaken by the awareness of how close he'd come to being shot—and most likely killed—by an experienced combat officer. But then the look in L'Que's eyes jarred Culver back into his own role.

"Your son's going to be okay, Colonel," he said, trying to be supportive and reassuring, but L'Que simply shook his head.

"I've seen too many critically injured men, Officer," he said in a low whisper that spoke of too many deaths in too many faraway places as they both watched the paramedics carefully lift the stretcher bearing L'Que's son up into the rescue truck. He paused for a moment and then closed his eyes and sighed deeply. "I would like to believe your words, but I . . . cannot."

Culver was still trying to figure out how to respond to Colonel L'Que's depressingly chilling statement when the excited voice of Jack Hattabaugh burst out over Culver's belt radio.

"Henry, southwest quadrant. I've got movement out here. Watch yourself in there!"

Then, moments later, the call that every patrol officer comes to anticipate and dread with almost equal fervor was broadcast on the police emergency channel:

"All units, clear for emergency traffic. We have shots fired."

Like Hattabaugh and Culver earlier, they came in slowly and carefully from opposite directions, one from the front and one from the back. But unlike Culver and Hattabaugh, neither of these men had ever worked in coordination with the other.

Which was perfectly understandable, because each of them *thought* that he was working alone.

But then too—thanks to hurried briefings by their misguided controllers—they also thought that this would be a quick and easy job. Couple of half-drunk, dumbshit burglars, with maybe a .380 semiautomatic pistol if they didn't leave it in the van. In and out, no sweat.

That expectation was immediately dispelled by a sudden and very loud explosion that shattered the icy calm of the crisp winter darkness.

The all-too-familiar sound of a high-velocity gunshot caused both men to divert from their respective plans and react immediately, each according to his own training, experience, gut instincts, and personality.

Charging up the porch steps in a manner best described as mindlessly aggressive and violent, the first and larger of the two intruders blew apart the front door lock with a twelve-gage deer slug from his Remington 870 pump shotgun, chambered another round, and then lunged forward, slamming the door open with his shoulder. Then, twisting and throwing himself forward to the tiled entryway floor, he made a complete 360-degree roll to his right, and ended up in a prone position on the living room carpet.

Sweeping the short-barreled shotgun back around to his

left, the black-masked figure came up swiftly on one knee and triggered a wallboard-shredding, number four buckshot round down the dimly lit hallway at a fleeting shadow figure who screamed and then immediately disappeared around the corner.

Eyes wide from the adrenaline, the huge intruder coolly jacked another Magnum round into the Remington's hot chamber with a loud *clack-clack*, started to stand up, saw the flash of metal out of the corner of his right eye, and then twisted away in the opposite direction with a good half second to spare before an equally blinding and concussive gunshot blew out about half of the double-glazed storm window just over his head.

Aware that he was incredibly lucky not to be sprawled out dead or dying on the thin, loose-pile carpet, the thick-shouldered man sent one of the thumb-sized deer slugs streaking through the semidarkness in the general direction of the blinding flash, his muscular arms jerking from the recoil.

And then immediately winced in pain as he realized that he'd lost the plug in his left ear.

There was a burst of movement at the far right edge of his vision. Twisting in that direction, he firing blindly at a lunging figure that vanished in an explosion of shattering glass. And then everything disappeared as every light in the house suddenly went out. Intent on covering himself, the black-masked figure triggered the last buckshot round in the same general direction—shattering more glass somewhere—and then rolled away to his right.

Hit the breaker box. Lucky shot, he thought as he tried to listen for the sound of movement over the incessant buzzing in his left ear.

At that moment, another high-velocity explosion ripped through the darkness, immediately followed by a trip-hammer burst of automatic weapons fire that seemed to send wall-piercing projectiles flying in every direction, causing the masked figure to flatten out and roll across the floor in a search for cover. He ended up crouched behind the questionable shelter of a large overstuffed chair in the living room.

Caught off guard by the unexpected weaponry, the hulking intruder dug his right hand into his jacket pocket, spilled the extra twelve-gage Magnum rounds—the ones that Digger had directed him to use—out onto the carpet, and then smiled calmly to himself as he began to feed the first of five more buckshot rounds into the magazine of the Remington 870.

"Three-eighty, my ass," he swore under his breath as he used his fingers to distinguish between the slug and buckshot rounds, wanting the buckshot now because things were probably going to get real close in the next few minutes.

As far as the first of the two intruders was concerned, he really didn't care about Bobby Morgan and Otis Lawnhart, or the crime scene that he was supposed to create with his shotgun casings anymore. At the moment, all he cared about was trying to figure out how many people with guns were still moving around in Bobby Morgan's house.

And more importantly, how he was going to get out of the house alive.

CIA Field Operative John Kregg, the second of the two intruders, had started out with a much more subtle plan that put more emphasis on his technical skills, which were as intricate and varied as they were deadly. A relatively small man, Kregg was extremely skilled in covert entries, which made the sliding glass door an obvious choice.

He was intent on slowly and quietly drilling out the soft aluminum latch lock with a small, battery-powered drill, when the first explosive gunshot from inside the house nearly caused the diminutive covert entry specialist to piss his pants.

Recovering immediately, however, Kregg jammed the whirring drill bit through the lock mechanism at full power, pulled the drill out and tossed it aside, fumbled at the latch, and popped it open. He threw the door open along its railed tracks, started inside with the stub-nosed Uzi in his right hand, and then found himself momentarily trapped when the sliding door bounced back off a chunk of firewood that was supposed to have stopped the door from opening at all—and would have, had it not fallen partway out of the lower aluminum track.

The subsequent high-pitched explosions that echoed throughout the small house—three from a shotgun at the front door, and the single pistol shot from the hallway?—sent Kregg into a frenzy of action as he tried to work himself loose from the door, duck down, and go back outside all at the same time.

He was still struggling with the door when the fourth shotgun round—the deer slug—ripped into the main junction box at the far side of the house, arced the 220-volt line, tripped the main breaker switch, and cut out all electrical power to the house just moments before a tight pattern of forty-one number four buckshot pellets blew out the safety glass panel in the door next to his head.

Panicked and confused, Kregg was still trying to decide which way to run when the first of three .357 slugs from Bobby Morgan's stolen revolver ripped through the drywall separating the hallway and kitchen and blew out the small kitchen window to his left.

That focused his attention nicely.

Lunging sideways to the floor, Kregg let loose with a long, magazine-emptying burst from the Uzi that sent thirty-two copper-jacketed nine-millimeter slugs ripping through wallboard, two-by-four studs and window glass, and empty casings bouncing across the linoleum floor.

On the other side of the house, guided by the sound of the exploding glass that he could just barely hear through his shrilly buzzing ears, Bobby Morgan dropped his aim and fired three more .357 rounds though his bedroom wall just as the oncoming burst of nine-millimeter slugs sent him tumbling frantically backward over his desk. Landing with a grunt, he tried to fire another round, and felt the hammer snap harmlessly against a fired primer. Stunned and afraid, he began to grope around desperately in the darkness for the stolen box of ammunition that had fallen to the floor.

In the next three minutes that followed, no less than 116 rounds—mostly nine-millimeter Uzi bursts, with sporadic twelve-gage and .357 replies—streaked through the dark rooms and hallways of Bobby Morgan's house, tearing through wood, glass, plasterboard, and, occasionally, human flesh.

One of those bullets, a lucky shot by Morgan, struck John Kregg's right forearm just as he was reloading the Uzi with the last of his thirty-two-round magazines. The impact sent the Uzi flying off into the darkness and Kregg staggering backward in shock. Then the glancing impact of another projectile—this one a ricocheting .24 caliber lead pellet from the twelve-gage—cut a furrow across his left rib cage, sending the grunting covert entry specialist reeling against the counter and then tumbling to the floor.

Lying in the ruins of the sliding glass door and kitchen window, and half out of his mind from the pain and shock, Kregg had to bite his tongue to keep from screaming—thereby giving away his position—as another .357 slug punched through the sink cabinet just over his head.

Groaning in agony, disoriented by the darkness, and terrified by the realization that he was probably very near death, John Kregg did the only thing that he could think of that might enable him to survive.

Fumbling awkwardly with his still-functional left hand, he scrabbled around until he found the Uzi. Then, after pulling himself to his feet, he stumbled forward through the glass fragments covering the linoleum floor over to the intersection of the hallway and the living room.

When he got there, he waited, leaning against the wall for support, until he could distinguish between dark and very dark shadows. Then, standing there in the hallway, he brought the small submachine gun up one-handed and emptied the thirty-two-round staggered box magazine at the first shadow that moved.

Chapter Nineteen

Friday, February 5, 0015 hours

Elliott Parkinson, red-eyed and weary but absolutely alert, sat in shocked silence as his shaken special assistant completed his report.

"Are you sure?" he rasped.

J. Winston Weathersby nodded. "As sure as we can be. The spotter team had strict orders to stay in position and observe. They remained in the area as long as they could, until the cops started showing up. They never had a chance to look inside the house."

"How many spotters did you use?"

"Two. I assumed that would be plenty. They . . ."

"How were they positioned?" Parkinson interrupted.

"Camouflage blankets, about thirty yards back in the woods. They were watching the back of the house when the shooting started," Weathersby replied quickly. He'd read the teletype twice before he brought the news to Parkinson, to make sure he had all of the details straight, but he still didn't know if his hasty orders had actually saved MEG, or simply broke the ten-year operation wide-open.

"Don't they have any idea what happened?"

"Kregg was making his entry through the sliding glass door when all hell broke loose. Their best estimate is that maybe 150 rounds were fired over a period of five minutes—mixed small arms stuff, high-velocity, with at least one shotgun. They heard the pump action," he added when Parkinson raised his eyebrows.

"What about Kregg?"

"He had an Uzi when he went in. They think he did most of the shooting."

"But he didn't come back out?"

"They didn't *see* him come out," Weathersby corrected. "They think they saw at least one person hobbling across the street right after the shooting stopped."

"But Kregg hasn't reported in yet, so now you're assuming he's still inside."

Weathersby nodded his head silently.

"Christ," Parkinson whispered, "two asshole burglars— no, let's be more accurate," he amended as he glared at his flustered assistant. "Two half-drunk, disorganized, and absolutely *incompetent* burglars, who were supposedly armed with one little goddamned .380 semiautomatic, took out one of the best field operatives in the whole fucking Agency."

"As far as we knew, that's all they had," the special assistant said defensively. "Marcus had a team in their house fifteen minutes after they showed up at the warehouse. One real old box of .380 ammo, less than half-full, in the desk drawer," he read from his notes. "One instruction manual and a holster for a Browning .380 semiautomatic pistol, but no actual pistol. That was it. No indication of any kind of shotgun in the house."

"There were two shotguns on the L'Que list. They could have taken three."

Weathersby shook his head. "Marcus is positive he pulled everything out of the back of that van except the copier. If they'd kept one of L'Que's shotguns up front, he's sure he'd have seen it."

"Then who the hell was firing that pump shotgun?" Parkinson demanded.

"I don't know." J. Winston Weathersby raised his arms in a helpless gesture. "Lawnhart was driving. Morgan got out to open the garage door. I suppose there could have been someone else in the back of the van."

"Or somebody could have come in from the front while your people were watching the back."

"It's possible," the special assistant agreed, noting the emphasis on the word *your,* and then stood there silently in front of Parkinson's huge executive desk, waiting to be told what to do.

"That goddamned Digger," Parkinson snarled, slamming his clenched fist down hard on his desk. "He couldn't have just gone ahead and done the job himself. He had to screw it up by sending a couple of . . . of incompetents," he seethed, staring down at his clenched fist for a few moments.

"All right," he finally said, shaking off the almost-overwhelming urge to panic. "Monitor the police reports and be ready to move the moment we hear something. We've got to be ready to control the body if it comes to that."

"Hopefully it won't," Weathersby replied solemnly as he started taking notes. "Oh yes, I almost forgot," he added. "Traynor called. He wants to talk with you."

"Did he say why?"

"No, just that it was important."

"All right, I'll call him in a few minutes. What's the latest on the L'Que boy?"

"They have him in surgery now, but he's listed as critical. It doesn't look good. Do you want a follow-up?"

"Yes, every half hour."

"Is it really that serious?" J. Winston Weathersby asked as he looked up from his notebook.

Elliott Parkinson blinked as he stared at his young assistant.

"Do you know anything at all about Charles L'Que?" he finally asked.

"No, not really," Weathersby admitted.

"Then I suggest you check his file out immediately, and read it very carefully," Parkinson said in a voice that betrayed his nervous tension. "And while you're doing that," he added solemnly, "you'd better start praying that Lawnhart, Morgan, *and* Kregg are out of the picture."

Parkinson's young assistant stared wide-eyed at his boss. "You *want* Kregg to be dead?" he whispered in disbelief.

"You're damn right I do," Parkinson said emphatically. "Because if L'Que ever discovers a link between Operations, those two burglars, and his son's death, the kindest thing I could ever do for you would be to put a bullet between your eyes right here and now."

The administrative offices of the Directorate of Science and Technology were located on one of the more pleasant aboveground level floors in a separate wing of the Central Intelligence Agency's new administrative building.

During the day, these offices literally buzzed with activities involving some of the most incredible and unlikely intelligence-gathering techniques imaginable. But unlike their counterparts in Intelligence and Operations, the Sci-Tech administrators were rarely found at their desks after midnight.

Tonight, however, was an exception.

The desk phone in the southeast corner office rang only once before it was answered.

"Traynor."

"This is Parkinson. Your wife said you might be at work," the Operations associate director explained, sounding almost—but not quite—apologetic. This was a major deviation, and the Sci-Tech administrator picked up on it immediately.

Good, Traynor thought, *you're finally starting to understand the situation. It's about time.*

"I'm glad you called," Traynor said. "We need to talk."

"About what?" Parkinson asked calmly, although Traynor could sense the underlying anxiety in his counterpart's voice.

"We found Paz."

"I see."

"Would you like a report?"

"I'd rather not discuss this on an unsecured . . ."

"This line is secure. We do our own checks."

Parkinson hesitated, and then said: "There are some other related problems—events that we didn't anticipate."

"Such as the shooting incident out in Clifton?"

Traynor thought that he could almost feel Parkinson cringe

over the intercom line. There was a long pause, and then Parkinson said, "One of our operatives may have gotten caught up in a local dispute that resulted in some shots being fired. Its a local law enforcement matter but we may need to cover the Agency on a few loose ends."

"That's all?"

"No," Parkinson said, wondering how much Traynor actually knew, and making a mental note to have the two spotters grilled mercilessly. The last thing he needed on this operation was a couple of loose mouths. "One of your . . . uh . . . assets may be involved in another matter."

"If you're referring to Henry, that would be a shame." Traynor spoke softly, but his eyes narrowed dangerously.

Not my *asset, Elliott. Henry's* your *asset now. You wanted him, you demanded him, and you got him over my strong objections. That makes you responsible, and God help you if you get him hurt with one of your asinine games.*

"My office?" Parkinson tried, seeking some degree of leverage.

"I think a neutral setting would be more appropriate," Traynor answered coldly.

"The west conference room, then," Parkinson agreed reluctantly. "Five minutes?"

"Fine."

Uniformed Crime Scene Investigation Officer Mike Quinzio, newly promoted to the rank of police officer first class as a result of his CSI work on the Kostermann case, stood beside the door of his marked station wagon, surveying the carnage and noting the alert postures of the four shotgun-armed patrol officers walking the outer perimeter on the south and east sides of the house, before turning to face the distracted detective standing at his side.

"You sure this scene's clear?" he asked suspiciously.

Homicide Detective Bradford Carpenter glanced up from his notebook, blinked a couple of times as he mentally changed gears, and then smiled.

"Come on, Quinzio, you really think Stewart and I'd let you go in there if we hadn't checked out the closets and looked under all the beds first?"

"Never stopped you before," the CSI officer said distractedly as the momentary flicker of a dark jacket and badge through the shattered living room window caught his attention. *One more inside. That makes five.* "So what're we playing with on this one?" he asked casually.

"Not sure yet." Carpenter shrugged as he continued to write in his notebook. "Probably a drug deal turned sour."

Quinzio's gaze shifted to the west side of the residence, where he observed two more shotgun-bearing uniformed officers and a sergeant, all facing outward with their backs to the smoldering house.

That makes eight, he thought to himself. *A whole goddamned squad off the streets to cover a free-for-all shooting over a dope burn. Yeah, right.*

"Anybody in the district still out on patrol?" Quinzio asked as he and Carpenter walked around to the back of his vehicle.

"It's a little light out there right now," Carpenter acknowledged. "They're pulling some guys over from Seven to cover. Probably going to have to hold the Eight-Charlie squad over, too, if you don't get your butt in gear and get this scene figured out," he added cheerfully.

"You guys going in there with me?" Quinzio asked as he snapped the trunk key ring off his heavy gun belt, "or do I get to go find out why we've got the National Guard surrounding this place all by myself?"

"Jesus Christ Almighty, Quinzio, the last few weeks, Stewart and I probably spent more time watching out for your scrawny ass than we did working cases." The black investigator grinned, perfectly willing to indulge in a little one-on-one with a fellow officer who was going to end up doing most of the dirty work on an unbelievably messy scene.

And that's exactly what the whole thing is, too—a goddamned dirty job, Carpenter thought, watching his breath condense in the freezing night air, as he went through it all in his head one more time: Couple of "good-oles" and a house shot to shit. Spent cartridge casings, splattered blood, glass fragments, and bullet holes all over the place. Back end of the house charred and smoky from a fire started at the junction box. Neighbors scared half out of their minds. Everything on the outside covered with slushy ice, and snow that was probably going to start dropping again any minute.

And the worst part of all, outside of the telltale shotgun casings, there wasn't a goddamned thing in the house to explain what had happened, much less why.

"Just what I need at ought-ought-thirty hours in the goddamned morning," Carpenter whispered.

"What?"

"Nothing. Just wondering what happened to Craven," Carpenter said, making a judicious sweep of the scene with his eyes to see if the infamous deputy commander of Major Crimes had made an appearance yet.

Little early yet, he decided. *Scene's still warm, still a lot of work for everybody to do, and no media boys sniffing around yet. Give him another fifteen.*

"Personally, I still think this is some kind of setup," the suspicious CSI officer groused as he finished loading a roll of film into his camera, snapped the back shut, and reached for the flash. "But what the hell, let's get it over with."

"Hey, you're a good man, Quinzio. Don't let anybody ever tell you different," Carpenter chuckled sympathetically, sending the slender uniformed CSI officer on his way with a shoulder slap. He glanced down at his notebook, then back up at the partially burned house, and sighed deeply.

"That's why we keep calling you out on these damn things," he added under his breath.

"Hey, Carp." Quinzio turned around when he realized that Carpenter was heading toward the patrol sergeant who was monitoring the perimeter detail.

"Yeah?"

"What about the lab. You got some people en route?"

"Stewart got hold of Gauss a few minutes ago. He's on his way now with a team. Ought to be here in about ten."

"Ah shit." Quinzio winced. "Hey, what about Henry?" he asked. "He's Eight-Forty-Charlie tonight. Think we can get him clear?"

"Already tried. They're holding him over on a res-burg with injuries over at Miller Heights." Carpenter shrugged sympathetically, knowing full well the animosity that existed between Quinzio and the new director of their crime lab.

The problem was, Carpenter reminded himself, they could all see Quinzio's point. Everybody in the Homicide detail had Gauss pegged as a habitual ass-kisser, especially around Craven. But that, as Carpenter and every other crime scene investigator on the PD knew, didn't make one bit of difference to Homicide Sergeant Alvin Stewart.

As far as Stewart was concerned, Crime Lab Director Theodore Gauss—like everybody else on the PD—had a job to do. And as long as he did that job, and did it without too much fanfare, the Homicide supervisor would see to it that every one of his investigators got along with the new lab boss just fine.

And *that*, Stewart had emphasized, was an order—which was all that Carpenter, Quinzio, and everyone else on the detail needed to hear, because none of them wanted to get crosswise with Stewart. Even the aggressively self-promoting Craven had enough sense to tread cautiously around the lantern-jawed ex–marine recon officer, who had a well-earned reputation for going down to the mat, or in through a door, to protect one of his men.

"Okay, I give up," Quinzio shrugged. "One of you guys want to give me a walk-thru on this thing? Maybe I can get the overalls shot and be out of here before the Pope and his entourage make their entrance."

Parkinson stared at the six 8x10 color photographs that Traynor had spread out across the conference table. The first two were overall shots of the front and back of the house that

Alberto Paz had rented. The third showed the open trapdoor in the middle of the living room floor. Four, five, and six were of Paz.

The last three photographs, obviously taken under cramped conditions in the far corner of the crawl space beneath the house were jarring, even for a man of Parkinson's extensive field experience, but he quickly put them out of his mind. He had far more pressing problems to consider.

"How did you find him?" he finally asked in a tight voice.

"Luminol," Traynor replied. "We sprayed the entire interior. He lost a little bit of blood from the dart wound. The fluorescent streaks stopped in the center of the carpet. Even so, it took us a while to spot the door. It was a very clean cut."

As he talked, Traynor continued to stare solemnly at the man who had been personally running the final phase of what he believed to be an incredibly dangerous operation for the past several months, using the code name of Topcastle. It was an operation that Traynor had done his best to stop, and one that he would now almost certainly be forced to support in order to protect the Agency.

"When was the last time one of your people checked the house?" Traynor asked when Parkinson remained mute.

"The next day," Parkinson said quietly as he continued to stare at the last three photos—the ones that showed the body of Alberto Paz dangling lifelessly from the crossbeams, secured, gagged, and suspended from the crawl space floor by lengths of wide nylon tape that stretched out in all directions from his arms, legs, head, and torso.

From a distance, the body of the covert field operative looked very much like a grasshopper that had been trussed up and put away for a later meal by a very large spider. Close up, he looked much worse. Parkinson was staring directly at his ex-operative's empty eye sockets, but the image was out of focus. His mind was miles away.

"That's the *last* time you were there?"

Parkinson nodded. "We didn't want to burn the house, just in case Digger might come back."

Traynor shrugged. "Probably wouldn't have mattered. You wouldn't have heard him down there anyway."

Parkinson nodded his head slowly, and then looked back up at the Sci-Tech administrator. "How long?"

"How long was he alive? Two days—maybe three at the most. Dehydration, shock, and exposure were the most likely causes of death, if it matters any."

"I see," Parkinson whispered, nodding his head again as he continued to direct his gaze at the close-up photos of Alberto Paz's ravaged face.

"What do you think?"

Traynor was silent for a moment. With Paz dead, and Digger now on the loose, Parkinson's entire operation was on the verge of turning into a disaster, just as he and several other members of the Directorate had predicted. It was time for someone to start making some serious decisions.

As far as Traynor was concerned, the only relevant decisions to be made now involved damage control to cover the Agency, and immediate action to protect people like Henry Culver, who might have unknowingly become a target. Recriminations would come later.

"What about Digger?" Traynor asked.

"What about him?" Parkinson blinked.

"Did your people help him get out?"

"No." Parkinson shook his head, mildly surprised that he was able to answer honestly. "We had intended to leave him in the Ward as long as possible. It was a convenient situation as long as the operation continued to run smoothly. We were making arrangements to have one of our medical people assigned to his case, and to ask for another month of observation, but he managed to get out first."

"You mean he was still working for you, even after the arrest?"

"Why not?" Parkinson shrugged. "His people are still functioning. We've had a few minor delays, but the crucial work is still being performed on schedule without any serious problems."

"Are you providing direction?"

"You mean now?"

"Yes."

Parkinson shook his head. "Not directly. We had a number of projects in the hopper before . . ."

"A number? How many, exactly?" Traynor interrupted.

Elliott Parkinson stared at his technically oriented associate for a few moments, and then seemed to sigh. He *needed* Traynor's help now. "Just under two hundred."

"You provided a maniac like Digger with operational plans and schedules for two *hundred* covert entries and burglaries?" Traynor said, incredulous.

Parkinson nodded glumly.

"And you last communicated with him when?"

"Not since he was picked up, about three weeks ago," Parkinson lied.

"Those photographs ought to be sufficient proof," Traynor said. "He's completely out of control. You need to resolve that situation immediately."

"We're trying, but it's a little difficult when most of our stateside operatives can be readily identified by local law enforcement. That's why we hoped that Culver would decide to be cooperative. These projects are very complex, and we . . ."

"Was L'Que one of those projects?" Traynor asked quietly.

"What?" Parkinson's head jerked up.

"I asked you if Lieutenant Colonel Charles L'Que was one of your projects," Traynor repeated.

"L'Que?"

"You may remember the name. Wahran. Nineteen-eighty."

"Certainly I remember the name. But what does a French Secret Service officer assigned to Interpol have to do with Digger and Paz?"

"Absolutely nothing, I hope," Traynor said softly. "L'Que was recently transferred to the French Embassy in DC for reasons which are undoubtedly related to the World Trade Organization and Interpol meetings beginning this weekend. A few hours ago, his home was burglarized. The people who committed the burglary may have critically injured his son."

"I . . . I'm sorry to hear that," Parkinson whispered.

Traynor nodded slowly. "Yes, I am too," he said, fixing his gaze on the blinking eyes of his bureaucratic archrival.

Parkinson knew that regardless of everything else, he still needed the technical expertise and resources of Traynor's Sci-Tech Directorate.

"I give you my solemn word that nothing we've done has anything to do with Charles L'Que," Parkinson said. "Absolutely nothing. We are simply running an intelligence-gathering operation."

"A *domestic* intelligence-gathering operation," Traynor corrected.

"Well, yes, I suppose that's true in a *technical* sense, but our targets are strictly limited to the international community. And besides, the operation is about to provide us with . . ."

"Is? You mean you're not shutting down?" Traynor's head came up sharply.

"No, we can't. The payoffs are just beginning to come in now, and some of the stuff's dynamite. We have to keep going."

"Whose decision?"

"Mine, for now. I'm expecting full concurrence from the director and all of the ADs."

"You won't get it," Traynor said flatly.

"But . . ."

"Let's move on. Is there any indication that the police might tie any of Digger's activities back to the Agency?"

Parkinson shook his head. "Not at this time. As far as we know, there are no links, direct or otherwise; but we may have lost another one of our operatives this evening. We'd like to have one of your damage control teams on standby, just in case."

"I'll arrange for it," Traynor said. "What about Culver?"

"At the moment, Mr. Culver has no apparent interest in being cooperative," Parkinson said stiffly. "I'm disappointed.

I expected an asset from your store to be more of a team player."

"Henry's different." Traynor smiled for a moment, but then his expression changed. "You said earlier that he may be involved now. How so?"

Parkinson hesitated. "You recall the incident at Digger's trial?"

Traynor nodded silently.

"We have reason to believe that Digger continues to hold a grudge against Culver and three other police officers—something to do with the evidence."

"He thinks that Henry faked the evidence." Traynor shrugged impatiently. "It's an idiotic idea. Go on."

"According to our sources, several of the officers involved in the investigation—including Culver—may have received threatening messages from Digger."

Traynor couldn't keep his eyes from flickering down to the photographs on the table. "Do they know he's out?"

"No."

"Then tell them."

Parkinson shook his head. "We can't take the risk. We'd be exposing the entire operation. And besides, we're fairly certain that he's left the area."

"Then what about protection, just in case he hasn't?" Traynor asked, virtually certain that he already knew the answer.

"We're maintaining a surveillance, but it's loose. We're a little short on people right now."

You sanctimonious little prick, Traynor thought to himself. *Why don't you just come out and admit that you're using Henry and the rest of them for bait to find your goddamned rogue?*

"You think that's a wise course?" Traynor asked, choosing to suppress his outrage for the moment.

"At the moment, we seem to be running out of options. Actually, we were hoping that you might . . . talk with him. He could be extremely useful to us in locating Digger, especially if he was able to get transferred, either back to the lab or into the Homicide detail. If absolutely necessary, I suppose, some information on Digger's escape might be offered as a sign of good faith."

"Henry needs to believe in what he's doing," Traynor said carefully. "That's why he left us. If you can't convince him that you're running a clean operation, then he won't be helpful, regardless of anything I might say."

"I see." Parkinson nodded slowly, his face solidifying into a tight-lipped frown. "Do you have any recommendations then?"

"Do you want my personal opinion?"

"Yes, of course."

"Personally, I'd shut the entire operation down, right now."

"Everything?"

"Absolutely everything," Traynor nodded.

"I . . . we can't do that."

"Then may I offer a couple of very serious *suggestions?*"

"Please," Parkinson said unconvincingly.

"First of all, you have at least one and possibly two rogue agents on the loose. Use everything you have to find them. And as soon as you do, bring them in or put them down *immediately.* Especially Digger. Don't even *think* about a rehab with that one. You can't afford the risk."

Parkinson nodded slowly, his face devoid of expression.

"Secondly," Traynor went on, "if you have any way of communicating with Digger's people, I would suggest that you try very hard to keep them out of Henry Culver's patrol area during his shift."

"Why so?"

Traynor smiled sympathetically. "I'm suggesting that you need to be careful with Henry. He may not seem the type, but he can be very dangerous, especially if you play on his emotions."

"I hardly think . . ." Parkinson started in, but Traynor raised his hand.

"Please take my word for it anyway, regardless of what

you or any of your associates may think," he said with barely restrained sarcasm. "If Henry chances to trip across *another* element of your 'project,' and starts putting pieces together, I believe you're going to find yourselves in a very precarious situation. I know him. Once he picks up the scent of something suspicious, he won't let it go."

Parkinson nodded indifferently. "I'll keep that in mind." He stood up from his chair and was starting toward the door when he was brought up short by a cold, menacing tone in Traynor's voice.

"There's one more thing, Elliott."

"Yes, and what's that?"

"I am very fond of Henry," Traynor said in a deadly calm voice, his narrowed eyes making direct contact with his bureaucratic adversary. "If you decide against a warning, and Digger does get through to him, I'm going to hold you *personally* accountable for his safety. Do you understand what I'm saying?"

"You can't threaten . . ." Parkinson started to bluster, but Traynor brought up his hand.

"You're not paying attention, Elliott," the Sci-Tech administrator said, shaking his head slowly. "I have no intention of *threatening* you at all."

Chapter Twenty

Friday, 0020 hours

Contrary to Mike Quinzio's sarcastic prediction, the arrival of Fairfax County Crime Lab Director Theodore Gauss to the scene of the bizarre Morgan and Lawnhart residence shooting really wasn't all that comparable to a visit by the Vatican.

More like a conductor walking out onstage, Detective

Bradford Carpenter decided as he watched the overweight scientist and his assistant unload their equipment from the glistening white lab van. Shaking his head and sighing, he called Quinzio to follow him over to the van.

Ten minutes later, Carpenter was leading Gauss and Quinzio through the still-smoldering ruins of the house. Typically, Gauss was trying to take everything in at once, his eyes sweeping the scene as he recorded some of the more pertinent details into his handheld recorder.

The first of the two bodies was lying faceup in the hallway. Male, white, mid-twenties, they all noted reflexively. The man's shirt and the torn waist area of his jeans were completely soaked with rapidly drying blood. The wallpaper above the body showed a partial pattern of five .24-caliber-sized holes at about waist level. The remainder of the twenty-seven-pellet pattern had nearly cut the slender man in half.

"Anything on this one?" Gauss asked, looking up from his tape recorder.

"According to his driver's license, his name's Otis Lawnhart. H-A-R-T. He and a guy named Morgan rent this place," Carpenter said.

"Anything to indicate they might be burglars?"

"Nothing yet." Carpenter shook his head, impressed that Gauss had picked up on the pattern that fast. Like many of the detectives in the department, Carpenter had been hoping that Henry Culver would get the job when the old lab director retired. They all found Gauss extremely difficult to warm up to, but everyone had to admit that the guy was sharp. "What about those shell casings?" he queried.

Gauss knelt down, examined one of the shotgun casings under the beam of his flashlight without touching it, and then stood back up.

"Four-ought buck, just like the others, but leaving the casings scattered all over the scene sure doesn't fit in with the M.O.," Gauss said after repeating the information on Lawnhart into his recorder and motioning for his trailing assistant to begin searching the area around the body. "Far as I can remember, there weren't any expended casings at the other scenes. Just the plastic cup wadding and shot."

"Couldn't that mean a double-barrel?" Carpenter asked as they all started down at the blood-splattered body of Otis Lawnhart. "Never had more than two shots fired at the other scenes. All straight-out hit-and-runs. Whoever it was could have just left the empties in the gun if he knew the targets were down. Nothing says he had to kick 'em out."

Gauss shook his head as his eyes continued to sweep the scene. "No, only one barrel," he said. "All the wadding we found had the same . . ."

Gauss hesitated as his assistant interrupted, coming over to drop a torn piece of semitransparent white plastic into his supervisor's hand. Gauss stared at it for a few moments and then looked up at the much taller detective, his fleshy cheeks breaking into a rare smile. "Yep, here it is. Twelve-gage plastic shot-cup wadding, with striations on the outside," he added, holding the cylindrical piece of plastic out so that Carpenter and Quinzio could see it.

"Yeah, so . . . ?" Carpenter said, his eyebrows furrowed as he stared at the telltale piece of powder-burned wadding.

"When you shorten the barrel of a shotgun with a hacksaw, you end up with a lot of burrs—rough edges inside the end of the barrel," Gauss explained. "Fire a round with a plastic shot-retaining cup wadding like this through that barrel, and the outside of the plastic gets gouged by those burrs. Leaves a pattern of parallel striations that are pretty reproducible."

"So that means we're dealing with a sawed-off here, too?" Carpenter asked.

Gauss nodded. "Sure looks like it."

"Wonderful," Bradford Carpenter muttered.

"You mean you can match the striations in that wadding like you can bullets?" Quinzio asked, impressed enough to momentarily forget his intense dislike for the habitually arrogant lab director.

Theodore Gauss smiled. "Not only that, but now that

we've got casings with extractor, ejector, and firing pin marks, we ought to be able to tell you something about the make and model of the weapon. Give you guys something to go look for."

"So the guy finally screwed up." Carpenter smiled in satisfaction.

"Maybe, if it *is* the same guy," Gauss said. "I'll be able to tell you more after we get everything back to the lab." He hesitated, blinking his eyes as if he'd momentarily forgotten something. "You said you had two bodies on this one. Is the other one Morgan?"

Carpenter shrugged. "We don't know yet. Probably have to ID him on prints since he hasn't got much of a face left. We'll get to him later. Thing I wanted you to see is in here." He pointed to one of the small bedrooms off the hallway.

As the three men moved carefully into the bedroom, their eyes immediately focused on the same object. Gauss was the first one to speak.

"A notebook computer?" he whispered, his voice clearly registering his disbelief.

"Or what's left of one," Carpenter said, stepping aside as Quinzio instinctively moved forward with his camera. "Looks like it got in the way of some of that buckshot, too," he added, nodding his head toward the torn wallboard. From all outward indications, at least three of the pellets from the hallway had penetrated two more layers of wallboard before punching holes in the portable computer's monitor screen. Two other projectiles had penetrated the plastic case.

Then Gauss turned and stared at the far wall of the bedroom that was opposite the kitchen. This wall appeared to have been hit by at least fifty or sixty bullets in discernible five-to-seven-round bursts.

"Where the hell did those come from?" the crime lab director asked.

"The whole kitchen floor's covered with nine-millimeter casings," Carpenter said.

"Anybody find the weapon?" Gauss asked, turning his

head slowly back and forth as he tried to determine angles of trajectory.

"Nope, just the brass."

"Christ, what a mess." Gauss shook his head in amazement. "These guys really must have pissed somebody off."

"So what do you think," Carpenter asked after Gauss remained silent for several moments.

"It doesn't make a whole lot of sense. From what I've seen so far—the house, neighborhood, clothes—everything adds up to these guys being a couple of beer-drinking, TV-watching, good-ole-boy rednecks," Gauss said quietly after a few more moments. "Just like the others."

"So what the hell're they doing with a computer, right?" Carpenter said.

"Exactly," Gauss agreed, scanning the bedroom quickly, and then blinking when Quinzio triggered his flash. "I don't see any computer books or manuals." He opened the desk drawers and then looked into the nearby closet. "Not even any floppy disks."

"Maybe they play video games with it?" Quinzio suggested.

Gauss shrugged. "Maybe, but I don't see any game boxes or instructions either."

"So what does that mean?" Carpenter demanded.

"I don't know," Gauss admitted, displaying a rare sense of humility and uncertainty that startled both Quinzio and Carpenter, "but I'll tell you what. I think we ought to get Henry Culver out here."

"Why, does Henry know something about computers?" Carpenter asked.

"Yeah, quite a bit," Gauss said. "He used to do all of our programming at the lab. Is he on duty tonight?"

"Fair Oaks District, but you'll probably have to get clearance to cut him loose," Quinzio offered as he started to wind the remainder of the film into the take-up reel of the camera. "They've got him out on a burg scene in Oakton."

"I'll see if I can get the watch commander to okay it," Gauss said. "Is there a phone I can use?"

"In the kitchen." Carpenter was still staring silently at the shattered computer. "You might check it for prints first."

"Yeah, right." Gauss laughed, again displaying a rare sense of humor that caused Carpenter and Quinzio to stare at each other with puzzled frowns as Gauss left the room.

Probably getting his rocks off figuring out this puzzle, the burly Homicide detective thought as he watched Quinzio start in to take some close-ups of the computer. The CSI officer had just finished setting up a tripod, and was in the process of focusing in on the shattered screen when Gauss came hurrying back into the small bedroom.

"I got . . ." he started to say behind Carpenter's broad back, and then the rest of his words were lost in the concussive explosion that sent all three men tumbling into the walls in a shower of pulverized glass and plastic.

Henry Culver was making a very determined effort to do at least two conflicting jobs at once—supervising the flow of people, information, and evidence in and out of the L'Que's house, and at the same time trying to figure out the meaning of the four deeply indented holes in the living room carpet that were too narrowly spaced to have been made by the missing TV—when one of the uniformed officers came running into the garage.

"Henry, have you been listening to the radio?"

"No, what's the matter?"

"That shooting scene out in Clifton. They just had some kind of bomb go off a few minutes ago. Sounds like a booby trap. Carpenter, Quinzio, and Gauss got caught in the blast."

"*What?* Are they okay?"

"I don't know. Stewart wants to talk to you, pronto. Said to use tac three."

Moments later, Culver was in his cruiser, punching the scanner-protected tactical frequency three on his radio and thumbing the mike.

"Eight-Forty-Charlie to MC-Ten."

"This is Stewart," Homicide Sergeant Alvin Stewart's voice echoed within the confines of Culver's cruiser.

"Al, this is Henry. Is everybody okay out there?"

"We don't know yet," Stewart replied, the strain and suppressed rage evident in his voice. "Gauss's got some pretty nasty bruises, but the paramedics said he's okay, outside of some ringing in the ears, and maybe needing a change of shorts. Carp got his bell rung hard. They're going to ship him out of here in a couple of minutes."

"What about Quinzio?"

"Transported him to Oakton Hospital a couple minutes ago. He's in pretty bad shape," Stewart muttered. "He was standing right next to the thing when it went off, but it looks like the main force went forward and up. Camera protected most of his face. He was talking okay a couple minutes ago, but he still can't hear anything."

"Jesus Christ . . ."

"Yeah, everybody's walking light around here right now. Hey, listen, do you still keep your CSI gear with you in that cruiser?"

"Sure, you want me out there?" Culver asked hopefully, crossing his fingers.

"Damn straight I do," the Homicide supervisor said, "but I got overruled by the watch commander. The word is, your Colonel L'Que is the head of some kind of hotshot, interagency counterterrorist unit on detail to Interpol, so the department wants to keep somebody with some experience on that scene until they can get an Army CID unit and the French Embassy to respond. Apparently they're worried that it might be some sort of retaliation hit. Sounds like you're going to be up to your butt in brass before too long."

"So what am I supposed to do, just stand around here and look important?"

"Sounds like it. Listen, Henry, I've got the bomb squad en route out here, but we're short on CSI and Gauss is still shocky, so I'm gonna need some help."

"I thought you said he's okay," Culver interrupted, momentarily concerned. He didn't care much for Gauss on a personal level, for a lot of very complicated reasons, but when something like this happened, it was a lot easier to remember that they were all on the same team.

"He probably is," Stewart said. "Just can't get his hands to stop shaking. And besides, Quinzio's camera got all screwed up by the explosion. Thought maybe you could take a look at it, or maybe lend us yours for a while."

"Yeah, sure, no problem" Culver said, trying to mask the disappointment in his voice while his subconscious was making a very determined attempt to get his attention. Something about bombs and booby traps and . . .

Russelli. Oh Jesus, that's right. The note from Digger. Russelli and the booby trap and . . .

Culver sat there in his cruiser, feeling the cold chill rise up his spine and out into his arms.

"Hey, Al, listen, I got this note . . ."

Then he stopped. He remembered that he and Russelli and Gauss and Quinzio had all worked the footprints out at the Kostermann scene, and then testified against Digger in court.

"Yeah, what about it?"

But it couldn't be Digger, because the bastard was still locked up in the County Ward, he reasoned.

"Uh . . ."

Make sure, he told himself. *Before you get everybody all stirred up, check it out and make goddamned sure.*

"Never mind, you've got enough to worry about right now," Culver said. "I'll tell you about it later. Soon as I clear it with the W/C, I'll be out there and take a look at that camera."

Fifteen minutes later, Henry Culver was standing in an isolated telephone booth next to a darkened gas station, trying to explain to the night duty nurse why a police emergency justified the release of confidential information on one of her patients. Assuming, of course, a patient by the name of John

Doe Thirty-three was still *in* the Ward, which was *not* beside the point because that was exactly the information that Henry Culver wanted. In fact, it was the *only* information he wanted. But he wasn't about to tell her that.

"I'm sorry, Officer Culver, I simply can't release that information to you," the nurse repeated for the fourth time. "You know the procedures."

Culver sighed deeply, starting to feel the effects of the extended shift already. It was going to be a long night.

"Would you please tell me how I *can* get that information?"

"The doctors would have to authorize the release," the nurse replied primly.

"Couldn't I get that kind of information directly from the patient?"

"You mean talk with the patient, directly?"

"That's right."

"Wouldn't you need some sort of court order to talk with someone under our care?" the nurse asked uneasily, suddenly finding herself treading on uncertain ground.

"Absolutely," Culver agreed. "A warrant *and* permission of his attorney. But Paul Radlick's a good friend and . . ."

Culver's words seemed to have an electric effect on the nurse.

"Oh, do you know Mr. Radlick?" she asked in a voice that seemed startled, delighted, and anxious all at the same time.

"Sure. Like I said, he and I are old friends from high school. In fact, I plan on seeing him this evening . . ."

"Oh that's wonderful!" the nurse interrupted. "He was supposed to come by here yesterday morning for a very important meeting, and the doctors were really upset when he didn't show up. I—we'd really appreciate it if you could have him call us right away."

"I'll be happy to," Culver said, smiling to himself now, "but the thing is, I still need to know about your schedule. If I go to all the work of tracking down a judge over the weekend, and then sweet-talk him into signing the warrant, is

John Doe Thirty-three going to be available at eight o'clock Monday morning? See, our warrants are only good for twenty-four hours, and I have to be in court on another matter at ten."

"At eight o'clock this coming Monday morning?"

"That's right." He could hear the rustle of papers in the background. *Come on, lady, don't stop to think about it. Just do it.*

"Yes, according to the schedule, he'll still be here at eight. But please, don't forget . . ."

Gotcha.

"I won't. Thank you very much."

Homicide Detective Bradford Carpenter was sitting on the curb in his shirtsleeves, a scowl on his face and a severely battered camera dangling from one large hand, when Culver drove up to the Morgan and Lawnhart shooting scene. Unlike every other cop out there, Carpenter seemed to be unfazed by the cold weather.

"Hey, I thought you were supposed to be at the hospital?" Culver said, eyeing the dried blood splatters that almost completely covered the front of the burly detective's light wool shirt.

"Shit, it's just a goddamned nosebleed. Get hurt worse'n this every time I try to chase my wife around the house." Carpenter grunted as he stood up slowly, trying unsuccessfully not to wince from the pain.

"Tough lady."

"And that's the damned truth, too."

"Didn't anybody ever tell you to stay away from things that might blow up?" Culver asked as he shut the door of his cruiser and walked around to the trunk, eyeing the bandages on Carpenter's dark cheek and forehead.

"Learned that from my platoon sergeant when I was nineteen. Taught me to walk real careful around bombs, but they never said nothin' about no fucking computers."

"What?"

Carpenter shook his head distractedly. "Stewart and Gauss'll tell you about it. I gotta get back to work before one of those goddamned medics talks Al into throwing me off the scene. So what about this camera?" He handed the battered instrument over to Culver. "I couldn't even get the back open. Think you can fix it."

Culver examined the camera under the trunk light of his cruiser for a few moments, used his flashlight for additional illumination as he probed a couple of likely places with his fingers, and then shook his head. He set the camera down on a folded blue wool blanket, and then reached for his own camera case.

"There's a fresh roll of 400 color loaded. You so much as *drop* this one and I'll see to it that you get assigned to the front desk for a year," Culver warned as he handed the case to Carpenter. "So what's this about . . . ?"

"Hey, Carpenter, get over here with that camera!" Al Stewart yelled out from the front door, interrupting Culver's query. "We got to get a couple shots before they turn the bodies over."

Carpenter sighed. "Okay, I'd better get back to it. I'll talk to you later. And in the meantime, you watch yourself. Lot of weird shit going on tonight," the somber Homicide detective added as he turned and started walking back toward the house.

Culver waited until Carpenter's broad back disappeared into the doorway, started to get back into his cruiser, and then changed his mind.

Three minutes—that's all, he promised himself. *Just enough for a quick walk-thru.*

Having given in to temptation, he quickly pulled the flashlight out of his cruiser and then walked over toward the front door before he could change his mind again.

He walked into the entryway using his flashlight beam as a guide, turned toward the hallway, and ran right into Theodore Gauss.

"Henry, they finally cut you loose?" Gauss said, the surprise on his face turning to what appeared to be genuine relief.

Culver shook his head. "Just delivering a camera to Carp," he said. "I'm supposed to be out of here by now."

"But you had to take a quick look, right?" Gauss grinned knowingly. "Never change, do you?"

"Terminally nosy." Culver shrugged, and then the question occurred to him. "Hey, how come Carpenter's running around here taking pictures instead of you or Ed? Carp's okay with a camera, but it's been a long time since he was in CSI."

"Watch commander had me send Ed out to the hospital to stand by on that L'Que kid. And me, I've got my own problems," Gauss said, holding his hands into the flashlight beam so that Culver could see the trembling.

"You okay?" Culver asked gently, not wanting to prod too hard, but at the same time not wanting to lose the opportunity to actually *talk* with Ted Gauss. He'd worked with the guy for almost twelve years, and had never once seen him really open up to anybody.

"Just scared the piss out of me," Gauss shrugged, staring down at his hands. "Literally," he added with an almost-choked laugh.

"What's the matter? You don't think that thing scared Carpenter or Stewart?"

Gauss shrugged. "Yeah, I guess it probably did. But if Carpenter hadn't stepped in front of me at the last second, I'd have walked right into it full on," the shaken lab director said in a tight voice. "I don't know, maybe I've got too much of an imagination."

"Occupational hazard," Culver said sympathetically. "We just all handle it differently. Carp's walking around looking like he's going to beat somebody to death with my camera, and Stewart acts like he wants to trade us all in for his old recon team."

"So now we've got to deal with goddamned bombs at crime scenes, is that it?" Gauss suddenly blurted out.

"Hey, why do you think I went back to patrol. Hell of a lot safer out there."

"Actually," Gauss said after a few moments of silence, "I guess I know why you did go back. Never quite knew how to tell you, but you deserved the director's job as much as I did—probably more, actually—and I really did want you to stay. Probably would have been you anyway if I hadn't got lucky on that Kostermann deal. But . . ."

"Hey look, don't worry about it—no big deal," Culver said, momentarily disoriented by the new, emotional Gauss.

"Yeah, I know, it's just that goddamned note . . ."

"Note? What note?" Culver interrupted, blinking his eyes as his head snapped up.

"Oh . . . uh, I got this threatening note in the mail a couple of days ago. Something about being a cheater, and that I should watch where I stepped. I figured it was just some sort of sick joke—probably one of the cops."

"Do you still have it?" Culver demanded, his eyes widening as his mind began to churn through the possibilities.

"Uh, no, I think . . . yeah, I'm sure I threw it out. It didn't seem like a big deal, but then . . ." His voice dropped off as he looked around the shattered house.

"So what do you think?" Culver pressed.

"What do you mean?"

"The note and the bomb. Are they connected? And if they are, then by who?" Culver said impatiently. "For Christ sake, Gauss, didn't it ever occur to you that this scene could have been a setup? That there might be some people out there trying to nail some cops, and that you might be one of them?"

Gauss blinked uncertainly for a moment, then chuckled self-consciously. "Actually, at first, that's exactly what I thought. But then I figured I was just getting paranoid. The Kostermann case was the first thing that came to mind because of the booby traps. I was even going to find out if that guy's still locked up, but . . ."

"He is, at the County Ward. I checked about a half hour ago."

"You checked? I don't understand. Why . . . ?"

"I got one of those notes too."

"You?"

"Yeah, me. So what about Quinzio? Do you know if he . . . ?" Culver started to ask and then caught himself, remembering that Gauss was the last person that Mike Quinzio would have gone to with such a problem.

"But the thing is," Gauss went on uncertainly, "now that I've had time to think about it, I'm pretty sure the bomb here was probably some kind antitampering device, rather than a trap. It makes more sense. But I don't understand why you . . ."

"Hey Gauss, get in here. We've got a whole bunch of stuff here for you to pick up!" Sergeant Al Stewart's voice echoed loudly in the darkness from the direction of the kitchen.

"Uh-oh, better get to work." Gauss sighed, starting down the hallway. Then he hesitated and turned back to Culver. "Hey listen, Henry, I just wanted you to know that you're welcome back in the lab anytime you want. But I realize you want a shot at Major Crimes, so if my recommendation means anything to Stewart, you've got it."

"Thanks, I appreciate that," Culver said, and waited until Gauss's flashlight beam had disappeared around the corner. He'd gotten about eight feet into the living room when something glistened in the path of the beam. Kneeling down, he brought the flashlight beam in close and recognized the object immediately.

"An ear protector," he mumbled to himself. "Now why the hell . . . ?"

At that moment, Brad Carpenter's distant voice caught Culver's attention:

"Think we should get Russelli out here?"

Russelli, on a shooting scene? Culver wasn't immediately sure that he'd heard the words correctly. But then he heard Stewart's growling voice answer: "Yeah, might as well. Just make sure you keep an eye on him."

Culver remained in place for a few more seconds, waiting

to see if any more information would be forthcoming. Then, as the implications of Stewart's words fully registered in Culver's mind, he stood up, turned away, and as quietly as he could, walked quickly out through the open door and across the slush-covered driveway to his waiting cruiser.

Lost in thought as he reached for the car door handle, Culver was completely unaware that his movements were being closely watched by a man who remained hidden in the cold darkness, his body pressed up tight against a rough, crumbly tree trunk as his mind churned furiously with thoughts of paranoia, anger, and vengeance.

Chapter Twenty-one

Friday, 0100 hours

By one o'clock that morning the sense of impotent rage and frustration that had nearly overwhelmed Digger when he first realized that he could no longer access his computerized burglary system had finally dissipated. In its place had come a growing sense of uneasiness and an absolute determination not to lose control.

Not now.

Not when he was almost there.

No matter what it takes, he told himself as he turned to his computer and began to type again, keying in line after line of program code that would eventually allow him to reactivate the meticulously complex programs that he had worked so long and so hard to create.

He knew how they'd done it now—how they *had* to have done it, because in spite of Alberto Paz's increasingly insistent demands, he'd never given the critical three-password sequence to anyone. Not ever.

They'd stolen his portable computer from the trunk of his

car the night of the raid, and then they had used the access information he'd left in the hard drive files to locate, enter, recode, and take over his system. And now they were running it themselves, and they'd screwed it up, and he couldn't do a thing about it because they'd transferred a copy of the program to another computer somewhere.

Even smashing his computer onto the floor—something he'd contemplated many times during the past hours—wouldn't have any effect. The only way he could stop them was to recontact his burglars, and he couldn't do that until he could figure out how to regain entry into the program *he'd* written!

"They'll all pay for this. Especially the cheaters," he whispered to himself.

Re-creating an access program was a horribly difficult and tedious task; but that was all right because it forced him to forget for a moment how hard it was to remain in place—to stay at his keyboard—when every protective instinct was screaming at him to run.

He *wanted* to go to ground, to go deep and stay hidden, just as he had done as a young boy, until his oppressors—initially his parents, but then more often his playmates—became distracted by more immediate and demanding problems, and left him alone.

But he couldn't do that anymore. He couldn't stop and he couldn't run because he'd already let it go too far. And unlike his parents, or his playmates, the police wouldn't stop coming after him. Not once did they realized what he'd done.

It helped to realize that there were others like himself—people who had been irrevocably twisted in their childhood by parents and playmates who had never bothered to *care*. So many others who had been forced to survive by building and sustaining a false wall of sanity around a core of smoldering anger that every now and then simply *had* to be released.

The amusing part was that the wall containing that anger, or at least *his* wall, wasn't all that difficult to build or sustain. The trick was to block out the sources of his frustration; and, if possible, not to think about them at all.

But to do that, he had to find something distracting.

Like the book. He nodded as he reached across his desk for the thick photo album and began flipping through the pages—the familiar bloodred pages of gore and mayhem, of Karl and Ingrid Kostermann and her children—that had proved to be so distracting in the past.

In doing so, he never heard the single electronic "click" that echoed sharply down the long dark tunnel that connected one of his homes with the other.

Ten minutes later, he shoved the album aside in frustration.

Normally, the visual sensation of reliving those incredible scenes would have vented away his emotions like a pressure valve. But now, the photographs that brought back the vivid memories of those blood-splattered rooms weren't enough to erase the past.

Then, at that moment, he knew what he was going to do.

Standing up from his desk in his low-ceilinged room, he walked over to the wood-framed doorway and entered his escape tunnel, determined to vent his rage in the only way he knew how. He moved faster and faster down the dark, narrow, head-high tunnel as he reached into the hidden recesses, one after another, to lock back the protective traps that protected his cherished hideaway from the cheaters.

People like Alberto Paz.

Paul Radlick.

John Russelli.

And Culver.

And then . . . in a moment of horrible realization, he let it all out in a roar of hate, and fear, and anguish that was beyond all control, with a scream that echoed and echoed down the long dark tunnel.

Chapter Twenty-two

At precisely 1:15 in the morning, while driving home from the charred and blood-splattered remains of Bobby Morgan's house, John Russelli's sleep-starved mind came to the perfectly rational conclusion that the past twenty-four hours had been one of the most bizarre and frustrating days he had ever spent as a police officer.

Which didn't even take into account the miserable goddamned weather, the exhausted investigator groused, blinking his eyes and shaking his head in a determined effort to stay awake for just a few more minutes so that he wouldn't drop off into a ditch and provide himself with some real grief.

But the hypnotic movements of his slush-laden windshield wipers were more than his preoccupied mind could cope with, and his eyelids had already started to open and close in cadence with the rhythmic sweeps when two spots of searing white light suddenly blasted into his retinas.

"Son of a BITCH!"

Blinded, disoriented, and surging with adrenaline, Russelli somehow managed to bring the heavy vehicle to a sliding sideways stop without actually going into the drainage ditch.

Enraged, he tried to blink away the after-glare as he groped around the detective unit's portable emergency light, intending to make a U-turn and chase the bastard down. But even as Russelli's thick fingers closed around the rotating light fixture, his vision returned, and he looked down and saw the blue indicator that told him he'd left his own brights on.

"Christ, I'm even starting to *drive* like a goddamned civilian," he mumbled to himself, quickly steering the unmarked cruiser back into his own lane as he tried to recover his night vision and his train of thought.

Wide-awake now, he remembered that he had arrived at the station early, intent on completing some long-ignored follow-up reports, only to end up in a heated discussion with his boss, Deputy Commander Morris Markham Craven, regarding his request to have another detective assigned to the residential burglary detail.

Lieutenant Morris Craven, or "M. Markham" as he preferred to be known, a master of the bureaucratic two-step, and a recognized "riser" within the department, had listened with sympathetic patience. He had also nodded understandingly at the appropriate intervals, and then firmly promised to "see what I can do."

"But in the meantime," Craven had cautioned the exasperated res-burg supervisor with just the slightest bit of nervousness, "your stats are atrocious. I want you to do something about them immediately."

"What the hell do you want me to do," Russelli had yelled before he could catch himself, *"go out there and start shooting the thieving bastards?"*

Looking back, Russelli decided, as he steered the detective unit around an especially treacherous-looking slush pile, it was a wonder that he hadn't lunged for Craven's throat on the spot.

"It makes us all look bad, you know," Craven had rambled on obliviously, while Russelli fought to control his hot-blooded Italian temper. The clear implication was that Russelli's diminishing arrest and clearance stats just might, God forbid, effect the chances of a certain well-deserving lieutenant to latch on to a pair of early captain's bars at the next selection board, and thereby become a full commander.

The incident with Craven had taken care of Russelli's morning nicely. It had also, he realized, been the impetus for his idiotic decision to trust the word of a goddamned snitch in formulating his desperate plan to nail Molly-the-Hun in the act while he still *had* a res-burg detail. The end result of that miscalculation, of course, had been the loss of both Molly *and* his snitch, not to mention the few remaining shreds of his reputation with the brass.

It was on that cheerful note that Russelli finally managed to pull the detective unit into his darkened driveway. He quietly let himself in the front door, double-checked the locks, and then looked in on his daughters, who were both fast asleep. Then he got undressed, brushed his teeth, and shuffled in near-exhaustion to his waiting bed.

When he checked the alarm clock, he discovered that he had a little less than five hours to divide up between his unfailingly affectionate wife and sleep, before his 6:30 A.M. alarm would start the whole thing over again.

All but unconscious as his head hit the pillow, Russelli resolved this final dilemma of the day by falling dead asleep before Sharon Russelli finished turning out the lights.

It was shortly thereafter that the phone in John Russelli's bedroom began to ring.

Given the events of the last twenty-four hours, Russelli wasn't the least bit surprised to find himself being wrenched awake from what promised to be a thoroughly pleasant and satisfying dream. But even so, it took three mind-jarring rings before his protective subconscious finally accepted the inevitable.

Groaning in futile protest, Russelli reached one fumbling hand out for the demanding phone, while at the same time lifting his head slightly from the pillow in an effort to focus his fatigue-blurred eyes on the brightly glowing face of his digital clock. To his absolute and utter dismay, the first blue digit was a two.

Groaning loudly, he dropped the telephone on the floor.

Sharon Russelli reached over her husband's broad back to retrieve the phone, thereby allowing the grateful detective to sink his head back into the warm confines of his pillow for a few more seconds.

"Hello?" she whispered sleepily.

For several long moments, Sharon Russelli listened to the raspy voice at the other end of the line, her body tensing as the words began to make sense.

"Who is it?" Russelli mumbled.

"Here," she whispered in a shaky voice as she slid the handset over her husband's shoulder, "this one's for you."

"Russelli," the exhausted burglary sergeant rasped as he tried to sort out the conflicting pieces of data that simply wouldn't register in his sleep-starved mind. Among other things, he couldn't understand why his wife was acting this way about another goddamned call-out.

"Detective Sergeant John Russelli?" a hollow-sounding voice whispered.

"Yeah," Russelli sighed, momentarily considering the idea of saying no, it wasn't *Detective Sergeant John* Russelli before finally shrugging off the thought. Wasn't worth it. They'd just call back.

"Sergeant Russelli," the voice whispered in breathless anticipation, "do you know what I'd like to do to your wife right now?"

Detective Sergeant John Russelli's eyes blinked wide-open.

Apparently not expecting an answer, the whispery voice went on to describe—in crude but effectively graphic detail—exactly what kind of amusement he had in mind for Mrs. John Russelli. For almost thirty seconds, Russelli tried to focus his attention on the voice that seemed to be penetrating the murky barriers of his consciousness from some place that was very dark and resonant—like at the bottom of a deep well.

Finally the distant voice hesitated, apparently running out of air or imagination. A few moments of uninterrupted silence passed before Russelli finally managed to find his voice.

"You—you're trying to tell me that you want to screw around with *my* wife at two o'clock in the fucking *morn-*

ing?" Russelli whispered the words in a voice hoarse with disbelief as he came up to a sitting position in the bed, while a more self-serving portion of his groggy mind came to the incredibly wonderful conclusion that this *wasn't* a call-out.

Which meant that he could go back to sleep.

But not just yet.

"Hey asshole, you still there?" Russelli inquired in a hoarse whisper.

There was an empty, hollow silence at the other end of the line, but Russelli could hear the faint sounds of labored breathing and occasional sounds of nearby traffic.

"You want to talk to her again?" Russelli whispered in a voice that should have caused any halfway intelligent pervert to drop the phone and run for his life.

More silence, but Russelli could hear the breathing sounds increase in intensity. Then he heard a barely audible "yeah."

"Good boy," Russelli said pleasantly, the words almost dripping with menace. "You just go ahead and talk to her and keep on playing with yourself, 'cause while you're doing that, *I'm* going to get dressed. And when I finish getting dressed, I'm going to go outside and follow the fucking wires all the way out to that fucking phone booth. And when I get there, I'm going to rip that little mouse dick of yours off with my bare hands and . . ."

The line went dead with a sharp click.

Much to Detective Sergeant Russelli's subconscious dismay, the flimsy tendrils of the distant, enticing dream had long since disappeared into the darkness, hopelessly out of reach, as he replaced the handset into the receiver and collapsed back into his bed, only vaguely aware that his wife had managed to snuggle the better part of her solidly conditioned torso against his back.

After a few moments, she whispered: "John?"

"Hummf?"

"Can you really do that?"

"What, rip his dick off?" he mumbled, keeping his eyes tightly shut as he tried one last time to draw the enticing images back.

"No, follow the telephone lines back to a phone booth."

"I don't know, ask Henry," Russelli sighed, his voice drifting away.

After a few moments of absolute silence, Sharon Russelli whispered softly in her husband's ear, "You really are a grumpy old bastard, aren't you."

"Uhhummf."

"You know what?" she whispered again as she snuggled in tighter against Russelli's warm back.

"Whummf?"

Sharon Russelli playfully nibbled at her husband's exposed earlobe. "Now that I'm awake, that *does* sound kind of interesting."

"You've *got* to be kidding," John Russelli whispered numbly.

In the cold, chilling darkness, the harsh, terrifying and all-encompassing awareness of self was suddenly and unexpectedly overwhelmed by a rising swell of sensation—of feeling!—that gradually and then more rapidly surged up into a searing wave of agonizing pain that rushed through his nervous system like hot acid.

Caught off guard by the sudden transition, the darkened figure whimpered—not only in response to the pain, but also from the certain knowledge of what was to come. There would be more pain, much more; but he had no choice, because the alternative was no longer thinkable.

No choice, do it! he told himself as he felt first the cold blade edge slice into his flesh, and then the strangely warm sensation of released blood.

The pain told him to stop—insisted that he stop—but he ignored it. There were worse things than pain.

No choice, he reminded himself again as the blade went

in deeper, and more whimpering sounds escaped through his tightened lips.

Absolutely no choice.

He had to move.

At precisely 2:51 A.M., according to the still-glowing clock face, a warm and sated but now vaguely worried Sharon Russelli shook her husband's shoulder.

"Uhhh . . . what . . . ? Again?" John Russelli mumbled incredulously, his blurred mind trying to focus on a confusing swirl of sounds and images, all of which seeming to be demanding things of his aching body that simply weren't possible. He could feel his heart pounding heavily in his chest—the predictable result of having been woken out of deep REM sleep—while his reeling mind tried to focus on one perfectly sound and rational course of action.

Gonna track down that little son of a bitch pervert, stomp his nuts . . .

"John, it's still raining."

"It's . . . what?" Russelli blinked his eyes. "You . . . you woke me up to tell me . . . ?"

"It's Ocha. I'm worried about him. It's so cold out there and I'm afraid he's going to get wet. You know, he's so old, and you never did get around to fixing the door to his doghouse."

"Ocha?" Russelli whispered groggily, "Who the hell's . . . the *dog?* You're worried about the fucking *dog* getting wet? Time is it? No, don't tell me, I don't wanna know."

"But it's raining."

"Dog's been getting wet . . . thirteen years," Russelli mumbled, keeping his eyes tightly shut. "Probably used to it by now."

"It's okay, you lie there and get some sleep, lover," Sharon Russelli whispered, giving her husband a gentle kiss on the neck. "I'm going to go let him in."

"Yeah . . . good idea. Let him . . ." John Russelli nodded

his head in his pillow, his last mumbled words drifting away as he floated back down into a gentle, welcoming darkness that suddenly, uncounted moments later, started yanking violently at his shoulder, whispering urgently . . .

"John, wake up!"

"Huh?! Wha . . . ?"

"He's dead."

"WHA . . . ? *What? Dead? Who's dead?"*

John Russelli sat straight up in bed, his heart pounding solidly against his rib cage again as he stared wide-eyed and openmouthed at his wife, who was almost invisible in the darkness.

"It's Ocha," Sharon Russelli whispered, her voice choked with emotion. "I . . . I went out to his doghouse and . . . he's lying in there, all stiff and cold."

"Aw Jesus," Russelli whispered, taking his wife in his arms and holding her tight against his heaving chest, wondering if this was how all those forty-year-old cops got heart attacks.

"I tried to pull him out, but he was so stiff, and I couldn't get him out."

"Yeah, I know," he said soothingly, working to bring his breathing back under control as he tried desperately to think of something nice that he could say about a dog that had driven him out of his mind for the better part of those thirteen years. "Listen, it's okay. Probably better this way. He was starting to slow down the last couple of months. Better he didn't suffer."

"But Michelle and Martine . . . ?"

"You get them off to school." Russelli yawned, trying to keep his eyes open. "I'll bury him out by the garden. Easier for them to handle it that way."

"You sure it's okay?" Sharon Russelli asked in a choked voice. "I mean, I know you're going to be late for work, but I don't think I could . . ."

"Yeah, sure, no problem," Russelli mumbled groggily as he let his head drop heavily back down on the pillow. "Noth-

ing much important going on at the station right now anyway."

Which wasn't altogether true, because at precisely 2:52 on
that cold and dismal morning, one of the men who had sent
a professional killer to Bobby Morgan's home made a very
important and absolutely irrevocable decision.

The project that he had labored on for so long was rapidly
going out of control; and it was becoming increasingly obvious that he could no longer afford the luxury of playing
with his most amusing—but at the same time most dangerous—adversary.

It was coming down to a matter of survival now, and that
made the decision easy.

In a matter of a very few hours, Eight-Forty-Charlie would
have to die.

Chapter Twenty-three

Friday, 0253 hours

"Check into the station about three and we'll let you know
if we're going to need to hold you guys over any longer."

Those had been the watch commander's last words before
sending Henry Culver and his squad back out onto the streets
to cover for the teams of patrol officers who had been pulled
out of their cruisers to protect the two hot scenes.

It had been frustrating for Culver to have to walk away
from both of those crime scenes, but he couldn't argue with
the watch commander's logic. They had plenty of competent
investigators at both locations, and they needed patrol officers on the street. Henry Culver was now a patrol officer,
which meant he got back in his cruiser and did what he was
being paid to do.

In about two minutes, he decided, anticipating the mildly exotic pleasures of a hot bath and a warm bed. He'd been thinking about both for the past half hour, mildly amused that the daydreaming hadn't included a warm body to cuddle up against.

Might as well get used to it, he thought to himself, glancing away from his casual search of the dark, tree-lined and ice-slickened country road to check his watch. And then yawning as he stretched his stiff and cold leg muscles (cautiously, one leg at a time) against the cruiser's solid fire wall.

The note that Tess Beasley had left in his unit back at Kathy Harmon's burglary scene had been direct and to the point. She was going to start dating a district attorney, and suggested that he ought to start looking around himself.

"How about a burg victim for a change?" Tess Beasley had added in a quick scrawl on the back of one of her report forms. "A pretty lady in distress? Just your type, Henry."

"Thanks, Tess, you're a great help," Culver thought as he remembered Kathy Harmon's enticing eyes. *Just what I need. Don't have time enough as it is.*

The time.

At 2:55, he'd start heading toward the station . . .

The dispatcher's professionally calm voice jarred Culver out of his daydreams.

"Scout Eight-Forty-Charlie and any cruisers in the area, an armed robbery, just occurred, Chalmer's Market in the Kings Park Shopping Center, eight-seven-two-nine Braddock Road."

"Eight-Forty, Fox Mill Road," Culver immediately called in over his mike.

"Eight-Forty has the call," the dispatcher advised. "All responding cruisers, two suspects observed westbound on Braddock in a dark foreign sedan, possibly a Toyota Camry. Virginia plates. First three only, Edward-Edward-David . . ."

Culver began to scribble hurried notes across his console-mounted clipboard pad as he accelerated the patrol cruiser down the narrow, two-lane road. The idea of a warm bed was completely forgotten as he forced himself to concentrate on glistening wet patches in the road and the dispatcher's voice.

". . . suspect number one described as male, white, curly brown, possibly eighteen to twenty. Blue jeans, white T-shirt, dark-framed glasses. Suspect number two, male, white, short blond hair, same approximate age, heavyset. Jeans and maroon football jersey, number four-four . . ."

Forty-four. Riggins's old jersey. Culver smiled as he glanced down at his clipboard to add the playing number of the Washington Redskin's rowdy ex-fullback to the abbreviated description of "S-2" on his clipboard notepad.

Automatically starting to construct mental images of the two suspects, Culver powered the solidly suspended patrol cruiser through a series of tight, climbing turns . . . and then momentarily snapped on his lights and siren as he made a sharp, tire-squealing left through the nearly deserted T-intersection at Highway 50 before floorboarding the cruiser on an interception course with Braddock Road now less than a mile away.

White T-shirt and a four-four Redskins jersey. Not much help. Gotta be ten thousand of those things in Fairfax County alone.

Culver shook his head, reminding himself to watch for the glasses and blond hair as the recessed radio speaker began its characteristic, static-filled squawking.

"Eight-Two-Zero, I'm west on Braddock from Stone Haven. Several vehicles in sight. Passing the store . . . now. Where y'all at, Forty?"

Moorestead. Culver smiled, easily recognizing the familiar, laconic voice of his patrol buddy in spite of the distorting speaker. Good man, Moorestead. Calm, cool, experienced—and, with any luck, moving up fast right behind the dumbshit bastards with his lights and siren off.

"Go get 'em, Billy Joe," he chuckled to himself, shaking off the fatigue as he reached for the microphone clipped to the side of the console-mounted car radio. "South on Jermantown from Oakton Road. Request confirmation that suspects are westbound on Braddock."

"All units in the pursuit," the voice of the dispatcher echoed in the patrol vehicle. "Affirmative on suspect direction. Last seen *west*bound on Braddock."

Stupid dumbshit bastards, Culver corrected himself, chewing on the inside of his cheek in uneasy anticipation. There was an on-ramp about a mile due east of the Kings Park Shopping Center connecting to the Beltway. A team of professional armed robbers who knew the area would have immediately turned *east* on Braddock, *toward* the Beltway, regardless of where they actually lived, and would have been long gone by now. West on Braddock suggested a pair of dumb or scared amateurs who would be completely unpredictable, and thus much more dangerous.

Culver requested information on any available backup cruisers from the adjoining Seventh Patrol District.

"Hold one," the dispatcher monotoned. "Any District Seven cruisers in the area, do you copy?"

"Seven-Five-One . . ." the speaker in Culver's car crackled weakly, ". . . clearing from Tysons Mall. Taking the Beltway in. ETA five to ten minimum."

Tysons Mall. A good five miles out. No help.

"I'm coming up on Chain Bridge now," Culver spoke into the mike, immediately focusing his eyes on the oncoming vehicles to his left—scanning the license plates for the Edward-Edward-David prefix—as he tapped at his brakes, quickly looked right to confirm clearance, and then power-turned left through the intersection onto Chain Bridge Road. "What about local units?" he added as the police cruiser's heavy-duty automatic transmission began to accelerate up through the gears once again.

"Be advised that Fairfax and Vienna units are setting up a check grid now," the dispatcher responded quickly.

"Ten-four. Any ID on the weapons?"

"Negative. Informant disconnected after calling in. We're attempting a recontact now."

If they stay west on Braddock, they're going to run themselves right into the Fairfax City traffic, and the City PD units. A dumb move, even for amateurs, Culver thought uneasily. The more logical alternatives were to make a run either north or south on Guinea, or try to hide in the maze of side streets branching off . . .

"Seven-Seven-One," the radio interrupted, "I'm north on Lake from Chapel Road. Want me to cross over and intercept at Guinea?"

"Seven-Seven-One was Patrol Officer Vincent Delacroix —better known as Vinny—from District Seven's overlapping 9:00 P.M. to 7:00 A.M. "graveyard" shift. Or at least he was *supposed* to be in the Springfield District—the densely populated patrol area just south of the Fair Oaks District.

Culver grimaced. *Out of his area, as usual. Wonderful, just what we need.*

"Scout Seven-Seven-One . . ." the dispatcher started in when Culver interrupted with his mike.

"Billy Joe, you spot 'em yet?"

"Negatory." Moorestead's gravelly voice echoed in Culver's ears. "Still moving west on Braddock, coming up on Sideburn now. No sign of the suspects."

Culver made the decision immediately, knowing that he needed every available unit in this area now, searching the cross streets before the suspects went to ground or hit a freeway, but still hesitant because he simply didn't trust Vinny Delacroix to follow orders. "Eight-Forty to Seven-Seven-One, negative on the intercept. Stay in the south to . . ."

"I GOT 'EM!" Delacroix's excited voice screamed out over the airwaves.

"Oh shit!" Culver cursed out loud, visualizing the gleeful expression on Delacroix's otherwise dark and foreboding face. Vinny Delacroix was one of those lead-footed, gun-*and* badge-heavy cops that most of the veteran police officers in Fairfax County tried to avoid whenever possible. Everybody *knew* that the crazy s.o.b. was going to kill somebody someday. It was just a question of who, when, where, and what poor bastard was going to find himself rolling in as the backup.

"Seven-One, what's your twenty?" Culver demanded, almost yelling the words into the microphone.

"I'M IN PURSUIT OF ARMED ROBBERY SUSPECTS," Delacroix screamed over the background sound of his sirens. "LIGHT TAN TOYOTA CAMRY, EDWARD-EDWARD-DAVID-THREE-ZERO-TWO. SOUTHBOUND ON LAKE ROAD FROM BURKE VILLAGE!"

Culver blinked. *South on Lake? What the hell . . . ?*

To get onto Lake, the suspects had to have turned south on Guinea from Braddock, and then turned off the main road to cut back east through the traffic hindering maze of narrow residential roads surrounding Braddock Lake before turning south on another main road. It sounded like they didn't intend to hide *or* run, which didn't make a goddamn bit of sense to Culver because there weren't a whole lot of cars on the road at three o'clock in the morning, and every second they stayed in the immediate area meant . . .

"Dispatch," Culver queried hurriedly, responding to an uneasily awareness that *something* about the call was wrong. "Is the chopper still down?"

"Affirmative," the dispatcher responded. "The flight crew advises they're still checking a fuel line problem. They'll be down at least an hour."

"What about the weapons?" Culver asked, feeling the tension beginning to knot his stomach.

"Car Eight is on a land line with the informant now. Hold one."

Car Eight was the single-digit call sign for Lieutenant Pete Christey, District Eight's swing shift watch commander.

Culver waited, one hand fidgeting with the microphone as the other tightened against the vibrating steering wheel of the accelerating cruiser.

"All units," the dispatcher came back quickly, "informant states he saw 'big handguns.' No further description."

Big handguns. Wonderful, Culver thought, unconsciously

brushing his free mike hand against the eighteen bulky layers of woven plastic under his gray uniform shirt. The Kevlar vests provided by the department were supposedly thin enough to be comfortable, but thick enough to stop anything up to a nine-millimeter or a .357.

It sounded nice in theory, but actual practice might turn out to be something else entirely, Culver knew. There were a lot of firearms experts who said that under certain conditions, a full-jacketed 9mm just *might* work its way through all that synthetic armor where a 9mm hollow-point wouldn't. That and the fact that a "big handgun" could mean damn near anything, including the .44 caliber Dirty Harry Specials that were capable of wrapping those eighteen layers of Kevlar right around a cop's backbone.

Culver left off on the gas as he came up over a small rise in the road and spotted the pair of much slower vehicles up ahead. *Hope the hell Pete gets some straight scoop out of the guy,* he thought uneasily.

"Vinny, did you copy on the weapons?" Culver queried, judging distances and approaching traffic before deciding that he had waited long enough to announce his presence to the suspects.

"Ten-four, big handguns!" Delacroix called out though the echoing electronic blare of his sirens.

Jesus, the son of a bitch sounds like he's having an orgasm. Culver shook his head in disbelief as he kicked in his light and sirens, sending a peacefully cruising sedan with two amorous teenagers scurrying for the side of the road as the whirlybirding reds and blues mounted over the roof of the rapidly moving patrol unit cut through the flickering street-light glare.

"Call out your location!" Culver demanded over the radio as he forced himself to concentrate on the roadway.

"South on Lake, approaching Burke Centre Parkway. SHIT, THEY BLEW THE LIGHT! OH GOD . . . T-C WITH SUSPECT VEHICLE AT LAKE AND CENTRE PARKWAY! TWO VEHICLES, ONE . . . JESUS, ONE'S ON

FIRE, HIT A LIGHT POLE . . . ROLL THE FIRE DE-
PARTMENT AND THE MEDICS, CODE THREE! SUS-
PECTS STILL GOING . . . WHAT DO I DO?!" Delacroix
screamed.

"Seven-One, keep rolling on the suspect vehicle!" Culver
shouted into the mike.

Jesus Christ, he thought, *there can't be more than a couple of dozen cars on the street in the whole goddamned district in this weather, and three of them manage to hit each
other?* "Dispatch, roll fire and rescue units, Lake and Centre Parkway, ten-three, and get us some backup out here!"

The dispatcher was on Culver's request immediately.

"Any cruisers in the area of Lake and Centre Parkway who
can respond for backup on a pursuit?"

"Command Eighty, I'm rolling from the station."

Then Vinny Delacroix's voice broke in: "I'M RIGHT BE-
HIND THEM!"

"Henry, I'm coming up on the T-C, about one behind
Vinny. Call it!" Moorestead transmitted over the radio static.

"Take the T-C," Culver directed, wincing in the realization
that he'd just cut his most reliable backup out of the pursuit,
but at the same time knowing it was the right decision. In
spite of everything else, Delacroix had the best chance at their
primary objective right now, which was to maintain contact
with the running suspects. "Vinny, I'm south on Chain Bridge
approaching Pohick."

"Still south on Burke Lake Road," Delacroix rasped, his
voice hoarse from the yelling, but still tense with excitement. "Suspects are . . . RIGHT ON POHICK!" he screamed
into the mike. "SUSPECTS ARE RIGHT ON POHICK!"

"Eight-Forty, I'm left on Pohick from Chain Bridge!" Culver yelled into his mike and then threw it on the seat, grabbing the steering wheel with both hands as he accelerated
through the turn. He fought to retain traction with the spinning rear tires of the cruiser before jamming the wheel to the
left and sliding the vehicle through the slush to a tire-

screeching perpendicular stop across the road. He ended up about two hundred yards ahead of the oncoming Toyota and the red-and-blue flashing lights of Vinny Delacroix's cruiser.

Seconds later, after yanking the Remington Model 870 twelve-gage pump shotgun out of its back wall mount; scrambling out of the unit; jacking a three-inch, forty-one-pellet, number four buckshot round into the chamber of the shotgun; and being just about ready to throw himself across the hood of the protective vehicle—all the while ignoring the insistent warning screams in the back of his mind—Henry Culver suddenly realized that the Camry *wasn't* going to stop.

Standing in the roadway with the stock of the shotgun braced tight against his cheek, Culver wasted another half second considering the idea of a windshield shot—a shot that could just as easily hit Delacroix, he realized—before the self-preserving instincts finally stopped screaming and simply took over.

Culver twisted away to his left and threw himself backward, just as the leading left edge of the oncoming Camry slammed into the front bumper of his marked unit. The metal-crunching collision sent the gray-and-blue cruiser spinning around counterclockwise, toward Culver, showering him with a light-reflecting spray of headlight lens particles as the sounds of tearing sheet metal and breaking glass echoed through the cold night air.

Ducking away from the flying glass shards, Culver scrambled forward on his hands and knees (barely in time as he sensed—rather than actually saw—the crumpled front end of his cruiser whipping past his back), came up to one knee, brought the shotgun up to waist level, swung the barrel left, and then squeezed the trigger in a single motion as the twisted and torn left side of the Camry came roaring into his field of vision.

Culver had never fired the Magnum twelve-gage rounds without ear protection before, and he wasn't prepared for the sharp, concussive blast that seemed to burst through the thin membranes of his eardrums. The momentary pain caused him to wince and close his eyes.

In doing so, he missed seeing the initial effect of the forty-one quarter-inch-diameter lead balls ripping into the Camry's left front tire, and never really heard the explosive release of compressed air as the spinning steel-belted radial tore away from the wheel rim.

But he certainly saw the aftereffects.

Blinking his eyes open, while instinctively drawing the foregrip of the shotgun back and then jamming it sharply forward to feed another round into the chamber, Culver watched the left front end of the Camry take a sudden nosedive. It dug into the road as the rest of the vehicle came roaring around in an engine-revving, 180-some-degree turn around the axis of the asphalt-shredding metal tire rim.

Still shaken by the violent, high-velocity impact that had occurred within inches of his own highly exposed and vulnerable body; half-blinded by the Camry's single functioning headlight, which was now shining directly into his eyes; and effectively deafened by the high-pitched whining in his ears; Culver never saw or heard Vinny Delacroix coming.

Instead, numbed by the sudden realization that he was standing out in the open, completely exposed to a pair of concealed armed robbery suspects, Culver was trying to divide his attention between the shadowy forms inside the Camry, intermittently illuminated by sweeps of the rotating red and blue lights mounted on the roof of his still-rocking cruiser, and the nearest point of cover, when he thought he heard the screeching sound of locking brakes behind his back.

Vinny Delacroix didn't have many attributes to his credit as a police officer, but the one thing he *did* know something about was pursuit driving. During his Academy basic training, he had repeatedly aced the pylon, "hound and hare," and the skid-pan scenarios; and as such, probably could have gotten out of the situation clean, in spite of his excessive speed on the rain-and-slush-slickened road, had there been any room at all.

But there wasn't.

The sudden, night-highlighted fireball erupting from Culver's shotgun, and the subsequent spinning nosedive taken by the Camry had distracted Vinny Delacroix in those critical moments when he should have realized that he was coming in much too fast. Thus, by the time he did start to brake, he was about a second and a half too late, which calculated out to be about 130 feet.

With an incoming speed of just over 60 mph, Delacroix had no time to think, and barely enough to react. As a result, he hit the brakes too hard and locked them up. He immediately sensed the loss of traction, and tried to regain it with instinctive play of steering wheel and accelerator in a desperate effort to avoid an uncontrolled slide. Only then did he realize, as the shrieking tires of his cruiser fought to regain their grip on the slippery asphalt, that in the backcountry darkness, the mixed pattern of rotating reds and blues from the two police vehicles had distorted the distance.

It came down to a matter of numbers—mass and velocity versus the diminishing yards of asphalt—that simply wouldn't match up. So Vinny Delacroix did the only thing he could do with the little time and distance he had left.

Henry Culver jerked his head around at the very moment that Delacroix floored the accelerator, jabbed right with the steering wheel, and then swung his shoulders into a full left turn that sent the back end of his cruiser swerving off the road in a violent, last chance effort to avoid a head-on with either the Camry or Culver's road-blocking vehicle.

For a brief moment, it looked as though Vinny Delacroix was going to pull it off. Then the leading edge of his sliding right rear tire caught the jagged end of an exposed tree root.

As Culver watched in stunned horror, Delacroix's cruiser seemed to leap into the air—beams of white, red, and blue light flailing wildly in the darkness as the gray-and-blue vehicle made a full one and a quarter twisting turn through its long axis. As Culver continued to watch helplessly, the cruiser slammed down hard against the asphalt road on its right side, and then seemed to lunge skyward again in a slow, stop-action roll before landing upside down in a windshield-shattering crash less than twenty feet away from the Camry.

Henry Culver was starting toward the overturned vehicle—to get Delacroix out of the wreckage before the gas tank burst into flames—when he remembered the Camry. He turned his head back to look into the glaring white light of the single halide headlight that was still functioning on the suspects' car, and saw a silvered reflection move inside the wrecked vehicle as the driver's side door started to come open.

Gun!

And then, out of the corner of his right eye, he saw Vinny Delacroix—blood streaming from his nose and mouth, and open gashes above both eyes—tumble out through the shattered side window of his overturned cruiser, try to stand upright with his duty revolver clutched loosely in one hand, and then drop to his knees in a delayed reaction to shock right in front of the opening door of the Camry.

Distinctly feeling his heart pound against his unyielding sternum as his mind and body went numb, Henry Culver reacted exactly the way that his Academy instructors had intended he would react in such a situation—according to his training, and to his deeply seated instincts to protect and survive.

A second pattern of .24 caliber lead pellets from Culver's shotgun blew most of the window glass out of the Camry's driver's side door.

The explosive effects of the third and fourth shotgun rounds from Culver's shotgun shattered the Camry's front windshield into hundreds of squarish, plastic-laminated shards that were still tumbling off the sloped hood of the crippled vehicle when Culver, tossing aside the now-empty shotgun in favor of his fully loaded .357 Smith & Wesson revolver, took five forward-lunging steps to put himself between Delacroix and the Camry.

In effect, putting himself in a position to protect his fellow officer.

And in a position to kill.

In a blur of motion, Henry Culver thrust the barrel of the weapon in through the shattered driver's side window frame with both gloved hands. He was a fraction of a second away from triggering the first of three hollow-pointed rounds into the face of the first suspect when his adrenaline-widened eyes registered the fact that the two robbers were not armed adult male suspects he was expecting . . . but rather two *unarmed* and absolutely terrified young boys—the older surely no more than fifteen—who were huddled together in mute, tear-streaked shock on the floor of the Camry amid hundred of small, squarish chunks of windshield safety glass and a half dozen light-reflecting, silver-coated bags of stolen potato chips and candy.

As it turned out, the series of events that took place at the scene, and the altercation shortly thereafter at Chalmer's Market between police officer Henry Culver and the store manager, who had falsely reported the "big handguns" (*"Because you cops always take your goddamned time getting here when I report a petty theft, that's why!"*), were monitored by several hundred Fairfax County citizens (mostly ham operators and scanner freaks), thanks to the frantic radio transmissions of Lieutenant Pete Christey, the District Eight watch commander, Patrol Sergeant Jack Hattabaugh, and four other patrol officers who managed to violate a half dozen traffic safety rules apiece in order to get to Chalmer's Market before they had an Internal Affairs–type homicide on their hands.

As far as the vast majority of these audio eavesdroppers were concerned, the fact that things seemed to be getting out of hand in the Fair Oaks Patrol District was, at worst, mildly disturbing. They were safe in their homes; the whole situation was far more exciting than TV; and even more importantly, they really didn't give a damn.

It went without saying, of course, that to these people, the name Henry Culver and the call sign Eight-Forty-Charlie meant absolutely nothing.

Which in and of itself was ironic, because the five individuals who certainly *would* have recognized Henry Culver's call sign, and who would have been absolutely *stunned* to learn of the incident at Chalmer's Market, had long since gone to sleep.

Three of these men had already made their positions regarding Henry Culver absolutely clear. Elliott Parkinson and J. Winston Weathersby would continue to use Culver as bait, in order to locate their rogue agents and to protect their incredibly risky but potentially rewarding operation. Arthur Traynor, on the other hand, would remain patient and watchful in the shadows as he continued to dig into the L'Que incident, prepared to intervene with every dirty trick in his tech agent's bag in the event that the life of Henry Culver or the welfare of his beloved Agency were ever threatened.

The fourth man was in no condition to care, one way or the other, about anyone except himself.

But as far as the fifth man was concerned, the events that would decide the fate of Eight-Forty-Charlie had already been set into motion.

Tomorrow afternoon, Henry Lucas Culver was scheduled to die.

Chapter Twenty-four

Friday, 0730 hours

Somehow managing to pull himself out of bed after his alarm had gone off for the second time, John Russelli washed, dressed, ate breakfast, waited for his wife and daughters to depart for work and school, cleared away the breakfast dishes, drained his coffee cup in one final bitter-tasting gulp, and then limped purposefully over to the sliding glass door that led out to the backyard.

Goddamned dogs, he thought as he stepped out into the cold, frosty air. *Dig up the yard, crap all over the place, and drive you out of your skull with their barking. Then, when you finally get used to having them around, they go and die on you.*

Shit.

Intent on getting the job over with quickly, Russelli hobbled over to the entrance of the new doghouse that he'd built one Saturday afternoon by simply cutting a twelve-by-eighteen inch hole through the insulated back wall of his garage. A magnetized rubber door flap provided the only access to a two-by-six-by-three-foot-high box—constructed out of half inch plywood, two bottles of wood glue, and at least five pounds of wood screws—that Russelli had bolted solidly to the garage wall studs.

The result, in John Russelli's view, was the premier doghouse of the neighborhood—an illusion spoiled only by the fact that up until last week, both of his dogs had steadfastly refused to get anywhere near the thing.

And then too, it hadn't occurred to Russelli that some sort of access from *inside* the garage might have made cleaning jobs—such as replacing shredded paper, or removing the rigored carcasses of family pets—a little easier. Such thoughts *had* occurred to Sharon Russelli, but she had wisely held her tongue, fearing that her impulsive husband might decide to cut a larger hole in the side of her house instead.

John Russelli was like that.

Although, in fact, the doghouse was only a minor example of the things that Russelli did to distract himself from the stressful demands of his job. As a rule, most of his projects were excessively large, absurdly solid, and jarringly imaginative. Or, as one of the neighbors who had witnessed the garage wall cutting with a mixture of stunned disbelief and judicious silence had put it diplomatically: there wasn't anything too outrageous that John Russelli wouldn't do for his wife and kids.

Of course the neighbor had made that comment while standing in front of a bright blue, eight-by-eight-by-twelve-foot-high castle (supported internally by four solidly braced twelve-foot four-by-fours, and complete with parapets, two levels of wooden decks over an open sandbox basement, internal and external ladders, eight rope-operated cannon ports, and an escape slide from the upper deck) that Russelli had built for his twin daughters about eight years ago.

There were any number of interesting speculations as to why a man like John Russelli would build a twelve-foot-high castle in the middle of his backyard. But the most rational view was held by Sharon Russelli, who simply believed that her inwardly warm and gentle husband had always wanted a castle as a child, and saw no reason why he shouldn't have one as an adult. It was as good a theory as any; but no one, least of all Russelli, had any idea as to why he painted it bright blue.

He just did it, much in the way that he allowed himself to be bullied and manipulated by a pair of small, slender, and absolutely gorgeous teenage daughters who—aside from a few unfortunate mental traits—bore almost no resemblance whatsoever to the hulking figure that stood out in the cold morning air, glaring down at a dog door that had been cut much too small.

This is it, John Russelli swore to himself as he squatted down painfully next to the rubber door, his back less than six feet away from the near wall of the looming castle. *I don't care if they scream, holler, beg, or cry. No more goddamned dogs!*

Trying to avoid having to lie down in the cold, slushy snow, it took Russelli several minutes before he was able to get into a position where he could see the hairy unmoving body with the use of his flashlight. After making several unsuccessful attempts to work his thick arm and shoulder in through what he now recognized as an incredibly tiny door flap, Russelli muttered a few appropriate comments to the world in general. Then he sighed, stood up, and walked over to the tool shed.

Better to get the hole dug first before that goddamned Nori wakes up, he told himself, remembering the young dachshund's annoying habit of chewing on anything it could get its small, sharp teeth into as he reached for the gardening spade, stopped, shook his head, and then grabbed the more practical heavy-bladed shovel.

At this time of the year, with the ground surface nearly frozen solid, he decided, the first five or six inches would probably involve some hard digging.

Which, of course, it did. But it hadn't occurred to Russelli that the next twelve might be worse.

After twenty minutes of grunting, chopping, bending, scraping, and cursing, the frustrated burglary sergeant stared bleakly into a ragged eighteen-inch hole that tapered down to an area approximately one foot square at the bottom.

Russelli had originally intended to go down about four feet, to keep the young dachshund from digging up his deceased mate and causing general havoc around the household. But four feet down meant chopping and scraping through about thirty more inches of rock and clay-based hardpan.

Russelli briefly considered the idea of tossing the dirt back into the hole, and then hauling the carcass to the dump; or even better, tossing it in the nearby woods. But he knew he'd never hear the end of it if his justifiably suspicious daughters ever found out that he'd done *that.*

It was his own fault, he realized. He was the one who'd made the big deal about the Russelli tradition of burying the family pets in the backyard, mostly because the girls had come home early from shopping before he'd had a chance to properly dispose of the son of a bitch cat that had pissed on his sweater.

It was some time after the cat episode that his daughters

had threatened to dig up and autopsy the next one of their pets that "died all of a sudden of old age."

Goddamn thick-headed little brats probably would, too, Russelli thought glumly. *Just like their mother.*

He took another look at the sorry depth of the hole. *Maybe another six inches or so,* he decided, stretching his aching shoulder and back muscles, and then leaning forward on the shovel to give his throbbing leg a rest and the entire matter some further consideration.

He was still leaning on the shovel, trying to come up with a reasonable compromise that would leave him with enough strength to get to the station and collapse at his desk, when he heard the dog door flap back and forth behind his back.

Grateful for any excuse to abandon the shovel for a few minutes, Russelli decided that he'd better lock the dachshund up before the single-minded little canine decided to chew off a piece of his former yard mate for breakfast.

"Come on, you mangy excuse for a dog," Russelli growled as he started to turn to glare at the offending animal, "get your butt out of . . ."

And then he stopped dead still.

As John Russelli continued to stand there in his backyard, mute and stunned, an elderly, stumpy-legged dog that resembled—as best anyone could tell—the unlikely cross of a collie, a German shepherd, and a bull terrier, slowly pulled himself through the door flap of his doghouse, stretched his arthritis-stiffened legs, and then walked over to Russelli.

Standing at the edge of the shallow hole, the long-suffering Ocha—who had absolutely *not* wanted to leave his warm doghouse in the middle of the night when Sharon Russelli had tried to rouse him—peered down into the rocky depths for a few moments, looked back up at Russelli as if to say "I could have told you this is a lousy place to dig, you dumb asshole," casually lifted one of his stiff rear legs to send a stream of urine trickling down the clay-smeared blade of Russelli's shovel, and then slowly wandered over to the patio deck to see if the early arriving crows had left anything in his food dish for breakfast.

When Detective Sergeant John Russelli finally limped into the Fairfax County Police Department's Central Headquarters building at 8:35 that Friday morning, the first person he saw was his immediate supervisor, Lieutenant Morris Markham Craven, the deputy commander of the Criminal Investigations Bureau's Major Crimes Division.

It was especially unfortunate that these two men should meet at this particular moment of time, because Craven was very much distracted by the possibility that he might be held accountable for some of the mind-boggling events that had occurred during the previous evening; whereas Russelli wasn't even *remotely* in the mood to be civil to a man that he had once described as possessing all of the supervisory and social skills of a rabid bat.

In effect, it was precisely that sort of chance encounter—of lethally armed but sorely mismatched antagonists—that in less civilized times would have quickly resulted in an out-and-out bloodbath.

"Little late this morning, aren't we, Russelli?" Craven suggested in a tight voice.

For a brief, uncertain moment, John Russelli half-seriously considered taking Craven out, right there in the Central Headquarters lobby. But then he considered the effect that such an act—meritorious as it might be—would probably have on his retirement pension.

Bound to be somebody around this goddamned place who actually likes the little prick, he reminded himself. *Screw it.*

"My wife wanted me to bury our dog this morning," Russelli muttered, reaching past his crisply uniformed boss to pull a stack of typed reports, letters, administrative memos, and crudely torn and folded teletypes from his mail slot. "Had to wait until the kids were gone to dig the hole."

"Oh . . . uh, sorry to hear that," Craven said, hurriedly switching mental gears in an effort to come up with some appropriate comment that would demonstrate his supervisory concern, even though he thoroughly despised—not to mention feared—the irreverent detective sergeant. "Must have been . . . uh, the old one."

Craven vaguely remembered Russelli mentioning something about having two kids and two dogs, and it stood to reason that the older one had kicked off. Viewing himself as a born-to-command type, Craven took pride in being "in tune" with his troops—something that he'd been told the selection board considered in making their cuts for the senior command ranks. The trouble was, Craven really didn't give a damn about his men—much less their kids and dogs—and it showed.

"You know," Craven finally said, setting his face with a properly sympathetic smile as Russelli continued to ignore his presence, "I think one of the hardest things I ever had to do when I was a kid was to put my dog in one of those holes."

"Yeah, I know what you mean," Russelli nodded absent-mindedly. "Couldn't get mine to get in the damned thing."

As Craven blinked in momentary confusion, Russelli finished scanning the last of the printouts and then looked down at his supervisor with a slightly unfocused expression in his reddened eyes. "Spent a half hour out there digging the fucking hole, freezing my ass off, and the ungrateful little bastard pisses on my shovel. You imagine that? Hell of a way to start out a day."

Craven blinked a couple more times, his mouth opening wide as he started to say something. But then he took another look at the glazed expression in John Russelli's eyes and decided against it. Instead, he put his arm out to block Russelli's way into the Criminal Investigations Bureau corridor.

"You've got company this morning," he said, gesturing with his forehead in the direction of Russelli's office. "The major wants you in the conference room, now. Oh, and you'll need this."

Craven handed Russelli a thick manila pouch folder

that looked to contain about forty or fifty pages of typed reports. The folder was sealed at the wide flap with two pieces of bright red security tapes imprinted with the words: CONFIDENTIAL—INTERNAL AFFAIRS DIVISION. The same words were stamped in bold red letters on both sides of the folder.

Russelli's tired eyes opened wide as they focused on the brightly stamped warning.

"I don't suppose you know what this is all about?" he asked with irrational hope, feeling his chest tighten with anxiety as his sleep-starved mind tried to figure out what he might have done—or more to the point, what he might have been *caught* doing—that would warrant an internal affairs investigation by the headhunters.

There were any number of possibilities, and one in particular that he didn't want to think about at all.

Craven shook his head emphatically, giving the distinct impression that in addition to not having any idea what this folder was all about, he didn't even *want* to know. The IAD had that sort of effect on departmental "risers."

"Better see for yourself," he advised unhelpfully. Then, before Russelli could say or ask anything else, he turned and began to walk hurriedly in the opposite direction.

Favoring Craven's rapid departure with an appropriate glare and muttered comment, Russelli shook his head, glanced down once more at the sealed folder, sighed deeply, and then limped down the bright green carpet that highlighted the pale green block walls of the corridor toward the Criminal Investigation Bureau's conference room. The heavy, sinking sensation in his chest grew heavier as he realized that the door was shut tight.

Taking in a deep, resigned breath, Russelli reached for the heavy brass doorknob, pushed the door open, and found himself staring at a number of all-too-familiar solemn faces, which included the commanders of the five operational headquarters bureaus of the department; Captain Harold Mays of Internal Affairs; Captain Mike Donahugh from District

Eight; Dr. Benjamin Scholtz, the county's resident psychiatrist; Patrol Sergeant Jack Hattabaugh; and the even more solemn and familiar face of Police Officer Henry Culver.

Molly Hunsacker was sitting back in her padded easy chair and sipping at an early morning beer, trying to figure out how to use a very complicated remote controller that she had just stolen, when a sudden high-pitched beep suddenly warned her that she had an urgent message waiting.

Grumbling to herself, Molly-the-Hun pulled herself out of the chair, grabbed her beer, walked over to the portable computer on her desk, jabbed impatiently at the enter key, and quickly scanned the message. Then she began to curse feverently as she dragged a chair over to the desk, sat down, and laboriously typed out a reply:

GODDAMN IT, WHY GO BACK AGAIN? WE GOT EVERYTHING THE FIRST TIME. THERE'S NOTH-ING LEFT WORTH STEALING.

For almost three minutes, while Molly Hunsacker sipped contemplatively at her beer, the portable computer on her desk remained mute. Then, with a beep that somehow seemed louder than the first, a second message flashed on the screen.

This time Molly read the words slowly, blinked, and read them even slower a second time.

Then, smiling widely for the first time that morning, she chugged the remaining six ounces of beer in one gulp, crumpled and tossed the can into the corner of her living room, and then started whistling as she picked up her wrench and headed for the door.

"Face it, Russelli, I screwed up."

Detective Sergeant John Russelli looked up from the last of the reports in the IAD's lengthy investigative file to peer inquisitively at the individual who sat slumped in the chair on the other side of his desk in his small, light green–painted block-wall room.

They were alone there. The other occupants had left the station ten minutes earlier to jointly inform the police chief of their decision.

"Oh I don't know," Russelli said after putting down the last page of the report. "Way I see it, you were doing pretty good, all things considered, right up to the point where you pulled out that Smith & Wesson and said, and I quote . . ."

Russelli hesitated a moment, reaching for the file again and fumbling through several dozen loose pages before he came up with the report he wanted.

". . . *'This* is a big handgun, you stupid son of a bitch.' "

Russelli peered over the top of the typed page to stare at Culver with a pleasant smile on his dark, craggy face. "You *really* say that?" he inquired hopefully.

Culver nodded glumly.

"Good for you." Russelli smiled approvingly. "Should of pistol-whipped him, too, while you were at it. Probably illegal, immoral, and unjustifiable, but definitely warranted. Fifty-fifty our old buddy Radlick would have gotten you off with probation."

"Russelli, I damn near blew away a couple of kids," Culver whispered in a weary and hoarse voice, the anguish visible in his eyes.

"But you didn't." The stocky burglary sergeant shrugged philosophically. "Damn-nears don't count for much in this business."

"Yeah, that's roughly what Scholtz and Donahugh said."

"Hey, buddy-boy, don't forget that Donahugh backed you up in there," Russelli reminded. "Way things are going right now, I'd give my left nut to have a station commander who'd go to bat for me like that."

Culver nodded. "Yeah, Donahugh's a good man."

"Hey, look at it this way," Russelli suggested. "Vinny deserved to die in that T-C, but he didn't. The parents of those two kids oughta be out looking for a lawyer to sue your ass off for shooting the shit out of their car at the very least, but the father's an ex-cop who's too embarrassed and pissed off to think straight. And, if nothing else, Donahugh should have put you on suspension, just to cover his own tail. But the thing is, aside from a little questionable behavior at the store, you did everything pretty much by the book. Fact of the matter is, all things considered, you came out of this whole thing pretty clean."

"You call this *clean?*"

Russelli shrugged. "Hey, the way it stands now, the department's looking to drop charges of petty theft, no driver's license, and felony-reckless on the kids; and felony false report with resulting injuries on your buddy Chalmers, all in exchange for a wash on a couple of excessive force and 'conduct unbecoming' counts against yours truly. Whereupon Chalmers generously buys the kid's father a new car, and we maybe have to overlook a couple of parental child abuse situations a few weeks down the road. Yeah, I'd call that clean. Best deal I've ever seen come out of the county attorney's office yet."

"So what you trying to tell me is that I got lucky?"

"That's it, buddy-boy." Russelli nodded. "Just one thing I don't understand."

"What's that?" he asked, his voice raspy from lack of sleep.

"How come you and Tess never got married?"

"What?" Culver's eyebrows furrowed in tired confusion.

"You, me, Tess, Sharon, Paul, and Doreen. How long did all of us run around together?"

"Russelli, for Christ sake . . ."

"Since tenth grade," Russelli said, answering his own question. "That's when Sharon's old man got transferred to the DC office. Crusty old bastard. Never did like me, did he?" He chuckled.

"No, not much." Culver nodded in agreement, the first vestige of a smile appearing on his face.

"Hey, remember in high school, when we all wanted to go

to that dance; but then we couldn't decide who was going to go with who, so we flipped that coin and you got Sharon, and then that prick—what was his name, the guy who wrestled heavyweight?"

Culver shrugged indifferently. "I don't know, Jim, John, Moose. Something like that."

"Yeah, anyway, remember at the dance, how he came up, trying to cut in on you and Sharon. You told him to shove off, and so he told them about the coin toss, and they flipped out, screaming at us, Sharon throwing the corsage in your face, and then you . . ."

"Yeah, wonderful night," Culver interrupted glumly.

Russelli sat in silence for a moment, reminiscing. "You know, all the things we did together—football, soccer, wrestling—I *never* saw you lose it like that. Didn't know you had it in you. Goddamned Henry Culver, skinny fucking kid who was going to be this hotshot mad scientist, biochemical electronics, something like that, save the friggin' world, couldn't fight worth a shit . . ."

"You trying to cheer me up or something?"

". . . puts the guy's head right through the auditorium wall," Russelli continued on. "As I recall, Paul and I had to keep pulling about half the wrestling team and a couple of teachers off your back 'cause you kept going after the guy. Wouldn't quit, even though you were getting your ass kicked. Just about turned the place into a friggin' riot until the cops showed up." Russelli smiled pleasantly at the memory. "Always figured the only thing that saved us from being thrown out of school was that the three of us were more torn up than all the other guys."

Russelli hesitated a moment. "Hey, remember what they used to call you after that? Killer Culver. Mad scientist, romantic, and general idiot. Rep like that, I thought the girls'd never go out with us again." The stocky investigator grinned.

"Hey listen, Russelli, do me a favor, okay?"

"Yeah, what's that?"

"Don't lay all that Killer Culver shit out on Scholtz, okay?

I already spent an hour with the guy this morning trying to convince him I'm not a flipped-out cowboy. Then I had to sit there and listen to him tell me how I've got to do everything exactly the same way the next time or else . . ."

". . . you're gonna be the one who catches a bullet, because the next one'll be for real," Russelli finished. "Scholtz is right, you know. Just because he's a nutcase himself doesn't mean he doesn't know what he's talking about."

"Yeah, I know. Get back up on the goddamned horse and try not to fall off next time."

"Exactly." Russelli nodded cheerfully. " 'Course they didn't exactly give you another horse, did they?"

Culver looked around the room with a resigned expression on his face. "Not exactly, no."

"More like a half-crippled, run-down mule with hemorrhoids, if you want to know the truth." Russelli sighed. "Anyway, quit dodging the question. How come . . . ?"

Culver shrugged. "It just didn't work out. I mean, we tried. I guess we still try. Going out to dinner or a movie every now and then, things like that."

"You two still shacking?"

"What? Jesus Christ, Russelli . . ."

"Hey, Sharon says she knows, but she won't tell me. Says it's none of my business. So?"

"Great, now I've got you worried about my sex life, too." Culver grinned tiredly. "Yeah, we get together every now and then. Thing is, we're still good friends and all that, but every time we try to make something stick long-term, it ends up coming apart."

"That's pretty much what Sharon said. I guess she and Tess still talk about it a lot. Something about how you're always playing around with the computers and electronics, always being called out all the time, never being around. Didn't realize you forensic-types worked the same hours as real cops."

"Yeah, hell of a job," Culver grumbled, looking around the room with some degree of interest for the first time that morning. "Okay," he said with a long sigh, "so now what?"

"You mean as in here?"

Culver just rolled his eyes toward the ceiling and nodded his head.

"Well, buddy, the way I see it, for a goodly portion of what little remains of our illustrious law enforcement careers . . ."

"We get to be burglary detectives," Culver finished glumly.

"That's exactly right. Culver and Russelli, comrades-in-arms, back to back, and all that shit. Just like the old days." Russelli grinned.

"Wonderful. Okay, so tell me, comrade-in-arms, just what the hell is it that we burg detectives do around here all day?"

"Very important shit," Russelli said reassuringly. "First of all, did you get any sleep last night?"

"Couple of hours on a cot in the briefing room. I'm okay."

" 'Bout all you'll ever get around this place anyway. Least-wise, that's all I ever get. Tell you what. After we get a few administrative details out of the way, why don't you head on home, take a shower, catch a couple more hours, and then meet me back at the house around two-thirty. Give us a chance to take a tour of the neighborhood, let you get a look at your new clients."

"Sounds good to me. Especially the sleep part."

"So anyway," Russelli went on, "you know the chain of command around here. We report to Craven. Craven reports to Bullar, and we don't give a shit about anybody else, right?"

"Got it." Culver nodded groggily. "So what about Craven? He as bad as I hear?"

"Worse. Typical lieutenant, only flat-ass dumb to boot. Useless as shit, but willing to stab just about anybody in the back to make grade. Fortunately for us peons, he's usually too busy dreaming about those captain bars and trying to tell Stewart how to run homicide investigations to care much about res-burgs. Long as we stay out of his way, we're fine."

"*I* may be fine, but what about you and your leg? I hear he's really been gunning for you lately about that physical."

Russelli nodded. "Yeah, that's another problem. The little

shithead and I don't exactly see eye to eye on what it takes to be a cop, but I've got a couple of ideas on how to work it all out.

"Anyway," he went on, patting the irregular stack of Xeroxed and stapled reports that overflowed his "IN" box, "what we do here is take these incident reports—two of which I happened to notice you wrote last night—log them into the system, put pins on the map board, put the stolen property into the computer, and check to see if there are any hits on numbers or prints. And then maybe, if we have time, we go out and talk to people."

Culver closed his eyes and nodded his head slowly. "I don't suppose there's any chance that, every now and then, we might actually go out and make an arrest?"

"You want to make an arrest?" Russelli asked, sounding surprised.

"Last I heard, that's what cops are *supposed* to do," Culver suggested hopefully.

Russelli shrugged expansively. "My partner wants to make an arrest, that's exactly what we'll do."

After rummaging through his "PENDING" box for a few moments, Russelli hesitated for a moment, reached into his desk drawer, pulled out a clipped together half inch stack of burg reports, circled a number with a half-chewed pencil stub, and then reached for the phone on his desk.

"Boone, that you?" Russelli growled into the phone. "Yeah, of course it's Russelli. Who the fuck you think it was? Yeah, well, listen up, shit-for-brains, I want to see you in my office at, oh, say about nine-thirty tomorrow morning. Yeah, I know it's a Saturday. So what? Didn't you know us cops work on weekends, too, just like burglars? What? Goddamned right you're gonna get arrested. What'd you think we're gonna do, swap brownie recipes? Mood I'm in right now, you'll be goddamned lucky if I don't rip your ugly head off and piss in the hole. Yeah, right, nine-thirty, my office. Bye."

Russelli hung up the phone and looked up at Culver with a beaming smile on his face. "There, how's that?"

Culver was staring at Russelli with a blank, disbelieving expression on his face.

"You've *got* to be kidding," he finally said.

"About what?"

"You think he's really gonna show up?"

"Always does." Russelli shrugged as he stood up. "Like I said, shit-for-brains. You ready to go?"

"Where?" Culver asked, resignation evident in his voice.

"Map room," Russelli said as he hefted the new pile of reports. "Gotta get those pins in."

"Oh yeah." Culver nodded as he got up out of his chair. "I almost forgot. The important shit."

"Right," Russelli said. He started for the door, and then stopped and put his hand on Culver's shoulder. "Hey listen, buddy, since we're gonna be partners and all that, you mind if I ask a favor, right up front?"

"You want me to put in the pins?"

"Naw, the sergeants do that," Russelli said seriously. "I just thought maybe, some night, you might get a call from Sharon saying I'm dead or stiff or something."

"Dead . . . or stiff?" Culver repeated, blinking his eyes as he tried very hard to keep from grinning because Russelli *looked* like he was serious.

"Yeah, right." Russelli nodded with an absolutely no change in his expression. "Anyway, it's no big deal. I just thought maybe, you know, you could stop by and make a double check, before she has me buried."

Culver just stared at his longtime friend, remembering as he did so the final words of the Internal Affairs division commander: "What we'd like you to do, Henry, is keep an eye on Russelli. See how he gets around with that bum leg. How he handles stress, things like that. Just keep an eye on him."

"You want me to . . ."

"No big deal," Russelli said, shaking his head distractedly as he reached for the door. "I just figured, you know, I might be a whole lot better off someday if somebody made sure she got a second opinion."

Chapter Twenty-five

Friday, 1030 hours

Thoroughly distracted by the events of the last twenty-four hours, Henry Culver parked his long-unwashed Mustang in his driveway, walked through about thirty feet of slush and mud to his porch with his Sam Browne gun belt and equipment bag slung over his shoulder, and then spent several seconds fumbling around for his keys before he finally looked up at his concealed alarm board and realized that someone was in his house.

His first impulse was to smile and reach for the doorknob, thinking that Tess Beasley had changed her mind about the district attorney, but in typical fashion had forgotten her key for the virtually pickproof stainless steel code locks that he'd installed on his front and back doors.

He considered that possibility for a few moments, and then slowly drew his magnetized key back out of the lock.

It was a nice idea, but Tess Beasley couldn't pick the push-button lock on her bathroom door, much less a code lock, Culver reminded himself as he reached over his shoulder to draw the heavy PR-24 baton from his Sam Browne belt. Then he hesitated once again as his self-protective instincts demanded attention.

But if not Tess, then who?

And more importantly, how?

At that moment, the courtroom image of John Doe Thirty-three thumbing through the grotesquely violent photo album flashed though Henry Culver's mind. The image jarred at his senses for a brief moment before he shook his head and smiled, remembering his phone call to the reluctantly helpful nurse.

Digger was still in the Ward, so it wasn't him.

It's the notes, he told himself. The note that Radlick had shown him, and the one that somebody had sent Gauss. That's what was setting him off.

The logical conclusion, Culver decided as he continued to stare at his securely locked front door, was that Radlick had given the original threatening note back to his client, and that Digger had mailed the notes from the Ward, just to let everybody know that he was still thinking about them.

But he's still in the can, so who the hell cares what he thinks. Culver shrugged. *No big deal.*

No big deal at all, except that he still had two red lights showing on his alarm system because somebody who *hadn't* come in through the doors or windows had been moving around inside his house tripping the sonics.

Yeah, wonderful.

Culver glanced down at the grooved handle of the baton, thought about the expression in Digger's pale blue eyes one more time, and then firmly moved his right hand over to the rubberized black grip of the .357 Smith & Wesson that had already gotten him into an incredible amount of trouble during the past twenty-four hours.

He had the heavy revolver halfway out of its holster when he remembered that he'd dumped the rounds, and put them in his right front pants pocket, before handing the .357 weapon over to the watch commander at Chalmer's Market. The loose cartridges were still in his pocket. He could feel them pressing against his thigh.

Quickly scanning the area around his porch for any sign of movement, Culver transferred the cold, blue-steel pistol to his left hand; carefully and quietly broke open the cylinder; and then dropped his right hand down to one of the speed-loader pouches on his Smith Browne belt—his ears acutely alert for the first sound of movement.

One through fourteen—every door and window in the house—all green, he thought, mentally decoding the pattern as he unsnapped the upside-down leather pouch and allowed the heavy, cylindrical, cartridge-filled speed-loader to drop into his hand.

Fourteen greens lights meant no entry, but reds on fifteen and sixteen confirmed movement inside the house—which could, Culver knew, represent a simple circuit problem, or even the movement of a small animal.

The problem with *that,* however, was that one, he had wired the motion detectors on separate circuits to avoid just that sort of problem; two, the sensors were mounted three feet off the floor; and three, he didn't *have* any small animals moving around inside his house—not even a goldfish.

Inside movement but no entry.

Hell of a trick, Culver thought, sweeping his eyes back and forth around his immediate area as he used the tips of his fingers to align the cylindrical loader, feeding and then releasing the high-velocity hollow-point rounds into the six chambers simultaneously. Then he closed the cylinder and allowed the empty speed-loader to drop out of his hand.

Some distant portion of his mind recorded the sound of the plastic loader bouncing off the porch and down the driveway as he slid the Sam Browne belt off his shoulder, gently placed it on the wooden floor of the porch, brought the Smith & Wesson up against the side of his head, and stepped softly over to the side of the doorframe.

Then he used his left hand to slide the thick magnetized key into the sturdy code lock.

So where?

Not the roof.

The doorknob turned noiselessly in Culver's left hand and then he paused, listening for any sound of movement as he felt his chest tighten.

Nothing. .

Not the garage door. He shook his head. It was wired too.

Stepping in closer to the left side of the door and placing the toe of his right foot up against the frame in the classic police barricade stance that left only the right side of his face and gun hand exposed, Culver took a deep breath and then pushed the door inward, letting it swing smoothly on well-oiled hinges into the padded doorstop.

Still nothing.

Not the air ducts—too small. He went on through the list in his head as he continued to search the semidarkened entryway.

Floor's solid. No way in through the crawl space.

Taking a deep steadying breath, Culver stepped slowly into entryway, and then spent several seconds staring into the portion of his darkened living room that was visible from the light coming in over his shoulder.

There was no sign of movement, no unusual noises, and no indication that anything had been disturbed—nothing at all to explain why the two red warning lights over his front porch were blinking ominously.

The beams cross right in the middle of the entryway and the hallway, Culver reminded himself. The entryway was clear, so that left the hallway, bedrooms and kitchen.

All the good hiding spots.

Shielding his eyes from the anticipated glare, Culver flipped on the hall lights, swept the barrel of the .357 in a rapid left-to-right arc that matched the sweep of his squinting eyes, started forward toward the living room, and then hesitated as he came up to the wall-mounted arming box with a matching three-by-five grid of green and red lights.

Oh for Christ's sake.

After examining the box, the lights, and the floor, Culver purposely walked forward into the living room, sat down in his recliner chair, placed the loaded handgun on the adjacent lamp table within easy reach of his right hand, leaned back in the chair, and then let his eyes drift to the darkened kitchen doorway.

He waited a few moments in silence, reminding himself that he'd better be right, and then spoke in the direction of the empty doorway in a tired voice.

"Hi, Traynor."

A dark, shadowy, heavyset figure appeared in the doorway, causing Culver to smile with a combination of relief and amusement.

"Glad to see it's you," the beefy Sci-Tech associate director commented as he walked into the living room and sat down in the chair on the opposite side of the lamp table from Culver. As he did so, he placed four frosty bottles of Michelob beer next to the Smith & Wesson. "I assume you rigged the sonics on a remote circuit?"

"That's right."

"Any backdoor routes I could have taken?"

"To make a complete reset without the code?" Culver shrugged. "I don't know, I guess you could have cut the ground wire coming out of the box, but you'd have to be pretty lucky. There's twenty identically colored wires in the cable. All but one power a drop switch to an audible. Bad odds."

Arthur Traynor nodded in agreement, but then stared at his ex-employee with a look of disapproval. "Even so, don't you think you were being a little careless, coming in and sitting down like that?" he suggested as he twisted the caps off two of the bottles.

"Not necessarily. Care for one of my beers?"

"Yes, thank you." Traynor nodded, taking a deep swig. "You knew?"

"Couldn't think of any B&E types around here who'd have the know-how to crack a code lock and rig a reset without setting off the fireworks," Culver said. "And besides," he added with a smile, "how many burglars have a fetish about cleaning up after their wire cuts?"

"Ah, very good," Traynor said, nodding his head in apparent satisfaction.

So what are you doing here, Traynor? Culver wondered

as he sat there and stared at his ex-boss. *Something to do with Forecastle, or the Chalmer's Market business, or what?*

"My predictable work habits aside," Traynor said as he placed the empty bottle back beside the deadly revolver and picked up a full one, "this might be a very bad time to be making careless assumptions about your welfare. I understand that you received a threat."

"If you're talking about some Ivy League kid who thinks his name is 'Forecastle,' he made it pretty clear that he's not real happy about my lack of enthusiasm for his project—whatever that might be," Culver added pointedly.

"Oh, our young Mr. Weathersby is nowhere near as threatening as he would love to have people believe."

"That's nice to hear."

"His boss, on the other hand, is something else entirely."

"And just who might his boss be?"

"Elliott Parkinson. A rather insufferable fellow who happens to be the new AD for Operations."

"Is that supposed to mean something to me?"

"Perhaps. Elliott Parkinson has the potential to cause people a great deal of grief if he really puts his mind to it. And for reasons that are not entirely clear to me at the moment, that mind seems to be focused on you."

"Me?"

"Among many others."

"What the hell did I do to get the AD of Operations for the CIA interested in me?"

"I don't know. That's one of the questions I'm trying to get answered as we speak."

Henry Culver was silent for a few moments, and then finally asked: "Is this something I should be concerned about?"

"Oh, Elliott's unpredictable, of course. That goes without saying for someone in his position. But fortunately for many people, you and I included," Traynor added with emphasis, "he seems to lack that certain sense of innate intelligence that would make him truly dangerous."

"But he *is* on our side, right?"

"Oh yes, certainly." Traynor nodded absentmindedly. "It isn't a question of ideology. That isn't the problem."

"I assume that's meant to be encouraging?" Culver asked with barely muted sarcasm.

Traynor paused.

"Henry, I find myself in a dilemma as to what I can tell you without . . ."

The ringing of Culver's front doorbell interrupted Traynor's comment and caused him to turn his head quickly in the direction of the hallway.

"Were you expecting company?" he asked, coming up to his feet in a smooth, easy movement that suggested a man of far fewer years and less mass.

"I wasn't expecting anybody, *including* you," Culver reminded as he picked a homemade remote up off the lamp table and aimed it in the general direction of the TV. Moments later, the image of a large black man wearing a rumpled suit and carrying a pair of aluminum cases filled the screen.

"Do you know him?" Traynor asked in a deadly calm voice.

Culver nodded. "Brad Carpenter, Homicide detective." Then he blinked in astonishment as he watched his ex-mentor slide a small semiautomatic pistol back inside his waistband.

"What's with the hardware? You starting to get jumpy in your old age?"

"As a matter of fact, yes," Traynor answered. "Can you get rid of him?"

Jesus, Traynor, Culver thought, *when did you start carrying a gun? What the hell's going on out there?*

"I don't know. Let's find out," Culver said in what he hoped was his normal tone of voice. He hit another button on his remote, and then spoke toward the TV: "Hi, Carp, what's up?"

The image on the screen turned around sharply, searching for the source of the unexpected voice.

"Hi, Henry," Detective Brad Carpenter finally said after he located the overhead speaker. "Hate to bother you at home, but we're still short on cameras out in the field and the one you lent me is kinda acting up. You left Quinzio's in your cruiser last night, but I can't get it to work either."

"You need it looked at right now?" Culver asked, eyeing Traynor.

"Yeah, really I do." The video image nodded. "Sorry to bust in on you like this, but things are really going to shit out there. Stewart told me to be back at the station in a half hour with either you or a functional camera, period."

Culver shut off the mike pickup and looked over at Traynor. "Is it going to cause you any grief to be spotted here?"

"Very possibly. That's all right, I'll get in touch with you later." Traynor headed toward the darkened kitchen doorway, and then paused and turned to face Culver.

"Just one thing, Henry. The threat you received. Not the one from Elliott's little assistant—the other one."

"The other one?" Culver said noncommittally, staring at one of the few men he truly respected with what he hoped was an appropriately blank and quizzical expression on his face.

You know about the note. Jesus Christ, Traynor, how the hell . . . ?

"Yes, the other one," Traynor said. "I understand your reluctance to discuss such things with an outsider, but if you would consider taking an old man's advice . . .

"Anytime, Arthur," Culver said, nodding slowly.

I trust you, Traynor. Or at least I trust you as much as I trust anybody out of that shop. But I still don't want to go back. And what's all this crap about the note? Digger's in the can, so who the hell are you talking about? Forecastle?

"It would be a very good idea if you could try to be a little more . . . careful for the next few days," Traynor said in an uncharacteristically hesitant voice that had a jarring effect on Culver's mental alarms. As far back as he could remember, Culver had never known Arthur Traynor to be anything other than completely self-assured and confident.

"Among other things," Traynor went on, "you should consider upgrading your security system immediately. I'd recommend at least another pair of detectors to cover the kitchen at the very minimum."

"An upgrade?" Culver said, incredulous. "You expect me to believe that you left your office in the middle of the afternoon, drove all the way out here, tapped though my security system, and then sat there in my kitchen for God knows how long, just so you could give me some friendly advice about keeping my doors locked?"

The dark shadow framed in the doorway shook his head.

"No, Henry, I don't. I only dropped by to explain a few things about Elliott Parkinson; however, I . . ."

"Yes?"

Traynor hesitated again, still reluctant to violate one of the Agency's basic rules, in spite of the threat that Digger represented to one of his favorite younger ex-associates. Then the doorbell rang again, and the decision was taken out of his hands.

"For the moment, just take my word for it, Henry," Traynor said firmly. "For the next few days, pay close attention to your surroundings—especially your *familiar* surroundings—and be very careful about who you let into your house. And that includes friends as well as associates."

"Familiar surroundings? You're saying I need to start watching my back in my own house?"

"I'm very serious, Henry. Your home, your workplace, your friends, everything. Even me. All I can tell you right now is that a very sensitive operation—one that Elliott Parkinson set into motion a long time ago—is starting to come unglued. It's a big operation; apparently much bigger than I expected—much bigger than I ever dreamed, for that matter—with many closely related elements."

"Elements? You mean . . . ?"

"People," Traynor said. "So what I'm telling you is that until everything settles down, you and some of the people you work with may find yourselves in a very precarious position."

"But why me?" Culver demanded. "Like I told that kid, I've been out of the business for a long time, and I intend to stay out."

"It's not that simple, Henry," Traynor said, shaking his head sadly. "As I understand it, you don't have much of a choice. Remember those elements I mentioned?"

"Yeah?"

"You happen to be one of them," Traynor said simply.

And with that, he turned into the darkness of the kitchen and disappeared.

"You got yourself a nice place here, Henry," Carpenter said, glancing around the spare bedroom that Culver had converted into an electronics workshop.

From floor to ceiling, all four walls were filled with shelves of electronic instruments, loose parts, and manuals of every description. A massive workbench that occupied most of the center floor space held a pair of computers, and a maze of cables, conduits, and assorted items of electronic test equipment.

"Yeah, I like it." Culver nodded absentmindedly, working his way blindly through the steps necessary to remove the partially exposed roll of film that had gotten jammed up in Mike Quinzio's damaged camera while Traynor's words continued to echo through his mind.

The entire camera was now safely enclosed in a black cloth darkroom bag equipped with multiple-banded sleeves that allowed Culver complete access to the inner mechanisms without exposing the film roll to any light.

Not that it matters much now, Culver thought. Given the damage that the camera had sustained in the blast, it was a better-than-even bet that the entire roll had been exposed. But he decided to go through the motions anyway, mostly because it gave him a few more minutes to try to figure out what Carpenter was really up to.

Whatever it was, Culver decided, it sure as hell didn't involve camera repair. He had already examined his own camera—the one he'd loaned to Carpenter—and as far as he could tell, it was functioning just fine.

"So what do you think?" Carpenter asked after a few long moments of silence.

"About what?" Culver asked, trying to concentrate on the problem of blindly popping the back of Quinzio's camera open without causing any more damage to the hinge mechanism.

Digger, Russelli, Gauss, Quinzio, Forecastle, Traynor . . . and now Carpenter. Come on, Carp, what's the link? Give me a clue. What the hell's going on?

"Hattabaugh said you had one hell of a night," Carpenter commented casually. "How close was it?"

"I was probably halfway through the trigger pull at a range of maybe two feet," Culver said, concentrating on the last corner of the hinged back, and then grunting in satisfaction as he heard it come loose with a slight pop.

"Too close," Carpenter whispered, nodding his head slowly.

"Close as I ever want to get to blowing away a fourteen-year-old kid for stealing potato chips and candy," Culver agreed as he rolled the film the rest of the way onto the take-up reel, opened the bag to expose the dismantled camera, and then pulled and sealed the exposed roll.

"Here," he said, tossing the sealed roll of 120 film to Carpenter. "Want to drop that off at the lab for Quinzio?"

"Yeah, sure," Carpenter said, catching the film roll and slipping it into his jacket pocket. "Way I see it, those little bastards gotta be the luckiest pair of juvies in the county. Anybody else in the department would've probably capped off six and then hit the ground. Cover their ass and leave it all for the coroner and the review board to sort out."

"Like you said, just plain lucky."

"Speaking of which," the black detective went on smoothly, "how do you like working for Russelli?"

Culver blinked.

My nearly killing a couple of kids, and cops covering their ass reminds you of Russelli?

Then his mind went back to the previous evening.

That's right, Carp. You were the one who wanted Russelli to come out on that scene last night, but Stewart told you to keep an eye on him—keep an eye on one of your old Homicide buddies that you used to trust with your life. Yeah, right.

Culver shrugged. "Guess it was my own fault. I told everybody I wanted Major Crimes. I should have been more specific."

"I understand you and Russelli go back a few years."

"Middle school, high school, college," Culver answered, and then blinked as he realized what the veteran investigator was doing. The standard interrogation procedures. Get the subject off guard with some small talk, ask a couple of trivial questions, and then zoom in. Works every time.

Even on cops.

"Hey, well that's good." Carpenter nodded. "Crazy job like res-burgs, it probably helps if the guys are tight."

You came out here to dig, Carp. You want to know something about Russelli, or maybe about Russelli and me, but you won't tell me what or why. Is that what's got you guys worried, that maybe the two of us are working together on something?

Is that it? You and Stewart don't trust me either?

Culver stared straight into the blank, unrevealing expression on Detective Bradford Carpenter's face for a few moments, and then shrugged.

"Russelli's a good guy," he said as he checked his own camera over again and then handed it to the detective. "We'll get along fine. And as for the camera, same warning as last time. Don't drop it."

"Yeah, well, I'll tell you what," Carpenter nodded, holding the camera indifferently, as though he'd forgotten how important it was to Stewart, "you just do like I told you before . . ."

". . . and watch myself?" Culver finished as he walked the burly detective to the front door.

So what am I, Carp—a suspect or bait?

"That's right," Carpenter nodded solemnly. "Especially your back. Lot of crazy shit going on around here these days. Might be a bad time to start getting careless."

Bait.

"Yeah," Culver whispered to himself, watching numbly as his longtime friend and fellow officer walked casually out to his unit, tossed the camera into the trunk, and then drove off slowly down the road, "tell me about it."

Chapter Twenty-six

Friday, 1115 hours

It was a dark sedan, foreign make, with Maryland plates.

Arthur Traynor spotted the car the moment that he stepped off the curb, but he pretended to ignore it. He continued to walk across the street with his hands deep in his jacket pockets and his head down against the cold wind, because there wasn't anything else that he could do now.

He'd already activated the tiny transmitter in his jacket pocket, which might give him a slight edge for a very few minutes. But in doing so, he'd also confirmed—even if they couldn't prove it—his deliberate violation of the director's recent orders.

And that was the serious part because the director had been very explicit in giving out those orders.

Elliott Parkinson's operation was sanctioned at the highest levels. No names, but you could draw your own conclusions. Parkinson had the lead and Sci-Tech would provide any necessary support. Under no circumstances, repeat, *no circumstances,* was any member of the Sci-Tech Directorate to contact or interfere with any operative, agent, or asset assigned to operation Mother Earth Green.

Was that understood?

Traynor had nodded his assent because the only other choice was resignation, and he wasn't ready for that yet—not while he still had a chance to save some of the things that he cared about deeply.

But taking that chance meant accepting the risk of losing it all—the Agency, his friends, and very possibly his life. It was a risk made all the more serious by the knowledge that they had most of the advantages.

He was a known profile, alone, on foot, and three blocks west of the subject's house, which meant it wouldn't take them long at all to make the logical assumptions and then try to get a radio message to Parkinson.

Traynor has made contact with Culver. Probably warned him. He's leaving the area now. What do we do?

That was the question they would *want* to ask Parkinson, but they wouldn't be able to because the tiny transmitter in Arthur Traynor's pocket would effectively jam the frequency range of their scrambled radios within a one-mile radius. Out of contact with headquarters, they'd have to get to a land line, and they wouldn't have much time for that because Traynor was moving, and by the time they got their answer back by phone, he'd be gone.

It would be a matter of degree now, the Sci-Tech administrator knew as he stepped up onto the sidewalk. A question of how badly their operation had deteriorated, and how desperate they were to keep it running.

Desperate enough to leave standing sanction orders against an Associate Director?

Arthur Traynor wondered about that as he turned to the right—walking away from the parked vehicle now—took an even dozen long steps, and then quickly turned left into a slush-filled alley.

He didn't think that Parkinson would make that kind of move at this stage of the game—or perhaps he just didn't *want* to think that way—but he also knew the associate director of Operations well enough to know that he would do virtually anything at all in order to win—or to survive.

Giving me some room, he noted. *A bad sign.*

The engine wasn't running—he knew that instantly, because the exhaust would have been readily visible in the crisp winter air—but Traynor discounted that as a ploy because Parkinson's team could rent all of the dark sedans they needed. And he also knew that the increasingly nervous AD would be perfectly willing to place a dozen teams in static positions around Henry Culver's house if he thought it might help him get Digger back under control long enough to complete his operation.

Or get Traynor and his Sci-Tech allies out of his way permanently.

Halfway down the alley, Traynor tossed the small jamming transmitter up on the roof of the nearest house to his right, figuring that it would take them at least a couple of minutes to triangulate on the signal, and several more to find a ladder.

Then, relying on his instincts to select the right fence, Traynor turned to the left, vaulted his considerable bulk over the flimsy redwood structure, and then crossed through the yard in the direction of the surveillance vehicle that was parked across the street against the curb, his faced reddened by the unaccustomed exertion and his ragged breath frosting the air.

Coming up to the equally flimsy gate, he took a quick look, noting that just the trunk of the vehicle was visible from the side of the house, slowly opened the gate, and stepped forward past a pair of trash cans, reaching into his deep jacket pocket as he did so for the pistol.

"Stop right there, Mr. Traynor," the whispery voice growled.

Arthur Traynor felt the thick barrel of the silenced pistol press against the base of his skull, just behind his right ear, as a strong hand shoved him up against the side wall of the house.

"Do you find yourself hanging around backyards a lot these days, Alex?" Traynor asked, for no particular reason other than to talk and keep his mind clear. There was nothing else he could do.

"Shut up, Mr. Traynor." The voice spoke gruffly as the shoving hand expertly frisked his pockets, taking the small pistol and then continuing to search when he failed to find what he was after.

"Why, did I say something to offend you?"

"No, not really." The man grunted with mild exertion as he put away the silenced pistol, took Traynor's right arm up behind his back in a tight wristlock, and exerted a moderate degree of painful pressure as his free hand continued to pat and probe the left side of Traynor's bulky frame. "I just happen to like you. Now where is it?"

"Where is what?" Traynor gasped, ignoring the comrade-in-arms gambit and refusing to give in, because time was the only weapon he had now.

"Jammer," the man replied as he increased the pressure on Traynor's wrist. "I want it, now."

"Any reason why I should cooperate?" Traynor asked in a shaky voice, and then gasped in pain as a solid fist slammed into his left kidney.

"Accidents can be quick, and they don't have to hurt," the man said with the casual indifference of a professional who really *didn't* care, one way or another.

"But in either event, they *do* have to be sanctioned," Traynor reminded, and then bit his lip as his arm was forced higher up his backbone.

"You think I would do something like this on my own, for amusement?" the brutally strong and self-assured man demanded, switching hands to work on Traynor's right side.

"Yes, I do."

The hand moving down toward the crotch of Traynor's pants froze in mid-probe. Traynor's assailant whirled around in a blur, struck out blindly at the source of the voice behind his back, and then cried out when the slashing edge of his callused right hand struck solid cast iron.

Stunned by the unexpected impact, and the pain of shattered bones and torn nerves, the man had only a moment to try to recover before he felt his wrist being twisted tight against the two-foot length of three-quarter-inch pipe in an incredibly painful pressure hold that nearly caused him to faint. A slight twisting movement of the pipe then sent him to his knees, gasping in agony, whereupon he brought his head up and stared through pain-blurred eyes into the impassive face of Lt. Col. Charles L'Que.

"Who gave the order?" L'Que demanded in a cold, hard voice.

"What order?" the man tried in a moment of desperation, but another twist of the pipe caused his eyes to bulge and his mouth to gape open in a silent scream. Then his spirit broke because there was nothing in the eyes of Lt. Col. Charles L'Que that even remotely resembled compassion.

"Who gave the order?"

"Parkinson," Traynor's assailant whispered.

"To kill one of your own people?" L'Que demanded.

The man whimpered in pain.

"Answer me!" The enraged Lieutenant Colonel tightened his grip on the trapped wrist.

"Yes!" If possible, the man's eyes seemed to bulge even farther out of their sockets.

"Have you reported in?" Another question that demanded an immediate answer, but Traynor's assailant hesitated again, sensing that survival was an issue now.

"Yes!" He nodded desperately.

L'Que looked up and saw Traynor slowly shaking his head. The question was asked silently, and answered with a shrug. Traynor could still feel the blunt end of the silencer against his neck, but he had always lacked the cold-blooded instincts that enabled a man to kill or maim without feeling.

L'Que had no such qualms, but even so, he had no specific reason to kill anyone.

Yet.

"Is he right-handed or left?" he asked in a cold, hard voice.

Traynor stared down at the man's pants, noting with some degree of interest that the thick white denim trousers were now soaked with urine as he observed the wallet bulge in the right rear pocket.

"He appears to be right-handed," he said softly, already turning away as L'Que crushed the man's right wrist with a sharp twist of the pipe, and then used the blunt end to shatter ribs, collarbone, and jaw.

They left Elliott Parkinson's professional assassin crippled, unconscious, and facedown in the frozen mud next to the trash cans.

The teenage girl who answered the buzzer stood in the doorway for a moment and blinked uncertainly before her youthful face broke into a delighted grin.

"Uncle Henry!"

"Hi, kid." Culver smiled, judiciously choosing to use the vague greeting because Russelli's twin daughters were notoriously difficult to tell apart.

"Hey Mom," the girl yelled back over her shoulder, "it's Uncle Henry, and guess what—he's wearing a coat and tie!" Then she turned back to Culver with a suspicious look on her face.

"Hey, you aren't sneaking off to get married, are you?"

"Didn't I take a sworn oath that you two would be the first to know?"

"Yeah, but you also promised to tell us how you could tell M . . . uh, my sister and me apart, and you never did." Then her eyes flickered as she seemed to remember something. "Hey, wait a minute, you called me kid. That means you're not sure who I am, right?"

"Well, let's see," Culver said, trying to look appropriately thoughtful, "who is it who never asks me to come in . . ."

The door swung open and Culver found himself being dragged into the living room where he was able to get a quick glance at the spirited teenager's tennis shoes before Sharon Russelli came hurrying in with a startled look on her face that matched her daughter's.

"Henry, what . . . ?"

"Wait a minute, Mom. I think I got him. He's already figured out that one of us has a mole on our elbow and the other doesn't, but that's not going to do him any good this time." She held up her jacket and sweatshirt-covered arms and grinned. "So go ahead, smart guy. Who am I?"

"Well, let's see, Michelle always offers me cookies . . ."

"We're out of cookies," the girl replied quickly.

". . . but when Martine walks somewhere, she always starts out with her left foot."

The teenaged girl glanced down at her feet and then back up at Culver with a look of quizzical disbelief on her face. She started toward him and then caught herself. Leaving her shoes planted firmly on the floor, she crossed her covered arms across her chest and glared at Culver defiantly. "Yeah, so?"

"So where's Martine?"

"Aggghhhh!" Michelle Russelli screamed as she threw up her hands in frustration, and then turned to her mother. "Gotta go, Mom, I'm late. Martine's waiting at the Mall."

"What time will you two be home?"

"Ah, midnight, latest?"

"Okay, but no later. Your father'll be waiting up," Sharon Russelli warned sternly.

"Yeah, we know." Michelle Russelli sighed. "Okay, see you later. Bye, Uncle Henry," she said as she gave Culver a quick hug and kiss, and then disappeared through the front door.

"And drive carefully!" Sharon Russelli yelled after her daughter, and then turned to her unexpected visitor.

"Henry, you . . . ?" She stared at Culver's sport coat, and then glanced down at her watch. "Aren't you . . . ?"

"Supposed to be on my way to the station?" he said. "Yes and no. Actually, it's kind of a long story, but I thought maybe if you had some coffee, and maybe a couple of Michelle's cookies hidden around somewhere . . ."

Then he smiled tiredly as he found himself being dragged by the arm into the kitchen of a long-trusted friend.

"I don't believe it," Sharon Russelli stated as she added a handful of cookies to Henry Culver's plate and then topped off his mug from a fresh pot of coffee. "The whole thing is just so . . . incredible."

"Weird stuff." Culver nodded agreeably as he helped himself to another cookie.

"You and John working together again," she whispered, shaking her head as her eyes seems to focus on something in the distant past. "Wouldn't it be something if . . ."

"Tess and I got back together again too?" Culver finished through a mouthful of crumbs. "Don't think so. You hear about the DA?"

Sharon Russelli nodded glumly as she sipped at her coffee.

"That's all right." Culver shrugged. "Tess never did learn to cook, and besides," he added as he gave in to temptation and took one more cookie, "the M-and-M twins are about all I can handle in the way of kids anyway. The way my luck's been going, the next thing I'd know, I'd be out in my backyard building blue castles, threatening oversexed teenage boys with death and dismemberment, and trying to bury dogs that won't stay put."

Sharon Russelli winced. "He told you about that?"

"In typical Russelli detail."

"Henry, do you think . . ." she started to say, and then hesitated.

"Do I think what?" he asked.

"Do you think John's been acting strange lately?"

Culver cocked his head and smiled encouragingly, telling himself, *Okay, here we go. Gentle and easy.*

"Russelli's been a nutcase as far back as I can remember. You knew that before you married him. And the fact is, now that I think about it, I seem to remember making a real serious effort to get you to run away with me instead. Never could figure out why somebody like Russelli should latch on to a nice motherly type while I end up dating a commando."

"I know." Sharon Russelli smiled, exposing her dimples. "He and I talk about that every now and then."

"About what—you and me?" Culver blinked, startled.

"Uh-huh. Sometimes I think he even gets a little jealous."

"Oh great." Culver winced. "That's just what I need right now—a maniac partner who doesn't trust me around his wife."

"Oh it's not like that. It's just that everything's been so . . . I don't know, I mean like for example, did he tell you about the computer he bought?"

"*John* bought a computer?" Culver blinked in disbelief, startled in spite of himself.

"For the girls. He just came home with it one night, right out of the blue. Said that the whole world is being taken over by computers, so they might as well start learning about them, too."

"That's not too far from the truth," Culver said, "but it's hard to imagine John actually walking into a computer store. We have a hard enough time making him use a radio."

"It's worse than that," Sharon Russelli went on. "The last few weeks, he's even been working with it himself. Sometimes he comes home early and spends hours in the den trying to figure out how the programs work. It's like he's afraid they won't let him be a cop anymore, so he's trying to find something else."

"John Russelli learning to use a computer. This I've got to see." Culver shook his head in amazement.

"But there's more," Sharon Russelli started to say, and then hesitated again.

"Like what?" Culver finally prompted.

"After he got hurt . . . he's been, I don't know—angry, depressed, moody, irritated, suspicious."

"That's pretty much the way he is every day around the station." Culver shrugged. "Anything specific?"

"A couple of things," Sharon Russelli said. "I mean, we've been getting these strange phone calls in the middle of the night, and . . ."

"Hey Culver, you in there hustling my wife?" Russelli's booming voice echoed throughout the house, causing both Henry Culver and Sharon Russelli to nearly spill their coffee.

Damn. Culver closed his eyes in frustration, realizing that he'd waited too long.

"You're too late, we're out here in the kitchen having cigarettes and coffee," Culver yelled out toward the front door entryway, settling back into the chair in resignation as they heard Russelli's heavy footsteps approach the kitchen.

"Cigarettes and coffee, my ass! Those are my chocolate chip cookies!" Russelli exclaimed in the doorway, his eyes bulging in mock-outrage.

"That's right, partner." Culver nodded as he deliberately took another large bite out of the chocolate-laden morsel in his hand. "That's what happens, you go off and leave your wife, kids, and goodies unattended."

"My wife and kids can take care of themselves," Russelli growled as he hurried over to the kitchen table, and then stared in dismay at the half-empty tin. "But you touch one more cookie and . . ."

"I'll wrap you up a dozen to take home," Sharon Russelli said reassuringly to Culver, her face visibly brightened by the awakened spirit in her husband.

"A dozen?" Russelli blanched, grabbing the cookie tin off the table and clutching it to his massive chest.

"At least." Sharon Russelli nodded firmly as she pried the cookie tin loose from her husband's protective arms and headed over to the kitchen counter. "Henry's had a traumatic day," she went on as she pulled a plastic container out of the cupboard and began filling it with the rich cookies. "First Tess dumps him for some two-bit district attorney, then he has the accident, and now he ends up working with you."

"Best thing that ever happened to him since I told him about girls," Russelli commented through a mouthful of cookie crumbs.

Sharon Russelli stopped filling the container and thought about that for a moment. "Maybe I should just give him all . . ."

"A dozen's plenty," Russelli broke in hurriedly. "Christ, you give him any more than that and he'll forget about sex entirely. And besides"—he made a show of looking at his watch—"we're late. Gotta get going."

"Actually, becoming a monk might not be such a bad idea," Culver said as he gratefully accepted the container of cookies under Russelli's baleful eye. "But as much as I hate to admit it, I may have found somebody . . ."

Both Sharon and John Russelli stopped dead still and stared at Culver.

"You found somebody you really like?" Sharon Russelli asked, her face beaming with delight. "Come on, Henry, tell us. Who is she? Where did you meet her?"

"Ah . . . I'll tell you what. If it works out, I'll bring her over and let you meet her in person. Fair?"

Sharon Russelli started to protest, but her husband shook his head.

"Don't worry, I'll have all the gory details out of him by lunchtime," John Russelli promised.

Sharon Russelli sighed in cheerful resignation. "How about this Sunday for dinner, six o'clock?"

Culver nodded agreeably. "If it all works out, six o'clock it is."

"Great." Russelli grinned widely as he grabbed Culver by the arm and led him toward the front door. "So in the meantime, let's go out and hunt us down some burglars. And since you've finally got your sex life figured out," he added as he kissed his wife good-bye, closed the front door, and then quickly yanked the plastic container out of his partner's unsuspecting hand, *"I'll* take care of the cookies."

Chapter Twenty-seven

Friday, 1545 hours

The names. They continued to echo in Theodore Gauss's brooding man's mind again and again, reminding him of how badly he had erred.

Morgan and Lawnhart.

The new team.

The ones who had managed, somehow, to screw up the L'Que job. And not only that, but then had the gall—the absolute *balls!*—to try to cheat him in the bargain.

"Goddamn them!" he seethed, furious because now he had to change his carefully made plans to make certain that people like Henry Culver, who might spot an elusive pattern where everyone else saw nothing but disarray, were kept as far away from certain burglary scenes as possible.

That is to say, away from *his* burglary scenes.

The fact that, in death, Henry Culver would escape the gruesome indignities that he had planned with such meticulous care irritated him immensely. But that was all right, because it was all so neat and simple now.

The trap had been set, and now, sometime within the next hour, it would all happen.

The bait would squeal and Henry Culver would respond. And when that happened, Culver would die, others would be blamed, and by the time the police managed to sort it all out, he would be gone . . . with everything he needed to start it up again at another location far away.

He had all of that to worry about, but there was something else too; something that had been eating at his subconscious and keeping him on edge all morning:

The fact that for the first time in a long while, he no longer knew the exact whereabouts of an ex-criminalist turned police officer named Henry Culver.

In point of fact, it would have been very difficult for *anyone* to have tracked down Henry Culver at that particular moment, because he happened to be sitting in the passenger seat of an unmarked detective vehicle with Detective Sergeant John Russelli at the wheel. And in his typical fashion, Russelli hadn't bothered to tell the dispatcher that he had taken his new partner along for the ride.

They had been driving for almost an hour, Russelli giving Culver an overview of the major residential areas being hit this month, when a call for routine backup on a breaking and entering came out over the air. The address was immediately recognizable as a sparsely populated rural section of the county.

Being seasoned veterans who knew better than to jump on every routine backup call, they continued to drive, noting with no great surprise that there didn't seem to be any cruisers available at the moment to respond to that particular address. Or at least no other cruisers whose neatly uniformed occupants wanted to spend the rest of this dreary winter afternoon getting wet and cold and muddy while poking through the slush-laden underbrush in search of a suspect who was almost certainly long gone.

Fairfax County police officers might have been many things to many people; but they weren't flat-ass dumb.

Russelli and Culver were within a couple minutes driving time of the location, but the call was for a scout car and a uniform—visual PR stuff to keep the public reassured that the police were out there doing their job. Thus the two detectives felt perfectly justified in continuing with their more casual investigative efforts—at least until the reporting officer came back on the air with the cheerful announcement that the breaking and entering was, in fact, a residential burglary.

"Well, shall we?" Culver asked, looking over at Russelli, who seemed to be muttering something under his breath.

Then, finally, Russelli shrugged his shoulders. "Sure," he sighed, "why the hell not."

Three minutes later, when Russelli and Culver arrived at the residence and walked in through the opened door (deliberately ignoring the pair of teenage juveniles loitering across the street—as if daring the cops to give chase or to call their truant officer), the first thing they noticed was the furniture.

Or, to be more precise, what was left of the furniture.

Russelli's low whistle said it all.

The initial impression was that the Oakton High School football team had decided to hold their afternoon scrimmage in the living room, with the front door being one goal and the kitchen the other. It was, in Henry Culver's view, the worst ransacking of a house that he had ever seen.

It was so bad, in fact, that for a few moments, he didn't even see her.

The woman was sitting on the one cushion still attached to the couch. She was dressed in loose smock, her hair askew, her elbows braced against her legs and her head resting heavily in her hands. Culver figured her to be in her mid-forties, but the numbed look in her eyes and the slump in her shoulders made any attempt to guess her age a futile gesture. She looked as though the weight of the world was going to keep her on that couch for the rest of her life.

Maybe she's really only thirty-five and has six teenagers living at home, Culver thought in a momentary flash of police humor that he immediately regretted. But as the reporting officer gestured for Russelli to follow him into the bedroom, Culver gave in to his emotions once again and walked over to the woman.

"Uh, Mrs. Hardy," he said softly, glancing down at the notes he'd made of the dispatcher's call.

Teresa Hardy brought her head up slowly and blinked. "Yes?"

"Mrs. Hardy, I'm pol . . . I mean I'm *Detective* Culver, and I just wanted to tell you how sorry I am that all of this happened." He gestured with one hand around the disheveled room. "We're going to do everything we possibly can to find out who did this. And perhaps after we're finished here, we can help you clean up."

"Oh, you mean the burglars?" she said in a quiet voice, looking up at Culver with weary eyes. "They just got into my bedroom. I don't think they did anything in here."

Culver was still standing there with his mouth partially open and his brain numb, trying to think of *something* to say to the woman, who seemed to have no real sense of what Culver had *already* said, when Russelli came up to him and patted him on the back.

"Listen, buddy-boy," he whispered next to Culver's ear, "unless you're real determined to set an all-time record for complaints filed against a cop within a twenty-four-hour period, why don't you just cut your losses and take a peek in the back room. Something you might be interested in seeing, now that you're a real live burglary detective."

As it turned out, Culver had actually come amazingly close for getting it so terribly wrong. Mrs. Teresa Hardy was actually thirty-eight years old, and only four of her five teenaged children still lived at home. The other one—the only girl—had gone off to college a couple of months ago. The house, as Mrs. Hardy sadly explained, was always a wreck.

Under normal circumstances, Culver might have said something to Russelli, but in this particular instance, he didn't—mostly because he was too busy staring at the spray-painted message on the bedroom wall.

The message that listed, in neat, black, block-printed letters, four very familiar names:

QUINZIO
GAUSS
CULVER
RUSSELLI

A crime scene investigator with nothing else on his mind might have found it interesting to note that the intruder had apparently gone to the trouble of bringing along a second can of paint to spray bright red X's thru the first two names on the list, but Henry Culver was well beyond that sort of clinical detachment.

In point of fact, he was much too busy trying to ignore the chill spreading rapidly down his spine as he continued to stand there and stare at the bright red circle that had been sprayed around one of the two remaining names on the list.

The name than began with a large, black "C."

"So what do you think?" Russelli asked as he backed the detective unit out of the Coffee Stop parking lot, and accelerated down the narrow, undivided two lane road.

"I think we've got somebody out there who's trying to screw with our minds," Culver answered, reflexively tearing away part of the plastic lid on his cardboard cup of streaming hot coffee as he made one more attempt to figure out how the X's and O's on the spray-painted list on Teresa Hardy's back bedroom wall might be related to the bizarre events of the past twenty-four hours.

Russelli nodded. "Yeah, I'll go along with that. Fact is, I think I know who did it."

"What?" Culver blurted out, almost spilling his coffee as he whipped his head around to stare at Russelli.

"IAD," Russelli whispered softly, almost to himself, as he sipped at his own coffee. "Give you two-to-one it was those goddamned headhunters."

"Come on, Russelli, think about it for a minute." Culver sighed as he settled his head back against the headrest and closed his eyes. "Quinzio and Gauss got nailed by an explosive device—a real live bomb—and they damn near got killed. You really think that Internal Affairs would rig something like that, just to put you out to pasture?"

Russelli continued to drive in silent contemplation for a few moments, and then nodded his head. "Maybe not IAD," he conceded, "but that fucking Craven'd do it in a second. Gutless little bastard's been sneaking around behind my back for the past three months trying to convince the chief that I can't do the job anymore."

"Russelli . . ."

"Trouble is, he's right."

Culver's eyes snapped opened as he turned around to stare at his new partner.

"What?"

"I mean it," Russelli insisted, paying the minimal amount of attention to his driving as he turned his head to stare at Culver. "You saw me hobbling around out there. You think I could run down one of those fifteen-year-old window poppers hanging around out there across the street, the condition my leg's in?"

"Russelli, you couldn't have run down one of those jackrabbits *before* you got hurt," Culver said reasonably.

"Yeah, well, the thing is, good old Craven managed to get me scheduled for a physical fitness battery next week. According to the memo, I either pass it or I'm gone."

"You don't think you can make it?"

"Shit, I couldn't run a mile and a half in sixteen hours, much less sixteen minutes." Russelli said, swerving back over to his side of the road at the last moment to avoid an oncoming trucker who honked indignantly.

"So what are you going to do?"

"You mean retirement-wise?"

"Yeah."

"Well, I . . ."

"Hey, wait a minute," Culver interrupted as he glanced down at the unit radio and realized for the first time that all the channel buttons were dark, "when did you turn the radio off?"

"Never turned it back on after we left the Hardy place. What do you want to do, follow up on every petty-ass door job in the county?"

"Right about now, I'd settle for a vehicle stop on a guy with a couple cans of spray paint in his car," Culver said as he leaned forward and thumbed the power switch on.

Russelli chuckled. "Yeah, right. Fat friggin' chance, but what the hell. Anyway, like I was saying," he went on, "in case things really go to shit, like they're probably going to, I was thinking that maybe if you and I . . ."

Russelli's "maybe if" was interrupted by the insistent voice of the Emergency Operations Center dispatcher who sounded anxious and irritable.

". . . EOC to MC-Eighty."

"Ah shit," Russelli grumbled as he grabbed for the mike. "MC-Eighty, go."

"We've been trying to raise you for the past ten," the dispatcher complained. "Do you have Henry with you?"

"Uh, that's affirmative."

"You're requested to respond immediately to six-three-niner-eight New Landing. Officers are on the scene now. Repeat, six-three-niner-eight, New Landing. Respond immediately. Do you copy?"

Russelli and Culver looked at each other and shrugged before Russelli finally acknowledged.

"Copy, on our way."

Deep in the hidden confines of his new Command and Control Center, Theodore Gauss sat at his desk and tried to ignore a growing sense of uneasiness as he stared at the glowing terminal screen that displayed the area patrol assignments for the Eight-Charlie squad.

"Damn it, Culver," he whispered, "where are you?"

Determined to prove that it was all some sort of mistake, he went through the code sequence again to request the patrol roster for the District Eight-Charlie squad. The squad that would be out patrolling the Fair Oaks District from three o'clock this Friday afternoon until one o'clock the following morning.

This Friday.

Today.

Feeling his mind going numb from a sense of impending disaster, he hit the enter key and then watched the data fill up the screen.

SQUAD:	80-C		
NAME:	RNK:	AREA:	ADDNL:
HATTABAUGH	SGT	80-C	
BEASLEY	P-2	840-C	
BRANCH	P-2	831-C	811-C
DROZ	P-3	830-C	OFF SICK
MOORESTEAD	P-2	820-C	
NOLAN	P-3	810-C	IOD
NOWOTNY	P-1	811-C	831-C
SUTHERLAND	P-1	850-C	

It was the right squad. He knew that because he recognized most of the names; but where was Culver?

"He's supposed to be Scout Eight-Forty-Charlie," Gauss whispered to himself. "He's *always* been Eight-Forty Charlie."

That didn't necessarily mean anything though, the crime lab director knew, because patrol officers were frequently shuffled back and forth between patrol areas to cover for people who had been injured on duty or called in sick.

But they'd added a new name to the roster, and hadn't marked Culver down as either IOD or on sick leave. And even if he *had* taken the day off, he reasoned, Culver still should have been listed as part of the squad.

They can't change that now, he told himself. *Not today!*

Stunned by the incredible possibility that his carefully devised plan might have been foiled by yet another random event, his hands flew at the keyboard, searching for the pathway that would take him into the Fairfax County Police Department's central personnel roster.

Minutes later, he found it; and with a few more keystrokes, he had Culver's duty status record scrolling up on the screen. Then he took one look at the data record, and froze in his chair.

NAME:	BADGE:	ASSIGN:	COMMENT:
CULVER, H.	337	MC-805	TRANSFER

"Transferred?" he whispered in horror.

For a few long moments, Gauss stared at the computer screen in disbelief, unable to absorb—much less understand—the significance of the message before his eyes. But the meaning of the word "transfer" was all too clear.

"They moved him! Goddamn it, they moved that bastard out of the Eight-Charlie squad and put him somewhere else!" he exploded.

But why . . . ?"

But then, in a flash of comprehension, he realized that "why" wasn't the operative. The thing that he cared about most of all right now was *where*.

What's the code? MC-Eight-Oh-Five? What's that? he asked himself, trying to remember all of the organizational codes of the Fairfax County Police Department as his hands went back to the keyboard to search more records—to search for anything that would tell him where Henry Lucas Culver might have gone.

"Where *are* you, Culver?" he whispered, feeling the pressure build—in his chest, and in his frenzied mind—as he brought screen after screen of data up on his monitor.

Searching every subsystem he could find.

Trying to find some trace of the man who had ceased to

be a mere obstacle, and had become, instead, his overwhelming obsession.

"*Dammit, Culver,*" he screamed. "*Where the hell are
you?*"

Settled back in the front passenger seat of Russelli's unmarked unit, Henry Culver suddenly found himself asking
the same question.

The address that the anxious and irritated dispatcher had
given out, and then repeated, had sounded vaguely familiar
to Culver, but he was tired and he had other things on his
mind, so he really wasn't paying much attention to where
they were going until Russelli made the westbound turn onto
Fairfax Station Road without ever taking his foot off the accelerator.

Then it hit him.

"Hey, what was that address again?" he asked, sitting up
in the seat and reaching in his coat pocket for his notebook.

"Uh, six-three . . . nine-eight," Russelli recited from memory.

"New Landing?"

"Yep."

"Oh shit," Culver sighed as he found the confirming address in his notebook and then sank back into the seat again.

"What's the matter, you know somebody here?"

"Uh-huh."

"You mind telling me what you're so all-fired happy about
all of a sudden?" Russelli inquired.

"Remember when I told you and Sharon that I'd found
somebody I kind of like, and that I might start going out with
her?"

"Yeah, so what?" Russelli grunted, and then he glanced
quickly over at Culver. "You mean . . . ?"

"Yeah, I'm afraid so."

"I don't get it. What's the problem?"

Culver shrugged. "She was kinda pissed off when I left the
other day. I figured I'd give her a little time to cool down,

and then maybe go back in a couple of days and smooth things out."

Russelli let his foot up off the accelerator until the unmarked cruiser dropped down to the legal speed limit. "You mean to tell me we've been hightailing it out here just so you can get another beef added to your jacket?"

"That's what it looks like." Culver nodded despondently.

"You know what, buddy-boy," Russelli said cheerfully as he eased his foot back down on the accelerator, "I think I'm gonna enjoy having you for a partner."

"Oh yeah, why's that?"

"Way I see it," Russelli said, starting to hum to himself as he took the turn onto New Landing, "you're the only guy I know who just naturally gets himself into more shit than I do."

After fifteen minutes of progressively frantic hunting within the electronic innards of the Fairfax County Police Department's computerized Law Enforcement Information Management System, Theodore Gauss sat motionless in front of the computer screen, feeling his arms and legs go numb with shock as he stared at the glowing letters:

CRIMINAL INVESTIGATIONS BUREAU

MAJOR CRIMES DIVISION

UNIT CALL SIGNS:

MC 100–190:	Homicide
MC 200–290:	Robbery
MC 300–390:	Sex
MC 400–490:	Auto
MC 500–590:	Check and Fraud
MC 600–690:	Fugitive
MC 700–790:	Child Services
MC 800–890:	Residential Burglary

"Major Crimes Eight-Oh-Five. My God," he whispered to himself, "they've assigned him to the residential burglary unit."

Fighting to hold back the growing sense of nausea welling up in his throat, his fingers jabbed at the keyboard as he quickly disengaged himself from the interface programs of the Fairfax County computer system.

Then, as his inflamed mind continued to churn with frantic indecision, Theodore Gauss began another search—only this time with an intensity that bordered on the maniacal.

HÄMMARCHOV, WHERE ARE YOU?

Nothing. The screen remained blank.

HÄMMARCHOV, REPORT IN!

Still nothing.

DAMN IT, HÄMMARCHOV, TALK TO ME!

Chapter Twenty-eight

Friday, 1645 hours

The moment that Detective Sergeant John Russelli turned his unmarked detective unit up the long, winding driveway off New Landing, he knew why the dispatcher had sounded irritated, nervous, and flustered all at the same time.

One fleeting look up that long, twisty stretch of icy gravel, and it was suddenly all too clear.

The new res-burg team of Russelli and Culver hadn't been dispatched to a "miscellaneous complaint" call after all.

Not at sixty-three-ninety-eight New Landing.

Not with four patrol cruisers, a marked station wagon, two unmarked detective units, and a pair of paramedic-equipped ambulance units scattered all around the upper driveway and front yard of the house.

The rotating sweeps of the distant red and blue emergency lights created a distinctive, bichromatic flickering inside Russelli's detective unit that caused Henry Culver to look up from his notebook and see the scene for the first time.

"Oh Christ," he whispered.

Like Russelli, it had taken Culver only a brief moment to absorb, evaluate, and then comprehend the horrible significance of the crime scene exhibited before his eyes—a scene that might have appeared perfectly normal to a casual observer of police activity, but to experienced CSI officers like Russelli and Culver, was anything *but*.

There were several telling factors, but three were especially unnerving.

First of all, in Fairfax County, Virginia, a follow-up complaint filed by a burglary victim *never* required the equivalent of an entire police squad response. In such cases, the supervising sergeant and the officer in question—with possibly a third officer standing by for backup—were expected to resolve the situation to everyone's satisfaction. The dispatch of *seven* marked cruisers was generally reserved for more significant events, such as an outlaw motorcycle gang party or a major neighborhood riot.

Less obvious, but equally unsettling, was the presence of the two paramedic units. The Fairfax County Emergency Operations Center would have been highly reluctant to dispatch one of their extremely expensive and constantly utilized lifesaving teams to a routine MI-COM call. A two-unit response in such circumstances simply didn't happen.

But the most aberrant factor of all was the certain knowledge on the part of Russelli and Culver that if such a dispatch ever *did* occur, the *last* thing that four of these highly professional and aggressive paramedic officers would be seen doing was standing around talking to each other with their backs to the scene, as if they had nothing to do, and nothing to say, but didn't want to leave just yet.

It was a sight that any police officer would have found incongruous. But Detective Sergeant John Russelli didn't have to see the bright red paramedic trucks, or the scattered pattern of marked and unmarked units, or the pairs of uniformed lifesavers standing around looking somber to understand why the dispatcher had sounded upset. He didn't even have to think about it. He'd been to so many dead body scenes during his five-year tour in Homicide that he could almost sense them blindfolded.

But even so, there was something about this one that was especially atypical, although Russelli couldn't quite put his finger on it.

Something about the pattern of cars . . .

"Russelli . . ." Culver started to say, but John Russelli had already sent the detective unit roaring, slipping and fishtailing up the driveway, and was braking to a mud-and-gravel-slinging stop next to the other two unmarked units that were parked farthest away from the house. Just as he'd done a hundred times before.

In the brief moment it took him to slam the gearshift into park, set the emergency brake, release the seat belt, and then reach for the door handle, he even recognized the license plates.

Stewart and Carpenter. He groaned. *Oh Jesus, not again.*

He'd been hoping against all logic to see the familiar plates of his other res-burg teams, but that had been a faint hope at best. He had already resigned himself to being put under the spotlights one more time.

But this one's different, he remembered. *Henry's got himself involved with this one . . . the poor son of a bitch.*

"Henry, if you're smart, you'll sit right here. You don't want in on this one," John Russelli warned as he turned to open his door, not wanting to see the expression on his partner's face. He'd seen that look on more occasions than he cared to think about, and it made him sick every time.

Everybody thinks it's the victim that suffers, but that's bull-shit, Russelli told himself for perhaps the fiftieth time in his career. *It's the ones that get left behind that do the hurting. You really don't want to go in there, Henry.*

But Henry Culver had already come out of the unit, and was following him stride for stride up the gravel driveway, so Russelli simply shrugged and kept walking, neither of them saying anything, until they came around the first of the sideways-parked cruisers and stopped.

At that moment, Russelli recognized the element that hadn't been quite right about this particular dead body scene.

The paramedics were by themselves, talking with each other, and keeping their distance from the cops.

Oh shit.

Russelli's gaze went immediately to the two bloody, sheet-covered forms—one almost twice the size of the other, and both lying next to the open driver's side door of the marked vehicle—and stayed there as he began to absorb and evaluate the scene out of pure reflex. Culver's eyes remained fixed on the side of the vehicle.

The side that looked like it had been hit by at least thirty or forty widely scattered shotgun blasts.

He'd already noticed the plate; and like Russelli and his all-too-familiar Homicide units, Culver knew those particular letters and numbers by heart. That was why he continued to stare at the side of the shredded vehicle as he felt the protective numbness take over and immobilize his limbs.

He couldn't bring himself to look down at the two sheet-covered forms. He couldn't even bring himself to say their names. Then, finally, it came out in a rush of emotion as the nausea struck with full force, and he found himself staggering over to the side of the gravel driveway and dropping to his knees.

Alerted by the all-too-familiar sounds of dry retching, the paramedics came running, grateful to have something they could actually work on; somebody that they could help; some excuse to get back in with the cops and feel like they weren't intruding.

One of them went for a blanket and towels, while another responded with a thermos of water and a cup.

They held the blanket around Culver's shoulders and helped him wash his face and rinse his mouth out with the cold water, all the while asking easy, soothing questions and soliciting nods to draw out critical information without insulting pride or dignity. They even offered him a ride out—up front, no lights or sirens, wherever he wanted to go—but Culver shook his head, stood up shakily, and then turned and found himself staring at Russelli.

"Where's Stewart?" he asked in a hoarse voice.

"In the house," Russelli said, his own voice tight with dulled anger and pain. Unlike Culver, John Russelli hadn't recognized the station wagon right away; and therefore hadn't been aware that the Fairfax County police officer lying under the blood-soaked sheet was Tess Beasley. Not until he'd lifted up the corner of the sheet and stared in shock at the face that was so horribly, tragically familiar.

"I want to talk with him," Culver rasped, gently disengaging himself away from the supporting hands of the paramedics as he walked toward the house on his still-shaky legs, glancing down at the bloody sheet-covered forms as he went by, and discovering—to his numbed dismay—that his defense mechanisms had already started to take him through the transition from stunned civilian to professional crime scene investigator, and the bodies had already started to become what they had always been in the past.

Simple objects.

Parts of the crime scene.

Things to consider, and evaluate, and measure, but always with logic and reason, never with emotion.

He didn't even notice that a shocked Russelli, responding subconsciously to eight years of intense training with the U.S. Secret Service, had taken up a protective position at his side.

You can't allow yourself to get emotionally involved. It

doesn't help and it doesn't work, Culver repeated to himself once again as he walked up to the front porch, only noticing the condition of the door lock mechanism and the surrounding wood frame when he reached past the uniformed officer guarding the door to let himself in.

He blinked and stared at the twisted chunk of metal that had once been a doorknob for several long seconds before that part of the scene, too, began to register in his mind—and to trigger his memory.

What had he told her?

You should call a locksmith immediately and have him put something more sturdy on this door; otherwise, I'm liable to be back here tomorrow filling out another report.

Then he stared at the shattered wood doorframe, staring at the deep impression marks in the relatively solid red oak that *should* have held the new tempered-steel bolt in place, but hadn't, because red oak doorframes weren't designed to absorb that kind of abuse.

So she'd called a locksmith, and they'd put a good, solid dead bolt in this time; only it hadn't done her any good, Culver realized numbly, because this time after the burglar had twisted the knob, he'd used the other end of the wrench to pound the whole mechanism out of the wall.

So I'm back here tomorrow anyway, only I won't be filling out any reports because they aren't going to let me work on this one.

Culver pushed the shattered door open, barely aware that Russelli had moved forward to shoulder his way in through the door first.

But that's okay, because they don't need me here anymore. I've already done enough. I'm the one who set her up by telling her that Molly-the-Hun wasn't usually violent—at least not toward people.

Yeah, right. Good thinking Culver. Not toward people. Just doors and dogs and police officers.

Except that everybody could tell that she was progressing, he reminded himself. *Getting more aggressive every day.*

Just a matter of time until she started after people, just like that prick Digger. Should have realized that.

Only I didn't.

The protective, foggy numbness that had insulated him from the worst of the emotional shock had almost disappeared by now. In its place had come a cold, hard, and unrelenting anger. Culver surged through the entryway of the familiar house alongside his partner, and into the living room, steeling himself to look at more bodies of people he knew, where he suddenly found himself staring at three very familiar faces.

Homicide Sergeant Alvin Stewart and Detective Bradford Carpenter looked up from their notebooks, but both remained seated, staring solemnly at the two police officers they had been waiting with growing impatience to interrogate for the past half hour.

The fact that the facial expressions and body language of the two oncoming officers—especially John Russelli—almost screamed out a warning of impending violence didn't seem to faze Stewart or Carpenter in the least. As Homicide investigators, they were ready, willing, and absolutely capable of dealing with a wide range of emotional behavior from their suspects—and on occasion, from one of their fellow officers.

But the third occupant of the room wasn't the least bit ready, emotionally or otherwise, for a hulking and frightening behemoth like Russelli to come charging into her living room.

Frightened and confused, she stood up quickly and started to move away from the sudden intrusion of two more aggressive male figures into her house. She backed up against the wall that had been desecrated in black and red spray paint with the names of four Fairfax County police officers:

QUINZIO
GAUSS
CULVER
RUSSELLI

But then something about the man who had followed Russelli in and was standing there next to his right shoulder seemed to catch Kathy Harmon's attention. She blinked for a moment, drawn off by the unfamiliar street clothes, and then her jade green eyes widened in absolute disbelief.

"Oh my God," she whispered, standing right beside the six black letters of the name that had been Xed out with violent slashes of red spray paint, and shaking her head as her face took on a distinct ashen hue, "I . . . I thought I killed you."

One more, Bobby Morgan told himself. *I can feel it now. Just one more.*

The sharply honed Buck knife was slick with half-congealed blood, and difficult to hold, but Bobby Morgan forced his nearly frozen bloody fingers around the slippery knife handle one more time.

Don't think about it. Just do it. You've got to do it because you've got to move. If you don't move, you're going to die.

He'd already gotten three of the pellets out, slicing his way lengthwise through the skin and muscle tissue of his upper right leg.

Trying to follow the path of the horribly destructive lead balls.

Trying to stop the immobilizing pain while screaming and moaning into a cloth-wrapped piece of branch that he'd forced into his mouth, to keep his teeth from clacking and grinding together.

And trying desperately to finish it so that he could move—so that he could get to some sort of shelter before he froze to death out here in the bleak red oak forest only a few hundred yards away from the charred remains of his house.

Come on, he raged at himself. *You don't want to die!*

He'd gotten three out, but the fourth one—the one that seemed to be pressing against a nerve, generating wave after wave of agonizing pain every time he moved—was lodged in deep and rubbing against the bone, and he'd already fainted twice and he didn't dare faint again because there was too much blood for the crude belt-and-stick tourniquet to stop completely.

Can't die yet, he told himself as he shoved the cloth-wrapped stick tight against his back teeth and then braced his hands together, trying to stop some of the shaking as he forced the blade in . . .

Not until I find him!

. . . and then he screamed once again.

"You want to hear it?" Detective Brad Carpenter asked as he walked over to the couch where Henry Culver had been sitting wordless for almost a half hour.

Culver looked up and then nodded silently.

"She was going to file a complaint, just like you thought," Carpenter said, flipping back through five or six pages in his notebook until he found the part he was after. "Comes home at 3:55 P.M., finds her place torn to shit again, sees all that crap on the wall . . ." Carpenter motioned with his pen over his shoulder.

"Wait a minute," Culver interrupted. "What about the little girl?"

"You mean her niece? She dropped her off at a friend's house after school."

Culver nodded in numbed relief.

"Anyway," Carpenter went on, "she gets on the horn to the station and throws a real shit fit, demanding that you get your ass out here pronto."

"She asked for me, specifically?"

"According to dispatch tape, she asked for the officer who was here before—Eight-Forty-Charlie. You give her that?"

Culver nodded, staring past Carpenter at the far wall. "I got a call on the radio while I was here," he finally said in a raspy whisper. "She heard the call sign. Wanted to know what it meant."

"You tell her it was your personal call sign?"

Culver shrugged. "I don't know, I might have. Why?"

Bradford Carpenter remained mute as he made a few more entries in his notebook.

Culver stared up at the black detective for a few long moments with a puzzled expression in his eyes, and then it all fell into place.

"Tess's call sign," he rasped the words out through a dry throat. "What was . . . ?"

"Eight-Forty-Charlie," Carpenter replied matter-of-factly. "They moved her into your vacant spot. The dispatcher was handling several calls at the time, so she didn't have a chance to call up the incident report and check names. Took the reporting party's word for it. Lousy procedure. Understandable, but lousy."

"Did Tess . . ." Culver forced the words through his constricted throat, feeling as though he was going to start vomiting again at any moment. "Did she get out any kind of message? Call for backup? Anything like that?"

"Nothing." Carpenter shook his head.

"How about a ninety-seven?"

"Yeah, it's on the tape. Voice normal, no stress. No other transmissions. They figure she never saw it coming."

"So she drove up here, called in her ninety-seven, and got out of the car . . ." Culver went on, ignoring Carpenter's attempt to make it easy.

". . . and she and Sasha got nailed by three claymores, rigged in series for a single detonation," Carpenter finished. "Whoever did it set it up so that they'd cover the entire upper driveway in a cross-pattern. Professional job."

"How was it wired?" Culver asked, finding a kind of mental sanctuary in the technical details that helped to block out the emotional ones.

"According to Stewart, it wasn't. Said it looked like some sort of remote trigger. Like maybe the front of the unit tripped a light beam or something—except they haven't been able to find the right pieces yet."

"It was set off by hand," Culver said quietly, shaking his head. "She probably even saw who did it."

"Oh yeah, what the hell makes you think that?" Carpenter demanded.

"She had released the dog," Culver explained, continuing to stare at the far wall. "The left side rear window was already down when it went off. Had to be. No glass in the backseat, and it's too cold to be driving that way."

"She had time to roll down the window?"

"No." Culver shook his head. "Tess carried an IR remote transmitter—sort of like a garage door opener—on her belt so that she could lower the backseat windows when she was outside the wagon. I know because I made it for her. It was on the ground, next to the front tire."

"You mean you think they knew . . . ?"

". . . that it wasn't me? Yeah, sure, of course they knew," Culver said bitterly. "Tess . . . her voice on the radio sounds rough. Somebody listening to a scanner might not have been able to tell; but they let her get stopped and call in—just to make sure, just like they'd planned to do, because otherwise it would have been a lot safer to rig a trip wire. Then she saw something that was serious enough to cause her to release Sasha."

"They knew it wasn't you, but they set it off anyway?" Carpenter asked, glancing back meaningfully at the crossed-out names on the wall.

"Yeah, right."

"Why? It doesn't make sense."

"Maybe because they wanted to. Maybe because they were waiting for me to get out of the cruiser, so I'd see it coming, and then saw it wasn't me, and all of a sudden Sasha was coming out the window." Culver shrugged, and then looked up at Carpenter. "Doesn't much matter now, does it?"

"It sure as hell ought to matter to you," Carpenter retorted, and then caught himself.

"Oh yeah, it matters to me," Culver whispered, his eyes staring blankly at the wall. "You'd better *believe* it matters."

"That's not . . . never mind. Stay here a minute," Carpenter said as he walked over to the closed kitchen door. After knocking, he entered and remained in the kitchen for several minutes as Culver continued to stare at the spray-painted wall. Then he and Stewart and Russelli returned to the living room.

"Henry," Stewart said, "do you feel up to going down to the station and dictating a report?"

"Yeah, sure, why not," Culver said, staring up at one of the few cops that he really, truly respected.

"Okay, Russelli's going to drive you there and stay with you until I get there," Stewart said. "You stick with him, and you don't separate, *under any circumstances.* You understand?"

"I'm all right . . ." Culver started to say, but Stewart interrupted firmly.

"I'm not asking for your opinion. Somebody seems to be making a very determined effort to kill four cops. You're one of them, and I'm not going to let it happen. *Do you understand?"*

Culver took in a deep sighing breath and nodded his head silently.

"Good." Stewart nodded in apparent satisfaction, started to go back to the kitchen, and then hesitated.

"Henry."

Culver looked up again at the crew-cut Homicide supervisor.

"You can't backtrack and play what-ifs on this. It doesn't work. You didn't do a single thing that put Tess on the line. She was a cop, and she took that call just like any other cop would have done taken it. Do you understand what I'm saying?"

"I . . . understand. I don't agree, but I understand."

"I'll settle for that," Stewart said evenly. "You want to help on this?"

Culver brought his head up sharply. "Yes, of course I do."

"Then keep a clear head," Stewart growled. "We're going to need it. Now get going."

You've got to move!

The searing waves of pain had finally dampened down into gentle swells of aching numbness, but it took several more minutes before Bobby Morgan could bring his ragged breath and shaking hands under control.

He'd lost the knife somewhere, but that didn't matter. He'd finished it, popping the last of the pellets loose, and then dropping everything when pain had almost torn through the top of his skull.

He wouldn't need the knife anymore.

Come on, don't just lie here!

He knew he had to move, but it felt so good, now that the pressure of that fourth pellet had been released, that he didn't want to take the chance that it would start up again.

The pain and the bleeding, both.

He's already lost enough blood to feel light-headed, and he didn't think that he could stand any more of the pain, so it was awfully tempting just to lie there and let the wet cold soak into the leg.

But if you do that, you're going to sit here until you die, he told himself. *There's only one way you're going to find out.*

Do it now.

Move!

Fitting the cloth-wrapped stick back into his mouth one more time, he bit down into the soft wood, and took several ragged breaths. Then he pulled himself up by the rough tree bark, took another deep breath, and took a step with his torn leg.

There was pain, and some more bleeding, but not so much of either that he couldn't take another step.

And another.

"We've got to tell Sharon, before she hears about it on the radio," Henry Culver said quietly, his eyes red from the tears that he couldn't blink back.

"I already called her," Russelli rasped in an uncharacteristically emotion-choked voice. "Martine's with her now. We get clear, we'll go home, stay with her, get her past all this shit."

Culver nodded a wordless assent.

They were less than five minutes away from the station, Russelli driving, with Culver in the front seat, when the dispatcher interrupted their numbed silence.

"MC-Eighty?"

Russelli blinked and then reached for the mike.

"What?"

"MC-Eighty, do you have Eight-Oh-Five with you?"

"Yeah, what about it?" he demanded, not really giving a damn about radio procedure at the moment.

"Be advised he has an urgent incoming call from the County Ward. Give me a transfer number as soon as possible."

"Yeah, all right," Russelli growled, and then turned to Culver. "You want to talk with anybody there?"

Culver shrugged indifferently.

"Okay." Russelli nodded. "Let's go find ourselves a fucking phone."

Three minutes later, Henry Culver was standing in a telephone booth at the corner of Ox Road and Braddock, listening in incredulous silence as a shaken security guard tried to explain it all in a way that halfway made sense. Then he ran back to the detective unit, got in, and slammed the door.

"Paul's house. We need to get there right now," Culver said, his face as ashen as Kathy Harmon's had been less than an hour earlier.

"You mean Radlick? What the hell do we want . . . ?"

"Look, just us over there, right now," Culver demanded as he fumbled around in the police equipment bag that contained, among other things, his shoulder-holstered .357 Smith & Wesson.

"What the fuck's the matter with you?" Russelli demanded, turning to stare at his partner.

"Digger." Culver almost spit the word out as he looked up from the heavy nylon bag. "He's out. The bastards let him get away."

Chapter Twenty-nine

Friday, 1835 hours

On the eve of that cold and drizzly Friday evening, the overcast sky was just beginning the transition from intermittent dark gray to uniform black when Detective Sergeant John Russelli brought his unmarked police cruiser to a slow stop about twenty feet away from the edge of Paul Radlick's fenced-in driveway. He gently pushed the gearshift lever into park, and then shut off the engine.

In the silence that followed, the only audible sounds were those of ice-laden raindrops slapping against the cold enameled skin of the cruiser, and the slow, controlled breathing of its two occupants.

Finally, Henry Culver whispered something that sounded like a resigned curse under his breath.

Russelli turned his head in response, but Culver didn't say anything else, so they both sat there in silence in the growing darkness and stared at the gloomy scene that told them far more than they really wanted to know—and suggested other things that they didn't even want to think about.

"You sure they didn't take off for the weekend?" Russelli finally asked in a strained and raspy voice.

John Russelli's face was set in a tightly controlled cold mask of professional indifference, but his vocal cords betrayed an underlying rage that threatened to send him lunging past the boundaries of commonly acceptable police behavior—and into that realm of mindless, reflexive violence that linked modern man back to his far-less-civilized ancestors.

All because of the bleak and dismal scene that was clearly visible through the front windshield of John Russelli's vehicle. A scene that spoke a thousand words of fear, and hopelessness and doom, all in a single gray-black picture.

Although, in truth, there really wasn't much of anything to see in the rapidly falling darkness.

No sprawled bodies this time.

No shredded vehicles.

No bloody sheet covering a fellow police officer they both knew and loved.

Not even a twisted doorknob; or at least none that they could see. Although, in fact, the house itself was just barely visible through the protective shield of bare oak limbs that surrounded the property, mostly because—unlike all of the neighboring houses—all of the windows were dark and all of the exterior lights were out.

In the rapidly fading light, the wood-and-brick structure appeared to have taken on an eerie and sinister cast, as though all traces of human activity had long since ceased to exist.

"Yeah, I'm sure," Culver whispered as he reached up to shut off the automatic interior light before quietly opening the front passenger door. "Hold on a minute, I want to check something."

Just an empty house, Russelli told himself. Quiet, dark and—from all outward signs—deserted, although there was nothing in that casual description that even began to explain the numbing sensations of rage and frustration that threatened to overwhelm the veteran police detective sergeant who continued to sit quietly and stare at the somber, melancholy scene before his eyes.

In a strange, horrible, and lifeless sort of way, it was very much like the scene outside Kathy Harmon's vandalized home, and Russelli knew it. And like Culver, his longtime friend, he could almost taste it.

But then it occurred to him. The other possibility. The one that made Detective Sergeant John Russelli blink his eyes for a moment, and then—in a terrible way—almost smile.

Culver was back in the car in less than forty-five seconds, gently closing the door and then tossing the newspapers and letters in a pile on the backseat. Russelli turned his head and saw that there were two thick, band-wrapped newspapers in the pile.

"Which ones?" he growled.

"Thursday and Friday," Culver replied in a steady, emotionless voice. "I just thought of something."

Culver's words were interrupted by the static-filled transmission of the EOC dispatcher.

"MC-Eighty."

Even the normally cheerful voice of Sally Henderson seemed to have taken on a foreboding air of portentous doom.

John Russelli slowly reached for the radio microphone while Culver returned his gaze to the house that had suddenly taken on an even more somber and threatening specter.

"Go to channel seven," Russelli rasped, and then reached down to switch the radio receiver to the scrambled tactical frequencies.

"EOC to MC-Eighty, channel seven."

"What do you want now?" Russelli demanded with audible indifference.

Sally Henderson hesitated, jarred by Russelli's blatant and continued violation of radio procedures—*like he doesn't even care about being a cop anymore,* she thought—but then she went on.

"We have the subject's secretary on the line. She says Paul Radlick did *not* show up at the office today, there was no prior call-in, and no response when they called to check. Repeat, no call-in, no show, no response."

Culver reached for the microphone, his gaze remaining fixed on the front of Paul Radlick's house.

"What about Wednesday and Thursday?" he asked for no

other reason than the simple fact that he wanted to know. It really didn't matter now, but he still wanted to know.

You bastard. You goddamned slimy, pervert bastard.

There was a pause of about fifteen seconds, and then Sally Henderson was back on the air.

"Subject was in the office all day Wednesday, but was checked out to the law library on Thursday. No contact with his office since Wednesday afternoon. Do you want a follow-up on that?"

Culver nodded his head slowly and closed his eyes for a brief moment before responding.

"Negative. Thanks, Sally."

Culver dropped the mike on the front seat, and then continued to stare at the darkened house for several more seconds before he finally spoke again.

"I think he's out here somewhere."

John Russelli's eyelids flickered, but his gaze never strayed from the front of Paul Radlick's house as the expression in his eyes slowly changed into something that wasn't even remotely civilized.

"You want to call in for backup?" he asked in a voice now completely lacking in warmth or emotion.

Backup, Culver thought, feeling his arms start to tingle in response to the first small infusions of arterial adrenaline; feeling the age-old anticipatory effects as his body began to prepare for the sudden, urgent need to survive.

Translation: do we want any witnesses if the goddamned slimy pervert bastard really *is* out here?

Or in there, Culver reminded himself. *Don't forget that. He might be inside.*

Yeah, right, but if he is, what the hell's he doing *in there? What's he waiting for?*

Us?

The thought of the pale-eyed, predatory Digger waiting patiently for them in the cold and rainy darkness caused Henry Culver slowly to turn his eyes away from the depressing sight of Paul Radlick's abandoned home, and to find the answer in the cold, passive face that mirrored his own. Slowly and carefully, as if wanting to be absolutely sure, he shook his head.

No, they didn't want a backup.

Not for John Doe Thirty-three.

They met together at the back of Russelli's vehicle.

Working quietly, Russelli carefully unlocked and opened the trunk lid, reached into the trunk, pulled out a twelve-gage sawed-off pump shotgun wrapped in a heavy blue denim jacket with a torn sleeve, a field jacket, two portable radios, two Kevlar vests, a pair of four-cell flashlights, a white cardboard box containing twenty-five number four buck twelve-gage shotgun shells, a similar box of fifty police-issue .357 hollow-points, and a roll of white medical tape. They set all of the items on top of the wheel wells.

Culver, in turn, pulled out one of his ever-present canvas equipment bags, and exchanged his polished work shoes for a pair of worn tennis shoes.

After checking to make sure they were turned off, Russelli and Culver hooked the small pack set radios to their belts against the small of their backs. Then Culver reached for one of the vests, a flashlight, and the denim jacket while Russelli checked the sawed-off shotgun, and then slowly fed the high-base rounds into the cylindrical magazine.

Making periodic checks of the gray-black shadowy areas surrounding Radlick's nearby house, Henry Culver exchanged his overcoat for the vest and the darker denim jacket, confirmed a full load in the chambers of his .357 revolver, and then transferred a pair of speed-loaders to his right jacket pocket.

They both tossed their loose change and house keys into the trunk, filled their right rear trouser pockets with a handful of .357 hollow-point rounds, wrapped short lengths of the white tape around their individual sets of vehicle keys, and then—at Russelli's direction—placed longer strips of the white tape around each of their left arms, just above the elbow, as identifiers, so that they wouldn't shoot each other.

Their preparations completed, they walked around to the right side of the vehicle, keeping the protective metal frame between themselves and any potential threat as they stared down the long, black asphalt driveway that led to the garage door and front porch of the darkened house.

He's been here. I know he's been here, Culver thought as his left hand tightened around the comforting grip of the heavy flashlight.

"Look for traps," he said quietly, as much to himself as to Russelli. "If the bastard's been here, he's set at least one."

"That's been his M.O. all along." Russelli nodded in agreement, ignoring the nagging pains in his lower leg. "No reason to think he'd change now. You going to need a light?"

Culver nodded. "Yeah, I think so. Thursday's paper is still there. If he was here, then he's had at least thirty-six hours—maybe forty-eight at the outside—to rig something. Hundred different ways he could do it if he's had that much time, most of them damn near impossible to spot."

John Russelli's many years of experience in dealing with crazies like Digger made him hesitate for a moment. The problem was that if both he *and* Henry went down without calling for a backup, then John-Doe Thirty-three, or Digger, or whoever the hell he was, was gone.

The thought of the pale-eyed Digger running loose—and nobody knowing about it for several more hours—caused Russelli to start to reach for his radio out of pure instinct, but Culver caught the motion and shook his head.

"I said damn near, not impossible. Don't worry, I'll spot it."

"What about the gate?"

"I already checked. It's clear."

"Okay, use the light, but keep it away from you," Russelli added as he scanned the driveway and the front of the house one last time. "Don't make yourself a target. I yell 'down,' you hit the deck and roll right. One of us ends up in a hostage situation, the other guy waits to hear his name and then double-taps the bastard, head and heart, clear or not. You got that?"

"Yeah, sure." Culver nodded absentmindedly, mentally walking himself through the most likely setups one more time as he secured the heavy .357 Smith and Wesson revolver back into its shoulder holster with his right hand. He moved his left hand out away from his side, and then switched on the flashlight with his left thumb.

"Okay," Russelli growled as he jacked a round into the chamber of his cut-down pump shotgun and then snapped the trigger safety to the OFF position, "let's do it."

The driveway was the obvious choice, but the icy tree limbs and brush in the surrounding darkness offered too many hidden trigger points, so they moved down the dark, slick asphalt as a linked team; taking it step by step as every sensory nerve in their bodies strained to catch the first sign of a beam, or a trip, or any movement at all.

Henry Culver was on his hands and knees now, ignoring the sharp-pointed bits of gravel that bit into his palms and knees, and the ice-encrusted water that soaked his clothes, as his eyes followed the flickering path of the narrow flashlight beam, searching for the trap that he and Russelli both knew—with absolute certainty—had to be there.

Somewhere.

As he continued to inch himself down the middle of the ten-foot-wide driveway, slowly and methodically scanning both sides of the asphalt strip, Culver was completely oblivious of the shotgun barrel that swept back and forth over his head . . . and of John Russelli's boot as it continued to brush against his leg, maintaining contact and position so that Russelli could concentrate completely on the house, and the trees, and anything at all that might move.

Henry Culver was no longer thinking about Russelli, or the shotgun, or pale-eyed freaks who liked to cut on people and then stare for hours at the bloody crime scene photos, because Culver's faith in his mercurial partner and longtime friend was absolute. If Digger was out there, then John Russelli would spot him—and deal with him—or die trying.

He's not going to use a beam, Culver told himself again as brought the flashlight beam back to a stray reflection that turned out to be an icy twig, but could have easily been something else, unaware that he had allowed the flashlight to inch closer to his body—causing some of the diffused light to illuminate the side of his face.

Have to be dual infrareds to be sure, and those systems draw a bunch of power. Lines have been going down all over the county, and it's too cold to trust a battery for—what is it, two days now?

A pile of icy leaves crunched in the darkness to Culver's left, jarring at his brain as his flashlight beam and Russelli's shotgun swung in unison, triangulating in on the pair of reflective eyes that blinked in shock and then disappeared as the thoroughly soaked and hungry feline changed its mind and its direction of travel in less than half a second.

"Jesus Christ, what was that?" Russelli hissed.

"Cat. Probably one of theirs," Culver whispered shakily, pausing a moment to swallow and take a deep, settling breath. "They had two—both of them green-eyed."

Russelli muttered something that Culver didn't even try to catch because he was too busy trying to shake off a sudden surge of nausea that had distracted his attention from the flashlight beam—nausea brought on by the sudden realization that he really didn't believe there was the slightest chance that Paul and Doreen Radlick were still alive.

Had two?

Knock it off, Culver swore at himself, *you don't know they're dead, so start paying attention to what you're doing. He's not going to use a beam, and he can't plant a sensor in asphalt, so he's going to have use . . .*

Halfway down the driveway now, and moving forward with his right knee and free right hand, Culver suddenly froze in position as he felt a sudden thin pressure against the upper portion of his forehead.

. . . a wire.

"Don't move!" Culver hissed, forcing himself not to move at all until he figured out which way was directly back and away from the almost-invisible wire that he *hadn't* spotted because he was too busy worrying about Paul and Doreen Radlick. He didn't dare put any more strain on it—not if it was a pull trigger.

"What's the matter?" Russelli demanded in a hoarse whisper.

"Trip wire, about thirty inches off the ground, running . . ." Culver brought his hand up very slowly until it just barely brushed against the thin, taut strand, ". . . about sixty degrees to the driveway."

"Where does it go?"

Culver was already running the flashlight beam down the length of the hair-thin strand of monofilament line until it disappeared in the rough brush to his right. He continued to sweep the beam back and forth until the disc of light suddenly stopped in the middle of a waist-high stack of split oak firewood.

Then Culver blinked because he wasn't seeing what he expected to see.

Instead of being absorbed and muted by the rough, porous wood surfaces, portions of the narrow flashlight beam were being reflected back in gleaming bits of sparkling light.

Three claymores, wired in series, Culver reminded himself, feeling his stomach start to churn as he remembered Sergeant Al Stewart's description of the explosive devices that had killed Tess Beasley. Hundreds of pellets apiece, backed up with enough C-4 to send them clear through the door of a K-9 unit station wagon.

Military issue, so he'd have to have access, Culver thought. *But how?*

Shaking his head, Culver forced the numbing images of the sheet-covered bodies into the back recesses of his mind as he continued to stare at the oddly reflective woodpile, remembering only then that the curved surfaces of claymore antipersonnel mines didn't reflect light.

Not supposed to be seen. That's why they cover them with dull green camouflage paint. So what the hell . . .

"Watch the light," Russelli whispered a warning out of the darkness.

"Yeah, right," Culver acknowledged, switching off the flashlight and then giving his eyes several seconds to adjust to the dim light from the neighboring homes before he began to move forward.

Then, trying not to think about the possibility of more invisible wires, Culver started crawling in the direction of the woodpile, using his free hand to sweep slowly and gently through the empty air, until his fingers finally brushed against a rough, wet, splintery surface. Then he turned the flashlight on again, and saw for the first time how the woodpile had been rigged.

"Jesus Christ," Culver whispered.

"What is it?" Russelli demanded as he shuffled his left shoe up against Culver's extended leg.

"Four-by-four-by-eight-foot pile. One row of logs in front, three in back, probably a hundred pounds of tenpenny nails, and at least a couple dozen sticks of dynamite that I can see from here in the middle. He's got electrical wire all over the place. If the whole cord's hollow, then there's probably a couple hundred sticks in there."

"No claymores?"

"No, just one big one," Culver answered, illuminating the setup with a quick sweep of his flashlight. "The back rows of logs are braced against those three trees. Assuming the driveway runs north–south, anything hits that wire, about two hundred pounds of nails and splinters go due west right on through it."

"Do you see any more wires?" Russelli asked, ignoring the fact that he was standing in the blast path of an incredibly lethal booby trap as he went back to searching the surrounding area for movement. As far as Russelli was concerned, dealing with the trap was Culver's problem. He wanted Digger.

"Don't see any." Culver shook his head as he used the flashlight once again to confirm his initial check, and then quickly shut it off again, uncomfortably aware that he and Russelli were targeting themselves by staying too long in one spot.

"Can you disarm it?"

"I can't see where the trip wire connects. It's probably a pull trigger, but . . ." Culver started to say, and then caught himself, remembering that as far as Russelli knew, he'd been working for the Army crime lab, analyzing dope all those years. "Russelli, I can't disarm this thing. I don't know a goddamned thing about . . ."

"Don't give me a line of shit, Henry," Russelli rasped in the darkness, never taking his eyes off the shadowy house. "Remember when they stuck me in Personnel after I got out of the hospital. Got so fucking bored in there, I finally popped the captain's safe for the pure hell of it one day while he was on vacation. Found out you've got one hell of a thick file for somebody who's supposed to have been some kind of U.S. Army dope chemist."

"That file was supposed to stay sealed," Culver whispered, feeling a sense of numbness flow through his arms that had nothing whatsoever to do with the nail-and-dynamite booby trap that was less than a yard away.

"It was, and I left it that way," Russelli replied. "But there was a real interesting list of expert qualifications on a separate sheet of paper that wasn't sealed. You ought to know something about disarming bombs, Henry."

Caught between a live and lethal booby trap, and the realization that his carefully constructed cover had been blown by his inquisitive partner, Culver closed his eyes for a moment and sighed.

"Russelli . . ."

"Look, Henry, I really don't give a shit about what you used to do to earn a paycheck, but it'd be real nice if you told

me you knew how to disarm that fucking thing before that
asshole starts wondering what the hell we're doing out here."

Culver hesitated a moment, and then shrugged mentally
as he turned the flashlight back on and then began to crawl
over toward the back of the woodpile. "I'll take a look."

Thirty seconds later, after the flashlight beam had flickered all around and above the woodpile, Culver suddenly
hissed out a frantic warning.

"Russelli, don't move out there!"

"I'm *not* moving, goddamn it!" he hissed. "What the hell's
the matter now?"

"Just stay right where you're at, I'll be right there."

"Jesus H. Christ," Russelli whispered. "Look, forget about
disarming the fucking thing. We can *step* over the goddamned wire. You keep this shit up and I'm going to die of
a heart attack before . . ."

"You go over that wire and you're not going to have a heart
to worry about," Culver whispered as he came up to his feet
next to his partner.

"What?"

"There's a second wire. It's a black thread about four
inches in back of the first one and about a foot off the
ground."

"Okay, so we jump . . ."

"Uh-uh, no jumping. The bastard rigged a pair of infrared
beams over the top to protect the system. You can see the re-
flectors over there, nailed to the trees. The lower one's about
five feet off the ground and the upper one's about seven, both
running parallel to the wires. As far as I can tell, all three systems are wired together at the dynamite—probably in sequence, to make sure a dog or cat doesn't set the thing off by
tripping one, but I can't be sure."

"What about cutting the wires to the dynamite?"

"Not a good idea. He's got protective circuits running all
through that wood pile. All I have to do is miss one, and the
whole thing goes."

"What about going around it?"

"He's got at least one more trip wire that I could see running into the woods. We've got to figure he's got the whole perimeter covered."

"Persistent little asshole, isn't he," Russelli muttered in a dangerously cold and humorless voice. "Any ideas?"

"I can think of maybe three or four ways we could do it."

"Yeah, I'm listening."

"One, we take our chances going through the trees—which, from what little I saw, is probably a real bad idea," Culver said quietly.

"Forget the trees," Russelli agreed.

"Two and three," Culver went on, "we could set off the whole mess at a distance with the shotgun. Or, if we've got any brains at all, we could put in a call to the station, and get some help out here."

Russelli stared at the house in silence for a while as he considered those options. Then he turned to Culver: "You said four."

"The last one isn't much better," Culver replied, feeling himself start to shiver in the cold darkness as he stared at the dark shadowy house that now seemed even more dismal and lifeless than before.

"What is it?" Russelli demanded.

"The wires and the infrared beams cover the entire driveway, and we can't go over, or under, or around them, right?"

"Yeah, that's about it. So?"

"So there's only one way left."

John Russelli's eyebrows started to furrow into a perplexed frown, and then it hit him. "You mean . . . ?"

Culver nodded his head slowly. "Right through the middle."

The two cross-stacked piles of wood Henry Culver created with the eighteen-inch-long, split oak logs he'd carefully removed from the booby-trapped woodpile, one by one, were each just slightly more that thirty inches high. Which meant that they were just slightly higher than the hair-thin monofilament strand that was now bordered, and theoretically protected, by the two parallel-running top logs in each pile. The second wire—the almost-invisible black thread—ran right between paired sets of cross-laid logs in the lower portion of the racks.

"You sure those things are solid?" Russelli whispered as he continued to watch for movement around the house.

"They'd better be," Culver grunted as he made a final check to confirm that there was no contact whatsoever between either of the wires and any of the logs.

"How much clearance do we have at the top?"

"It looks like a little less than twenty-four inches, but don't count on more than twenty. The beams run in a straight line, but the driveway curves down at both sides. Hard to tell for sure."

"Great," Russelli muttered dourly.

"Just keep your weight balanced, your back straight, your butt down, and take it slow," Culver advised with far more reassurance than he felt himself. "You ready?"

Nodding silently, Russelli slowly took several backward steps along the slushy wet driveway, sweeping the sawed-off shotgun back and forth in the general direction of the house, until he came up against the front bumper of the parked detective unit. Crouching down against the opposite side of the vehicle from the woodpile, Russelli reached around his back for the pack set radio and triggered the transmit button twice.

Back at the racks, Henry Culver waited until he heard the two clicks on his own radio, and then went to work. With slow, careful movements, he passed the radio, his holstered revolver, the flashlight, and then finally Russelli's denim jacket through the gap between the top of one of the wood stacks and the invisible line representing the lower protective edge of the rectangular infrared circuit. The circuit that he didn't dare interrupt, even for a second.

Not if I want to stay alive, Culver reminded himself as he removed his shoes and socks, and passed them through the gap also, to give himself a little bit more of a grip, just in case.

Then, after taking a couple of deep, steadying breaths, Culver slowly got down on his hands and knees, set himself parallel to the direction of the wires, and then ever so carefully put first his right leg and then his right arm into the gap and then on the two slightly wobbly racks, balancing himself on the slippery wet asphalt with his left leg and hand.

Okay, he told himself, *nice and easy now.*

Taking in and holding a deep breath, he transferred as much of his weight as he could onto the two racks with his right arm and foot, trying to judge the stability of the entire system one last time. Then he pushed himself up onto the stacked logs in one smooth motion that left him extended over the wires in a lizardlike position, with the left side of his face pressed tight against the rough, splintery surface of one of the logs and his chest and stomach not quite brushing against the tight monofilament strand.

Better the wire than the beam, he thought as he let his arms and legs take his weight evenly for a few seconds, to ease the strain on his trembling muscles. *I can feel the wire. Don't even want to think about the beam.*

He took in another deep, steadying breath, and then began to move his fingers and goes in toward the center of the outer perpendicular logs at the top of the racks, trying not to move them out of position to where they'd fall on the wire.

Come on, get it over with. Don't worry about it, just do it.

After positioning the fingers and toes of his left hand and foot to what he hoped was the center balance point of each rack, Culver slowly brought his trembling and nearly frozen right foot up from the log until he could just barely feel the rough surface. Then, straining to maintain his balance, he extended his leg out in a parallel direction to the ground, and then slowly dropped his bare foot down to the asphalt.

Moments later, he was sitting on the wet, slushy driveway on the other side of the trip wires and quickly putting on his shoes as John Russelli warily approached the jury-rigged bridge.

"Just take it slow," Culver repeated as he finished tying his shoelaces, hearing the soft clattering noise as Russelli passed the sawed-off shotgun through the gap and set it down gently onto the hard, wet asphalt.

Then, as Russelli finished divesting himself of anything bulky, Culver drew his .357 out of its holster, and moved forward as far as he dared up the driveway toward the house—trying to watch for Digger, keep an eye on the shadowy figure of Russelli, and stay as far away from the potential blast zone as possible, all at the same time.

"That's it, take it slow and easy, and keep your face down tight against the logs," Culver hissed, turning his own head back and forth as though he was watching a tennis match, trying not to wince at the creaking sounds as Russelli slowly muscled himself up onto the crosshatched racks of split wood.

"You on?" Culver whispered.

"Yeah, I guess so."

"Okay, body straight, stomach tight, butt down, transfer your weight to your left hand, and then . . ."

The horrible sounds of clattering wood and Russelli's frantic curse jarred at Henry Culver's brain, causing him to spin around and stare numbly with some indeterminate portion of his consciousness at what he knew would be the last thing he ever saw. And then he scrambled forward, the .357 forgotten somewhere on the asphalt driveway.

What he saw made the rest of his conscious mind and his entire body go numb.

In the instant that the rack of logs under his head started to go, Russelli had thrust his long arms and legs down onto the spilling logs, and was now caught in a fully extended push-up position on his fingertips and toes, straddling the exposed upper trip wire with an arm and leg on either side and his muscular chest and stomach sagging against the strand. Miraculously, the lower black thread hadn't been pushed or broken by the still-protective lower logs.

"Jesus, Russelli . . ."

"Tell me about it later," Russelli rasped, his deep voice almost breaking from the mental and physical strain of keeping his heavy body upright and immobile. "What the hell do I do now?"

Fighting against an almost-overwhelming desire to panic and dive away from the deadly explosion of nails and oak splinters that could come at any moment, Culver forced his mind clear.

"Keep your arms extended . . ."

"Yeah, no shit," Russelli gasped between rapid breaths.

". . . and lift your left leg up, a little more. Okay, now bring it to the middle, straight across . . . okay, I've got it," Culver grunted as he reached through the gap between the wire and beam, and took the weight of Russelli's left leg and lower body in both hands. "Okay, now bring your right leg around to the right—watch it, stay up! Okay, that's it, so that you end up perpendicular . . . right. Okay, now brace yourself in a three-point stance—right arm and both feet. Yeah, okay. Now come back . . . there!"

John Russelli collapsed face forward on the wet driveway, and lay there for several long seconds, taking in deep, shuddering breaths. Then, finally, he shook his head, came up to a sitting position, pulled the shotgun next to his right side, and began to put on his boots.

Moments later, he was standing next to Culver, about ten feet from Paul Radlick's front door, with the shotgun in his hands.

"Any second thoughts about calling for backup?" Culver asked, keeping his eyes on the dark house.

"You think the little prick wired the door too, don't you?" Russelli asked, still breathing heavily, and pointedly ignoring his partner's sarcasm.

"Yeah, probably."

"Fine." Russelli nodded. "Then to hell with the door."

Before Culver could say or do anything else, John Russelli uttered something that sounded far more animal-like than human, took several lunging steps forward, and then launched himself sideways through Paul Radlick's living room window.

Chapter Thirty

Elliott Parkinson was on the phone, making cryptic notes on a green legal pad as he listened to a status report from one of his senior field operatives, when J. Winston Weathersby came hurrying into his office.

Looking up and immediately recognizing the worried look on his young assistant's face, Parkinson held up a cautioning hand and then turned his attention to the phone.

"Marcus, let me call you back. Yes, in five minutes."

After making one more notation on the legal pad, Parkinson put down his pen and looked up.

"Well, what is it?"

"Several things," Weathersby said, setting himself down in one of the plush visitors chairs—the first time he had ever done so without being invited—and worked to get his labored breathing under control.

"Take your time," Parkinson advised calmly.

"First of all," Weathersby said, after taking in a deep, steadying breath, "I finally managed to get in contact with our friend at the PD. Turns out the victim on that bombing wasn't Culver after all."

"Thank God for that," Parkinson whispered as an image of the unnerving expression in Arthur Traynor's eyes flickered through his memory.

"Yeah, right now, he's about the only link we've got left to Digger." Weathersby nodded, completely misreading his supervisor's concern.

"Who was it then?"

"Some female patrol officer. Odd thing about it though, she was apparently assigned Culver's old call sign—

Eight-Forty-Charlie. They're not sure if that means anything."

"It would be an incredible coincidence if it didn't," Parkinson said uneasily. His right index finger started to tap nervously on the polished surface of his desk.

"You mean you think Digger went after him?"

"I would consider that to be a reasonable assumption. Wouldn't you?" the AD retorted, favoring his special assistant with a glare that nearly caused J. Winston Weathersby to forget the most important part of his presentation.

"Oh, uh, yes—of course. But, uh, the reason things got so confused," Weathersby went on hurriedly, "it turns out that Culver was transferred over to one of the Major Crimes units this morning."

Parkinson's pale lips suddenly blossomed into a wide smile. "It's about time we had some good news for a change. No wonder we couldn't locate him. So where is he now?"

"One of the spotter teams just reported in a few minutes ago. He and another detective are out at the house of an attorney named Paul Radlick."

"Radlick?" Parkinson's eyebrows furrowed. "Wasn't he . . . ?"

"Digger's attorney," Weathersby finished.

Parkinson blinked in surprise. "What in the world is Culver doing talking with Digger's attorney?"

"Well, actually, I don't think he has—or at least not yet anyway," Weathersby corrected. "According to our spotter, as of a few minutes ago, Culver and another detective were still trying to work their way in toward Radlick's house. As best he can tell from his position, it looks like the driveway's wired."

"What?" Parkinson sat upright in his chair. "What do you *mean,* 'wired'?"

"I'm just telling you what they reported in," Weathersby said hurriedly. "I don't—"

"You mean 'wired' in the sense of the Kathy Harmon situation? Another *bomb?*" the AD demanded.

"Possibly . . . I guess. I mean, I guess he really couldn't tell because it's pretty dark out there, and I guess, from the sounds of it, he can't get in too close because the cops—Culver and this other big guy—are acting pretty spooked, like they're going to shoot the first thing that moves."

"For Christ's sake, what the—?" A look of palatable fear suddenly flashed across Parkinson's tanned face. "Not us? For God's sake, don't tell me one of our people—"

"Oh no, of course not." Weathersby shook his head quickly. "Culver is still hands-off. I made sure everybody got the word."

"Good," Parkinson nodded, visibly relieved. "If Digger does get to Culver, it must be absolutely clear that our fingerprints are not on it." But then his expression shifted to one of piqued interest. "Digger's attorney," he said, mostly to himself. "That's fascinating."

Weathersby nodded. "Especially if that driveway really *is* wired."

"Is there any indication that Digger's out there?"

"No, but everybody's on the alert."

"Good." Parkinson nodded in apparent satisfaction. "What else?"

"L'Que's son was rushed into emergency surgery about twenty minutes ago. Something about pressure on the brain. They're working on him right now. L'Que's there at the hospital."

"Go on."

"Then there's Alex—the operative that Traynor, uh, injured."

"Yes, what about him?" Elliott Parkinson's eyes suddenly focused on those of his special assistant. "Has he decided to start talking?"

"The most we're ever going to get out of him in the next couple of months is a written statement, assuming he changes his mind and starts being cooperative," Weathersby said, shuddering inwardly as he remembered the mass of wiring that had held the field operative's severely broken jaw shut.

"I want to know what happened out there," Parkinson emphasized with a pointed finger. "I refuse to believe that Arthur Traynor could do something like that to an experienced operative like Alex."

"Traynor claims to know nothing about it," Weathersby said, "and he certainly doesn't *look* like he's been in a fight, but it's not that simple anymore. According to Security, the director just had Alex transferred into protective custody."

"*What?*"

"I'm still looking into it," Weathersby said defensively, "but that's not the worst of it."

Elliott Parkinson shook his head in disbelief. "Then what, pray tell, *is* the worst of it?"

"The word in the halls is that the director's really pissed about something," Weathersby said nervously. "Supposed to be an emergency meeting of the director's council being scheduled sometime soon."

"Then maybe you should find out what it's all about, don't you think?" Parkinson suggested sarcastically.

At that moment, the white phone on Parkinson's desk rang.

"Yes, Marge," he spoke softly into the handset, and then listened for a few moments. "Yes, of course, nine o'clock will be fine," he said, nodded his head as he acknowledged his special assistant's hasty exit.

Then he paused, lost in thought for a moment.

"Oh, and Marge," Parkinson added as the door to his office closed gently, "would you please get hold of Marcus for me. Yes, please, right away."

Given the hazards of a daily lifestyle that involved stealing from neighbors, short-weighing friends, snitching off competitors, and playing very dangerous games with cops like John Russelli, the sudden, unexpected explosion of window glass behind Molly Hunsacker's back *should* have sent the professional burglar, car thief, dope dealer, occasional informant, and general con artist diving for the .22 caliber Browning target pistol she kept in her backpack.

Or, at least, that would have been the intelligent thing to do.

But while Molly-the-Hun was well-known throughout Fairfax County for her feats of strength, aggressiveness, and beer-drinking, nobody had ever accused her of being overly intelligent.

She verified that assessment by simply turning in the direction of the crash with a puzzled expression on her face, just in time to see an explosive spray of glass fragments and a dark, bearded, shadowy figure tumbling forward on her living room floor.

That got Molly-the-Hun's attention, and finally sent her scrambling in the direction of her backpack and pistol. But by that time, of course, it was much too late.

She never even got close.

Instead, the bowel-loosening roar of a .357 Magnum pistol being fired in the confines of the twelve-by-sixteen-foot room—not to mention the added impetus of seeing her mildewed, canvas backpack spin away under the high-velocity impact of a .357 expanding hollow-tip bullet—sent the mind-shocked burglar sprawling to the floor with her arms wrapped tightly around her head.

For a few panic-stricken moments, Molly Hunsacker continued to cower on the floor in a futile effort to ward off the expected second bullet. Then, finally, her eyes widened with fear and rage, she opened up her arms in what amounted to resigned surrender, and saw for the first time the face of her assailant.

"Bobby?" She whispered in shocked disbelief as her arms dropped to the floor.

"That's right, *Bobby,* you goddamned double-dealing, two-faced *bitch,*" Bobby Morgan managed to snarl through his chattering teeth as he hobbled forward to stand over the woman he had once almost thought of as a friend. "Bet you're real surprised to see me, aren't you?"

"Surprised? You shithead! You break into my house . . . !" Molly started to scream, mad and scared all at the same time as she started to come up . . . and then immediately changed her mind when Bobby Morgan stuck the long barrel of the still-smoking revolver right between her glowering eyes.

"Come on ahead—*do it!*" He sneered.

"Bobby, what's the hell's the matter with you?" Molly-the-Hun demanded, her stunned mind racing furiously. "You come breaking into my house like a crazy person, yelling and screaming—and your pants . . . look at them. They're covered with blood. You must have cut yourself on the glass when you—"

"*Cut myself?*" Bobby Morgan raged, holding on to the wall to keep from falling as he glared down at Molly Hunsacker. "Is *that* what you think all this blood is about—that I *cut* myself on your goddamned window?"

"Bobby—"

"Thanks to you—*you!*" Bobby Morgan gestured furiously with the pistol barrel as he stammered on in a mindless rage, "I nearly got my goddamned leg blown off by a bunch of crazy assholes who broke into *our* house and started cranking off rounds like it was the goddamned Fourth of July!"

"What?"

"You heard me. They shot the shit out of our place. And then I end up hiding out in the woods, in the goddamned freezing rain, trying to cut a whole shitpot full of lead outta my leg just so I can stay on my feet long enough get away from there. And you want to know if I got *cut?*"

"Bobby, listen to me." Molly Hunsacker blinked, shaking her head. "Honest to God, I don't understand any of this. What are you *talking* about?"

"What am I *talking* about? What the fuck do you *think* I'm talking about, you slimy, back-stabbing bitch!" Bobby Morgan yelled, his bloodshot eyes bulging with rage as he stared to reach for Molly-the-Hun's long hair with his free clenched hand. But then, before he could carry out the intended pistol-whipping, Morgan suddenly screamed "Ah SHIT!" and twisted to the floor as a nerve-searing bolt of agonizing pain surged up from his shattered leg and into the back of his head.

"Bobby—!?"

"What's the matter, you don't like the sight of blood?" Morgan gasped, bracing himself against the wall with his shoulder, and using his free hand instead to press against the blood-soaked bandage just above his right knee where his self-inflicted surgical wounds were starting to bleed freely again. "Well that's too goddamned bad," he choked out between rapid, shuddering breaths, "because the way I see it, this—this whole mess is *your* fault."

"*My* fault? What are you talking about? *What's* my fault?" Molly Hunsacker demanded.

"I'll *tell* you what's your fault," Bobby Morgan whispered, his bearded face a pale, ashen color from the nearly overwhelming pain. "Me and Otis, we did just like you said. We hooked in with that bastard what's-his-name, that friend of yours, and he sent us that computer, just like you said he would. And then we waited—Christ I don't know how long, two or maybe three months—until he finally gets around to sending us some instructions, and we did the job for him, just like you and Otis and I talked about."

"You guys did a job for *Digger?*"

"Yeah, that's the name. Digger." Bobby Morgan whispered softly. "Knew it was something weird like that." The severely injured burglar was finding it more and more difficult to talk in complete sentences, and his eyes had taken on a distinctly glassy look.

"But—"

"Anyway, we did the job okay." Bobby Morgan rambled on, ignoring her. "It got a little screwed up because the kid came home early, but we took care of him, and then got out of there okay. But then we went off in a ditch 'cause of all that ice and rain, and I damned near broke my leg with the jack, and we almost got nailed by the cops, and then—*then,*" he added with savage emphasis, "*we* get fined for being a couple minutes late by some smart-ass, old fart nigger who thinks he's Lord God Almighty himself."

"Bobby . . . I don't *understand,"* Molly-the-Hun whispered, shaking her head in absolute disbelief.

"And that wasn't even the end of it. No, by God, it wasn't. You want to know what that goddamned Digger friend of yours did to us *then?"*

Molly-the-Hun just sat there on the floor and stared at the wide-eyed, bloody figure.

"No? Well I'll *tell* you what he did," Bobby Morgan raged, his bulging, bloodshot eyes threatening to pop out of their sockets. "First of all, he sends us a computer message calling *us* a bunch of dumb bastards. *Us.* Can you believe that? Otis and I, we lay our butts out on the line for that bastard, damn near get ourselves killed and arrested, and that's the kind of thanks we get."

"Bobby, goddamnit, I *told* you—" Molly started in, but Morgan refused to listen.

"And *then,* after that, he—or maybe a couple of his goons, I don't know—anyway, somebody comes busting into our house, middle of the night, shoots Otis, and then nearly kills me too!"

"Otis is dead?" Molly Hunsacker's normally suntanned face was starting to turn pale.

"Is he dead? They nearly cut him in half, shot him in the face. 'Course he's dead. Whadda ya think, that I'd leave him back there for the cops to find if he wasn't?" Morgan demanded, pointing the shaking barrel of the .357 directly at Molly Hunsacker's prominent nose.

"No, no, of course not," Molly said carefully, very much aware that this was definitely the wrong time to be getting into Bobby Morgan's face.

"Yeah, well, anyway," Morgan went on, "there's this cop in the deal, too. Think his name's Culver. Yeah, that's it, Henry Culver. Heard a bunch of cops call him that last night."

Molly Hunsacker, who hadn't really understood much of anything that Bobby Morgan had said up to this point, and who was widely viewed by her peers as having the constitution of a lumberjack, looked like she was about ready to pass out at any moment.

"Now you're saying that a *police officer* broke into your house . . . and killed Otis?" She whispered, unable to believe her ears.

"See, what it is," Morgan continued on, starting to look completely out of focus now as he ignored Molly-the-Hun's incredulous response, "I think this Culver guy's involved with you and Digger in all this, 'cause he was the one who shoulda nailed us when we were off on the side of the road. And he would have, too, except that all of a sudden he just went away, for no particular reason. And then I see him again at our house, after everything really went to shit. Only this time, all the other cops *except* him stay there, and he goes away again.

"I mean, I'm asking you," Morgan mumbled, staring straight down at Molly Hunsacker with his glassy eyes, "does that sound suspicious or what?"

Molly Hunsacker furrowed her eyebrows in confusion, and then shook her head as she stared up at her former employee. "Bobby, please, you *gotta* slow down, 'cause I don't understand one goddamn thing you're saying. You're trying to tell me that Digger is working with a police officer named Culver, and that the two of them killed Otis?"

"Thas' what looks like to me," Morgan said, the slurring of his words becoming more and more pronounced. " 'Cept what I'm thinking, now . . . is maybe you got a part in it too."

"That's bullshit! You know I'd never—"

"Goddamned right it's bullshit," Morgan interrupted, vaguely aware that his eyes were blinking shut more and more frequently. Then he started to weave back and forth and had to grab at the wall again before he fell. "And thas' exactly what I'm going to tell him, too," he whispered hoarsely as he rested his forehead against the crudely painted wall, "just as soon as you take me there."

"As soon as I do what? Take you—?"

"You and me, Molly baby, we're gonna go out to see your friend Digger, have ourselves a little talk," Bobby Morgan rasped as he tried to focus his eyes on the blurry figure who was still sprawled out on the floor. "Just a little conversation, get everything straightened out real nice and easy like. Then, soon as we finish doin' that, I'm gonna kill him to make it up to Otis."

"Bobby, listen to me," Molly Hunsacker said cautiously, "I *can't* take you to see Digger, even if I wanted to—even if you threaten to kill me, I still can't—because I don't have the slightest idea where he lives. I've only talked with him once over the phone, the first time, and that was a long time ago."

"So call him up, talk to him again."

"It doesn't work that way. I've explained this to you at least a half a dozen times. Everything is done through the computer now. Digger never talks to anyone face-to-face. I don't know his address, his telephone number, or anything. God as my witness, I don't even know what the bastard *looks* like. That's just the way he runs things."

"Oh yeah, right, forgot about that goddamned computer shit," Morgan mumbled as his eyes slowly closed and his chin dropped against his chest.

For a brief moment, Molly-the-Hun thought she might have a chance. Bobby Morgan seemed to be slipping into a merciful state of unconsciousness that would either allow her to run for it, grab for his gun, or go for her own gun in the backpack. But before she could begin to make her move, Morgan jerked his head back up and pointed the .357 revolver at her head again.

"Where's your van," he slurred, trying to blink his eyes open.

"In the garage. Why?"

"Gimme the keys."

"Bobby, I told you . . ." Molly started to protest again, but Morgan cut her off.

"Listen, maybe you don't know what he looks like, but you still work for him, right?"

"Yeah, sure I do, but . . . ?

"And you probably hit a place for him tonight, right?"

"Yeah, as a matter of fact, I did." Molly-the-Hun nodded her head slowly, making an effort to smile agreeably. "Which reminds me, I gotta get going, make my drop before they start wondering—"

"Okay, good," Bobby Morgan nodded, "and you got all the stuff in your van, right?"

"Yeah, sure, but—"

"Gimme the keys, *right now,*" Morgan emphasized, gesturing with the .357 for Molly-the-Hun to get up off the floor.

He waited until Molly carefully handed him the van keys. Then he transferred them to his own pocket and smiled.

"See," he rasped, "what I'm gonna do is, I'm gonna drive out to that goddamned warehouse, drop of your stuff, let 'em figure it all out, just like they did with us. And while they're doing that, *I'm* gonna go have me another talk with mister God Almighty, and get *him* to tell me where I can find that son of a bitch Digger."

"Bobby, listen to me. This is crazy. You gotta believe me—the last thing we want to do is cause trouble with these people."

"Oh no, trouble's 'actly what I want to cause them," Morgan said, slurring his words and having to work hard at not letting himself slip away again. He knew he couldn't trust Molly. Not for a second. Not on something like this.

Bitch'll go for my throat, first chance she gets, he told himself, as he blinked his eyes rapidly, trying to clear away the gathering fog. *Oughta shoot her right now. Ought to—come on, goddamn it, stay awake!*

"Molly, listen to me," Morgan whispered in a raspy voice. "This friend of yours—this Digger—he killed Otis. Killed him like a goddamned dog, over a miserable 307 dollars cash money that wasn't his to begin with. You understand what I'm saying?"

"No, Bobby, honest to God, I don't know what you're talking about."

"What it is, see," Morgan patiently tried to explain, "this Digger asshole, he thinks we cheated him out of some bread, but the way it worked out—"

"You . . . you *cheated* Digger?" Molly-the-Hun whispered the words in horrified disbelief.

"Cheated him, shit." Morgan shook his head. "He owed us *at least* that for not warning us the kid might come home early. Hell, we're the ones who almost got caught. Anybody got cheated, it was Otis and me."

"Oh my God—"

"So what we're gonna do, after I get back from the warehouse," Bobby Morgan went on, "is we're gonna tell him that. Tell him that he really screwed up when he killed Otis. I wanna make goddamned sure he understands that before I put a bullet through his fucking head. And after I do that," he added, blinking his glassy eyes wide-open and forming his dark-bearded lips into a tight smile, "you and me, we're gonna go out and find ourselves a cop named Culver."

Chapter Thirty-one

Friday, 1910 hours

A sudden echoing creak of distant floorboards in the gloomy darkness brought Culver and Russelli to an immediate halt along the far interior wall of Paul Radlick's dining room.

Reacting in unison, they both switched off their flashlights and waited.

Ten seconds later, there was a sharp, cracking noise.

Culver and Russelli responded to the second creak by turning their backs to the wall, crouching down, and bringing their weapons to bear on the three possible approaches:

the kitchen to their left, or the hallway and living room to their right.

They waited for a long sixty-count with their flashlights extended out and away from their bodies, ready to blind, distract, and shoot the instant that they had an identifiable target. But the first minute went by, and then half of another before the strain on John Russelli's ankle finally forced him to move.

"Where?" he whispered as he slowly straightened up into a standing position.

"Don't know," Culver said softly as he came up out of his own crouched stance. "Maybe the den."

The den was at the far diagonal corner of the house from the dining room, and was accessible from either the kitchen, the hallway, or the living room. That meant Digger, if he was the source of the creaking floorboards, could come at them from virtually any direction.

John Russelli's first thought was to take the hallway at the fastest speed he could maintain with his bum leg, and then burst through the door of the den—depending upon the element of surprise, his own reflexes, and the limited protection of his Kevlar vest to flush and neutralize the psychotic killer. At least that was what he *wanted* to do; but he knew better than to give in to his aggressive instincts on this one.

Tactics of that sort might have worked against a man on the run, desperately seeking a place to hide or a means of escape. But they wouldn't work with John Doe Thirty-three, for the simple reason that Digger was *not* on the run—at least not in the desperate sense. The trip wires across the driveway, and the elaborate triggering device Culver and Russelli had discovered wired to the inside of the front door were evidence enough of that.

What Digger was doing, in his own perverse way, was hunting. And it was becoming increasingly evident to John Russelli and Henry Culver that they had walked right into his trap.

All of which meant that Russelli and Culver had to make

a very quick decision: circle back around to confirm that the ground floor was clear, and thus leave themselves exposed to an assault from the wide, overhanging stairwell; or take the stairs, clear the top, and then work their way back down.

There was a third and much more logical option—the one that involved going back outside and calling for backup—but they'd already shrugged that option off.

Russelli took one last longing glance down the hallway toward the partially opened den door, and then motioned with his hand for Culver to follow.

"If he's in here, he knows where we are," he whispered. "Use the light and watch the hallway and the den until I can clear the stairs."

"Right."

John Russelli approached the stairwell with his back tight against the wall, the sawed-off shotgun held out and ready in his right hand, and the glary flashlight out and away from his body as the probing beam swept up the empty stairwell.

"Stairwell's clear. See anything?" Russelli whispered.

"Den door hasn't moved. Nothing in the hallway," Henry Culver replied in a soft voice as he inched himself backward along the wall in the semidarkness, the beam from his flashlight and the barrel of his .357 continuing to sweep back and forth across the dining room and the hallway as he searched with a tightly focused intensity for the first sign of movement—the first sign of Digger trying to make a back-door move.

The streaks of bright red blood began to appear on the wall just as Culver felt himself bump up against John Russelli's broad back.

"Russelli, check your arm," he whispered. "You still bleeding?"

"Yeah, probably, don't worry about it," Russelli muttered as he started up the stairs, his right index finger caressing the trigger of the sawed-off twelve-gage as his flashlight beam cleared the way.

Moments later, he and Culver were up at the top of the

stairs, watching the three closed doors that led off into the upstairs bedrooms as they paused to catch their breath and steady their nerves.

"What do you think?" Russelli rasped as he swept his flashlight beam across the carpet of the upper stairwell, searching for any sign of Digger's presence.

"First of all, I don't think he's here anymore. And secondly, I think this is probably the dumbest stunt we've ever pulled," Culver whispered in a barely steady voice, "and that includes your John Wayne bit with the window."

"Front door was wired, wasn't it?"

Culver nodded. "Yeah, the front door was wired."

"And the breaker box too, right?"

"Yeah, probably," Culver replied quietly. There wasn't any "probably" about it. The circuit breaker box *was* rigged, and he wasn't about to get anywhere near it. That was why they were using the flashlights.

"And you wouldn't have gotten through that door with any of your goddamned log-stacking tricks either, would you?" Russelli whispered again as he slowly pushed the first bedroom door open with the barrel of his shotgun.

"No, probably not."

"I just figured he wouldn't take the time to wire all the windows, too," Russelli went on in a muted whisper as he stepped inside the room, scanned it quickly with his light, and then stepped back out into the stairwell. "Besides, everybody knows cops like to kick doors."

"Yeah, well, we're still acting like a couple of dumbshits," Culver muttered as he went past Russelli—who remained in place, providing cover with his shotgun—and then stepped quickly into Paul and Doreen Radlick's bedroom.

There was a long pause that was finally broken by Culver's urgent voice: "Russelli, get in here!"

"Christ," Russelli whispered as he came in behind Culver and swept the beam of his own flashlight through the room.

Paul Radlick's bedroom looked like it had been the site of a major free-for-all. Articles of clothing were scattered everywhere. The bed covers were strewn across the carpet. The dresser was overturned, and both reading lamps were lying on the floor, lampshades crushed and bulbs broken. From John Russelli's viewpoint, the room looked exactly like the scene at the Kostermann home, with two glaring exceptions:

There were no bodies to be seen.

And equally unnerving, there was no blood.

"What the hell happened in here?" Russelli demanded, but Henry Culver was already down on his knees, laying the .357 aside and using his flashlight to search the carpet for any clue as to what might have happened.

"Henry . . ."

"I don't know." Culver had the side of his face almost touching the carpet as he swept his flashlight bream across the woolly surface, oblivious of anything other than his determination to work through the scene, trying to reconstruct the events, trying to . . .

"He's been up here and he got at them" Russelli whispered menacingly as he reached down with his flashlight hand to lever the dresser back up against the wall.

"Don't touch the dresser!" Culver suddenly warned.

"Why not?" Russelli demanded, pulling his hands back as the lens end of his flashlight just barely brushed against the polished wood surface.

Culver's flashlight beam steadied on the underside of the dresser for a few more moments before he went back to examining the carpet. "Mousetrap."

"What?"

"He's got it wired to three sticks. Lift the dresser and the spring wire snaps forward, makes the connection," Culver explained in an absentminded tone of voice as he continued to sweep his flashlight beam along the surface of the carpet.

"That asshole . . . !"

"Don't worry about it" Culver advised as he continued to search the carpet with oblique light from his flashlight. "It's stable, just don't move the dresser."

"That miserable, stinking, low-life bastard," Russelli muttered in a cold, malevolent voice as he slowly backed away from the booby-trapped dresser, and then spun around as he realized that he hadn't been watching the door.

"Russelli, don't move!"

"What the hell did he do, wire the fucking carpet, too?" Russelli demanded as he quickly scanned the area around his feet with his flashlight and saw nothing.

"Let me see the bottom of your shoes," Culver said, ignoring his partner's comment.

"*My* shoes?"

"Yeah, let me see them. Hurry up and . . . okay, thanks," he nodded after sweeping the beam of the flashlight across the underside of Russelli's shoes and then his own.

"What the hell was that all about?"

"Dirt. Red clay dirt. It's all over the carpet," Culver explained as he moved toward the door on his hands and knees, following the faint trail.

"Yeah, so what? There's red clay all over the place in Fairfax County. Paul and Doreen probably tracked it in from the yard."

Culver shook his head. "No, those two always took their shoes off every time they came in the house, and Doreen vacuumed at least once a day. Besides, I helped them landscape their yard last year. The soil's real good out here. You've gotta go down at least four feet before you hit clay."

"Yeah, so what does that mean?"

"I don't know, but I want to see where this stuff goes. Watch my back, okay?"

"Yeah, right." Russelli nodded, glancing once more at the overturned dresser before he followed Culver back out the bedroom door.

Five long, nervous minutes later, Henry Culver and John Russelli stood in the middle of the den and stared silently at the end result of their long, nerve-wracking search: the closed door of Paul Radlick's den closet.

"You sure?" Russelli whispered, keeping the barrel of the twelve-gage rock-steady on the center of the door.

Culver nodded. "Yeah, I'm sure," he said, feeling the tingling numbness start to spread up his spine.

That's where he went. I can feel it.

"What do you want to do?" Russelli growled. The unnerving image of the mouse-trapped dresser was the only thing keeping him away from the door.

That's a good question, Culver thought. *What do I want to do?*

"Henry?"

Nothing. I don't have to do anything because he wouldn't have wired this one. Culver nodded to himself in sudden understanding as he continued to stare at the door with a sense of numb fascination that made the back of his neck tingle.

"Henry?" John Russelli's whispery voice became more insistent as his index finger tightened on the trigger of the shotgun.

Something in the hidden recesses of Russelli's subconscious was screaming at him to shoot, to pump the five rounds of number four buckshot right into the closet at staggered, twelve-inch intervals, but his professional training would not allow him to open fire at an unobserved target. Paul and Doreen Radlick had to be somewhere.

"Henry, for Christ's sake . . ."

Then, in a moment of decision that he didn't even try to justify, much less understand, Henry Culver stepped forward until he was right in front of the closet door, brought the .357 Smith & Wesson up to waist level, tightened his finger on the trigger, reached forward with his flashlight hand, tensed, and then yanked the door open in one swift movement.

For a long three or four seconds, Henry Culver stood there and stared into the closet.

Then, from John Russelli's point of view, both of Culver's arms suddenly seemed to sag, causing both the flashlight beam and the barrel of the Smith & Wesson to point down at the closet floor in front of his feet.

"Henry, what the hell . . . ?" Russelli rasped as he started to move up behind his partner.

Then Detective Sergeant John Russelli felt his entire body go cold when Henry Culver motioned him back with his flashlight, and he suddenly realized that the .357 Magnum revolver in his partner's hand wasn't being held loosely, but rather was being tightly gripped and aimed down at a gaping black hole in the closet floor.

"Russelli," Henry Culver whispered hoarsely. "Get us some backup . . . right now."

Chapter Thirty-two

Friday, 2000 hours

"Where is he?" Homicide Sergeant Al Stewart demanded as he stomped into the darkened family room of Paul Radlick's home with an expression on his face that, in the shifting, shadowy light of five flashlights, made even Patrol Sergeant Jack Hattabaugh and Detective Sergeant John Russelli blink and hesitate.

Stewart had been chosen as the supervisor of Fairfax County's Homicide investigation unit because he was invariably calm, controlled, steady, methodical, persistent, protective of his men, essentially fearless—and if necessary, perfectly capable of killing a man without a moment's hesitation.

In effect, he was precisely the sort of investigator that a police chief could turn loose on a renegade homicide suspect like Digger, and still sleep at night.

But on this particular evening, Sergeant Al Stewart didn't appear to be the least bit calm, controlled, or steady. Instead, he looked exactly like a very frustrated and dangerous man who had been pushed right up to the edge of his breaking point.

The immediate implication—which Russelli and Hattabaugh recognized instantly—was that the next misfortunate soul who got in his way, regardless of size, rank, or allegiance, was going to risk being taken apart at the seams.

And it was equally obvious to everyone in the immediate area that the man who had followed Stewart into Paul Radlick's darkened living room was likely to be that unfortunate soul who finally caused the furious Homicide unit supervisor to snap.

Lieutenant Morris Markham Craven had a talent for affecting people that way.

"Over here, in the den," John Russelli gestured with his head, knowing exactly who and what Stewart was talking about as he favored Craven with a steady glare. Russelli was standing just outside the doorway to the den with a useless circular power saw in his huge hand, looking helplessly enraged and frustrated—and, like almost everyone else in the house, just about ready to kill something.

"Well, is he down there?" Craven demanded.

"Is who down where?" Russelli muttered. Like Stewart, Russelli was in no mood to deal with a self-important horse's ass like Craven. Not now. And especially not under these circumstances.

"The goddamned freak that got away from you people, that's who," Craven hissed. "John Doe Thirty-three. Is he down there in that hole, or isn't he?"

It took a few moments for the full import of Craven's words to sink in. But even so, John Russelli still wasn't completely sure he'd heard them right.

"Got away from us?" Russelli repeated, his hoarse voice nearly overcome by a rush of disbelief and outrage that nearly caused him to miss the spine-chilling look that flickered across Al Stewart's chiseled face. But Russelli had spent too many years with the Presidential Security Detail to miss an emotional surge like that—the look in the eyes, and the clenched hand that, had it not been for Stewart's almost-inhuman degree of self-control, would have been at Lieutenant Morris Craven's throat.

"That man is our responsibility until he's put away for good, *Sergeant,*" Craven said emphatically, completely unaware of how close he'd come to pushing Stewart over the edge as he glared up at his subordinate res-burg supervisor. "He walked away from the Ward on our watch, and we didn't know about it for a week. *Seven goddamned days!* Do you realize how that makes us look? Like idiots!" Craven almost screamed the answer to his own question.

"Lieutenant," Sergeant Al Stewart whispered the warning in a cold, emotionless voice that nearly caused Hattabaugh and Russelli to lunge between Stewart and a man who was obliviously teetering on the edge of self-destruction. But Craven wasn't paying the slightest bit of attention to Stewart or anyone else. At the moment, he was completely focused on what he thought might be a serious threat to his own bureaucratic survival.

"Do you know what O'Reilly is doing *right* now?" Craven raged on, referring to one of his fellow lieutenants, and still completely unaware of the effect that he was having upon every man in that room. "At this very moment, he's putting together a special enforcement team that will be sent in to assist *us* in dealing with a simple escaped criminal who is supposed to be *our* problem, and I want you to understand that I'm not going to have any of that. As long as I'm in charge, we will take care of our own problems *without* outside help. Now I'm asking you once more, Sergeant. *Is he down there?*"

Detective Sergeant John Russelli stood there in the darkened living room, fingering the heavy, sawtoothed chunk of metal in his hand and thinking for a moment that he just might save Stewart the trouble and take Craven out himself, before he finally answered. "We don't know."

"You don't *know?*" Craven almost shrieked. "You mean

you people have been out here all this time, and nobody's had the balls to go down there and *look?*"

Russelli saw Stewart's clawed hand lunge forward out of the corner of his eye. Reacting out of pure reflex, he dropped the power saw and stepped between the two men, absorbing the jarring impact of Stewart's hand with his own muscular back as the heavy power tool clattered against the bare wood floor with a jarring metallic crash that echoed throughout the darkened house.

"Russelli! What the hell are you . . . ?" Craven started to yell when he found himself suddenly being propelled away from Stewart and toward the door of Paul Radlick's den by a firm come-along grip that Russelli had on his arm. Before Craven could respond, or scream for help, or try to wrench himself loose, Russelli had shifted his hand so that his arm was now wrapped tightly around his supervisor's narrow shoulders, guiding him in through the doorway in a manner that was no longer overpowering but was still effectively irresistible.

"Tell you what, Lieutenant," Russelli whispered in a voice so calm and controlled that he didn't even recognize it as his own, "why don't you step inside here and let us show you something."

John Russelli and Henry Culver had argued about it for almost ten minutes before the first of the blue-and-gray cruisers began pulling up next to Russelli's unit at the end of the cul-de-sac. Then, after making sure everyone knew how the traps were rigged and how to follow the safe—and carefully marked—back way into the house, they stationed a pair of officers at the gate, and a second pair just outside the closet door with loaded shotguns and flashlights aimed down into the eerie, gaping hole.

Then they'd spent another fifteen going over the same ground with Patrol Sergeant Jack Hattabaugh while they waited for Stewart and Carpenter to arrive.

It had been a pointless argument from the start because

they all knew that the primary question—*who* or *what* was waiting for them down there in the crawl space—couldn't be answered until somebody actually went down there and looked.

The trouble was, in this particular case, the difference between a *who* and a *what* was significant; and it was also the crucial factor in determining who was going to make the entry.

They were starting with the assumption that whoever did go down through that hole in the closet floor would probably find Paul and Doreen Radlick. Henry Culver had spotted drag marks in the dirt under the door, so the only real question was whether they would be found dead or alive. If they were still alive, then any delay in getting them out might turn out to be critical. If not, then time wasn't a factor and they could all stand back and wait for the arrival of Lieutenant O'Reilly's Special Enforcement Team to take the house apart board by board.

All very fine except that they wouldn't *know* if they had time to wait for the SET, and daylight, until somebody crawled down in that hole and found out *who* or *what* was waiting for them down in that cold, musty darkness.

And that brought them back to the crux of the situation.

The "who" or the "what."

If the crawl space under Paul Radlick's house was wired like his driveway, then Henry Culver was the logical one to go in. He was the only one of the officers at the scene who possessed the ability to spot and disarm a concealed triggering device (other than the county demolitions expert who was very busy at the moment trying to secure the surrounding neighborhood from trip-wired explosives), and therefore was the only one who stood a reasonable chance of spotting and surviving a trap.

But if Digger was down there—in what was probably a dark, familiar habitat—then someone like Henry Culver *wouldn't* stand much of a chance at all. In that situation, the logical entry man was Russelli or Stewart or Carpenter, all three of whom were perfectly willing and capable of going down in a dark hole and taking a malicious freak like Digger apart with their bare hands. Assuming, of course, that they could get their hands on him without stumbling into one of his merciless traps—which, in the narrow, confining, and unfamiliar darkness, was not a sure bet at all. ·

Stewart had already made the decision to go in himself, trusting his own military experience with a recon team to spot the traps, and Russelli had still been arguing with him over the secured channel, not realizing that Craven was also en route, and well into the process of formulating his own self-serving plans, when Henry Culver had made the first of two very crucial observations.

The first had sent John Russelli tearing into Paul Radlick's garage in search of some sort of saw, which he finally located just in time for Culver, using a piece of broken mirror and his flashlight taped to Hattabaugh's baton, to make his second and even more crucial discovery.

A discovery that had caused John Russelli to be standing there in the adjacent living room with the saw in his hand and a look of cold helpless rage on his face when Craven and Stewart arrived.

As Craven and Russelli walked into the den, followed by a murderously calm and composed Stewart, they all saw a dark figure sitting on the floor in front of the closet. It took Craven a moment to recognize the face in the dim, flashlight-illuminated darkness.

"Culver?" Craven looked startled, as if he couldn't understand why John Russelli's new partner was sitting there on the floor behind the two shotgun-bearing officers, in the process of removing Russelli's heavy denim jacket and his own Kevlar vest.

"Hi, Lieutenant." Culver acknowledged Craven with a distracted nod of his head as he finished taking off the vest.

"What are you doing here?" Craven asked, still confused, irritated, and distracted by John Russelli's blatantly insubordinate behavior.

"Getting ready to go down into a hole and get dirty," Culver replied, trying to keep his mind away from the distracting images of sheet-covered bodies on Kathy Harmon's driveway.

"You?"

"That's right."

"You two are letting a . . . a *scientist* go down there after that son of a bitch?" Craven almost stuttered as he turned to stare at Russelli and Stewart. "That's ridiculous. Absolutely ridiculous. I'm ordering both of you, right now, to go down there and . . ."

"Sorry, Lieutenant, but they can't," Culver interrupted before either Russelli or Stewart lost the last vestiges of their self-control.

"What do you mean, they can't?" Craven spun around on his heels and glared down at Culver. "I happen to be in charge here, and if I tell them to go jump into a goddamned hole, then that's what they're going to do. Period."

Culver shrugged indifferently. "Doesn't matter what you tell them. They still can't go down there."

Craven looked as though he couldn't believe his ears. "Would you care to tell me why not?" he demanded, his voice almost cracking from the strain.

"The guy who cut that hole happens to be a skinny little bastard," Culver explained as he reached for a roll of duct tape next to his feet. "Looks like he made it just big enough for somebody his size to get through. Outside of me . . . and I guess maybe you," he added, glancing up and down Craven's spare frame as if seeing him for the first time, "nobody else around here is going to fit."

"So make the hole bigger," Craven interrupted hurriedly before anybody had a chance to suggest that *he* go down in that hole. Morris Markham Craven had an exceedingly generous opinion of himself as being a man born to lead, but he had no intention at all of being *that* kind of leader. "Russelli, you've got a saw. Use it!"

"A nice idea, but we can't do that either," Culver said calmly, staring up at Craven again.

For a brief moment, Lieutenant Morris Markham Craven, deputy commander of the Major Crimes Division and up-and-coming riser in the department, looked like a man who was about to have a seizure. But momentarily stunned and speechless as he was, he recovered quickly.

"That's the second time you've told me that I can't do something, *Detective* Culver," Craven said in a clearly threatening voice. "While you still have a job, would you care to explain yourself?"

Culver looked over at Stewart and Russelli for a brief moment, shrugged his shoulders, and then nodded his head agreeably. "See, the thing is, Lieutenant," he explained as he went back to work, using the roll of duct tape to secure his pant legs tightly around his ankles, "we can't make that hole any bigger—even if we had power, which we don't right now—because whoever cut it in the first place ran wires around the underside edge."

"Wires?"

"Wires. Just like the stuff outside." Culver nodded as he wrapped the roll of tape around his right ankle three times, tore it off, and then began working on the left. "Spotted them when I was trying to look around down there with the mirror and flashlight routine. Couldn't see where the wires go, but it looks like there's at least two separate sets, and probably several more. All the wires are the same color, interwoven and tacked to the underside of the flooring at about six-inch intervals. No way to tell them all apart. From what I could see with the mirror, it looks like he's got the stuff running all over the place down there."

"Would you mind telling me *why?*" Craven asked in a quietly infuriated voice, apparently still not catching on to the implications of Henry Culver's description.

"Why the wires around the hole? I'm not sure." Culver shrugged. "The obvious answer is that he doesn't want anybody making the hole any bigger, probably so that whoever goes in there—me from the look of things so far," he added without any apparent trace of sarcasm, "will have to go in either head- or feet-first right in that spot. I can't see why that matters—I used a mirror, and I can't see anything else rigged around the hole—but . . ."

"You mean this *house* is booby-trapped?" Craven interrupted as his face suddenly took on a distinctly ashen look.

Culver nodded. "That's what it looks like. I haven't been able to spot any explosives so far, but Hattabaugh found an empty box labeled dynamite in one of the trash cans. Label said it held a hundred sticks and we only found a couple dozen in the woodpile, and a few upstairs, so . . ."

"Do you realize that this . . . this is a threat to . . . to the entire neighborhood," Craven whispered. "My God, we've got to do something. I . . . I've got to get the chief on the horn immediately. With that, Craven spun around and almost ran for the door. Moments later, the sound of the garage door being slammed open against the wall and Craven's rapidly disappearing footsteps echoed throughout the house.

Russelli stood there staring at the empty doorway for a few seconds, smiling to himself, and then turned back around to find himself under the dark, silent scrutiny of Al Stewart.

The unasked question hung in the air.

"Wouldn't have been fair," Russelli said as he met Stewart's cold, even stare. "I've had the little prick in my sights for a long time now, just waiting for him to do something really stupid. Wait your turn."

They both stood there, staring at each other for a few moments, no one saying anything, until Stewart finally nodded. "Appreciate it," he said, and then turned to a perplexed but silent Culver.

"If you've got any better ideas on how to handle this thing without going down there yourself, I'd like to hear about them, right now," Stewart said as his gaze shifted over to the gaping black hole in the closet floor.

"Russelli wants to get a generator set up and power-cut bigger holes most of the way through the floorboards at random spots, and then cut through the rest of the way by hand," Culver said as he put the heavy denim jacket back on, zipped it up, and then began wrapping duct tape around the end of the torn sleeve, and then the other one. "That might work if we go at it real slow, but I don't think we can take the risk. Not if there's any chance at all that Paul and Doreen are still alive down there," he added softly, staring down at his taped wrists and legs.

"But you don't think they are, do you?"

"No, I don't." Culver shook his head, continuing to stare down at the floor.

"You see anything at all down there? Any sign of a body?" Stewart asked after a few moments.

"Not a thing. Foundation walls stick up about six inches off the ground, and crisscross in what looks like eight-by-twelve-foot rectangles. Just barely enough room to crawl between the concrete and the floor joists. I can't see more than about fifteen feet in any direction. Drag marks head due north. Lots of hiding places. Lots of . . . possibilities," Culver added in a hesitant voice.

"Is that your vest?" Patrol Sergeant Jack Hattabaugh demanded as he entered the room, looked down at the floor, and saw the discarded Kevlar vest.

Culver nodded.

"So what's the idea of taking it off?"

"Too much bulk. I'm afraid I'll get hung up in one of those gaps. Besides, it probably wouldn't do me much good down there anyway," he added as he tossed the tape aside and reached for his flashlight.

"Come on, Al, let's forget about this entry crap," Hattabaugh said, turning to Stewart. "It's not worth the risk. Let's just use gas and flush the bastard out."

"That's not going to help," Culver said as he began unscrewing the head of the heavy three-cell flashlight.

"Why not?"

"Found a mask bag under the desk." Culver continued talking as he went through the steps of replacing the partially used batteries with new ones. "Gotta figure that if he *is* down there, he's got one and they don't. I know Paul reacts pretty badly to the gas, and Doreen's had asthma problems all her life. If they're in bad shape already, that might be enough to do them in. And besides," he added, "if I have to wear a mask, it's going to be that much more difficult to spot anything."

Stewart stared down at the floor and muttered something under his breath that Culver couldn't quite catch, but it didn't matter. He knew exactly what the veteran Homicide sergeant was thinking—mostly the same things that Russelli had been saying out loud for the past fifteen minutes.

Finally Stewart brought his head up and stared at Culver. "He's already got you marked as a target, and he knows you and Radlick were tight. So you've got to figure that this one was meant for you. Knowing that, you still want to go down there?"

"The way I see it, the setup at Kathy Harmon's place was meant for me, too. I just got lucky, or Tess got unlucky, depending on how you want to look at it," Culver replied with a bitter edge to his voice.

"That's not what I'm asking."

"I'd rather be home on the couch, drinking a beer, and watching a ball game," Culver acknowledged quietly, "but I'll be fine if I take it slow. Russelli disagrees with me, but I don't think he's down there anymore. I called Scholtz a couple minutes ago, and he's pretty sure that Digger's not the suicidal type. Doesn't think he'd put himself in a hole without a back door."

"He may have one down there."

"Yeah, maybe, but we've got the place surrounded, and if he's down there, he can probably hear us talking and he knows it. According to all the crap he's been writing on walls, he's still got Russelli and me targeted. I don't think he'll try to make a stand unless he's sure he can get both of us."

"That's comforting," Steward commented dryly.

"Listen, Henry," Hattabaugh advised from the dark corner of the den, "that guy's still a freak, and no matter what anybody says, there's no way you can predict one of those bastards. You can't depend on some headshrinker's opinion down there."

"Yeah, I know," Culver acknowledged, "but if he put Paul and Doreen down there, and they're still alive, he's sick enough to really make it rough on them. I don't think we can wait."

Stewart stood there quietly for several long seconds, and then nodded his head. "Okay," he nodded solemnly, "do it."

The first thing that hit Culver, once he'd finally managed to work himself between the first wood-and-concrete barrier with both of his hands out in front of his head—the three-cell flashlight in his left and Russelli's sawed-off shotgun in his right—was the dank, musty smell of moist dirt and cobwebs in the cold, tight, confining darkness.

That and the sudden, claustrophobic, and almost-overwhelming sense of being alone and trapped beneath a huge and oppressive mass, confined within a narrow crawl space that seemed to go off into dark infinity in all directions, was almost enough to send Culver scrambling back up out of the hole.

Culver glanced back over his shoulder, past the incredibly narrow gap between the rough concrete foundation wall and the splintery support beam that he'd already navigated, and saw how far he'd come from the dim, flickering rectangle of light that poked down into the shallow crawl space like an eerie, geometric ghost.

The light that was almost blocked out by the hanging flap of the gently swinging trapdoor.

Jesus, it looks like a lighthouse beacon back there.

Except that it wasn't the same thing, Culver reminded himself, because that was the direction he had to go if things went to shit down here.

There wasn't all that much light coming down through the trapdoor now, mostly because Culver had been forced to tell

Russelli to pull his flashlight back in because the unpredictable beam was both blinding and distracting, and he couldn't afford that.

Not when he had to watch for one of Digger's twisted traps.

It had taken Culver almost fifteen minutes to get this far—little more than three times his body length—because he had to check every niche and cranny with the flashlight beam, and then feel every square inch of the ground beneath his fingertips before he dared to inch himself forward, using the barrel of Russelli's shotgun to push his way through the sticky, dusty sheets of spiderwebbing that seemed to be everywhere.

What does that make it, about a foot a minute? Wonderful. I'm going to be down here all night at that rate. Jesus, how big is this house? Four thousand square feet, two floors . . .

"Henry?"

The voice seemed to scream out at him from the darkness, and he had to put the flashlight down for a moment and then twist around—his shoulder wedged against the overhanging floor boards—to get at the volume control of the pack set radio that Russelli had attached to the side of his right thigh with several loops of duct tape. He had also secured a microphone under his shirt collar and the earphone wire to the side of his neck.

Wrong hand. Should've put the shotgun down instead of the flashlight, but I didn't. Can't even convince myself. Have to tell Scholtz about that. Make his day.

"Yeah, what?" he finally whispered into the shirt mike.

"Check in once in a while, goddamn it!" Russelli's voice rasped in his ear.

"It's okay so far," he said softly. "There wasn't anything rigged around the hole. I'm in the first section past the hole going due north, following the drag marks."

"Can you see anything?"

"Negative, unless you want to count about half the spider population of Fairfax County. Must be where they hibernate during the winter. Section I'm in now looks like a goddamned haunted house."

"Forget the fucking spiders," Russelli whispered. "Can you cut any of those wires?"

Good idea, Russelli. I wouldn't mind some company down here.

Culver twisted back around and used the flashlight to try to follow the ends of the interwoven pairs of wires, but each set disappeared off into the darkness over a piece of concrete or around a support beam.

Shit.

"Negative on the wires," Culver whispered with as much casual indifference as he could muster. "Can't see the end points. Give me a little more time."

"Can you find a clear spot in the flooring?"

Even better idea. You're a good man, Russelli. No wonder Nixon wanted you between him and a bullet. You'd have probably taken it, too.

"Uh, hold one," Culver whispered into the mike as he searched around with his flashlight, trying to find a spot under the flooring that wasn't crisscrossed with one of the overlapping and tied-together lengths of wire.

Jesus, look at all the wire the guy used. Culver shook his head in amazement. He'd already worked his way past six empty thousand-foot spools, and could see at least two more in the distance with the flashlight beam.

Bastard must have burged a hardware store to run all this stuff.

He managed to pull and wiggle himself through the narrow gap into the next twelve-by-sixteen-foot section, almost snagging and losing his radio in the process. Then he saw them.

Oh shit.

"Hey, Russelli," he whispered again, feeling his heart pounding in his chest as he tried to make a count and then gave up. There were too many.

"What?"

"You guys better start helping Craven wake up the neighborhood."

"What're you talking about?" Russelli demanded.

"Remember that box Hattabaugh found?"

"Yeah?"

"Well, tell Jack he must have missed about four boxes," Culver said. "This place looks like its wired to go into orbit."

There was a long pause, and then Stewart's voice came over the radio.

"Henry, I've got the EOD guy here. Tell him what you see."

"Okay." Culver discovered that he was having to make an effort to control his breathing . . . and to ignore the almost-overwhelming sensation that the entire floor of the house was starting to settle down onto his chest. "I'm in the second section, still due north, maybe thirty feet from the hole. Probably right under the family room. There's at least three or four hundred sticks down here that I can see. They're taped together in small groups and nailed to the beams. Five, six, eight sticks each."

"Can you see any detonators?" an unfamiliar voice asked.

"Yeah, some of them are exposed, but most of the wires run behind the bundles," Culver finished as he scanned bundle after bundle of the orangish brown, waxy-looking cylindrical sticks with his flashlight. "Some have two or three sets of wires running to them."

"How about timers or switch boxes?"

"Negative—nothing like that. Just wires running all over the goddamned place."

"Okay, take it easy," the unfamiliar voice said in a steady, even voice. "Don't try to move anything. Real good possibility that he put release switches under the bundles."

"Right, I'm not touching a damn thing," Culver promised.

"Okay, hold one."

There was another pause and Culver caught some pieces of the conversation through the open mike. Something to the effect that Stewart should get him out of there, right now.

Yeah, good idea, Culver thought as he continued to search though the mass of light-reflecting cobwebs with the flashlight beam until he finally found what he was looking for.

"Hey, Russelli."

"Yeah?"

"Listen, from where you're standing, at the trapdoor, about twenty feet due north and fifteen east, there should be a bathroom. Looks like it's probably the one in the hall.

"Yeah, so?"

"He missed that spot. No wires. There's a clear radius of about six feet all around the sewer pipe that goes up to the toilet. Keep it in mind."

"Got it," Russelli responded. "We're hooking up a generator right now. Be down there in a couple of minutes."

"Okay, great, I . . ." Culver started to say when a sudden, barely audible crunching sound from somewhere in the darkness to his right sent warning messages screaming through his brain.

What?

Almost numb from shock, Culver froze in place as he swept the flashlight beam back and forth across the dark shadowy gaps beneath the multitude of crisscrossing floor joists, listening with every ounce of concentration he could muster as he tried to pinpoint the direction.

Nothing.

"Russelli," Culver whispered.

"Hold your horses, buddy, we're . . ."

There was another crunching sound, this one louder and more distinct. Something large was definitely moving in the far reaches of the crawl space to Culver's right.

Jesus Christ . . .

"Russelli, I think I've got company down here!" Culver hissed into his shirt mike as he twisted himself around under the confining floor joists to point the flashlight and the shotgun in what sounded like the vector point of the noise, and in doing so smacked the end of the flashlight against a piece of solid concrete foundation.

Suddenly, Culver couldn't see anything, and he started to panic before he finally realized that the bulb in his flashlight had gone out.

"Where?" Russelli raspy voice demanded.

"I don't know, northeast quadrant, I think," Culver whispered as he shook the flashlight, causing it to flicker brightly for a brief moment before going out again. "Can't tell, flashlight's going out on me."

"Henry, get back up here, *now,*" Al Stewart ordered, his voice snapping loudly through Culver's earphone.

"Right, I'm heading back . . . oh shit," Culver whispered as out of the corner of his eye he caught the movement of something that, for a brief instant, blocked out the narrow rectangle of diffuse light underneath the distant trapdoor.

"What's the matter?" Stewart demanded.

"I'm blocked off," Culver whispered. "Between me and the hole."

"Did you see him?"

"No, just the movement. Shadow."

"You see him, you see anything, shoot. Don't hesitate," Stewart ordered. "You hear me?"

"Oh yeah, I hear you," Culver whispered shakily.

"I'm cutting through now," Culver heard Russelli yell in the background.

"No, wait," Culver whispered urgently. "My light's out. You start cutting and I won't be able to hear him coming! I'm moving back . . . putting myself in a corner . . . far northwest side. Tell you soon as I get there. Then start cutting!" Culver grunted as he jammed the useless flashlight into his belt and then used his free left hand to help pull himself frantically through the next rough gaps in the concrete that seemed to be getting narrower and narrower as he worked himself deeper into the cold, claustrophobic darkness of the spider-webbed crawl space, trying to listen . . .

There!

He twisted over to his right, jamming his left shoulder up against one of the splintery joists, grabbed for the flashlight, and rapped it against the rough-cut wood, sending another intermittent beam of bright light into the web-streaked darkness.

Nothing.

Shit!

In his desperate determination to reach that protective corner, Henry Culver had completely forgotten about watching out for traps or triggering devices. His only concern now as he scrabbled his way on his stomach across the rough, crumbly pieces of concrete, his face and arms and shoulders now completely covered with overlapping pieces of spiderweb, was to get himself wedged back against those corner blocks.

If he could just get there before . . .

The fingers of the hand that brushed against the side of Culver's face seemed to be going for his eyes, but they never completed the movement because Culver slashed at the arm with the shotgun . . . and felt the end of the barrel catch on something that felt like a big nail or a bolt head.

Panic-stricken, Culver thrashed the shotgun around to work the barrel loose and then lunged forward, losing his flashlight in the process as a vicious snarl born out of shock, and fear and rage escaped through his clenched teeth.

In the narrow, confining space, there wasn't any room to maneuver, and he couldn't see, and something sharp was jabbing into the side of his face, so Culver did the one thing that he could do, which was to continue driving his legs forward as he slashed out again with the heavy sawed-off shotgun and felt the impact of steel against flesh and bone.

He heard a voice, but his earphone had come out of his ear, and the brief flash of red light behind his back meant nothing to him at all.

So he continued to drive forward with his legs and slash at the invisible form with the shotgun until suddenly his free hand grasped and then sensed the cold, congealed flesh.

Oh God, no.

The sudden high-pitched tearing sound of a saw blade ripping through linoleum-surfaced plywood echoed throughout the crawl space, and there was another flash of red light behind his back, but none of that registered in Henry Culver's mind because he was still scrambling about wildly for his flashlight.

Then he had it, and he was pounding it madly against the overhead joist, trying to force one last spark out of the hopelessly damaged bulb when the third flash of light behind Culver's back briefly illuminated the cold, still face of Paul Radlick in a pale reddish glow that finally registered in Culver's shell-shocked mind.

The dying glow of the third red light bulb mounted on the far distant floor joist was still visible as Culver twisted around in time to see the fourth bulb come to life in brilliant display of scarlet light that briefly illuminated the first three bulbs in the series, the remaining two, and one more that didn't look like a light bulb so much as a . . .

The fifth bulb surged into life, sending its reddish glow out against Henry Culver's web-covered face.

. . . *relay switch!*

And then suddenly, the echoing shriek of the saw blade disappeared in a series of retina-blinding and eardrum-shattering explosions that pounded at Henry Culver's fragile brain as he sent five concussive fireballs roaring out from the barrel of the sawed-off shotgun into the web-strewn darkness.

Chapter Thirty-three

Friday, 2055 hours

The emergency meeting of the Central Intelligence Agency's directorate council had been set for 9:00 P.M. sharp. But at five minutes before the hour, the director—a meticulously neat, poised, and punctual man who rarely deviated from a schedule—looked up from his notes, saw that seven of the twelve chairs around the leather-surfaced conference table were filled, and then turned to the man sitting to his immediate right at the head of the T-shaped table.

"Sam, would you please close and lock the door?"

Sam Nokes, the deputy director, a grayed and wrinkled survivor of countless Washington, DC skirmishes who still harbored visions of reaching the top spot in the Agency before he retired, rose obediently from his chair, walked over to the heavy oak door, pushed it firmly shut, and set the bolt lock.

Then, instead of returning to his traditional head table position, he chose an empty chair directly across the long span of the conference table from Elliott Parkinson, and right next to Arthur Traynor.

It was a simple, low-key action that spoke volumes to the other attendees in the secured room. Something serious was in the wind. Something that involved Nokes, Traynor, Parkinson, and the director . . . and the deputy director had just planted his flag in the ground. The attention of the other four associate directors in the room picked up noticeably.

The director, a white-haired graduate of Yale Law School who had mastered the nuances of bureaucratic infighting many long years ago, responded by blinking his steely eyes with amused interest before turning his attention to the group as a whole.

"Starting tomorrow," the director began in a quiet voice as he thoughtfully stroked his smoothly shaved jaw, "joint meetings between the standing committees of the World Trade Organization, the Convention on International Trade in Endangered Species, Interpol, and approximately twenty environmental orientated nongovernment organizations—the NGOs—will begin. In all, including the six plenary sessions, a total of seventy-two separate meetings are scheduled to deal with a wide range of cultural, religious, and trade issues. I don't think I need to remind anyone in this room that these meetings are unprecedented in modern history. Nor do

I need to remind you that they have the potential to cause a complete and unpredictable realignment of both economies *and* alliances with the global community. Essentially, it is one of those once-in-a-century opportunities to alter the playing field . . . ideally, in a manner that ends up to our long-term advantage and benefit," he added with a slight smile.

Everyone around the table nodded their heads solemnly . . . and cautiously.

"Accordingly, I have been advised by the highest authorities that any . . . information . . . that we may happen to come across, *prior to or during these meetings,* with respect to positions and bargaining points of the individual members of these standing committees, would be of inestimable value to our representatives and allies at these meetings."

Again, all seven heads nodded in understanding. No one needed to ask what the term "highest authorities" meant. There was only one "highest authority" as far as the director of the CIA was concerned, and that was the individual who could fire him on a moment's notice: the president of the United States.

Then, before anyone could make any comment, Deputy Director Sam Nokes cleared his throat.

The director of the CIA turned to his normally loyal but frequently outspoken deputy. "Yes, Sam, is there something that you'd like to add at this point?"

"I was just thinking," the deputy director said calmly, "that before we go on, this might be an excellent time for Elliott to give us a briefing on one of his operations that may be of some direct relevance to this discussion."

"Oh really? And what project might that be?" the director asked.

"I was thinking of Operation MEG."

Elliott Parkinson forced himself not to react visibly as the other four associate directors looked at each other in confusion. None of them had ever heard of an operation by that title.

"Actually, MEG is more of an interesting side project than

an actual operation," Parkinson said hesitantly. "We don't really . . ." he started to add when the director interrupted.

"MEG is something that Elliott has had simmering on the back burner for a number of years," he explained in careful, measured words. "The international environmental groups—the 'Greens,' if you will—have long been recognized as having tremendous emotional appeal to the European community at large. The opportunity to have some influence within that community, and to monitor their activities—"

"At meetings such as the WTO, CITES, and Interpol talks here in Washington?" Nokes asked pointedly.

The director nodded his head, the expression in his eyes turning measurably colder. "That *was* one of the interesting options," he said. "But we're still looking at this as a back burner option. The pot is simmering, but we haven't decided to bring it forward to a full boil as yet."

"That's probably just as well." Sam Nokes offered a slight smile as he turned to face Elliott Parkinson. "I understand there may have been a few spills?"

Parkinson turned to the head of the table for help. The director visibly hesitated, and then said: "Go ahead and describe what you and *your* staff have done on Operation MEG to date, Elliott."

The director's words had the effect of a verbal body blow on Elliott Parkinson. He hesitated, took a deep breath, and then reluctantly began to speak.

"We, uh, became aware of the growing influence of the environmental community upon international affairs some years back. It seemed like an excellent opportunity to get in on the ground floor, so we . . . did." He looked around the table. "I've had a small team of agents monitoring the activities of these groups for some time now, so, when we heard that the WTO, CITES, and Interpol organizations were going to be getting together here in DC to discuss international *sanctions*—"

"You decided that it would be disruptive, and ultimately

harmful, to discontinue an ongoing monitoring process?" one of the other associate directors offered helpfully.

"Uh, yes, that's right." Parkinson nodded his head slowly. "Actually, I think if we interpret the intent of the restrictions in the broadest sense, from the standpoint of the 'hot pursuit' doctrine, we—"

"There are some extremely limited international precedents with respect to the 'hot pursuit' doctrine, Elliott," one of the other associate directors who was responsible for interpreting legal issues interrupted. "But we can talk about those later. What about these 'spills' that Sam mentioned?"

Elliott Parkinson took in a deep breath.

"We've had some setbacks," he admitted, maintaining a calm demeanor in spite of his inner confusion and nervousness. "One of our primary assets broke away from his leash for a few days, at the same time that three of our operatives turned up missing. But as of this evening, I have been advised that the entire situation was resolved, and that we're back on schedule. We expect to have full coverage on all seventy-three meetings."

"Seventy-*three?*" One of the associate directors to Parkinson's right turned to the director. "I thought you said seventy-two?"

"There are only seventy-two *announced* meetings," Parkinson acknowledged as he made a pretense of referring to his notes. "However, we have reason to believe that the French may have scheduled an *ad hoc* session on their own. They recently positioned one of their military attachés . . ."

"Charles L'Que?" Sam Nokes interrupted.

"What?" Parkinson blinked, unable to control his reaction this time.

"Lieutenant Colonel Charles L'Que," the deputy director said. "He was transferred to the French Embassy in DC a few weeks ago. Is that who you're talking about?"

"Uh, yes," Parkinson nodded, feeling his diaphragm tighten.

"Incredible."

The director turned to face his deputy, the icy expression in his eyes in direct contrast to the measured warmth of his vocal tones. "Why do you say that, Sam?"

"I hardly think . . ." Parkinson tried, but the director put up a silencing hand. His self-preserving instincts were fully alert now.

"According to one of our sources on the Hill," Sam Nokes went on in his own calm and measured voice, "sometime tomorrow, three senators from the Select Intelligence Committee, and the president's national security advisor will be taken to an unspecified location in Fairfax County. Presumably to one of the seventy-two—or perhaps seventy-three—meeting sites that Elliott just mentioned," he added, eyeing Parkinson for a brief moment before going on.

"There, I'm told, they expect to be introduced to an individual who will have solid proof—documents, tapes, *and* photographs—to the effect that, back in the early eighties, one of our cooperating agents in Algeria *was directly involved* . . ." he emphasized those words clearly, ". . . in events leading up to the 1985 assault on the *Rainbow Warrior* in New Zealand by elements of the French Secret Service."

"Come on, Sam, that's old news," one of the associate directors commented with a chuckle. "The French have been making those claims for years."

"Yes, that's true, they have. But unfortunately, the situation now seems to be a bit more complicated. Apparently, this same informant is also prepared to offer proof that this 'cooperating agent' of ours is now directly involved in running an international environmental group . . ." Sam Nokes looked down at his notes, ". . . *Terre-Mère Vert,* which, as I understand it, is expected to have a significant voice in directing sanctions against member nations of the WTO for violating a wide range of environmental laws."

The room turned deathly silent as Sam Nokes looked around at the stunned faces for several long moments.

"Does anyone happen to know," he finally asked, "what *Terre-Mère Vert* stands for?"

"It's French, or some reasonable facsimile thereof, for 'Mother Earth Green,' " Arthur Traynor said. "I believe the appropriate acronym would be M-E-G."

Every head in the room turned to face Elliott Parkinson.

"Operation MEG." Sam Nokes nodded his head slowly. " 'Directing sanctions against member nations of the WTO for violating a wide range of environmental laws.' " He paused for a long moment, and then said: "I assume it's obvious to everyone in this room that if the French can show a direct connection between the destruction of the *Rainbow Warrior,* and *Terre-Mère Vert*—"

"—our position becomes untenable," the director finished, the icy glare in his eyes visibly melting. He was listening carefully now.

"That's exactly why . . ." Parkinson started to interrupt, but the director waved him off impatiently. He wanted to hear more on why his bureaucratically astute—albeit outspoken—deputy had openly chosen sides on this issue.

"And *because* of that rather frightening possibility," Sam Nokes went on with a solemn expression on his wrinkled face, "I think we all agree that it would be extremely useful to have a transcript of everything discussed at this specific *ad hoc* meeting."

Every head around the table nodded with varying degrees of assent, all of them clearly understanding that the word "transcript" actually meant a tape recording only. An intercept like that would never be transcribed.

"Unfortunately, there's still one outstanding element that may have an extremely serious impact on all of this." The deputy director hesitated for effect. "It seems that Lt. Col. Charles L'Que, of the French Secret Service, may be directly involved in this unannounced meeting."

"Should that really concern us?" the director asked.

"I think so." Sam Nokes nodded. "Were you aware that Elliott arranged to have his son killed?"

"That's not true! The boy is still alive, and I didn't . . ." Parkinson started to say, and then caught himself, much too late.

The director's feral eyes locked on the paled face of his associate director for Operations.

"What Elliott is saying," Sam Nokes explained for the benefit of at least four confused faces around the table, "is that Lieutenant Colonel L'Que's *youngest* son—who, by some interesting coincidence, was critically injured during a burglary of his parents' home yesterday evening—hasn't died yet. It was L'Que's older son, Jacques, who was shot and killed in Wahran, Algeria, by one of Parkinson's agents approximately eighteen years ago, while in the process of contacting his controller . . ."

"We had no choice. He was about to expose one of our critical operations, and we had verification!" Parkinson protested, but every eye in the room was on the deputy director.

". . . who happened to be his father—an individual who is now considered to be one of the top counterterrorist experts in the French Secret Service. An individual who, at the time of his son's death," Sam Nokes finished, "was apparently investigating a radical environmental group called *Terre-Mère Vert,* and had sent his son in to infiltrate the group."

"Jesus," someone in the room whispered.

For almost fifteen seconds, the room was completely silent as each of the men worked out the ramifications from their own perspective.

"If L'Que is involved with this informant, he'll crucify us in the eyes of the American public, simply out of an understandable desire for revenge," the director whispered, effectively summarizing the unspoken conclusions of every man in that room. Every man, that is, except one.

"There's one more aspect of this situation that hasn't been considered yet," Traynor spoke out from the far corner of the room.

"What's that?" the director demanded in a voice hoarse from the effects of delayed shock.

"Do you recall the name Henry Culver, the ex-employee we talked about earlier?" Traynor asked.

"Yes, what about him?"

Then, to the absolute dismay of Elliott Parkinson, Traynor began to explain.

"Feel like talking?"

Startled out of his meditative daydreams by the sudden, unexpected voice, Henry Culver jerked his head around and then blinked for a few uncertain moments at the sight of Homicide Detective Brad Carpenter's dark face poking through the window of the unmarked police car before he finally nodded his head.

"Yeah, sure," he said, his voice dull and rough, "why not?"

Culver had been sitting alone in Carpenter's unmarked vehicle for over an hour, wrapped tightly in a woolen police blanket and lost in his tangled thoughts as he continued to monitor the arrivals and activities of the specialized teams— the Homicide investigators, the bomb squad, the uniformed CSI officers, the coroner's investigator, and the mortuary body-baggers—with a curious lack of emotion that he couldn't even begin to understand.

Like they're all actors, silently playing out their roles on a dark, cold, and desolate stage, he thought morosely. He liked the idea and wanting to hold on to it, because it implied the eventual dropping of a curtain that would signal the return of everything, and everyone, back to normal again.

Culver knew better, or at least he was pretty sure he knew better. But the familiar characters on the other side of the windshield were still walking through their all-too-predictable motions, and the images that continued to materialize out of the dark catacombs of his memory still didn't make much sense. So he continued to sit in Bradford Carpenter's unmarked cruiser and observe the entire operation with a sense of emotional detachment that was almost scary, just to see if he really *was* wrong.

He had even watched Theodore Gauss, the new director of the Fairfax County Crime Laboratory, step down out of the familiar lab van with what used to be *his* CSI kit and *his* recorder and *his* clipboard . . . and discovered to his amazement that *that* didn't bother him either. Instead, he'd found himself feeling curiously sympathetic toward the visibly shaken forensic scientist.

You were looking bad out there, Gauss—overweight, limping, and the way you were acting, probably scared out of your mind that you were going to walk into another bomb. And I don't blame you one bit because that's exactly the way I'd have felt, too, if they wanted me to go back down there.

In fact, if anything, the sight of Theodore Gauss hesitating at the garage door and looking around nervously before he finally entered the dynamite-laden house had only served to reinforce Culver's feeling that he was just part of the audience now—alone and isolated and apart from it all.

Like he really didn't *belong* at a homicide investigation anymore.

Or at least not at this one.

He found it very strange to feel that way because he'd tried to follow it all from his distant viewpoint at the end of the driveway, mentally walking himself through the predictable steps—the establishment of the scene perimeter, the initial walk-thru, the overall photographs, the start of the scene sketch, the note-taking, and the locating and marking of the obvious evidence items—all in a futile attempt to block out the images that kept flashing through his head.

The images of Paul and Doreen Radlick, their pale, frozen faces reflecting the agony of their last desperate efforts to work themselves loose before they succumbed to the cold, or their injuries, or whatever drugs the coroner's lab might find in their blood and tissues; almost certainly knowing, as they fought against the unbreakable nylon webbing, that they'd been left there as bait.

And Tess.

And the dark shadow of Digger crossing in front of the light from the open trapdoor ("probably a racoon," somebody had said, but Culver couldn't remember who, or when or where).

And the dynamite sticks, almost dripping with thick, resinous drops of purified nitroglycerin that had already begun to crystallize in the cold night air, bundled together and waiting with passive indifference for someone to provide the slightest, shearing jolt that would send them, and everything else in the immediate area, roaring into white oblivion.

And a more distant memory: Digger's face as he sat there at the defense table, flipping through the unimaginably gruesome photograph album in a state of almost-orgasmic bliss as somebody—Radlick, Toledano, Judge Mauser, or himself, he couldn't tell which—kept insisting that the exhibit labeled John Doe Thirty-three was clearly tainted, because everyone had cheated, and was therefore inadmissible.

And the lights.

Especially the lights.

The pulsing string of bright red lights that, one by one, had drawn his eyes across the length of the beam to the relay switch that would have killed them all. The lights that had visibly timed the detonation sequence in a slow, precise, and terrifying cadence until they suddenly disappeared behind the retina-burning brilliance of the fireballs that erupted from the instinct-guided muzzle of Russelli's sawed-off shotgun.

Culver had tried to block all of the images out, telling himself that the remnants of shock were still playing games with his sense of reality. But it wasn't working because the images kept coming back, reappearing over and over again in the dark recesses of his mind.

And so he had continued to sit there in Carpenter's cruiser, alternately shivering and sweating in the bone-chilling darkness, as he waited for the players to walk themselves through the one critical scene that would make it all absolutely and irrevocably clear.

It had taken the coroner's investigator and the two grim-faced mortuary attendants, working in careful conjunction with the three ATF bomb disposal experts in their distinctive orange overalls, almost an hour before they were finally able to transfer the plastic-encased bodies of Paul and Doreen Radlick up through the ragged five-by-five hole that John Russelli had cut through the downstairs bathroom floor.

They brought the stretchers out to the mortuary van one at a time, the heaviest one first.

Paul.

And by the time the two attendants finished shoving Doreen Radlick's plastic-encased body into the back of the van, Henry Culver was nodding his head and blinking back the tears, and trying to decide if the overwhelming sense of numbed relief that accompanied his jarring return to reality meant he really *was* insane, after all; or just cold and callous and . . .

. . . and what? Glad that they're dead, because now everything makes some kind of sense? So what does that make me? Just another variation of John Doe Thirty-three? Some kind of freak who doesn't react to the sight of two more bodies because after they're dead they're just sticks of furniture. Part of the scene. Something to be considered, measured, photographed, and evaluated . . . and then discarded.

Shit.

They'd backed the van slowly out of the driveway a few minutes ago, which was why Brad Carpenter now had time to walk over to his official vehicle and conduct a casual interrogation of the one person—a friend and a cohort—who, wittingly or not, had somehow become a focal point of a growing number of supposedly unrelated deaths that had too many overlapping edges that didn't even begin to make sense.

Carpenter settled his heavy frame into the front passenger seat, closed the door, and turned to face Culver, wincing at the sight of the bloodied and swollen lower lip, and the thick streaks of spiderwebbing that still covered most of Russelli's denim jacket, and the spots along Culver's head, face, neck, and hands that the paramedics hadn't had time to wipe away. He tossed the .357 Smith & Wesson down on the seat.

"You left that down there. Thought you might want it."

"Thanks," Culver whispered indifferently, making no effort to reach for the dirt- and mud- and spiderweb-encrusted handgun.

"You look like a momma spider's bad dream," Carpenter commented. "How you feeling?"

"They really weren't crystallizing, were they?" Culver asked in a soft, steady voice, as he stared straight into the Homicide detectives eyes.

"What are you talking about?" Carpenter's dark brows furrowed in momentary confusion.

"The dynamite sticks," Culver explained patiently, almost certain that he had it figured out now. "They really weren't oozing nitro, right?"

He really wasn't *down there. Stupid to panic. Should have realized that. Not the way that bastard works.*

"It was all brand-new, just out of the factory. Guy out in Warrenton reported it stolen last Wednesday, along with a couple hundred detonators and about fifteen thousand feet of wire" Carpenter said, trying to get a look at Culver's eyes without being too obvious about it. "I miss something?"

Culver shook his head. "I just got a little confused down there. Wanted to make sure I had it all straight. I seem to remember trying to give Russelli and Stewart a hard time."

"They forgot to wear their good-guy hats when they went down in there after you." Carpenter shrugged. "Way I heard it, you couldn't see or hear on account of all those rounds you cranked off, and probably figured it was Digger making a move on you."

Culver nodded. "Yeah . . . right. Did I . . . uh, do anything?" he asked hesitantly. His lower lip was still tender, and he could taste the dried blood. But a split lip didn't even *begin* to account for all of the blood he'd discovered on his shirt and the sleeves of Russelli's jacket.

"Russelli's supposed to have one hell of a bloody nose, and Stewart's got some interesting bruises for a guy who spends his weekends training recon marines. Said to tell you, after this thing's all over with, he and Russelli are gonna take you out to the training center and stomp the shit out of you, just on general principles."

"Yeah, sound's like a reasonable idea." Culver nodded absentmindedly, distracted once again by the mental image of the sequencing red lights. Only this time they weren't threatening; just interesting because he understood why now. And *that* bothered him too.

Funny, I'm really starting to understand the bastard. Have to tell Hattabaugh about that. Really make his day.

"Oh yeah, I'm supposed to ask you how your ears are doing?" Carpenter went on. "Still ringing?"

Culver nodded. "It sounds like a cicada uprising in the back of my skull. Probably go away after a while. Guess I should have worn ear protectors down there, but I wasn't really planning on doing any shooting. Just thought I might find them . . ."

Ear protectors? Where . . . ?

"Yeah, I heard you cut it kinda close on those shots," Carpenter said, gently changing the direction of the conversation. "One of the ATF guys took a good look at that relay box a few minutes ago. He said he thinks you had maybe a couple seconds left at the outside. Which reminds me," he added, "you able to see what you were shooting at?"

The house out in Clifton. Somebody went in there with ear protectors and lost one. So what does that make it, a professional hit?

Culver shook his head. "No, I couldn't see anything at all after the first shot. Just kept jacking the rounds and pulling the trigger, hoping I was close."

"Turns out you weren't," Carpenter shrugged. "Nice grouping, but they all went high left by about five or six inches. Tore the shit out of the beam though."

"I missed the relay box?" Culver blinked and turned his head to stare at the smiling investigator. "But how . . . ?"

"Believe it or not, you managed to cut the critical wires." Carpenter smiled. "Had to go down there and see it for myself."

"Jesus Christ," Culver whispered.

"Yeah, exactly." Carpenter nodded in agreement. "I wouldn't count on getting any medals for crappy shooting like that, but I hear Hattabaugh's planning on giving you his, just as soon as he goes home and picks up a change of shorts."

"Poor old Hattabaugh," Culver whispered softly. "Guy's gonna drive himself crazy, trying to watch out for us rookie cops."

"Yeah, well, you didn't help the situation any, telling everybody that you were knee-deep in dynamite down there just before you started capping off rounds. Damn near gave Jack and Al heart attacks. Which reminds me," Carpenter added with a pleasant smile, "they had to medevac Craven out of here with a torn-up ankle. He took off running soon as he heard the first shot. Went right into a culvert."

For the first time in several hours, the faint glimmer of a smile appeared on Henry Culver's bloodied lips.

"And speaking of supervisors going ape-shit," Carpenter went on easily, "I understand Russelli just about took the house apart trying to get you out of that crawl space."

"Russelli's a good guy," Culver said softly, nodding his head. "He's been backing us up ever since we were kids. You'd think he'd get tired of it by now."

"Us?"

"Paul Radlick. He and Russelli and I all went to school together," Culver explained in a distant voice. "Oakton High and then George Mason. Paul and I were always getting ourselves into some kind of shit, and Russelli would always manage to get us out."

"Ah."

"Worked out fine as long as we all stayed together," Culver went on in a voice that had suddenly turned hard and cold.

"Should have never let ourselves get separated. That's how that bastard Digger works. Plays games with your head, splits you up, and then takes you out when you're not paying attention."

"Easy, Henry," the Homicide detective cautioned. "We haven't even made the guy to any of this yet. Gauss is still rummaging around in there trying to find something that'll put him in the house."

"Digger killed them," Culver repeated, shaking his head slowly. "You know it and I know it. Doesn't matter if Gauss finds anything or not. Digger killed Tess and Paul and Doreen. He put Quinzio in the hospital, and damn near took out you and Gauss, too. And he's going to keep on coming after Russelli and me until somebody puts him away for good."

"I'm not arguing with you."

"Carp," Culver whispered hoarsely, "all I want to do right now is kill the bastard. Walk right up to him, look right in those goddamned, washed-out eyes of his, and then put him right out of his misery."

"Don't need to feel like the Lone Ranger." Carpenter shrugged indifferently. "There's a couple hundred guys on the department right now who're looking to be first in line when we kick that door."

"But you know what really bothers me, really tears the shit out of me?" Culver continued on, caught up in the momentum of his confession.

"No, what?"

"Right now, right here in this car, I honest to God don't see anything wrong with it."

"I don't either," Carpenter said calmly. "Only difference is, most of us already worked ourselves over that hurdle a long time ago. You're still looking at it. Fact is, you may never get over it, and you're probably a whole lot better off if you don't."

"I don't follow."

"You want the truth? Or at least the truth as I see it?"

"Yeah, sure."

"Fact of the matter is, you shouldn't be a cop. You're not cut out for it."

"What?"

"Henry, guys like Stewart, Russelli, Hattabaugh, and me, we never went through all that forensics ethics training you're always talking about. All that stuff about how the people working in crime labs have to be absolutely straight, 'cause you're the check on the system."

"What the hell does *that* . . . ?" Culver started to interrupt, but Carpenter held up his hand.

"Henry, if one of us ever manages to get Digger in our sights, we're going to drop him. No question about it. Unless our boy pops up with his arms wrapped around a circuit court judge like they're a couple of newlyweds, he's gone, period."

"Okay, so . . ."

"But the thing is," Carpenter interrupted, "Stewart, Russelli, Hattabaugh, and I, we don't have some kind of scientific conscience running around in our heads saying we have to do it fair. Legal—yeah, we'll keep it legal. But fair? That's a different ball game."

"You guys are going to kill him *legally?*" Culver almost smiled again. "Come on . . ."

"Absolutely legal," Carpenter said, nodding with emphasis. "When we find him, he's gonna resist, 'cause that's the way he is. And the first second he does, he's going down because we're not going to screw with him anymore. End of story.

"But the thing is," the black detective went on insistently, "right now, you want him just as bad as we do—maybe more, because of Tess and Paul. But even so, if it really comes down to it, if you ever *do* get a shot at the guy, every cop in the station, from the chief on down, knows you'll try to take him clean. You'll sight in on him and then hesitate, because you'll want to do it right, and if you pull that kind of shit with a goddamned crazy freak like Digger, he's gonna kill you."

Culver sat there in silence for several long moments, staring at the solemn face of his friend.

"So what do I do, Carp?" he finally asked. "Try to talk Russelli into sleeping on my couch for the next few months until one of you guys hunts him down?"

"That wouldn't be such a bad idea. Russelli knows how to keep a guy like that off your back. And speaking of Russelli, you happen to know where he got off to?"

"I saw him leave in one of the cruisers a few minutes ago. I think he said something about going home to check on Sharon and the kids." Culver shrugged. "Said he'd be back."

Carpenter nodded thoughtfully. "Yeah, that's probably a real good idea."

They sat there in silence for a few moments, seemingly oblivious to all of the surrounding activity, and then Culver took in a deep breath and let it out slowly.

"Hey Carp," he whispered, staring out at darkened house that was now being illuminated by a pair of fire department generators. The ATF crew still hadn't figured out how to get into the booby-trapped breaker box.

"Yeah?"

"Mind if I ask you something personal?"

"Why not," Carpenter shrugged. "I've been digging around in your head all this time. Fair is fair."

"Why would Stewart want you to keep an eye on him?"

Carpenter was silent for a moment.

"Who's this 'him' we're talking about?"

"Russelli."

"Ah." The black detective nodded noncommittally. "Where'd you hear something like that?"

"I was standing around where I didn't belong at that shooting scene the other night, heard you guys talking. You didn't answer my question. 'Ah', meaning what?"

" 'Ah', meaning . . . ah shit." Carpenter shook his head, torn between his loyalty to Stewart and his friendship with Culver. "Henry, take my word for it. You don't want to be involved in this."

"I don't want to get *involved?*" Culver whispered incredulously. "Carp, there's a guy out there writing my name on walls and booby-trapping cops and killing my friends because he thinks Russelli and I cheated him. The guy kills his own attorney and uses him for bait to lure one of us down in that hole, and you don't think I should want to get *involved?*"

"Henry, Russelli's a different issue . . ." Carpenter started to protest, but Culver wouldn't listen.

"Different, my ass. The guy ripped a goddamned toilet out of the floor with his bare hands so he could get down there in that crawl space and get me out!"

"Yeah, so . . . ?"

"So I figure that maybe it's time somebody started watching *his* back for a change," Culver said, "before somebody besides Digger puts a knife in it."

Carpenter glared at Culver for several long moments, and then shook his head firmly. "It isn't like that."

"Convince me."

Carpenter hesitated again before finally shaking his head and taking a deep, sighing breath. "Listen, just give me some time to talk with Stewart. We've got something going on right now—a sensitive operation that's kinda touchy, and I can't . . ."

". . . can't trust me either because Russelli and I are tight?" Culver finished.

A sensitive operation?

The words jarred at Culver's subconscious.

What was it that Traynor said? Something about a sensitive operation that was coming unglued. An operation that involved Topcastle, and had several closely related elements.

And that I was one of those elements?

Christ, Traynor, what have you guys got yourselves into now? And more to the point, what have you got me into? Where the hell's the connection?

Aside from a momentary flash of something in his eyes, and a visible tightening of his jaw muscles, Bradford Carpenter remained absolutely calm and controlled. And in watching as best he could in the darkened vehicle, Carpenter realized that Henry Culver, too, was now in full control of his emotions. In full control and probing, trying to get a reaction that might tell him more than the words.

That's the way, Henry, Carpenter thought to himself. *You're learning. Make a Homicide investigator out of you yet, if we don't have to arrest you and Russelli first.*

"Like I said, Henry," Carpenter said as he started to get out of the car. "Let me talk with Stewart. He gives the okay, then we'll talk about it."

Culver thought about that for a few moments, and then nodded his head. "Yeah, okay," he sighed, "that's fair."

"Just take it slow, buddy," Carpenter advised as he shut the door. "Everything's all screwed up right now. Give it time to settle down."

"Yeah, okay, I understand." Culver nodded somberly, and then called out as the Homicide detective started back down the long dark driveway. "Hey Carp, mind if I use the car? I'll leave it at the station."

"Sure, go ahead. I'll get a ride back with Stewart." Carpenter shrugged as he tossed his key ring in through the open window, and then hesitated as something occurred to him. "Where you going?"

"Home, take a shower, get some sleep, try to get my head straight," Culver mumbled, trying not to think about anything at all as he slid the key into the ignition and started up the engine, knowing full well that the mind-wrenching images of his three dead friends would be waiting for him later, in his dreams.

"Henry." Even over the masking rumble of the V-8 engine, the concern was evident in Brad Carpenter's voice.

"Yeah?" Culver blinked, looking up.

"Listen, just stay tight with Russelli and don't worry about Digger, okay?"

"Don't *worry* about him?"

"That's right." The heavyset detective nodded, his dark facial features masked by a look of malicious determination.

"Al's got this thing under control. As far as Digger's concerned, the next time that cat sticks his head up, he's history."

In the tightly secured confines of the director's sixth floor conference room, seven men sat in absolute silence, each lost in his own turmoiled thoughts as they all waited for a decision from the one man with the power and authority to say yes or no.

That man, the director of the Central Intelligence Agency, continued to sit motionless with his hands in his lap and his head bowed as he continued in his own methodical way to work through the likely ramifications of each option.

Then, finally, he nodded slightly, as if to reassure himself that he had considered every possible variable, and raised his head up.

"Elliott," he said, applying a commanding tone to his voice that brooked no further arguments, "your operation will continue as planned. You are to make every effort to determine the time and the location of this *ad hoc* meeting, penetrate the security *without* detection, and acquire recordings of all conversations regarding our Algerian asset. Those recordings are to be a number one priority. Is that clear?"

Elliott Parkinson nodded his head, unable to conceal the flush of victory.

"Arthur," the director continued on without pause, "Sci-Tech will stand by in a support mode to provide any necessary equipment."

Arthur Traynor nodded his red-bearded head in acquiescence. He'd made his objections, and now he would do exactly what he had been hired to do: function as ordered. "Do you want a team for the penetration?"

The director turned his head to face his chief field executive. "Elliott, what is the current status on Digger?"

"We're back in contact," Parkinson said in a voice vibrant with renewed confidence. "He was extremely apologetic over the L'Que incident. Assured us it won't happen again. From now on, he'll handle everything himself."

"Have you physically located him yet?"

"No, but we will. We have teams monitoring the individual that we believe is his primary objective now."

"Culver?" the director inquired.

"Yes."

"And he agrees to our stipulation that he will terminate his, uh, extracurricular activities regarding Mr. Culver and any other Fairfax County police officers until *after* our operation is completed, thereby resolving Arthur's concerns?"

"Yes, he's fully agreeable to that stipulation."

"Whereupon you will *immediately* terminate his employment in an appropriate manner."

"Yes."

"Arthur," the director said, still keeping his gaze on Elliott Parkinson, the man with whom he had just entrusted the remainder of his political career, "do you have anyone on your staff with better qualifications to make the entry?"

Traynor hesitated.

"I have any number of people who are far more stable than Digger, but none with equivalent technical skills, myself included," he finally said, somehow managing to keep the sarcasm out of his voice.

"What about R.C.?" one of the men at the table asked.

"He and Henry Culver are close friends," Traynor said quietly. "R.C. is aware of Digger's intentions. He won't help."

"Will he accept a direct order from me?" the director asked.

Traynor shook his head. "No."

"Then Digger is the logical choice," the director said. "We'll discuss the loyalty of Mr. Cohen at a later date. Any further questions?" He surveyed the table and saw Elliott Parkinson raise his hand slightly.

"Yes, Elliott?"

"One more thing. What about the police?"

"What about them?"

"They are now aware that Digger has escaped from the Ward, and have reason to believe that he was involved in the recent death of one of their officers, as well as an attorney and his wife."

"All three of whom were close friends of Henry Culver," Traynor reminded in a tightly controlled voice.

"Yes, we understand that," Parkinson said impatiently. "In any case, an extensive manhunt could hinder our ability to remain fluid during the end phase."

"You said you have a reliable source in the Fairfax County Police Department?" the director reminded.

"We have someone very well placed for this particular operation." Parkinson nodded.

"Then see to it that he monitors the situation carefully." The director looked at his watch. "According to our latest report, the meeting with L'Que and the Congressional committee members will occur sometime during the next twenty-six hours. During that time period, no one is to be allowed to interfere with Digger or any portion of Operation MEG. That includes Lieutenant Colonel L'Que, Henry Culver, or any other Fairfax County police officer. Do I make myself absolutely clear?"

All seven heads nodded.

"Good, then get it done."

Chapter Thirty-four

Friday, 2200 hours

Henry Culver had just finished transferring his gear from Carpenter's unmarked cruiser to his own snow- and-ice-covered Mustang when one of the uniformed station officers walked up to him in the Central Headquarters parking lot.

"Package for you," the officer said, handing Culver a heavy, sealed manila envelope. "Hey, man, really sorry about Tess."

"Yeah, thanks," Culver mumbled as he slid the package into one of his equipment bags. He quickly started up his car, backed out of the parking space, and headed for home.

Don't think about it right now, he told himself as he methodically took the long back road route to his house. *Just go home, take a shower, get into bed, and hope the hell you don't dream. Think about it tomorrow.*

He stopped to make a couple of phone calls at a local gas station; the first to Arthur Traynor's home, and the second to Traynor's Langley office. When he got to his driveway, he paused at his mailbox to pick up his accumulated mail, stuffing the handful of envelopes into his equipment bag.

At his front porch, he transferred the Smith & Wesson to his already-encumbered left hand in order to reach for his keys. When he looked up, he saw the two small red lights glowing brightly among their fourteen emerald green counterparts under the main crossbeam of his entryway.

Oh no, not again.

One through fourteen, all green—no entry. Fifteen and sixteen red—confirmed movement inside. Same as last time.

Not the roof—too visible.

Not the garage door—no access to the wires.

Not the air ducts—too small.

Not the floor—

Why not the floor?

Because the floor was solid and there was no way in through the crawl—

The stony expression on Culver's face never altered. Only his eyes blinked.

For one brief moment, as his heart began to pound in his chest and his hands and arms began to tingle, Henry Culver actually smiled.

The image of Digger's face, his pale blue eyes widening in shock under the square, aligned sights of Culver's Smith & Wesson, was starting to come into a clear, satisfying focus . . . and his right hand was starting to reach for the pistol held loosely in his left when he suddenly remembered something.

Ever since the Kostermann scene, John Doe Thirty-three—the consummate game player—had been setting the rules and picking the stage; and they'd all been going along with it, letting him call the game his way the whole god-damned time.

And where the hell has that got us?

Culver stood there and stared at his locked door, knowing that he was exhausted and hungry and pissed, and could hardly think straight because he'd just lost three of his best friends.

And a couple hours ago he'd almost blown himself up, along with everybody else in Radlick's house, because he hadn't been paying attention, he remembered. And in spite of all that, he was getting ready to walk right in through his front door, just so he could find out what kind of game Digger had set up this time.

So what do you think about that, Traynor?

A foolish question, because he knew *exactly* what Arthur Traynor would say in a situation like this.

You keep on playing his game, Henry—keep on letting him set the rules—and one of these times he's going to win.

Yeah, right.

And then something else occurred to him.

What if it wasn't Digger?

Last time it had been Traynor, the CIA penetration specialist.

But it wasn't Traynor this time because Culver had just talked to him at his private office number.

What was it Traynor had said?

Take my word for it, Henry. For the next few days, pay close attention to your surroundings—especially your familiar surroundings—and be very careful about who you let into your house.

Freaks, friends, or associates. It doesn't matter, don't trust anybody.

Culver looked up at his concealed warning light grid once more, just to reassure himself that he wasn't seeing more of those blinking red light images. It hadn't changed. Fourteen greens and two reds. No entry, but confirmed movement.

Don't trust anybody. Good advice, Traynor. So why do I trust you, even when you warn me not to.

A horrible possibility suddenly occurred to Culver, but he immediately shook it off, because he couldn't even begin to believe that Traynor—or, for that matter, even a bureaucratic idiot like Forecastle or his presumably more intelligent boss—would be stupid enough to get involved with a freak like Digger.

No, no way. Culver shook his head firmly. *You could always count on the fact that the people in Operations were going to come up with some pretty weird shit; but even* they *drew the line at homicidal maniacs.*

And besides, he reminded himself, for something like that to be going on in the county, there'd have to be links all over the place, and there aren't any—or at least none that he'd ever seen.

So don't even *think* about that.

Okay, Traynor, so what the hell do I do now? Stand around out here on my front porch like a chunk of bait, and wait to see if I get chewed on?

And then, at that moment, he knew exactly what he was going to do.

Arthur Traynor was in the process of hanging up his phone when he looked up and saw the director standing silently in the doorway of his office.

"Who was that?" the prim, white haired executive asked quietly.

Traynor hesitated, and then said "Culver" in a calm, neutral voice.

The director nodded silently as if he'd expected that answer all along. "What did you tell him?"

"Nothing."

The director raised his white eyebrows.

"This phone is connected to the central recording system," Traynor replied evenly. "You can have the tape on your desk within thirty seconds if you wish."

"Did he call you?" the director asked, ignoring the offer.

Traynor nodded.

"Why?"

"Henry knows that he and some of his police associates are being targeted by a technical expert, and he's concerned about his ability to spot the traps. He asked for assistance."

"Did you offer to help?"

"Yes."

"I assume you realize that, in point of fact, you *can't* help him, because if you did, you would put Elliott's operation— and therefore the Agency—at an unacceptable risk."

"So I'm told," Traynor said coldly.

Traynor had no idea how much the director actually knew about Elliott Parkinson's latest act of desperation, or L'Que's last-minute intervention, but one thing was absolutely certain. Any charges of attempted murder against a fellow member of the Agency would require irrefutable proof, and Traynor wasn't about to bring L'Que in to provide that proof.

Not yet anyway.

The director paused for a long moment, and then said: "Elliott is very concerned about your personal involvement in his operation, Arthur. He's made some accusations which I find very difficult to take seriously."

"Such as?"

"That, among other things, you violated my direct order not to contact Culver. Of course, that seems to be a moot point now," the director added, glancing meaningfully at the telephone on Traynor's desk.

"Your orders were very specific. I was not to tell him of our connection with Digger," Traynor reminded. "And in spite of my objections, I haven't, and won't, even though I'm absolutely convinced that your decision to continue with Operation MEG is one hundred percent wrong."

"I understand that one of Elliott's operatives was attacked and severely injured earlier this morning, somewhere in the area of Mr. Culver's home," the director probed, ignoring Traynor's comment.

"So I heard. Any word on his condition?"

"Serious but not critical. Several broken bones, a badly fractured jaw, and a concussion. Apparently he wasn't able to identify his assailant."

Or doesn't want to, Traynor thought, smiling inwardly at the realization that the well-deserved reputations of some of his exceptionally loyal and maliciously innovative Sci-Tech operatives had probably saved his career once again.

"It's a dangerous world out there. Even experienced CIA operatives can get mugged if they're not paying attention to their surroundings. Elliott ought to remind them to be more careful."

"Yes, I suppose he should." The director nodded absent-mindedly, and then stared at the multitude of plaques on Traynor's wall for a few seconds before going on.

"I'm sure I don't need to remind you how sensitive this operation is, Arthur," he said quietly, as much to himself as to Traynor. "We're dealing with some very serious issues here. To disrupt everything at this juncture could mean a public relations blowup on an international scale—the loss of crucial assets that simply cannot be replaced. Inflamed public reactions. Human lives placed in jeopardy."

Traynor tried to say something, but the white-haired director continued.

"Arthur, if an incident *does* break out as a result of all of this—in Algeria alone, we could be talking about thousands of innocent casualties, at a minimum. On the balance, one individual, or even a dozen . . ."

"I understand the issues," Traynor interrupted, "And I know all about body counts and balances. But do you know what I'm *really* afraid of?"

The director shook his head slowly, watching Traynor's face carefully.

"What really scares me is the possibility that this operation has been redirected to protect asses rather than assets,"

Traynor said. "And if that truly is the case," he added, fixing his unblinking gaze on the director's anguished features, "then the possibility that someone like Henry Culver might learn something unfortunate about one of our rogue agents is going to be the very least of our problems."

The problem, Culver told himself as he continued to stand there on his front porch and stare at his code-locked front door, was actually very simple—once you looked at it from the right perspective.

The reason Digger was finding it so easy to target a bunch of cops who *should* have been able to watch out for themselves, was that all of them—Russelli, Gauss, Quinzio, Tess Beasley, and himself—had been committing the classic rookie mistake that trainee police officers were warned about time after time at the Academy.

In simple terms, they had allowed themselves to become predictable.

Start falling into a pattern in the way you patrol an area, or respond to a call, or stop for coffee, and within a matter of days, the instructors had warned, the people on your beat are going to have you down cold before you even know they're out there.

And how long had it been since Digger conned his way out of the Ward?

Seven days.

Christ, he thought, *no wonder the guy's got us pegged. Might as well have sent him a set of duty rosters and a copy of the Departmental Manual.*

It's just that simple, Culver told himself. *He knows our schedules, our operating systems, and exactly what it takes to lure one of us into a trap. And that means he gets to make the first move every time.*

Unless . . .

Unless he and Russelli broke themselves loose from Digger's progressively encircling game plan—whatever that plan was—and regained some degree of control over the situation, and their own lives, while they still could.

And that was when Henry Culver made his decision.

Forcing himself to ignore the telltale red lights on his alarm board, and the enticing possibility that the pale blue-eyed freak who had bobby-trapped Tess Beasley really *was* in there, waiting for him on the other side of that locked door, Culver slowly stepped back off his porch and then paused for a moment to listen for any sound of movement.

Nothing.

You still think Russelli and I cheated you on the Kostermann scene, don't you, you bastard?

Then, moving as cautiously as he could with his eyes and ears alert for the slightest sound of footsteps, or a door opening, or any movement at all, Henry Culver began to move backward along his walkway at a slow and steady pace toward his car.

Well you're wrong. But that's okay, because we're not going to play your games anymore.

Something snapped at the far side of his house, and he turned his head quickly in that direction, but the subsequent crackling noises sounded very much like a rotten tree branch breaking and falling under the weight of the icy snow, so he ignored it.

You got at Radlick and Quinzio and Gauss, so now there's just Russelli and me left. But if you really want us that bad, you're going to have to crawl out of whatever hole you're in and come out in the open after us . . . and that will be just fine as far as we're concerned.

He hesitated as he reached for the door handle, remembering that Tess Beasley had died in a very similar driveway beside the door of her station wagon. For a brief moment, the numbing image of the two sheet-covered bodies returned, but he immediately shook it off.

Don't think about it. He hasn't had time to set anything. And besides, if the driveway was wired, he'd have touched it off as soon as you drove in. Don't think about it at all. Just go. The direction probably *didn't* matter. The important thing was to make random, unexpected jumps. Be unpredictable.

Long way around. Go left.

Henry Culver was no longer thinking about Digger as he backed out of the driveway. Instead, he was trying to focus his mind on his next jump—the one that he hoped was going to tell him something.

But something in the back of his mind kept trying to get his attention by whispering a single word.

Wire.

What about the wire?

There had been a lot of it in Paul Radlick's driveway and a whole lot more in the crawl space of his house. All the same brand, which probably meant something. *Later,* he told himself as he pulled into the parking lot next to the Fairfax County Police Department's Central Headquarters building. *Plenty of time later.*

There, in the parking lot, under the cover of darkness and the intermittent downpours of icy rain and hail, he made his second random jump by exchanging his distinctive Mustang for one of the spare unmarked detective vehicles—a dark brown Honda Accord, just acquired from a DEA seizure—that didn't look like a cop car at all.

In doing so, and in transferring some of his gear from one trunk to the other, Culver was very careful not to attract the attention of any Fairfax County police officers who occasionally hurried in and out of the station.

He accelerated the Honda out of the parking lot, made his way to the eastbound Highway 66 on-ramp heading to DC, and watched his rearview mirror closely as he drove.

At the Theodore Roosevelt Memorial Bridge, he crossed the Potomac and then immediately took the left lane turn onto the Whitehurst Freeway.

Okay, first let's see who's out there.

Pulling over sharply into the right-hand lane, he accelerated the Accord into the tight, looping turn through the off-ramp that put him right in the middle of the slowly cruising, Saturday-night-in-Georgetown traffic.

And then maybe we'll find out why.

Two minutes later, he broke away from the congested cross-mix of vehicle and pedestrian traffic by turning sharply onto a very familiar, single-lane, one-way street. Humming to himself now, he continued to drive at a steady twenty miles per hour for about a quarter of a mile, until the darkened road suddenly curved around to the left and he found himself coming up alongside the driveway of a brightly illuminated service station on the left-hand side of the road.

After glancing up at the mirror to confirm that he was clear, Henry Culver suddenly braked to a full stop, shut off all his lights, reversed gears, and then quickly backed up into the driveway of the gas station until the rear of the Accord bumped up against the huge metal trash Dumpster adjacent to the rest rooms.

He shifted the Accord into park, left the motor running, and then settled back into the driver's seat with his right hand across his chest on the rubberized grip of his shoulder-holstered .357, waiting to see who—if anybody—would drive by.

Less than twenty seconds later, he had the answer to at least one of his questions.

The three chase cars, each nondescript and unremarkable—if you ignored the fact that there were two dark figures in each of the front seats—drove by in single file, one after the other, at a slow, steady, twenty miles per hour.

Red Escort, white Mazda, and green minivan, Culver noted. *Okay, Traynor, where's the big boy?*

A few moments later, a vehicle that Culver immediately recognized as a RDF—radio direction–finding—van rumbled past the gas station in what appeared to be a desperate effort to catch up with the three smaller vehicles. Culver smiled, knowing that the van was essentially useless now because the small but powerful transmitter he'd discovered on the underside of his Mustang was still screaming out its electronic homing signal from the middle of the Fairfax County Police Department's main parking lot—and they already knew where *that* was.

What was it you said, Traynor?

A very sensitive operation, involving Elliott Parkinson—the AD of Operations for the CIA—that's starting to come unglued.

There was something else, Culver remembered. Something about the operation being a lot bigger than Parkinson or anyone else at the Agency had expected, with a lot of closely related elements. And even though he'd told Parkinson's assistant very clearly that he *wasn't* going to do any work for them again, and even though he *hadn't* been involved in an Agency project for years, he—Culver—was still considered to be one of those elements.

So whatever it is happened a long time ago—which means that it isn't Digger, thank God, Culver realized with a sense of relief that told him just how afraid he'd really been of that possibility.

So maybe Parkinson had a change of heart and decided to put a half million dollars' worth of surveillance on my tail, just to keep me out of trouble.

Yeah, right.

He watched the van drive past with a detached sense of interest that almost bordered on amusement, now that he was no longer concerned about Digger and Parkinson being linked together. It had been especially enjoyable to watch eight professional trackers trying to pretend that they weren't the least bit interested in a little Honda Accord butted up against trash Dumpster as they drove on by, mostly because there wasn't anything else they *could* do.

Although actually, Culver knew, they could have turned into the service station and parked right here next to the Dumpster, if all they wanted to do was harass him. But that obviously *wasn't* why somebody had put them on his tail.

And nobody had bothered to tell them their target was an

alumnus of Sci-Tech, or they would have never let themselves get bunched up like that on a one-way street.

And now that they'd been blown, Culver smiled, they'd be frantically radioing in for instructions and backup units because they would have just discovered that the road was all one-lane, one-way, with no exits for another three blocks . . . which meant that by the time they all managed to get turned back around, their target would be long gone.

Henry Culver knew all about those frantic radio calls. He'd made more than his share.

And that eliminated Arthur Traynor as a suspect, he decided, because Traynor would have made *sure* that the entire team knew all about the training and expertise of their quarry, and would have threatened everybody with immediate transfers to Moscow if they lost him.

Which leaves us with that classic model of bureaucratic paranoia, Elliott Parkinson, complete with batboy Forecastle. Exactly the kind of operational director who would deliberately hamstring his tracking teams with incomplete information, just so they wouldn't know what he was up to.

Unless they already . . .

At that moment, another vehicle—this one a dark blue pickup which looked just as unremarkable as the first three chase vehicles—drove past the driveway to the service station at a slow, steady twenty miles per hour.

Oh . . . shit.

Henry Culver knew that from long experience that the Agency tracker teams almost always worked in groups of three or four chase cars, and so the abrupt appearance of yet another slow-moving vehicle on this well-traveled Georgetown road normally wouldn't have caused him any concern at all.

But there were three significant things about this particular pickup truck that suddenly caused his entire bloodstream to turn cold.

First of all, the small telltale antenna.

And secondly, the fact that every one of its exterior lights were off.

But third, and most chilling of all: instead of looking straight ahead like the others, the driver of the dark blue pickup deliberately turned his head and stared in the direction of the darkened Honda Accord as he slowly cruised past the driveway entrance to the station.

Chapter Thirty-five

Friday, 2315 hours

It wasn't a MOSS team. Culver was certain of that now. Or at least not in the classic sense, because the Agency's mobile search and surveillance units had a very limited set of functions, which were—in essence—to locate, follow, observe, and record without being spotted, and then transmit the raw intelligence back to the people who got paid to make the big decisions.

Culver had worked dozens of such assignments for Traynor during his stint with the Agency, and therefore knew precisely how the MOSS teams operated—in a very straightforward, low-key, and extremely cautious manner. And almost always by themselves.

But every now and then, as Henry Culver had discovered to his everlasting dismay, an operational field director would decide to play it cute and put all of his devious eggs into one handy basket, so that the subject could be located, the intelligence gathered, and the follow-up response delivered like a one-two punch.

In the parlance of the Agency planners, it was known as the Mossy Rock Option. And when the desired follow-up response was an Agency hitter armed with a gun, knife, bomb, dart, or some devious form of poison, the option amounted to a highly organized and very efficient assassination.

The basic idea was to attach the hitter to a MOSS team, and thereby take advantage of the team's locating capabilities to obtain a direct fix on the target. The problem—from the planner's standpoint—was that this usually had to be done without informing the trackers, because the search and surveillance teams preferred to think of themselves as professional collectors of intelligence, rather than as thugs or assassins.

Culver had unknowingly been assigned to a Mossy Rock unit during an operation in Wahran, Algeria, and had spent several hours working himself into a perfect position to monitor and photograph what was supposed to be a routine exchange of information between a deep-cover foreign agent and a young exchange student courier. He had been about to snap the crucial photo—showing the actual exchange of a manila folder full of secret goodies—when the courier had suddenly been flung backward into a nearby wall, and then fell face forward onto the ground, leaving a bright red pattern of blood on the concrete bricks, and a bloody, fist-sized hole in the middle of his upper back.

The immediate assumption was that one of the players in Algeria's ever-shifting game of political espionage had decided to change sides, meaning that all of the other players had to quickly reassess their own status and loyalties. Accordingly, Culver and the rest of his MOSS team immediately went to ground in four different directions, regrouped three days later in Tangier, and only then learned what had really happened.

Henry Culver had resigned from the Central Intelligence Agency that same day. And since that time, he had never once even considered the idea of being involved with another Agency surveillance team in any manner or form.

But then, too, up until this evening, Henry Culver's feelings about the deployment of the Mossy Rock teams were based solely on his experience as a tracker, when he and his cohorts had been cool, calm, professional, and relatively safe from harm.

Looking at it from the perspective of the target was a different situation entirely.

A long and nervous twenty minutes later, Henry Culver was standing in a remote telephone booth near the American Airlines lobby of National Airport, waiting for someone to pick up the phone at the other end of the line.

"Four-one-two-five."

"This is Hotel Charlie," Culver spoke in as calm and controlled a voice as he could muster. "I need to talk with Traynor."

"Sorry, but you've got the wrong . . ." the gruff voice responded, but Culver immediately interrupted.

"No, I *don't* have the wrong number," he said firmly. "Pay attention. Arthur Traynor is working in his office this evening. I know that because I just talked with him a few minutes ago. Put him on, *now.*"

There was about a sixty-second delay, which seemed much longer to Culver because he was having to scan the dozens of faces that were continually moving around and past his telephone booth.

"Hello?" a higher, more resonant, and absolutely more threatening voice answered, and Culver recognized it at once.

Forecastle.

He hesitated for a moment, thinking of all the things he wanted to say to the youthful special assistant who had tried to drag him back into working for the Agency again, but then he shook his head because he didn't have that much time.

"This is Culver. I'd like to speak with Traynor."

"Mr. Traynor is out of his office at the moment. Can I take a message?"

"You can tell him that I'm running out of quarters."

"All right," J. Winston Weathersby said agreeably.

"But that's okay because I hear the *Washington Post* is pretty good about letting people borrow their phones," Culver continued on with a forced sense of casual indifference. "Especially people with interesting backgrounds. You want me to call back from there?"

There was a brief pause, and then Weathersby was back on the line—still controlled, soothing, and audibly dangerous. "No, actually, we don't."

"Then call him off."

"Call who off?" Weathersby inquired evenly, as though they were discussing a potential change in the weather.

"Mossy Rock."

"I have no idea what you're talking about."

"Fine, then you won't care if the paper gets his picture as a bonus."

"That would be a very bad idea," Weathersby said after a moment's hesitation. "Don't even think about it."

"It's a large brick building. Real easy to find," Culver pressed, feeling more confident now that he was into it. "Very homey. Even has an old printing press in the front window. I hear they're really nice people, too. Like nothing better than to sit around all night listening to war stories."

A longer hesitation this time. Then finally:

"That would be an incredibly bad move on your part, Mr. Culver."

"Yeah, you're probably right. Better to have them come to me instead. That way you guys won't have to worry about finding enough parking spaces."

"That's really *not* going to be necessary," Weathersby went on soothingly, but there was a distinct, underlying edge to his words now.

Starting to lose it. Things must be getting tight. Come on, somebody in there get word to Traynor.

"Convince me."

"Culver, you don't *want* to talk to the goddamned *Washington Post*," J. Winston Weathersby snapped. "Traynor needs to talk with you, but he's in an important meeting with the director right now. He'll be out in a couple of minutes. Just hold on . . ."

At that moment, the needle gage on the cigarette pack–sized device in Henry Culver's hand swept off the scale.

In a series of practiced movements that in total took less than fifteen seconds, Culver hung up the phone, detached the alligator clips and rubber-cupped leads from the receiver and handset, stuffed the device into his kit bag, and then quickly walked out through the sliding glass door of the lobby toward the glary darkness of the huge airport parking lot.

At precisely 11:45 that Friday evening, Bobby Morgan slowly drove Molly Hunsacker's van up in front of an isolated garage in northeast Washington, DC, shut off the headlights with a trembling, blood-streaked hand while leaving the engine running, and then waited.

He had started out four hours earlier, intent on getting to the hidden warehouse on time so that he'd have at least a little leverage to work himself in with Molly's load—because all he wanted to do was to talk to somebody who could tell him how to find that bastard Digger, so that he could avenge the gruesome death of his boyhood friend, Otis Lawnhart.

But somewhere on the way to Highway 66, Bobby Morgan realized that he was starting to black out, and he just barely managed to get the van over to the side of the road before everything *did* turn black. And when he finally came to, it was a little after eleven and he felt like he'd already died at least twice, and he couldn't even *begin* to think of what he was going to tell the people at the warehouse. So he just started up the van and continued to drive, and tried not to pass out again, and told himself that he'd think of something when the time came.

The trouble was, Morgan realized as he closed his eyes, the time *had* come, and he still couldn't think of anything to say that made the least bit of sense.

A few moments later, a dark figure hurried up to the side of the van and pounded on the driver's side window, causing Bobby Morgan to jerk his head up painfully.

"What the hell's the *matter* with you, showing up this late?" the man demanded as he started to thumb the transmitter to raise the garage door—*another black dude, not the same one,* Morgan realized, trying to focus his blurry eyes—but then the man took a closer look through the rain-streaked side window of the van and yelled, "Hey, wait a minute!" and Bobby Morgan did the only thing that he could think to do.

He shot the man in the forehead with Molly-the-Hun's .22 caliber target pistol, aiming the thick barrel through the open wind-wing, and then somehow managed to stagger out of the van, pick up the transmitter, and climb back into the van without fainting again.

Smiling to himself, ignoring his trembling hands and horribly throbbing leg, Bobby Morgan then used the transmitter to open both garage doors. Marcus Grey and his men were busy unloading a heavy television monitor and a pair of matching speakers, wondering as they did so what the hell had happened to Molly Hunsacker.

To further complicate matters, Morgan didn't know that he was supposed to use the transmitter to shut the doors behind him. So when he drove the van into the almost-empty loading dock area, braked to a stop, and rolled down his side window, he effectively turned the hidden warehouse into a very efficient echo chamber.

This became a critical factor a few moments later when Marcus Grey started toward the van and then stopped immediately when he saw a familiar face that was definitely *not* Molly-the-Hun lean out of the driver's side window.

Bobby Morgan intended to wait until the gray-haired black man came closer, but then somebody from up above above yelled *"Marcus, watch out!"* so he decided to hell with it, stuck the target pistol out through the open window, cranked off a pair of sharply cracking .22 caliber rounds in the general direction of the rapidly scrambling Marcus Grey, and then heard a curious noise that sounded like exploding glass before he thought to wonder about the source of the shouted warning.

Much too late, he remembered the men in the rafters with the deadly-looking assault rifles.

Determined to do something right for a change, Bobby Morgan tried to bring his arm up and around to center the gunsight of the incredibly heavy target pistol on one of the distant dark figures who—for some strange reason—seemed much higher up and much farther away than he remembered.

But then the window of the van disintegrated in a rapid and sustained burst of eardrum-shattering automatic weapons fire that slammed the luckless dark-bearded burglar back against the torn seat, and sent a rolling thunder of echoing explosions tumbling out into the dark, empty streets of northeast Washington, DC, and in through the open window of a passing District patrol cruiser.

Knowing that the first thing they'd do was try to run a trace on the phone, Henry Culver had chosen National Airport to make his call for a very specific reason; or actually, a number of specific reasons—those being the number of different ways that he could make his next jump.

He ticked them off in his head as he hurried up the crumbling concrete steps in the semidarkness to the next terraced parking lot level.

Bus.

Metro.

Shuttle.

Limo.

Taxi.

Rental car.

Or even an airplane, he thought. *It's stopped snowing, so maybe there'll be a couple of flights going out late. Hope so. Make it more difficult for the bastards.*

But the thing was, it really didn't matter if there were any more flights going out or not. If they really wanted him bad enough, they'd still have to check out all the other possibilities, too, and it would take a lot of time and people to do it right.

Probably everybody they've got in DC, including some of the old fart desk jocks, Culver thought as he got into the car, started it up, and headed for the rear exit. *That ought to really piss everybody off.*

He really didn't care where they searched, or whom they upset, but the one thing that he hoped they *wouldn't* do was expect him to get back into his readily identifiable Honda and drive back into Fairfax County, because that was exactly what he was doing.

Finally, forty minutes later, feeling very alone and vulnerable in the rural Clifton darkness, he turned the Accord onto New Landing Road and made a dry run past the house at as slow a speed as he dared.

He couldn't see any movement, but there were a lot of trees in the way, and there weren't any streetlights. So after he turned around about a half mile down the road, he drove past the house again and then turned up the next gravel-strewn driveway.

Hope the neighbors don't mind some unexpected company, he told himself as he accelerated up the long, bumpy, single-lane dirt and gravel road, watching the bouncing sweep of his headlights for any sign of movement.

At the top of the hill, his headlights illuminated a pickup truck parked next to an old, weather-dulled, two-story wood house.

The house was completely dark, and aside from the presence of the pickup, apparently empty—no barking dogs, no porch lights coming on, no sign of life.

Culver shuddered momentarily when he realized that something about the dark shadowy house reminded him of Paul Radlick's desolate home; but he had too many other things on his mind right now to be concerned about gloomy shadows, so he quickly parked the car beside the pickup, cut the engine and lights, grabbed his two equipment bags, exited the car, and put on the helmet and goggles.

The original model of Culver's night vision system had been designed for helicopter pilots in Vietnam who were crazy enough to fly around in the dark without lights or radar, but frequently needed both hands to operate their aircraft—which made it awkward to deal with the heavy handheld scopes.

The early helmet systems were crude, and prone to flare-outs, but they worked. The third generation systems, however, had several interesting improvements that made it possible for Culver to pick his way through the closely spaced bare trees and dense underbrush—that all appeared as varying shades of bright green under what little star- and moonlight filtered through the clouds—and still be able to check his progress by looking out at the distant but progressively closer house lights.

He had a flashlight in his hand, but he had no intention of using it unless he had to.

He was more than halfway there, with less than a hundred yards to go, when he heard a rustling of brush to his right that was definitely *not* caused by a falling tree branch.

Jerking his head around and bringing the flashlight up in a protective stance, he searched through the bright green images of tree trunks and bare branches for the expected human form, saw nothing, felt himself step onto something soft and yielding . . .

And then almost yelled out loud as the needle-sharp teeth buried themselves into his ankle.

His mind was screaming "snake!" and he had already started to swing the flashlight down at the head of the thrashing, reptilian form when he realized that the long skinny body attached to his ankle was covered with fur.

Reaching down, he pulled the attacking animal loose from his leg and held it up in front of the tubular goggle lenses. An oddly distorted, ratlike face glared back at Culver in fearless defiance.

What the . . .?

"Spanky?" Culver whispered hoarsely, and then almost screamed again when the twisting ferret sank its teeth into his thumb. As Culver dropped his flashlight and grabbed for his hand, the ferret twisted loose, dropped to the ground, and scampered toward a nearby patch of dense brush.

Culver started to lunge after the rapidly disappearing mammal, not altogether certain of his intentions, when he suddenly felt himself step down on something soft and yielding again. Lifting up his foot as he looked down, he saw something in the slushy ground cover that looked remarkably like . . .

Jesus Christ!

. . . a badly mangled human hand.

Chapter Thirty-six

Saturday, 0030 hours

Approximately a hundred yards west from the spot where Henry Culver had made his startling discovery, a dark shadowy figure stepped out of the woods and moved forward, slowly and carefully, until he was on the porch of the rural, isolated, two-story house, with his back up against the wall next to the doorjamb.

Then, after looking around once more to make absolutely sure that he was alone, he rapped on the wooden door.

By the count of thirty, there was still no response. But then an interior light snapped on, and he thought he heard movement inside, so he rapped on the door again. This time, he did get an answer.

"Yes, who is it?" a shaky voice demanded from the other side of the door as the dim porch light came on.

"Fairfax County Police," the dark figure mumbled, holding a badge up in front of the newly mounted peephole in the door. "Security check. Just making sure everything's okay."

"Wait, don't leave yet, I want to ask you something," the voice said as the dead bolt mechanism began to rattle, and then went on hesitantly. "Oh . . . ah, hold on just a second, what's your name?"

"Hattabaugh. Sergeant Jack Hattabaugh."

There was a short pause.

"Okay, thanks," the voice replied faintly as the lock rattling continued. "They gave me a list and said to make sure . . . there!"

Finally managing to work the unfamiliar dead bolt loose, Kathy Harmon pulled open her heavy wooden door, unlatched the screen, and then stepped out onto her back porch saying: "I thought you guys were going to . . . *huummmff!*"

A strong, dirty hand clamped around her mouth, and suddenly a very shocked and terrified Kathy Harmon found herself being forced back into her house by a dark shadowy figure in a blue denim jacket covered with cobwebs.

At five-foot-six and 120 pounds, Kathy Harmon was no match for the longer arms and added weight of her assailant, but like the gutsy girlfriend of Michel L'Que, who had battled Bobby Morgan to a near-draw on a cement garage floor, she wasn't about to give up.

At least not without a fight.

What she didn't realize, however, in her frenzied effort to tear, bite, or kick herself loose, was that her assailant really didn't want to hurt her.

Moreover, *he* knew the noise factor could be critical, so he deliberately absorbed the full punishing effect of Kathy Harmon's fingernails, teeth, knees, and elbows for almost a full minute, his right hand clamped tightly against her mouth as they twisted around on the carpeted floor, before he was finally able to work his left arm into a partially effective carotid chokehold, pin her down with the weight of his upper torso, and get the side of his face up against her right ear.

"For Christ's sake, ease up! It's me, Henry Culver," he hissed in her ear, and then sighed in relief as she finally responded to either the sound of his name or the chokehold and released her full-jawed grip on the fleshy part of his right hand.

"*What the . . . ?*" she gasped as Culver started to release the chokehold, and then quickly clamped his injured hand back over her mouth.

"Don't talk," he whispered urgently against the side of her head. "Very important. Don't talk, don't scream, don't yell. Do you understand?"

Kathy Harmon shook her head violently, her green eyes bulging with rage as she tried to twist her flannel night-gown-clad body out from under the weight of Culver's muscular frame.

"Kathy, listen to me!" Culver hissed as he clamped down on the struggling woman. "The police officer who was killed in your driveway. Remember?"

Kathy Harmon's firmly conditioned body was still tensed in her effort to pull herself loose form Culver's grasp, and she was still glaring up at him, but she was also listening. She nodded her head.

"That was Tess Beasley, the canine officer who helped you with Bear."

Her eyes blinked in disbelief.

"She was also my girlfriend."

It took a few moments for Culver's whispered words to register, but then Kathy Harmon's eyes opened wide in shock as her entire body relaxed.

"No noise, right," Culver whispered once more as he slowly drew his hand away from her mouth.

She nodded her head.

Ten minutes later, wrapped in a thick bathrobe to ward off a chill that had very little to do with the outside weather, Kathy Harmon sat on her upstairs bed and watched in confused silence as Culver knelt down beside the nightstand and carefully began to disassemble her telephone with a pair of needle-nose pliers and a small screwdriver.

Shaken by the flashback images that were almost impossible to reconcile—the friendly, curly-haired Tess Beasley, who had been so gentle with her dog, and the bloody, uniformed figure on her driveway that had barely looked human, much less female—Kathy Harmon's gaze kept returning to the glistening pistol that Culver had set down on the carpet next to his right leg. For reasons that she really didn't want to think about, the deadly blue-steel weapon now seemed far more comforting than sinister.

Her eyes kept shifting back to the pad of paper and pen lying next to Henry Culver's knee, and to the words he had written there.

TRIED TO KILL ME, GOT TESS INSTEAD.

And then the second line.

SOMEHOW YOU AND LISA ARE INVOLVED.

After a few seconds of work with the screwdriver, Culver finally looked up at her, nodded his head, and then reached for the pad of paper and quickly scribbled another message.

SAME AS THE ONE DOWNSTAIRS. VOICE ACTIVATED. TRANSMITS ANYTHING SAID IN THIS ROOM THRU THE PHONE LINE.

Kathy Harmon took up the pad and wrote her own note:

WHY US?

DON'T KNOW, he responded. THAT'S WHY I'M HERE.

WHAT NOW? she scribbled.

Culver thought about that for a moment.

I CAN'T STAY HERE, AND YOU SHOULDN'T. TOO
DANGEROUS.

BUT THIS IS MY HOUSE! Kathy Harmon protested
with deep, hurried strokes of the pen.

I KNOW, BUT THEY MAY COME BACK TO CHECK
THE PHONE.

That got Kathy Harmon's attention. For about fifteen seconds, she seemed to consider the entire situation in detail before finally nodding her head.

WHERE DO WE GO?

CAN WE USE YOUR CAR? MINE'S KNOWN.

Hesitating only slightly this time, Kathy Harmon nodded
her head again.

IS LISA HERE?

She shook her head, and then reached for the pen again.

NO, AT NEIGHBOR'S HOUSE. AFRAID TO HAVE
HER HERE.

GOOD. WHAT ABOUT BEAR?

Harmon shook her head.

STILL AT VET CLINIC.

Another quick nod.

OKAY, WE'LL GET THEM TOMORROW. READY TO
GO?

Harmon stared at Culver in wordless disbelief, and then gestured with open palms as she looked down at herself, as if to say 'like this?'

BETTER GET DRESSED FIRST. TAKE CLOTHES FOR TWO OR THREE DAYS. OKAY?

A much slower, uncertain nod this time.

DOWNSTAIRS, Culver quickly scribbled. FIVE MINUTES. HURRY.

In the dimly lit confines of his office, Elliott Parkinson sat in his high-backed executive's chair and listened to his special assistant's telephoned report with a numbing sense of absolute dismay.

"How could Marcus have possibly let it get out of control like that?" he demanded when J. Winston Weathersby finally stopped talking.

"Apparently the van threw them off," the young bureaucrat explained, shivering from exposure in the open telephone booth as he watched three more District police cruisers pull up in front of the open garage door across the street. "By the time they realized it wasn't Molly, the shit had hit the fan. The doors were open, so the shots were probably heard for miles. And then the cops started showing up almost immediately, so I guess there wasn't anything else they *could* do."

"Jesus Christ Almighty!" Parkinson swore, stunned by the unthinkable possibility that a single deflected .22 caliber bullet just might have destroyed the entire operation, not to mention his career.

"I know, but what do we do now?" Weathersby pressed nervously.

"How soon can you move everything out of there?"

"I don't know. I don't think they're going to let anything or anybody leave here until they get some satisfactory answers."

"All right, I'll get some pressure put on from this end," Parkinson said. "We've *got* to get that stuff back to him as soon as possible, and properly dispose of everything else."

"But what about the damage?

"Start arranging for a replacement immediately, and have the technicians standing by."

"But . . . but the stores, they're all closed."

"Then you'd better goddamn well open one up, hadn't you?" Parkinson snapped.

"Yes sir." Weathersby gulped.

"One more thing," Parkinson growled, his voice reduced to a furious whisper. "Tell them, whatever it takes, I want Culver found, and I want him tagged, and I want it to happen *right now.* We have to locate him before Digger does. Do you understand?"

"But . . ."

"Right now," Parkinson repeated.

"Yes, but . . ." J. Winston Weathersby started to say, and then winced as Parkinson slammed the phone down.

"Why do I have to go in there?" Kathy Harmon demanded as she stared out through the front windshield at the neon-framed office.

"Because if these people are really serious about trying to find us, they'll start calling around to all the places within a fifty-mile radius," Culver explained as he rested his head back against the side window frame of the Jeep. "They've got a picture of me in their files. Height, age, hair color, the works."

Then, too late, he realized what he'd said.

"Files? Criminals keep files now?"

"Some of them do." He shrugged noncommittally.

"And these people that are trying to find you—you don't know who they are, but you *do* know that they've a picture of you . . . in their files?"

"Right," he said, too tired to care about trying to come up with a plausible story to cover his mistake.

Tired . . . talking too much. Watch it.

"And they're not after me?"

"I don't think so. Whoever wired those phones obviously knows where you live. If they wanted to, they could have picked you up anytime."

Assuming it was one of my ex-CIA-type buddies—and not Digger—who burged your house and tapped your phones, Culver corrected himself, although it still didn't make any sense because he'd already decided that it *had* to be Digger who had wired her driveway and killed Tess Beasley. Had to be, because he couldn't come up with a single reason why Traynor or Parkinson or anybody else in the Agency would even *think* about wanting to do something like that.

And besides, Digger's had Quinzio and Gauss and Russelli and me lined up all along. Why do something stupid like that?

But it wasn't quite that simple, of course, because the evidence indicated that Molly Hunsacker, a.k.a. Molly-the-Hun—who had no known association with Digger or any likely access to the highly sophisticated Mod-VIII phone bugs—had almost certainly hit Kathy Harmon's house at least once in the past twenty-four hours, and possibly twice.

Oh yeah, and don't forget Russelli. Digger and Molly are both res-burglars, so Russelli's probably involved in all this shit, too. Or at least Stewart and Carpenter think he's involved in something, and he might as well be, because everybody else sure the hell is.

God, Culver thought fervently, *it sure would be nice to know what's going on.*

"So why didn't you just go to the police instead of coming back to my place?" Kathy Harmon demanded.

"Because you—or your house—keeps popping up as a common denominator, and I want to know why. And besides," Culver added quietly, his eyes almost completely shut now, "I *am* the police."

Wire was another common denominator. Something about the wire.

Kathy Harmon blinked. "You think *I'm* involved in all of this?"

Culver shook his head. "No, I think you're being used. I just want to know by who and why. Why you, why Tess, why a lot of things."

"So why don't we just drive down to the police station and get some help? More policemen, or detectives or SWAT teams, or whatever the hell it is you people use?"

"Trust me, it's not that simple."

"*Trust* you?" Kathy Harmon exclaimed, incredulous. "In less than twenty-four hours, my house has been broken into twice, my dog nearly beaten to death, and a police officer killed by a bomb in my driveway. Then *you* show up in the middle of the night, grab me, throw me on the ground, and tell me that somebody's been putting bugs in my phones. And *then* you talk me into leaving my house in the middle of the night to go to some sleazy motel just because you *think* somebody's trying to kill you—only you don't know for sure and you don't want to go to the police station to get more help. Have I got it right so far?" she demanded.

"Close enough." Culver sighed.

"Okay, so then why the hell should I trust you when you don't . . ."

Then it occurred to her.

"That's it, isn't it? You don't trust the police either. You think some of them might be involved in all of this, don't you?"

"I'm not sure who's who anymore, if that's what you mean."

"But you're expecting *me* to trust *you* anyway, right?"

Culver nodded. "Yeah, I guess that's about it. You going to get us a room, or are we going to sleep out here in the parking lot?"

Kathy Harmon hesitated, as if trying to decide whether she should continue to go along with the cobweb-streaked police officer sitting in her Jeep, or simply go into the motel office and call for another cop.

But then she realized that she would have absolutely no way of knowing if the cop who showed up was part of it, too.

She looked over at Culver for a brief moment, and realized that he was almost asleep.

Lisa likes him, she thought to herself. *And Bear . . . oh SHIT, what the hell am I supposed to do?*

"Can't we find a . . . better place?" she finally asked.

"You walk into any halfway decent hotel lobby with me looking like this," Culver said in a voice almost overwhelmed with fatigue, "and they're going to think you roll derelicts for a living. They're also going to remember us—especially me."

He had wanted to take the time to shower and clean up at her house, to get rid of the cobwebby reminders of his journey through the crawl space under Paul Radlick's house, but the presence of the phone taps had changed his mind quickly. Without access to some of his more sophisticated electronics equipment, he couldn't tell how thoroughly the house had been wired, and he hadn't wanted to wait around there to find out.

"But . . ."

"It'll all work out okay," Culver whispered sleepily. "Just trust me."

Five minutes later, she was back in the car. "Number twenty-two," she said in a voice that was now tight with suppressed rage as she slammed the door shut.

"Nice guy?" Culver inquired as he started up the Jeep.

"I . . ." Harmon started to say, but then shook her head.

He nodded sympathetically. "They don't get many MBA types to run these places. So where do we go?"

"All the way to the end. I told him we wanted . . . some privacy," she added with a grimace as she glared back at the neon-lit office.

"Yeah, that'd do it." He drove the Jeep down to the far end of the seedy motel complex, and then pulled into the parking space in front of number nineteen.

"I said twenty-two."

"I know," Culver said as he stared out through the snow-streaked windshield over at the darkened door of room twenty-two, "but I want to give us some distance, just in case they put your Jeep on their surveillance list."

"Oh," she whispered, still staring at the dismal-looking building.

"Maybe it'll look better inside," he suggested as they opened the doors and stepped out into the cold darkness.

It didn't, but Culver noted with some measure of relief that the original door lock had been replaced with a more practical model that looked like it might stand up to at least a couple of solid kicks. And much to his surprise, the adjoining bathroom had a tub as well as a shower.

Apart from that, the room was pretty much what he expected, with one exception—which wasn't what he expected at all. The question was how to broach the subject without sending his new partner running off screaming into the night.

"I take it they ran out of rooms with twin beds?" Culver asked casually as he placed his equipment bags against the door and then carefully set the dead bolt.

Kathy Harmon stood on the opposite side of the small room with her travel bag in her hand, looking as though she couldn't even *begin* to understand how she'd ended up in a place like this.

"I don't think that . . . *man* has ever heard of a motel room with twin beds," she finally answered. "Do you want to know what else he said?"

"Something about the hourly rate and extra towels?"

"That's right."

Culver shook his head. "I don't think so. The extra towels would have been nice, but I think we can make do."

"This is . . . crazy," Kathy Harmon said.

"Yeah, I know, but I've got to get some sleep. Mind if I use the shower first?"

"Be my guest," she muttered as she cautiously lifted up one edge of the turned-back sheet and thin blanket covering the double bed that took up most of the small room.

Twenty minutes later, after Kathy Harmon finished brushing her teeth and shuddered once more at the sight of Henry Culver's dirty, cobweb-covered clothes lying on the floor between the incredibly filthy toilet and the cracked tub, she turned off the bathroom light, walked slowly out into the small studio bedroom, determined to set things straight about the sleeping arrangements, and discovered to her surprise that Culver was already in bed, nude at least from the waist up, and snoring.

Wary, confused, and tired all at the same time, she finally turned off the lamp on Culver's side of the bed—making an effort to keep her hand as far away as possible from the .357 Magnum that he had placed on the nightstand—walked around the bed, got in and slid her legs under the thin covers, and then lay there on the far edge of the bed, tense and alert, for several seconds until she couldn't stand it any longer.

"Hey, Culver," she whispered loudly into the darkness.

"Uhmm, what?" he mumbled.

"Tomorrow, you're going to come up with an explanation for all of this, right?"

"Yeah, sure," Culver said, his voice drifting away, "explain everything—tomorrow."

Sometime in the middle of what remained of the night, Culver woke up shivering, only to find a soft, feminine body cuddled up tight against his back.

At first, he thought that Tess Beasley had decided to stay the night, which didn't seem right somehow, because she was supposed to be seeing that attorney . . . and besides she was dead. But Culver was still too tired to make sense of it all, so he simply turned over and wrapped his arms around the firm, warm, and enticing flannel-covered body that unconsciously turned over and repositioned itself snugly against his front torso as he nuzzled his head against the warm and fragrant hair and drifted off back to sleep.

Only to be woken up with a heart-stopping rush of adrenaline when a high-pitched scream echoed through the small, cold, and darkened room.

"What the hell?!" Culver yelled, grabbing for the .357 blindly and twisting away from the noise—only to tumble to the hard floor as he rolled off the bed.

He came back up immediately with the pistol in a two-handed grip, bracing his arms against the protective mattress; and then saw Kathy Harmon backed up against the door, holding a thick manila envelope and several smaller ones in one hand and pointing down with the other at one of Culver's equipment bags.

"There . . . there's a hand in that bag!" she whispered, her voice almost breaking.

"Hey, keep it down in there!" a muffled voice yelled as someone pounded on the thin wall.

"No, no, keep it up!" another more distant voice laughed.

At that moment, the telephone rang. Culver reached for it, and then winced as he realized that his right hand was severely bruised, cut, and swollen.

"Yeah, it's okay," he said into the phone, still groggy from the shock of being woken up like that. "She just got a little carried away. Yeah, I know, we'll keep it quiet. Yeah, right, thanks."

"That was the management," Culver said as he hung up the phone, put the .357 back on the nightstand, and then turned to face a still wide-eyed and openmouthed Kathy Harmon. "They'd appreciate it if you would be a little less enthusiastic."

"You—there's a hand in that bag," Kathy Harmon repeated numbly before blinking her eyes and shaking her head in sudden realization of what was going on in and around their room. "What did you say?"

"Less enthusiasm," Culver repeated. "You're waking up the guests." As if in confirmation, a muffled voice on the other side of the wall giggled loudly.

"But . . ."

"I *know* there's a hand in my bag. It's probably in better

shape than mine," he added as he massaged his swollen fingers. "You and that damned ferret have a lot more in common than you might think."

"Ferret? What fer—you mean Spanky?" Kathy Harmon blurted out, her mind still whirling from the combined shock of waking up in a small, smelly motel room to find herself sleeping with a police officer who had a severed human hand in his equipment bag. "Where is he? Is he all right? I've been trying . . ."

"If that was Spanky who bit me, you don't need to worry about him," Culver said soothingly as he sat back down on the bed, apparently unconcerned that he was only wearing a pair of thin white boxer shorts. "From what I saw, outside of a little swelling on one side of his head, he was doing just fine."

Culver then had to explain how he had parked in her neighbor's driveway, and made his way through the woods to avoid being spotted by any surveillance that might have been placed on her house, and then ran into what was undoubtedly her missing pet.

"So," Culver finished, "I figure he probably found the hand somewhere in the woods nearby—which means, among your other assorted problems in life, you may have a dead body lying around on your property somewhere."

"What?"

"It's not likely, but if you'll toss me . . . never mind, I'll get them myself," Culver corrected as he stood up, walked over to his equipment bag, and pulled out the extra pair of jeans, shirt, socks, and running shoes he'd taken from the trunk of his Mustang. Then he went back to the bed and put on the clean clothes, seemingly oblivious of the presence of Kathy Harmon and all of the creaking and giggling that was taking place in the room next door.

Finally, after tying his shoelaces, he looked up at Harmon, who was still standing there with the manila envelope in her hand, looking thoroughly confused, shaken, distraught, and decidedly sexy in the thin flannel nightgown.

"Kathy," he said calmly, "unless you're planning on hopping back into bed and getting into the spirit of things around here, maybe you'd better get dressed. We've got a lot of work to do."

Forty-five minutes later, Henry Culver hurried out of the Fairfax County Coroner's Office and quickly got back in the driver's side of Kathy Harmon's Jeep, rubbing his hands together and shivering. He was still wearing Russelli's blue denim jacket, but with Kathy Harmon's help, he had managed to get most of the cobwebs off.

"You ready for some breakfast?"

"What did you find out about the hand?" Kathy Harmon asked apprehensively, not wanting to even think about breakfast.

"They're going to check it out," Culver said as he started up the Jeep and then pulled out onto the main road.

"That's all, just check it out?"

"They're not exactly desperate for more work. They've got two more autopsies to finish up this morning, then they'll take a look at it. Outside of being chewed up, the hand was in pretty good shape. If the victim's got prints on file, they should be able to make an ID on him."

"It was a man? You're sure?"

Culver shrugged. "Based on the short fingernails and the hairy knuckles, male gender is probably a good guess. Not sure about the age, though. It's been cold the last few days. It could have been out there a while."

"Oh thanks." Kathy Harmon shuddered.

They drove for several minutes, the silence broken only by Henry Culver's soft whistling, before Kathy Harmon finally decided that she couldn't stand it any longer.

"I don't understand you," she blurted out.

"That's okay, I don't understand me either," Culver said matter-of-factly as he made a routine check of the coming intersection, watching for any sign of the trackers.

"The police officer who was killed yesterday—you said she was your girlfriend, right?"

"Ex-girlfriend. Same thing," Culver said as he continued to drive with reflexive movements, watching the street.

"And she was in that morgue room, the one you were just in, wasn't she?"

Culver nodded.

"Somebody you cared about was killed yesterday—blown up by a bomb in my driveway—and today, all you've been doing is making jokes and smiling and whistling like nothing's wrong at all. And you just took a human hand that you found in the woods into a morgue room where she—" Kathy Harmon shook her head, unable to finish her sentence. "And now, you want to eat breakfast?"

"I'm hungry and I'd like to eat breakfast. Something wrong with that?"

Kathy Harmon took in a deep breath and released it before going on. "I guess my question is, are you really that warped and crazy, or is it just that you've been a cop so long that you don't feel anything anymore?"

"I feel a lot better this morning than I did last night," Culver answered as he made a quick lane change and then an immediate, smooth right turn, "and you're right, I probably *have* been a cop too long. But as for the warped and crazy business, that's just part of the game. Makes everything you run into a lot easier to stomach."

"But doesn't it hurt? Don't you feel anything?" Kathy Harmon pressed, looking like she was about ready to either scream or burst into tears herself.

"To lose Tess? Yeah, it hurts a lot. More than I want to think about," Culver said, watching his rearview mirrors as he made another series of random turns. "Tess was a wonderful, warm, and fun-loving person; but she died doing exactly what she wanted to do—and what she was good at. So maybe that part's okay."

"It's okay that she was murdered?"

"No, that's the other part." Culver smiled grimly. "See, the thing is, the guy who rigged that bomb—or at least the guy I *think* rigged it—wasn't trying to kill Tess Beasley."

"I don't understand."

Culver nodded. "I hope not. When you called in to report the second burglary, you didn't ask for me by name, did you?"

"I asked them to send . . ."

"Eight-Forty-Charlie," Culver finished. "Right?"

"That bomb was meant for you?" Kathy Harmon's eyes widened in horror.

"I told you that Eight-Forty-Charlie was my call sign, but I never did explain how they're used. If somebody calls in sick, or goes on vacation, or gets transferred out—as I did Thursday night—then somebody else gets assigned to their patrol area and takes over their call sign."

"Oh my God," she whispered in disbelief.

"So what I think happened," Culver went on, "is that he timed the second burglary so that Eight-Forty-Charlie—supposedly me—would have to respond, because your house was in my patrol area."

"I killed her."

Culver shook his head. "No you didn't. Car Eight-Forty-Charlie was going to have to respond to that call, no matter what. That had nothing to do with your asking for me by my call sign. Even if you'd asked for me by name, they'd still have sent Tess. It wasn't an emergency, so there wouldn't have been any point in pulling somebody in from another area. They would have just waited until she cleared.

"But . . ."

"See, what he didn't know—what he *couldn't* have known," Culver interrupted, "was that I got involved in something the night before that got me transferred out of patrol. So Tess shows up for duty yesterday afternoon and gets assigned my area and call sign by Hattabaugh. Could have been any of the other guys, but she and Sasha were a rover unit—worked the whole district—so it was probably easier just to make the one change."

Kathy Harmon shook her head slowly, her face visibly paled.

"So," Culver went on calmly, "Eight-Forty-Charlie responded to your call, just the way he planned it, only it wasn't me. I think he knew that at the very end, but he killed her anyway."

"Why?"

"I don't know. Maybe she spotted him and was getting ready to release the dog, or maybe he just didn't care. Knowing him, probably the latter. But it doesn't matter, because the important thing is, he made a mistake."

"You keep saying 'he' like you know . . ."

"Huh? Oh, yeah, that's right, you don't know about him, do you?" Henry Culver whispered. "John Doe Thirty-three, a.k.a. Digger. Residential burglar turned psychopath. He's probably got some help out there, maybe one or two guys, but he's the one who screwed up."

"What are you talking about?"

"He should have let Tess go and waited for Russelli or me to show up for the follow-up investigation. That would have been the smart way to play it. He'd have gotten at least one of us easy—better me, because I'm starting to understand him now. Probably even starting to think like him."

"But see, the thing is," Culver went on as he turned into the parking lot of the restaurant, ignoring the stunned look on Kathy Harmon's face, "he didn't wait for us to show because he's a game player, and he's smart, and he really thinks he's going to get away with it."

"How do you know that?"

"That's what they all think. Especially the crazy ones. Surprises the hell out of them when we put all the pieces together and then knock on their door. Paul Radlick, my ex–school buddy used to tell me that. He used to be a Fairfax County cop too, before his wife—Doreen—talked him into going to law school, which is how he ended up being a defense attorney for all these freaks. Of course, that was before Digger killed them too."

"He's killed . . . others?"

"Five that we made him on before all this started. A family with three kids. Eight if you count Paul, Doreen, and Tess. *Three* people I cared a lot about, not just one."

There was a long pause that lasted for almost thirty seconds as Culver parked the Jeep, set the brake, and then turned off the ignition. Then Kathy Harmon spoke again.

"When you find him, you aren't going to arrest him, are you?"

"I don't know," Culver said, shaking his head slowly. "The way I see it now, I think that's going to be up to him."

Chapter Thirty-seven

Saturday, 0715 hours

Elliott Parkinson was staring out his window when the telephone on his desk jarred him out of his meditative trance.

"Yes?"

"You'd better get down here, right away," J. Winston Weathersby whispered, the urgency in his voice broken by a sudden fit of sporadic coughing.

"What's the matter?"

"They called L'Que."

"They? Who's they? What the hell are you talking about?" Parkinson demanded.

"The DC Police."

"*What?*"

"I tried to tell them . . ." Weathersby started in, but then his explanation got lost in an uncontrollable sneeze—which really didn't matter because Parkinson wasn't listening anyway.

"*Why* did the police contact L'Que," he asked in a raspy whisper, but his shell-shocked mind had already begun to churn through the data, and he knew the answer even before his special assistant stopped sniffling.

"One of their detectives started pulling serial numbers on the stuff they found in the warehouse, and . . ."

"Didn't Marcus explain to them that this was a multiple-agency sting operation?" Parkinson interrupted.

"I guess he tried, but then the medics had to sedate him on account of the bullet in his knee, and that's when the whole thing started coming apart. See, Marcus and I are the only ones with police credentials—and they're okay, but we had to do them quick, so they won't stand up to a real close look, especially if these guys start making calls to New York—and our DC contact is on vacation until Monday, and the guy you said was supposed to be here from Fairfax to back us up still hasn't gotten here yet."

Parkinson blinked. "He was supposed to be there hours ago. What the hell happened?"

"I don't know. When I called to check on him, he started giving me a bunch of shit about his leg hurting, and how he was goddamned sick and tired of getting phone calls in the middle of the night, and I . . ."

"He'll be there immediately. *I'll* see to it," Parkinson snarled. "Now what about L'Que?"

"From what I heard, I guess he's on his way out here now, to ID and pick up his stuff."

"Why would they want him to do that?" Parkinson whispered, unable to comprehend how and why it was all coming apart so badly.

"Jesus, Elliott, *I don't know,*" J. Winston Weathersby almost yelled out of pure frustration, "maybe because we've got a goddamned dead body out here, and a whole shitload of shots fired, and when the cops show up, they find all this stuff in the warehouse that traces back to a burg two days ago where the owner has diplomatic status, and his kid is still in a coma from being beaten half to death. I mean what the hell do you *think* they're gonna do, just let everybody go home and report back in the afternoon? Christ, the only reason they're still letting *me* use a phone is because they think I'm the liaison guy from New York who's supposed to be coordinating this whole mess."

"But today's the day. We can't . . ."

"Elliott, listen to me," J. Winston Weathersby pleaded, "they've got the warehouse roped off like it's a presidential assassination site, and the guy in charge says he's not letting *anything* go out of here until he starts getting some answers that make sense."

"We can't wait. There's no more time," Parkinson whispered, his mind churning feverishly now as he tried to think of some logical approach to the problem that didn't involve the ultimate cutout option of severing all of the links—which they couldn't do anyway, because they still hadn't located Culver or Digger. "We *have* to get that stuff moved immediately."

"Elliott, I know it's Saturday morning, and I know about the time factor. But unless you get somebody out here *right now* to talk with these people, we're not going to make it."

"All right," Elliott Parkinson agreed, having finally thought of an alternative that *might* work. "Stay there, watch for L'Que, and try to say as little as possible. I'm on my way."

"So what's it like, being a burglary detective?" Kathy Harmon asked in a quiet voice, trying to come up with something to talk about that didn't involve dismembered bodies or psychopathic killers.

They had just finished eating breakfast and were sipping the last of their coffee, neither of them the least bit anxious to leave the warmth, comfort, and security of the restaurant.

"To tell you the truth, I really don't know. I haven't been one long enough to find out."

"You don't sound all that enthusiastic."

Culver shrugged. "It's not exactly what I had in mind as a career goal, but it's probably better than a lot of other things I could be doing right now."

Like being hunted down by a blue-eyed freak with a mossy

rock, he wanted to add, but couldn't—and then he blinked in confusion because that wasn't right.

Or was it?

Digger and Parkinson are two separate deals, he told himself. They had to be, because he hadn't found a single bit of evidence to the contrary.

Kathy Harmon started to say something else when she looked down at her purse and realized that she still had all of the envelopes that she'd taken out of Culver's equipment bag back at the motel room.

"Oh . . . uh, I guess these belong to you," she said softly, dropping the smaller envelopes and holding up the larger manila packet for Culver to see. "I forgot to give them back to you this morning."

"No big deal." Culver shrugged indifferently, picking up a handful of the smaller envelopes as he gave in to temptation and signaled the waitress for another round of coffee.

He opened one of the envelopes, froze for a moment in shock, and then quickly tore it open. The note he pulled out read:

HENRY,
SOMEBODY MADE OFF WITH DIGGER'S COMPUTER. I NEED TO FIND OUT WHO. GIVE ME A CALL.
PAUL

"Is something wrong?" Kathy Harmon asked, watching the expression on Henry Culver's face shift from mild curiosity to bewilderment.

Culver silently handed her the letter, and then quickly examined the envelope. He was looking for a return address—not that it really mattered, because Paul Radlick's distinctive form of block printing was easily recognizable—or some other form of identification, but all he found was the cancellation stamp.

February 4. Thursday. Two days ago. Probably the last thing he wrote before . . .

Then he shook his head, trying to blank out what seemed to be an almost-overwhelming sense of depression.

"What's *that* all about?"

"I don't know. Just a friend trying to tell me something, I guess," he shrugged. "Go ahead and open that one," he suggested, hoping that the thick manila envelope would offer at least a mild distraction from the horrible images that kept flickering around in the back of his head.

"This isn't more of your . . . evidence, is it?" she asked, shuddering at the memory of the severed hand.

"I doubt it," Culver said, absentmindedly nodding his thanks to the waitress as she filled their cups. "Probably just a bunch of reports I'm supposed to read."

"Nope, photographs," Kathy Harmon said as she pulled a quarter inch stack of eight-by-ten color prints out of the envelope.

Culver blinked curiously. "Oh yeah? Of what?"

"I don't know, some kind of house . . . oh my God," she whispered, visibly recoiling as she turned her head away from the gory images on the second photograph in the stack.

Culver quickly took the photos out of her hands, and then nodded his head in immediate recognition.

"This is the shooting scene I told you about. The one that happened last Thursday evening—the two guys who got nailed in their own house."

"Did you ever find out why?" she asked, taking a hurried sip of her hot coffee in an effort to erase the vivid memory of the torn face.

"Not as far as I know. Probably a drug deal that went sour."

"I don't see how you can even look at pictures like that, much less take them," Kathy Harmon whispered.

"It's not that difficult once you learn to blank things out. Just frame, focus, and shoot. Worst part is usually the smell, and you get used to that pretty quick," he added as he began to thumb through the photographs, noting the professional wide-angle framing and exposure.

Definitely Q-quality, he nodded to himself, wondering how the police photographer was doing.

"But as it turns out," he went on, "I didn't shoot these. They're probably the ones that Mike Quinzio—one of our CSI officers—took just before he got hurt."

By a bomb.

Culver blinked.

That's right, he remembered as he continued to stare at the photographs. *This was the scene where Gauss and Quinzio and Carpenter ran into the booby trap. Coincidence? Two unrelated bombings and all that shit at Radlick's place in one day?*

The fifth photograph showed the two bodies in relation to each other. Culver stared at that photograph for several long moments, thinking: *So what if it isn't just a coincidence. What if they're related. Would that mean these two guys are tied in to Digger?*

Culver shook his head, trying to think, and trying to remember—something that he had meant to ask Carpenter about. Something important.

Everybody had been acting like the victims were a couple of drug dealers, he remembered; but Stewart and Carpenter hadn't asked for a Narcotics team to respond on a follow-up. They'd asked for Russelli.

And if those two were tied in with Digger . . . Jesus, I didn't even think about that. A couple of goddamned burglars. But who the hell would want to go around killing burglars?

"What's the matter?" Kathy Harmon asked, but Culver ignored her as he continued to look through the photographs.

A pissed-off cop?

Russelli?

The overall shot of the partially burned garage was the eighth one in the pile, and it caused Henry Culver—who was

trying very hard *not* to think about Detective Sergeant John
Russelli executing residential burglars—to blink in surprise.
The photographic image, for some reason, seemed haunt-
ingly familiar.

He'd seen hundreds of vans during his law enforcement
career, but something about this specific van was tugging at
his rattled memory. Then he remembered that somebody at
the shooting scene had described the victims as being a couple of good ole boy rednecks.

*But when did "good ole boys" from Virginia start running
around with copy machines in the back of their vans?* Culver asked himself.

The photograph showed the van's sliding panel door
pulled back to the full open position, and he could see the
copy machine in the back of the cargo area, clear as day, sitting there right next to the wall-mounted spare tire and the
packet of . . .

Road flares.

Jermantown Road.

"Henry?"

The two guys who ran off the road?

Ignoring Kathy Harmon's query, Culver quickly flipped
back to the pictures that showed the frontal views of the two
bodies, but he'd only seen the face of one of the men at the
Jermantown Road accident—*the other guy was where, under
the van?*—which wasn't going to help any, Culver realized,
because the faces of the victims had been torn apart by shotgun blasts.

*Okay, so what was he wearing when I saw him that night?
Overalls? Yeah, right, and both guys in the photos are wearing jeans, but they could have changed when they got home—
and probably would have because his overalls were soaking
wet.*

Then he saw the small Confederate flag earring in the
lower edge of one of the gruesome close-up photographs.

"I'll be a son of a bitch," Culver whispered as he looked

up and found himself staring into the bewildered eyes of Kathy Harmon.

"I don't understand," Harmon said as she stood on the edge of Jermantown Road in ankle-deep slush, and watched Henry Culver stumble back to the Jeep with a jack and six long red road flares in his hand.

"I don't either," Culver said as he carefully placed the items into the back of the Jeep. "They had flares in the van, but they must not have wanted to open the door while I was there—which meant they had something in the back that they didn't want me to see, and it wouldn't have been that copy machine, unless it was stolen."

The guy even started to raise his hands, as if he expected to be arrested, Culver remembered as he sat in the driver's seat of the Jeep and stared out into the chilled and icy morning, grateful that he'd thrown an old summer patrol jacket into one of his equipment bags. The nylon was thin, but it was still better than wearing Russelli's cobweb-streaked denim jacket.

Culver knew that he could go back and check the log, see what kind of crimes had been committed in this area of Jermantown Road at about that time of night—to see if there were any commercial or residential burgs—but he didn't have to do that, because he already knew about one.

The guys who hit the L'Que house? Had to be. In a hurry, in the immediate area, at the right time of night.

Jesus.

"Can we stop at a phone booth? I need to call Lisa, to make sure she's okay," Kathy Harmon said.

Actually, Henry Culver thought, nodding his head absentmindedly as he put the Jeep into motion toward a nearby gas station, *the more relevant question is: what does a lieutenant colonel—what was he, a military attaché from the French Embassy?—have to do with a couple of redneck burglars who managed to get themselves shot to death a few hours after they'd burglarized his house and probably fatally injured his son?*

The obvious one? Revenge?

Culver parked in front of the phone booth and then sat there in silence, considering another, equally relevant question.

What about the bomb that nailed Quinzio, Gauss, and Carpenter?

Was it theirs—accidentally detonated during the search, or deliberately set to protect something? Or had somebody—Digger?—put it there in an attempt to nail Quinzio and Gauss because their names were on a very short list of targets? Or was that just some kind of weird coincidence that didn't have anything at all to do with the bomb that killed Tess and the list of names on Kathy Harmon's wall, because how the hell would somebody like Digger know who was going to be at the scene, or when to set it off?

Oh yeah, and one more question while we're at it. Do I still believe in coincidence?

He allowed that very relevant question to circle around in the back recesses of his consciousness until Kathy Harmon returned to the Jeep.

"They're not home, but she left a message on my answering machine," she said. "She'll be at basketball practice at the school, and then she's going over to one of our neighbors. Wants me to pick her up there. Is that all right?"

"Yeah, sure," Culver nodded absentmindedly. He was still trying to work all the steps through in his head.

"You still want to know what it's like, being a burglary detective?" he finally asked.

Kathy Harmon blinked her eyes in confusion. "Uh, sure, I guess so."

"Fine," he nodded. "Let's go."

When they arrived at Lt. Col. Charles L'Que's home at ten-thirty that morning, Culver was surprised to discover the colonel in his garage, unloading what appeared to be an expensive stereo system.

"Colonel," Culver said as he got out of the Jeep and walked over to introduce himself, holding his badge case open for identification, "I'm Detective Culver from the Fairfax County Police Department, and this is my—uh, associate, Kathy Harmon."

"Yes, you look—familiar," Colonel L'Que said as he put one of the stereo components back into the back of his Bronco and turned to stare at his casually dressed pair of visitors with an alert but puzzled expression on his face.

"I was one of the uniformed officers who responded to your house last Thursday," Culver said. "I wanted to stop by and inquire about your son, to see how he is doing."

"Yes, of course," L'Que nodded with a sudden half smile of recognition, glancing down at Culver's old patrol jacket as he first shook Kathy Harmon's hand, and then Culver's. "The police officer who sometimes does not wear his badge on his jacket. My apologies. And your name is, again, please?"

"Culver. Henry Culver."

L'Que blinked, but his face remained expressionless.

"Ah yes, that is correct." He finally nodded, as if slowly reconstructing his memories of the previous evening. And then: "I am very glad you are here, Officer. I would like to thank you for your help, and to apologize for my behavior that night. It seems that the quick response of you and your paramedics may have saved my son's life after all."

"Your son's going to be all right?" Culver asked in surprise, remembering the severity of the boy's head wound, and the gloomy pronouncement of his war veteran father.

"He is stable, and perhaps—according to the doctors, who seem very optimistic—starting to recover," L'Que nodded, continuing to stare at Culver as though he were a particularly fascinating example of a United States police officer.

"That's wonderful." Kathy Harmon smiled.

"Yes, it is," L'Que agreed. "He regained consciousness last

night and was able to say a few words. The surgeons are calling it a miracle, but I think they are being modest. It is an interesting trait that you Americans possess. I do not wish to
sound patronizing, but I am continually amazed by the effi-
ciency of your doctors and scientists and police—even in
such a trivial matter as all of this," he added, gesturing at the
pile of stereo equipment in the back of his Bronco.

"I'm sorry?" Culver said, not following the conversation
in spite of the Colonel's very passable English.

"We have many burglaries in France also, but I do not believe our *gendarmes* would have been able to retrieve stolen
property in two days, even for one of your Ambassadors—
much less a military attache'."

"Uh . . ." Culver started to say as Kathy Harmon's eyes
blinked wide open, but L'Que interrupted.

"*Detective* Culver, I am extremely grateful to you, and I
do not wish to be impolite, but I am most anxious to return
to the hospital as soon as I possibly can. So perhaps, if you
could help me unload—?"

"Of course," Culver replied, stepping forward and gently
lifting one of the large speakers out of the Bronco, his mind
whirling with the sudden flood of contradictory information.

"You got your stolen property back in *two days?*" Kathy
Harmon asked L'Que in a tight voice.

"Yes. Actually, a day and a half," the colonel said as he
picked the stereo amplifier back up and started walking toward the garage doorway to the kitchen.

"But I thought you told me—?" Harmon started to say to
Culver, but he stopped her with a quick shake of his head.

"Colonel," Culver asked as he followed L'Que into his living room, "did you happen to get the names of the officers
who recovered your property?"

"I have their names in my briefcase. Would they be useful to you?"

"Very much so."

"One moment, I will get them."

L'Que returned to his living room about a minute later to

find Culver staring down at the four deeply indented holes that were still visible in the thick carpet. He handed Culver a small, handheld transmitter, and a piece of paper with two names, badge numbers, and an address.

"I found that in our garage," he said, nodding at the transmitter. It does not belong to us, but I discovered that it opens all three of our garage doors. I assume that is how they got into our house."

Culver examined the familiar transmitter model, noting that it was identical to the one he'd programmed for Tess Beasley, and that the switch was set to AUTO SCAN FAST.

"Mostly likely," he agreed, slipping the device into the deep right-hand pocket of his black nylon patrol jacket.

"It seems that they tried to sell our television and stereo in Washington, DC, to what I believe you call a 'sting' operation," L'Que explained as Culver copied the information from the slip of paper into his notebook.

Culver looked down at the names and badge numbers for a few more seconds, and then back up at L'Que. "And these officers—the ones who called you up and said you could pick up your property at this address—they were from the New York City Police Department?" he asked, holding up his notebook.

"Yes, that is correct," L'Que said. "I wanted to wait until this evening, but they said that they needed to get some details cleared up immediately. Apparently there was a shooting incident last night at their warehouse."

Culver's head came up. "A shooting?"

L'Que nodded. "When I arrived, there was a covered body and evidence of considerable shooting, most of it certainly by automatic weapons. I have no idea if the man who was killed had anything to do with the injuries to my son, but perhaps this will give the police some more information."

"Very likely," Culver said. "Uh, Colonel, would it be all right if I used your telephone?"

"Certainly." The military officer gestured toward the

phone on the sofa end table. "Call whomever you wish. But now, if you will excuse me, I must get back to work." L'Que walked away in the direction of his garage, clearly impatient to finish unloading his recovered property so that he could return to the hospital and his son.

Walking quickly over to the sofa, Culver sat down and reached for the phone. He dialed a number from memory and then sat there staring at the four indented holes in L'Que's carpet as he waited for someone to answer.

"Property."

"Gus?"

"Yeah, who . . . hey, is that you, Henry?"

"Right. Hey, listen, You still think you owe me a favor?"

"Goddamned right I do," the retired NYPD street cop turned property officer growled in his characteristically thick New York accent. "You want twenty 'keys,' come on over and pick 'em up. Even help you carry them out to the car."

Culver grinned. "Craven'll love to hear that."

"That little pissant can take that pretty gold badge of his and . . ." the grizzled property officer started to describe some extremely painful manipulations, and then suddenly switched gears. "Hey, so what's the deal?"

"I've got a couple of names from NYPD, and an item of evidence I need some information on."

"Give 'em to me."

Culver read from his notebook.

"Hey, pal," the property officer almost whispered as he finished copying down the names and badge numbers, "I heard about Tess, and I'm really sorry about that. I really liked that crazy broad."

"Yeah, me too." Culver nodded, momentarily shaken as he had to work to force the images back into his subconscious. The emotions were still too raw and he didn't want to try to deal with them . . . not now.

"Listen," the property officer muttered, "you ever find the crazy fuck who did it, you make sure you call me before you take him down, understand? Show you guys how to kick a door New York style."

"You help me track down this information, and you've got a deal," Culver said agreeably.

"Gimme the case number."

"Two-five-five, nine-seven-eight," Culver said, reading from his notebook. "The van from the shooting Thursday."

"Yeah, sure, we picked it up yesterday."

"There was a copy machine in the back. Did you guys log it in?"

"Put it on the shelf a couple hours ago," the property officer acknowledged.

"Here's what I need you to do," Culver said, and then spent another thirty seconds giving the property officer specific details, and L'Que's phone number. Then he checked his notebook one more time while he waited. *Twelve by eighteen. Come on Gus, give me the link. They brought it in here, right in the house. I know they did. I just don't know why.*

Ten minutes later, the phone rang. L'Que answered it and then handed the receiver over to Culver.

"Henry?"

"Yeah."

"You interested in trying to get in touch with those NYPD dicks?"

"Yeah, sure. Is that going to be a problem?"

"Depends on how much you like to dig. According to the central records computer, they're working down here in DC on some kind of special assignment. But I got a buddy in personnel who happens to think that might be just a little bit difficult, seeing as how both of them got shot and killed on a dope bust in Harlem about five years ago. Sounds to me like somebody else has got the problem."

Culver nodded. "Kinda looks that way, doesn't it. What about that copier?"

"The legs are exactly twelve inches by eighteen inches apart, on center, and about three quarters of an inch deep. That what you wanted to hear?"

"Yeah, Gus," Culver whispered, "that's *exactly* what I wanted to hear."

The man slouching down in the blue Chevy pickup parked in a long, concealed driveway approximately a hundred yards south of L'Que's house waited until Kathy Harmon's Jeep had driven past on Miller Heights before he brought his head up and keyed his radio.

"Mike-Romeo-Five, advise Topcastle we have Hotel Charlie in sight. Repeat, we have Hotel Charlie."

"Mike-Romeo-Five, we copy your advisory on Hotel Charlie," a distant voice responded. "Don't lose him this time."

Smiling pleasantly to himself, the man clicked the transmit key twice, tightened his safety belt, adjusted the scoped 7.65mm Model 70 Remington bolt-action rifle on the floor under his legs, and then accelerated the blue Chevy pickup down the driveway.

The address that L'Que had given them turned out to be an isolated warehouse in a run-down section of northeast Washington, DC.

Culver made a wide circle around the entire block, noting the presence of several late model sedans in a parking lot across the street. He came back around and parked Kathy Harmon's Jeep about a block away from the warehouse, in a position where he was partially concealed, but still had a clear view of the front loading door. Then he pulled a pair of small binoculars out of his equipment bag, put them on his lap, and waited.

"What do you expect to see?" Kathy Harmon finally asked after several minutes had gone by.

"Probably nothing," Culver admitted, "but if we're real lucky, we just might see some extremely dumb burglars delivering some stolen property to a bunch of cops running a storefront operation, posing as fences—dealers in stolen property," he added in explanation.

"They're going to do that in broad daylight?"

Culver shrugged. "Sure, why not? That's when they steal most of it."

"So the things they stole from me could be in that warehouse right now?"

"That's a possibility, but don't get too hopeful. There are a lot of fences in the DC Metro area. And besides, this thing ought to be shut down by now."

"I guess I still don't understand," Kathy Harmon said. "These burglars are going to deliver all the things they've stolen to some police officers who are pretending to be crooks in that warehouse, and then they're going to be arrested?"

Culver shook his head. "I doubt it. Unless we're really lucky, the shooting L'Que talked about probably screwed everything up so that they had to shut the operation down. But to answer your question, usually the cops just pay the going rate for the merchandise, and send them back out on the street."

"You mean these burglars are actually working for the police?" Kathy Harmon rasped, her mouth dropping open and her eyes flashing in outrage.

Culver shrugged. "I suppose that's true, at least in a technical sense. But in reality, the police are just functioning as temporary middlemen until they can gather enough intelligence to put a bunch of them out of business all at the same time."

"But that's . . . that's crazy," she exclaimed. "You just let them go right back out and burglarize other people's homes. Not only are you not stopping them, you're *encouraging* them!"

"Yeah, but this way, at least we find out who's doing the jobs, we get most of the property back, and—hopefully—we document enough break-ins to convince a judge to put the idiots away for a few months."

"But . . ."

"Hold it!"

At that moment, a brand new panel truck with big red letters on the door panels that read: DE GUELLE'S GLASS—WE DELIVER on the side pulled up to the front of the warehouse, waited to be recognized, and then drove in under the slowly rising roll-up door.

"That's a new twist," Culver said continuing to watch. About twenty minutes later, the same panel truck drove out of the warehouse, immediately followed by a weather-beaten, late model van that Culver immediately recognized as belonging to Molly Hunsacker.

"Well I'll be damned."

"Who was that?"

"A Fairfax County burglar by the name of Molly Hunsacker," Culver said as he made a notation in his notebook. "We call her Molly-the-Hun, for reasons that would be fairly obvious if you ever actually met her." Culver smiled. "Good old Molly. You can always count on somebody not getting the word."

"So now what?" Kathy Harmon said after a few moments.

"What do you mean?"

"Aren't we going in?"

"No, of course not."

Kathy Harmon blinked her eyes in disbelief. "Why not?"

"Because it's still in operation."

"What, the sting business?"

"Apparently."

"So?"

"So the guys working in there wouldn't be real thrilled about having a police officer from Fairfax County walk in there and identify himself," Culver explained. "No way of telling who's going to be in there."

"But they let that man—that Colonel what's-his-name—pick up his property," Kathy Harmon protested.

"Yeah, I know. That's the part I don't . . . wait."

The small metal door adjacent to the much larger roll-up

door suddenly opened and three men who looked much more like bodyguards than three-piece-suit businessmen stepped out onto the sidewalk and took up protective positions around the door.

"Okay," Culver said as he quickly brought the small binoculars up to his eyes and adjusted the focus, waiting for the other two men who were just barely visible in the shadow of the doorway to step out into the light, "here we go."

"Who are they?"

"Doesn't matter who *they* are. What matters is . . . oh shit," he whispered, as one by one, three men stepped into the protective phalanx formed by the three neatly dressed guardians.

One was a man that Henry Culver immediately recognized as the young man who had used the code name "Forecastle." The second was a neatly dressed older man who, in Culver's opinion, looked very like a grown-up version of the young bureaucrat. *Elliott Parkinson, I presume?* Culver thought to himself, remembering Traynor's comment as the face of the third individual suddenly appeared in the field of the binoculars. A very recognizable face that belonged to . . .

Fairfax County Detective Sergeant John Russelli.

Henry Culver was still looking through his binoculars, numb with shock, when he saw one of the protective guardians suddenly bring his right hand up to his ear and then turn to say something to Parkinson and his special assistant.

Then, to Culver's horror, all six men turned their heads to stare intently down the block in the direction of Kathy Harmon's partially concealed Jeep.

Chapter Thirty-eight

Saturday, 1125 hours

"WHAT ARE YOU DOING?" Kathy Harmon screamed as Henry Culver suddenly accelerated the small Jeep into a sliding 180-degree turn, fishtailed his way through the slippery slush for about fifty feet, and then took the next left in the wrong direction on a one-way street.

Moments later, only the Mossy Rock team's blue Chevy pickup and a green minivan were still within sight of Kathy Harmon's rapidly moving Jeep as Culver made another sudden right-hand turn that sent a small delivery truck bouncing onto the sidewalk and pedestrians scattering for their lives in all directions.

"You're going to get us killed!" Kathy Harmon screamed again as she grabbed for the off-road safety strap.

"I'm trying to *keep* us from getting killed!" Culver yelled as he headed south, right through the porno and business districts of DC, keeping one eye on the rearview mirror all the way.

Goddamn you, Traynor, why didn't you tell *me? Digger's working for you bastards all along . . . and Russelli too?*

A brightly flashing set of red and blue lights of a black-and-white cruiser suddenly filled the better part of his rearview mirror as the familiar shriek of a siren filled the cold air.

"Henry, stop, pull over! It's the police!"

"I *know,* but . . . !"

Henry Culver was still in the process of trying to decide between stopping in DC, or running for the more familiar territory of Fairfax County, when the flashing lights of the pursuing District cruiser suddenly disappeared out of his review mirror—to be replaced by the relatively bland front end view of a green minivan.

Shit, Culver thought as he glanced in his side mirror just in time to see the District black-and-white spin away from the sideswiping impact of the van, and then smash into a shiny black limo parked along the curb.

Nice move, asshole, whoever the hell you are, he thought as he accelerated around a blocking sedan full of gawking tourists, blew a pair of stoplights, and finally managed to head west, back toward the Theodore Roosevelt Memorial Bridge.

"Goddamn it, Henry, *talk to me!* Where are we going?" Kathy Harmon demanded, her voice alternating between frustrated anger and visceral fear.

A quick check of his rearview mirror confirmed that the minivan and the pickup were still hanging tight a couple of cars back.

"We've got a problem," he finally said as he continued to blow yellow and red lights in his desperate bid to get across the Potomac River and back into his home territory.

"Now what?"

"Green minivan and a blue pickup behind us. Can't get rid of them."

Kathy Harmon glanced over her shoulder, and then quickly turned back to brace herself as Culver swerved sharply around a relatively slow-moving Cadillac.

"Who are they?" she gasped once the Jeep was accelerating in a straight line again.

"I don't know about the van, but I've seen the guy in the blue pickup before, and *he* sure as hell isn't friendly," Culver said, concentrating on the road ahead, and trying not to think about all of the little pieces of the puzzle that were starting to come together.

As they crossed the bridge, the signs started listing off his options—the new Highway 66, the older and much slower Highway 50 that ran through downtown Arlington, or the scenic George Washington Parkway that went right past the CIA Headquarters Building in Langley.

Yeah, right.

He took the 66 turnoff, trading higher visibility on the open road for added advantage of increased speed, and hoping that Kathy Harmon's Jeep could maintain the pace for a few more miles without throwing a rod. He couldn't see either the van or the pickup in his rearview mirror anymore, but his gut level instincts told him that they were back there and closing in fast.

They passed the 495 Beltway going due west at something approaching eighty-five miles per hour when Culver spotted a flash of green in his side mirror. He took less than a second to record the fact that the van—with its front windshield mostly broken out—was about six or eight cars back, and that the blue pickup was right behind it.

"Kathy, there's a police radio in one of my equipment bags. Get it out, right now!"

"Which one?" she yelled back as she reached for the black nylon bags at her feet.

"I don't know, just find it!"

Moments later, she held the small rectangular radio up in triumph, and then passed it quickly over to Culver.

"Code ten-thirty-three! Any cruisers in the area of sixty-six and one-twenty-three, code ten-thirty-three!" Culver yelled out, broadcasting the Fairfax County emergency call sign. This is Mike-Charlie Eight-Zero-Five. I'm in a tan Jeep Cherokee with a civilian passenger. I am being pursued by a pair of possible homicide suspects—a green minivan and a blue pickup. The minivan's got a broken front windshield. Unknown license plates, unknown number of occupants. Repeat, ten-thirty-three . . ."

"Mike-Charlie Eight-oh-Five, copy your thirty-three," the EOC dispatcher broke in. "Give us your location for intercept."

"I'm coming off sixty-six at one-twenty-three now, heading east," Culver called out as he tossed the radio to Kathy

Harmon, downshifted, and then used both hands to control the vibrating steering wheel as he took the off-ramp at a much-too-high rate of speed. He was grinning now as he listened to the familiar voices of the Bravo shift scout cars calling in their positions.

Then his head slammed forward into the steering wheel as the green minivan suddenly rammed into the rear of the smaller Jeep, nearly causing both vehicles to go sliding off the road. Culver heard Kathy Harmon screaming something, but he was too busy trying to maintain control of the Jeep to pay any serious attention. Then they were through the intersection at Jermantown and heading into Vienna when he heard the faint voice of one of the responding cruisers call out "Henry, take Miller!"

Hills are blocking him out. Shit!

"Kathy, stick that radio out the window and tell them we're going north on Miller from one-twenty-three!" Culver yelled as he power-turned the Jeep Cherokee into a left-hand sliding turn in front of the new shopping center.

Kathy Harmon opened her side window, fumbled with the unfamiliar radio for a few moments, and then screamed "north on Miller! We're going north on Miller!" and then screamed again and lost her grip on the radio as the fishtailing of the Jeep slammed her head into the doorframe.

"I lost it!"

"Never mind, just hang on!" Culver yelled, glancing once more into the rearview mirror and seeing the minivan less than two car lengths back. Then he saw the red-and-blue flash of a pair of oncoming cruisers in his side mirror about fifty yards back as they power-turned onto Miller Road.

"Come *on,* guys," Culver muttered.

The rear window in the Cherokee exploded, causing Henry Culver to curse and twist away as a bullet streaked into the console between the two front seats, demolishing the stereo radio in a spray of plastic shards.

Two more bullets slammed into the back door of the Jeep with a pair of sharp, metallic thuds.

Kathy Harmon started to bring her head up over the seat, but Culver pushed her back and yelled *"Stay down!"* as a large pond appeared at the left edge of his peripheral vision. At that instant, he jammed the accelerator pedal to the floor in what he hoped would look like a desperate effort to get up enough speed to make the upcoming hill.

No brakes, he reminded himself. *Don't give him a warning.*

Then, at the last second, seeing the flash of red-and-blue light coming from the top of the hill, Culver rapidly downshifted once, twice, and then clenched his teeth and accelerated into a sharp left-hand turn that sent the wildly lurching and swaying Jeep tearing up the narrow one-lane dirt road in a spray of ice and mud and rocks—leaving behind a wildly intersecting array of a blue-and-gray patrol cruiser whose screeching brakes and glaring headlights and flashing red and blues now pinpointed a battered green minivan that had come to a sliding, ninety-degree sideways stop right in the middle of Miller Road.

"Where are we?" Kathy Harmon whispered after Culver had guided the sorely abused Cherokee around intermittent pastures and though about a half mile of dense, old growth oak and fir trees, where the extremely narrow crisscrossing dirt paths appeared to have been made by and for horses.

"This place belongs to some friends of mine," Culver said, the exhaustion evident in his voice. "A hundred and eighty acres. They use it for boarding horses. Nice place to ride, but their daughter grew up, so hardly anybody ever comes here anymore."

"So we're safe if we stay here?"

Culver shook his head. "No, I don't think so," he said as he slowly maneuvered the Jeep through the last stand of trees, through a mostly tree-covered and unfenced backyard, in between two very expensive-looking homes, and out onto a residential road whose identifying sign read Blue Roan.

"So now where are we going?" Kathy Harmon asked, her face pale and drawn.

"I don't know," Culver said. "Right now we're just going to try to get out of this neighborhood without being spotted. Maybe once we do that, I'll be able to figure out something that makes sense."

They talked themselves through it all again and again until there wasn't anything more to talk about, so Culver continued to drive the bullet-torn Cherokee aimlessly through the historic Civil War town of Manassas, trying to clear his head of all the extraneous data that only seemed to be confusing the issue.

He had been trying to convince himself that there were really *two* puzzles, with separate and distinct pieces, but he knew now that wasn't the case at all. The problem was that he didn't even want to *try* to put those last big pieces together because he was afraid of what he was going to see.

Finally, he parked the Jeep in front of another service station pay phone, and then sat there and stared at it for a another minute or so—until he couldn't stand it any longer.

Mumbling something unintelligible, he got out of the Jeep, put on his light patrol jacket, feeling the transmitter that L'Que had given him in the right pocket, walked up to the booth, and then made the call he'd been dreading for the past hour.

"Carpenter."

"Hi, buddy," Culver said softly.

"Henry?"

"Yeah, it's me."

"Where the hell are you?"

"Out driving around, trying to clear my head. I need to talk to you."

"There's a bunch of people around here who want to talk with you," Carpenter said, "starting with the watch commander. He's got a couple of interesting questions for you about a green minivan out on Miller Road."

"Did they get him?"

"Your uniformed buddies took the driver and a passenger into custody, if that's what you want to know. Trouble is, watch commanders tend to get a little upset when their patrol officers start arresting FBI agents in pursuit of a felony suspect."

Culver blinked in momentary confusion, and then shook his head. "Carp, the guys in that van are no more FBI agents than you and I are."

"That a fact?"

"When's the last time you saw a Feeb deliberately ram a District cruiser off the road in downtown DC in the middle of a pursuit?"

"Not beyond a couple of FBI guys I know."

"Listen, you guys check that van, and then call the District," Culver said heatedly. "The whole left side of that damned thing should be covered with black and white transfer paint, and there ought to be a really pissed-off DC cop out on Fourteenth Street right now still trying to dig his cruiser out of a stretch limo."

"Yeah, well, that might be kinda difficult to prove," Carpenter allowed.

"You guys let them go, didn't you?"

"When a special agent in charge shows up and starts flashing the federal gold, us local types usually pay attention, whether we like it or not," Carpenter said. "Yeah, *of course* we let them go, along with some very sincere apologies and a promise to help find the asshole driver of a certain Jeep Cherokee."

"They give you a license plate?"

"No, they couldn't get it. Said you were driving like some kind of maniac, and they couldn't get close enough."

"Carp, those guys rode my bumper for fifteen goddamn *miles*. They rammed me at the one-twenty-three off-ramp, and then put three rounds in our back end from about ten yards. All that, and they couldn't read the plate? Come on, you know that's bullshit!"

"Yeah, well, that may be true, Henry," Carpenter said after a moment of hesitation. "But I'll tell you what, you sure didn't help your case much when you disappeared over the horizon after calling in that ten-thirty-three."

"Yeah, I know." Culver sighed. "Listen, I still need to talk to you and Stewart, and I don't want to do it over the phone. You guys willing to meet me somewhere, like at the heliport, in about an hour?"

"Yeah, I could arrange that," Carpenter said after another moment of hesitation. "You got Russelli with you?"

"No, why?"

"We've been looking for him too."

Culver held his breath for a moment. "What for?"

"Henry," Bradford Carpenter said in a strained voice, "a little over an hour ago, the Commonwealth Attorney issued a warrant for his arrest."

For some strange reason, Henry Culver thought that he could feel his blood rushing through all of his veins and arteries. He stood there for several moments, silent and numb, as he allowed his mind to drift in the empty hope that it would all go away somehow.

"Henry?"

"What's the warrant for?"

"Homicide, burglary, theft, conspiracy," Carpenter recited tonelessly. "Basically, it looks like Russell's been knocking off his burg suspects to cut his stats so maybe we'd keep him on. Latest ones are probably going to turn out to be Molly-the-Hun and a couple of her asshole burglar buddies."

"Where'd you find them?"

"One of the workmen out at the County Dump found a pair of size ten tennis shoes with a couple of legs attached sticking out from under a bunch of plywood. So Gauss and Stewart and I spent the whole goddamned morning digging through bags of rotten garbage to see what else we could find. We were just packing up and getting ready to leave when patrol spotted Molly's van parked off by itself on the other side of the drop-off ramp. Found blood and glass all over the front seat, and another body in the back, but it wasn't Molly, so now we've got another search team tearing the place apart trying to find *her.*"

"What makes you think Russelli did it?" Culver asked numbly, trying to remember exactly when he'd seen Molly Hunsacker's van coming out of that warehouse.

"Direct physical evidence."

Culver stood there in the booth and stared out at the dismal weather.

"Craven must be having an orgasm," he finally whispered, not knowing what else to say.

"Oh yeah, the bastard's out there hobbling around on crutches and kissing ass with the press right now, making it sound like he wrapped the whole thing up single-handed."

"Only fair, I guess." Culver nodded his head slowly, his mind almost completely blank now. But then one of the words that Carpenter had used finally registered in his mind. "Wait a minute, you said conspiracy?"

"We figure Russelli had help."

"Yeah, no shit."

"There were two warrants issued," Carpenter said. "The second one has your name on it."

For a few long moments, Culver wasn't certain that he'd heard Carpenter right.

"Me?"

"We've got a team in here from the FBI Lab right now putting all the pieces together. Gauss said he doesn't want to touch it . . . doesn't believe it."

"Believe what? What are you talking about?"

"Kostermann. The FBI's going over the entire case, reexamining all the evidence."

"Yeah, so?"

"Initial report says there's no way those Reebok shoes you and Russelli took from Digger's place match that footprint cast from Kostermann's garden."

"What?"

"Henry," Carpenter said in a tight-voiced growl, "they

went back and made sixteen-by-twenty blowups of Quinzio's CSI photos. Hell, even I could see the difference."

"What do you mean, 'see the difference'?"

"It was obvious. They don't match."

"If it was so goddamned obvious, then why the hell did *I* think they matched?" Henry Culver demanded.

Carpenter remained silent.

"Carp," Culver went on, trying to keep from being overwhelmed by the surge of conflicting information and emotions, "those photographs. Did you show them to Quinzio?"

"No, he's still out of it, but it doesn't matter anyway. The Feebs say they're absolutely sure that none of the negatives were altered, but that's not the big issue around here right now."

Not a match, and absolutely certain that there wasn't any tampering. Very impressive, Traynor. You guys must have found yourselves one hell of a photographer.

"I almost hate to ask."

"We found your bank accounts."

"My bank *accounts,* as in plural?" Culver laughed.

"According to the auditor, you and Russelli each have a total of approximately"—Carpenter paused for a moment to check his notebook—"$138,000 and change apiece. Matching deposits on matching dates—"

"—that just happen to correspond to within a few days of some of our major burglaries?" Culver finished.

"That's right."

"Carp, the last time I looked, I had something like 250 dollars in my checking account, max. I don't even *have* a savings account."

"Yeah, well you might want to take another look. It's a bunch of money, but not all that much, when you stop to think about it." Carpenter sighed heavily. "I'm really disappointed in you, Henry."

"Yeah, I can see where you would be, if you believed all of this shit."

"Listen, man, do yourself a favor. Let me walk you in."

"What?"

"It'd be a lot better that way. Bunch of people around here really liked Tess. Some of them are out on the street right now, looking for you and Russelli. The money angle really tripped everybody out."

"Oh yeah, right . . . forgot about that." Culver nodded to himself, not trying to make any sense out of it anymore, but just trying to keep up with the flow. "Yeah, I guess all things considered, I appreciate the offer."

"You still going to meet me at the heliport?"

"Yeah, sure, why not," Culver said, and then thought of something else. "Hey, Carp, tell me something, how'd they make Russelli?"

"Mostly because of you."

"Because of *me?*"

"Yeah. We've been picking up shell casings and plastic wadding from all the shooting scenes where we've been finding dead burglars. Pretty obvious from the striations on the plastic shot-cups that it was a sawed-off; but we couldn't get at Russelli's shotgun, so we couldn't make any test fires for comparison. What we ended up doing was using those rounds you capped off under Radlick's house for knowns. So far, everything matches up perfectly."

Culver's eyes blinked in confusion as he considered all of that for a few moments, the memory of the crawl space under Paul Radlick's house coming back in vivid detail. The cobwebs. The darkness. The shadowy movement. Slashing at the cold, lifeless hand of Paul Radlick with the shotgun, and then snagging the end of the barrel on that bolt or nail—or whatever it was—and thrashing around desperately to work it loose, because he'd been sure that Digger was coming. Digger the freak. The crawl space burglar who killed animals because he hated them . . . and people because he liked to.

"Carp?"

"Yeah?"

"About Molly-the-Hun and the other guy, whatever his name is."

There was a pause at the other end of the line. "You mean Morgan? Yeah, what about them?"

"Morgan?" Culver's eyebrows came up. "Wasn't one of the guys who was killed at that house in Clifton last Thursday named Morgan?"

"Yeah, that's what we thought at first. Otis Lawnhart and Bobby Morgan," Carpenter said. "Only it turned out the second body was somebody else. Haven't ID'd him yet."

"But this guy Morgan, the one they found in Molly's van—you're sure he was killed with a shotgun?"

"He was full of small holes, and Gauss found casings and wadding at the scene. What do you think?"

"Fired from *Russelli's* shotgun?"

"That's right. The Feebs just matched the casings a few minutes ago."

"When?"

"What do you mean *when?* I just told you . . ."

"No, listen, it's important. Do you have a time of death?"

"According to the coroner, sometime between ten last night and one this morning."

"So *after* we were at Radlick's house, right?"

"Yeah, sure, have to be. So what? Russelli took his shotgun back, remember?"

"I don't remember shit," Culver said. "But I want to know something else. When the Feebs made the match, did they check the casings *and* the plastic shot-cups?"

"Does it matter?"

"Maybe. Can you think of any reason why an ex–Homicide investigator like Russelli would leave empty casings at a scene *knowing* that firing pin impressions and ejector marks could be matched back to his shotgun?"

Carpenter hesitated again, and then muttered: "Give me a couple of minutes."

He was back on the phone in less than one.

"All of the twelve-gage shotgun casings at the dump were positively matched to the rounds you capped off under Radlick's house—firing pin *and* extractor marks," Carpenter stated flatly. "And Russelli did take his shotgun with him. I've got confirmation on that from Stewart."

"What about the shot-cups?"

"They only examined the casings."

"Carp, listen, ask them to go back and compare the striations on the plastic too."

"What the hell do you want them to do that for?" Carpenter demanded. "All that's going to do is nail the lid down tighter."

"Look, just ask them to do it, will you? Tell them it's important."

"You're still going to meet me, right?"

"Yeah, sure. And if you'll give me an hour, I'll try to bring Russelli in too," Culver added.

Carpenter hesitated then, and Culver thought he heard Stewart's muffled voice in the background.

"Okay, one hour. We don't hear from you by then," Carpenter warned, "you're on your own."

The phone clicked dead in Henry Culver's ears.

They picked Bear up at Pender Veterinary Clinic, Culver remaining in the vehicle while Kathy Harmon went in. When she came out with the huge dog in tow, Culver braced himself for a confrontation. But instead of being threatened by a pair of teeth-studded jaws, he found himself being licked and pawed and jumped upon by ninety-some pounds of deliriously happy black shepherd.

"He remembers you." Kathy Harmon smiled as she strained to calm the dog down and get him into the backseat. "I think he likes you now."

"Good thing," Culver grunted as he scratched the shaggy head one last time before turning back to the steering wheel. "They way things are going, I'm going to need all the friends I can get."

He started the engine and then looked over at Harmon, who was still rubbing Bear's long muzzle. "You sure you're ready for this?"

"Absolutely," Kathy Harmon said, her face now set in an expression of grim determination.

"Okay," Culver nodded, "let's go teach you how to be a burglar."

Fifteen minutes later, he and Kathy Harmon were parked down at the end of the street where Molly Hunsacker lived. They were both sitting there in silence as they watched a short, squat, muscular figure run out of the house with an armload of clothes.

"Who's that?" Kathy Harmon asked.

Culver slowly dropped the binoculars away from his eyes. "Molly Hunsacker, also known as Molly-the-Hun," he whispered. "The burglar who hit your house."

"But I thought you said she was dead?"

"Yeah, she's *supposed* to be," Culver said as he put down the binoculars and reached for the ignition key.

Molly Hunsacker had just finished loading the few possessions she truly cared about into the back of her old VW Bug, and was going back for her cherished plumber's wrench, when she stopped and stared at the Jeep Cherokee roaring down the street in her direction.

She managed to turn around and get herself in through the doorway, and was just turning around to slam the door shut when Henry Culver took a running leap and threw his 175 pounds into the heavy, solid core door. The resulting crash sent both Molly-the-Hun and Culver tumbling into the living room floor in a tangle of thrashing arms, legs, knees, and elbows.

"Police officer!" Culver yelled in Molly Hunsacker's ear as he twisted himself around the short, muscular burglar and drove his left arm under her thick neck, going for a carotid choke submission hold. "You're under . . . agghhh!"—and then lost the chokehold when Molly lunged upward with her short, weight-trained legs, lurched forward, and then slammed Culver into the living room wall with a heaving roll of her shoulder.

Pulling herself loose from Culver's loosened grasp, Molly-the-Hun slammed her right elbow hard into Culver's ribs and then uttered a feral growl as she swung her callused left fist around in a full-shouldered swing, intending to nail the staggered detective with a wicked roundhouse to the jaw—only to end up gasping in pain when Culver swung a blocking right forearm against her wrist, and then slashed back with a tight-fisted backhand into the side of the res-burglar's exposed jaw.

Stunned by the blow, Molly Hunsacker started to go down, but then recovered and caught Culver with an off-balance left to his already-injured ribs that sent them both tumbling to the floor again—only this time with Molly ending up on top.

Laughing in bloody-lipped glee, Molly Hunsacker saw Culver's shoulder-holstered revolver under his patrol jacket. She grabbed for it, got it partially worked loose, tearing his jacket in the process, and then screamed in rage as Culver twisted around and straight-armed her to the side, off-balance, and then followed through with an armlock takedown hold that nearly snapped her arm at the elbow. Twisting around to get the necessary leverage, Culver savagely slammed the struggling res-burglar face first into the carpet.

"Kathy, grab this!"

Unable to resecure the .357 back into his shoulder holster with his free left hand, Culver pulled the weapon loose with a reverse grip and slid it along the thin carpet into the far corner of the living room near Kathy Harmon, and then grunted in pain as a stunned and bloodied but still-fighting Molly Hunsacker drove her knee up into Culver's abdomen, just missing his groin.

"You goddamned *bitch!*" Culver snarled. Twisting around, he slammed the palm of his hand across the side of Molly Hunsacker's stubby nose—the impact snapping her head back in a spray of blood—and then found himself underneath again as the muscular burglar wrenched him over and dropped her 180 pounds of muscle on Culver's chest.

They were both reaching for each other's throat, Culver

trying for one last chokehold before resorting to a killing strike that might be necessary to save his life, when the horrendously explosive sound of a .357 Magnum revolver tore at their eardrums and blew the front window out over their heads.

"Shit!" Culver and Molly-the-Hun screamed in unison, both twisting away and then looking up to see Kathy Harmon standing there in the middle of the living room with Culver's revolver clenched in two hands.

"Jesus Christ, don't *shoot* her!" Culver yelled.

"She tried to kill Bear!" Kathy Harmon snarled, still blinking her eyes in response to the terribly LOUD and concussive gunshot that had sent her staggering backward and left her with a shrill ringing in her ears. She started to aim the heavy pistol at Molly Hunsacker's head, which forced Culver to scramble painfully to his feet and grab the gun away from her.

"Bear? Who the hell is Bear?" Molly-the-Hun demanded through bloody, split lips as she started to come up, but then hesitated as Culver motioned her back down.

"You stay put," Culver warned as he leaned back against the wall, trying to catch his breath and shake off the shrill ringing in his own ears, "or I'm gonna give her back the gun and let her dump you."

"But I didn't try to kill anyone!" Molly Hunsacker protested as she glared murderously at Kathy Harmon. "What's this broad talking about?"

"Maybe she's upset because you damn near beat her dog to death when you burged her house last Thursday," Culver suggested, wincing as he probed gingerly with his left hand at his painfully bruised ribs.

"What?"

"I said . . ." Culver started to say, but then he stopped and just stood there, staring in disbelief as the huge black shepherd bounded in through the door, trotted up to Molly Hunsacker with a wagging tail, and then started to lick the blood off her bruised and reddened face.

Chapter Thirty-nine

Saturday, 1400 hours

"It's always been that way, ever since I was a kid," Molly Hunsacker explained, her deep voice echoing from the kitchen. "Dogs and I have always got along. That's why it's been easy, you know, doing what I do. Want one?"

"A beer would be nice," Henry Culver replied as he sat back in the ancient rocker, closed his eyes, and wondered what the hell had ever made him think he wanted to be a police officer.

Molly-the-Hun returned from her kitchen with three opened, long-neck Budweisers. She handed one of the chilled bottles to Culver, a second one to Kathy Harmon, who was sitting with Bear on the floor, and then dropped into the grimy padded easy chair with a grateful sigh.

"Up yours," she said with a bloody grin, and then proceeded to drain about half the bottle down her throat in a single gulp.

"Likewise," Culver said, nodding agreeably as he took a cautious sip of the wonderfully soothing brew, noting out of the corner of his eye that Kathy Harmon didn't even bother to wipe off the end before bringing the bottle up to her lips.

Molly Hunsacker finished off the remainder of her beer, dropped the empty into the nearly full wastebasket next to her chair, and then turned to stare suspiciously at Culver.

"You look familiar," she finally said. "Have I seen you somewhere before."

Culver shrugged noncommittally. "It's possible."

"Are you really are a Fairfax County police officer?"

"You want to see the badge again?"

"No, that's okay. It just seems kinda odd, you know, me sitting here drinking brewskis with a cop."

"It is a little unusual," Culver admitted.

"But you said I'm not under arrest, right?"

"No, you're not under arrest. Not yet anyway."

"So if I tell you to haul ass, you're just gonna go, just like that?" Molly-the-Hun asked with a decidedly skeptical expression on her bruised and blood-smeared face.

"Sure. As long as you understand that when I leave, I'm taking the wrench with me."

Molly Hunsacker's eyes narrowed. "So I'm not off the hook after all."

"*You* are," Culver corrected. "Your wrench isn't."

"Why bother? You guys're always taking it away, and then you always end up giving it back 'cause you can't ever prove I used it on a job." The res-burglar smiled cheerfully.

"You mean because the teeth got filed down right after each job?"

Molly Hunsacker shrugged easily, still smiling.

"Actually, the way I understand the situation," Culver responded, "a guy named Bobby Morgan is supposed to have used your van to drive a load of stolen property out to your fence this morning. And after that, things apparently got a little confused, so I'm figuring the odds are pretty good that you probably forgot all about filing those teeth. Might be real interesting to see if we can get a match on any doorknob twists that happened"—Culver looked at his watch—"oh, let's say during the last twenty-four hours."

"How do you know about . . . ?" Molly Hunsacker started to demand, then she looked at Culver more closely. "In court. *That's* where I've seen you before. You're the crime lab guy who testified against me."

"Which means I'm also the guy who taught you all about filing the teeth on that damned wrench, right?"

Molly-the-Hun thought about that for a few moments.

"So what're you saying? Like I'm supposed to owe you

one, or something like that?" The res-burglar's bushy eyebrows furrowed in confusion.

"You might look at it that way. Or you might think about what's going to happen if I decide to arrest you for three counts of residential burglary. Kathy Harmon's home, twice, and Teresa Hardy's place yesterday morning, the first of which happens to be directly related to the murder of a Fairfax County police officer."

"That's bullshit!" the res-burglar protested. "I never killed nobody!"

"I believe you," Culver said. "But I think you know who did."

Molly Hunsacker stared first at Culver and then over at Kathy Harmon, who seemed to be more interested in rubbing the black shepherd's head than in following the conversation.

"Hey, you." Molly Hunsacker gestured with her head at Henry Culver's companion. "Are you a cop too?"

Kathy Harmon looked up and blinked her eyes. "Who, *me?* No, I'm not a cop."

"So who are you, then?"

"Harmon," she replied evenly. "First name Katherine. As in burglary victim."

Molly Hunsacker blinked.

The now thoroughly confused res-burglar considered that latest bit of information for a few quiet moments before turning her attention back to Culver. "This whole deal is nuts," she said.

"I think that's a fair assessment."

"So if I'm not under arrest, then maybe I ought to just tell you to haul ass right now?" Molly Hunsacker suggested, moving her head around as if to loosen up her neck muscles.

"Molly, you and I can bounce off the walls all day long if that's what you want. Personally, I'm just about in the right frame of mind to really enjoy it. But if I understand the situation correctly," Culver added, gesturing with his head in the direction of Kathy Harmon, "no matter how much you and dogs get along, if you so much as *touch* this young woman here, that shepherd's likely to rip your arm off at the shoulder and bury it out in your front lawn."

Molly Hunsacker blinked her eyes, made a rapid re-assessment of Bear—who was resting his head in Kathy Harmon's lap and slapping his heavy tail on the carpet, but nevertheless keeping his dark eyes fixed watchfully on the res-burglar—and then turned back to Culver.

"So that's all this amounts too—just another goddamned Fairfax County twist, right?"

Culver nodded agreeably. "Any cooperation you might be willing to provide the Fairfax County Police Department will be greatly appreciated."

"Yeah, bullshit," Molly-the-Hun muttered. And then, after a moment: "So what the hell do you want to know?"

"Let's start with the dog. Was he in the house when you broke into Kathy's place last Thursday?"

Molly Hunsacker hesitated, still uneasy. "I don't think I should be saying shit without my lawyer here."

"Who's your lawyer?"

"Mr. Radlick."

"Paul Radlick?"

"Yeah, that's right."

"Then you don't need to worry about calling your lawyer," Culver said calmly, "because he's dead. Your buddy Digger killed him."

Molly Hunsacker's eyes blinked wide open.

"And how about Bobby Morgan? You know him, too, right?"

"Yeah, of course I know Bobby, but . . ."

"Then I've got more bad news for you," Culver interrupted, "because Patrol just found his body lying in the back of your van out at the dump."

"Bobby's dead . . . out at the dump . . . in *my* van?"

"The interesting thing is, with all the blood and glass on the front seat, the homicide guys figured you were probably dead, too. Fact is, they're tearing up the whole goddamned dump right now, trying to find you."

Molly Hunsacker eyes were blinking rapidly now. "God-damn it, I don't understand . . ."

"Paul Radlick and his wife are dead," Culver explained patiently, "and I'm reasonably certain that Digger killed them. I have no idea who killed Morgan, but I figure that whoever did it was probably expecting you to be driving that van."

Molly-the-Hun's face turned deathly pale.

Bingo.

"Molly, listen to me," Culver pressed, determined to maintain his momentum, "I never did read you your·rights, and I don't have a warrant for your house, so that means anything you say in this room can *never* be used against you, no matter what. You even have a civilian witness here—who really doesn't like cops very much—who can back you up," he added, gesturing with his head at Kathy Harmon. "So tell me about the dog."

"He was there," Molly Hunsacker nodded, having to swallow to get the words out, "but he was lying there on the floor, out cold, when I broke in. It kinda pissed me off, you know, 'cause like I told you, dogs and I always get along, and I don't like to see them hurt or anything like that. So you can tell that asshole Russelli . . ."

"Hold it a minute," Culver interrupted. "What's Russelli have to do with any of this?"

"You know him?"

"Yeah, I know Russelli."

"Well, take it from me, he's an asshole," the res-burglar muttered.

"Most of the cops around the station think he's a pain in the ass to work with, too," Culver replied. "So what?"

"The guy hates animals. Everybody knows that."

"He's not real fond of residential burglars, either. I repeat, so what?"

Molly Hunsacker stared at the black shepherd for a few moments, and then looked up at Culver.

"You want me to give you something. What if I give you a cop?"

"Who, Russelli?"

"That's right."

"What do you know about him?"

"That maybe he's a fucking murderer."

Henry Culver sat there for a moment and stared at the beefy, disheveled residential burglar, the overheard words of Brad Carpenter and Al Stewart at the shooting scene of the two rednecks echoing in his ears.

Think we should get Russelli out here now?

Yeah, might as well. Just make sure you keep an eye on him.

And then in Paul Radlick's driveway, listening with Carpenter.

We got something going on right now, a sensitive operation that's kinda touchy.

Something touchy enough that they didn't want one of their ex–Homicide investigators wandering around a homicide scene.

A sensitive operation.

Jesus, Russelli, what the hell did you do?

"Start talking," he finally said.

Molly-the-Hun shook her head. "Uh uh. I want immunity on this first. Immunity *and* protection."

"If you have specific proof that Detective Sergeant John Russelli is involved in a homicide, I'll see to it personally that you get put into the Witness Protection Program," Culver said.

"You can guarantee that?"

"I can call the Commonwealth Attorney's Office right now, and have you in the program within twenty-four hours," Culver said. "New name, identity, location. The works."

"You'd do that for me?"

"I'm sitting here drinking your beer, aren't I?"

Molly Hunsacker stared down at her lap and chewed on her bloody lower lip for a few moments. Then, finally, she sighed heavily and nodded her head in resignation. "Okay,

you've got a deal. The guy I used to work for, he—" she
began.

"Who was that, Digger?"

"Oh yeah, that's the guy all right. Far-out freaking Digger. The word is, he and Russelli are working together."

"Russelli, working with Digger?" Culver started to laugh,
and then caught himself, trying to ignore the chilling sensation that was traveling up his spine.

"Doesn't make a whole lot of sense, right?"

"Very little," Culver agreed.

"Yeah, well, the way I heard it, thanks to Digger and one
of his fucking traps, Russelli's leg got so torn up, you guys
weren't gonna let him be a cop anymore. And also, that you
guys were gonna fire or demote him anyway, 'cause he
wasn't solving any burgs . . . mine, mostly, I guess. So," the
res-burglar shrugged uneasily, "word is on the street, he and
Digger made a deal."

"A deal?" Culver rasped, not at all sure that he wanted to
hear the next part.

"That's right. A deal. He and Russelli have it all worked
out. Digger sets up the burgs for people like me, works out
all the details, and Russelli scares off the competition by
knocking somebody off every now and then. Always uses a
sawed-off shotgun, too, so that everybody out there understands the situation. Work with us, or don't work, period."

Henry Culver just sat there and stared at the nervy but still
clearly shaken burglar.

"And just so you understand," Molly Hunsacker went on,
"the main reason I'm doing this—the main reason I want
out—is we think they're starting to knock the rest of us off,
too."

"Who else?"

"Pogo, for one."

"You mean Pogo Waters? Russelli's snitch?"

"That's right. I mean, it's not like anybody didn't *know*
Pogo was Russelli's snitch, for Christ sake. The stupid little
shit would even brag about it when he got drunk, but nobody

really cared 'cause he always warned us, too . . . even though he kept on saying that Russelli was going to kill him someday for working both sides."

"Jesus," Culver whispered.

"Yeah, exactly. I mean, everybody could understand why Russelli would want to kill Pogo. Hell, I wanted to kill him a couple of times myself. But now everything's completely screwed up 'cause we all thought Bobby and Otis were already dead."

"Bobby and Otis?" Culver was having trouble following the thread of the res-burglar's recital.

"Yeah, right, Bobby Morgan and Otis Lawnhart. One of my new teams. Or at least they were. Somebody kicked the door on their place Thursday evening and blew them away—with a shotgun," she added meaningfully.

"And they worked for Digger, too?" Culver asked, going through the motions now because the pieces were starting to fall into place in his head faster than Molly Hunsacker could talk.

"What do you think I've been saying all this time?" Molly-the-Hun demanded. "Hell, yes, they worked for Digger. We all did. Him and Russelli. But you want to hear the really good part?"

Culver nodded his head slowly. "Keep talking."

"The kicker is that Russelli's supposed to have somebody working for him in your crime lab—some guy named Culver—who helps him fake evidence so that nobody on Digger's team gets caught."

Culver saw Kathy Harmon's head come up out of the corner of his eye, but he didn't dare say anything that might stop Molly Hunsacker from talking.

"That's a nice trick," he said.

"Pretty damned smart, if you ask me, and I happen to hate the bastard. The thing is, see, we figure this lab guy is the one who probably nailed Bobby."

"You think *Culver* killed Bobby Morgan?" Henry Culver was having trouble believing his ears.

"Yeah, sure. I mean, it makes sense 'cause, see, Bobby said he was gonna kill this guy Culver, too, after he got back from the warehouse. So what I figured happened is . . . hey, wait a minute, you said you worked in the police lab too, so you must know this Culver guy, too, right?"

Culver nodded. "I know him. Go on."

"I mean, that's why this whole deal confuses the shit out of me," Molly Hunsacker said, shaking her head. "I always kinda figured the crime lab guys were supposed to be straight arrow. I mean *you*, for example. You could have probably faked evidence on me anytime you wanted, said those teeth marks matched when they really didn't, but you never did."

"Who told you all this, Molly?" Culver asked in a quiet voice.

"Digger, of course." She shrugged as if to say "who else?"

"You've talked with him, recently?"

"We don't exactly talk," Molly-the-Hun said, smiling. "You wanna see something you ain't gonna believe? Come on in my bedroom."

Henry Culver stood there in the middle of Molly-the-Hun's bedroom and stared at the portable notebook computer sitting there on the ancient wooden desk for almost a minute, feeling it all fall into place in the back of his head like a line of dominoes.

The computer had been the missing element all along, and he'd known about it for almost thirty-six hours now because Homicide Detective Brad Carpenter had told him about it out on the curb that night.

Taught me to walk real light around bombs, but they never said nothin' about any fucking computers.

Yeah, I bet they didn't, Culver thought to himself. *And if Sharon hadn't told me that Russelli bought a computer, I'd have never . . .*

Bombs?

Oh shit.

"Kathy," Culver said in a tight voice, "my equipment bags.

The ones in the Jeep. Get them for me, please. I need them right now."

Kathy Harmon had been staring at Culver from the entryway of Molly Hunsacker's bedroom, trying to make sense out of what she had heard, when Culver's words finally registered.

"What?"

"Go get my equipment bags out of the Jeep and bring them in here, *right now!*" Culver said emphatically, never taking his eyes off the computer.

"What's the matter?" Molly Hunsacker muttered through bloody lips as Kathy Harmon and Bear disappeared through the bedroom door.

"Have you got a medium-sized Phillips screwdriver and a set of hex wrenches?" Culver asked, ignoring Molly's question as he cautiously examined the two sliding panels on the sides of the computer case, and then quickly disconnected the telephone cord between the internal modem and the phone jack.

"Yeah, sure, but . . . ?"

"Go get them," Culver said softly, "and hurry it up."

Thirty minutes later, Henry Culver double-checked the two settings on the relay switches in the partially dismantled computer, removed the remote transmitter that he'd found on the driveway next to Tess Beasley's shattered car from one of the equipment bags, set the switch on the back to AUTO SCAN SLOW, and then handed it to Kathy Harmon.

"Walk over to the far corner of the room," he directed. "Then turn your back and aim it at the wall."

"Like this?" she asked.

"Exactly." Culver nodded. "All right, now see those two switches in there?" he said to Molly as he pointed into the innards of the computer.

"Uh-huh."

"Watch the one on the left. Okay, Kathy, push the button."

The relay switch on the left closed with a loud "CLICK!"

that echoed in the small room and caused all three of them to wince.

"How did you do that?" Molly Hunsacker whispered as she watched Culver quickly reach into the computer, change the code of the left-hand relay switch, and then manually reset the switch to the open position.

"It's standard hardware," Culver said distractedly as he took the transmitter back from Kathy Harmon and started to take it apart again. "They use this kind of transmitter for garage door openers. This is one of the earlier models that's been discontinued. It uses a three-digit code that you can set internally," he removed the top cover from the device and pointed out the three LED boxes showing three red sixes, "to send out a signal that activates a relay switch set to the same three-digit code."

"Wouldn't it be easier if they put the numbers on the outside so you can see them?" Kathy Harmon asked.

"Sure, but then everybody would know the code setting on your garage door."

"I used to have a remote just like that," Molly-the-Hun said. "A friend of mine gave it to me. She said it would open almost any garage door in the county."

Culver smiled. "She was probably right. And to have it do that," he said as he turned the opened transmitter over and pointed to a recessed knob on the back that was marked at three positions: LOCK, AUTO SCAN SLOW, and AUTO SCAN FAST, "what your friend probably did was to switch this knob here over to AUTO SCAN FAST position."

"Yeah, so?"

"You set the three-digit code on this model just like you'd set a digital alarm clock. Use the AUTO SCAN FAST to get close to the number you want, and then switch to the slower scan speed to get the exact number that matches the code on your relay switch. Then you turn the knob back to the LOCK position and you've got yourself a garage door opener that's set to your own personal code . . . or at least one out of a thousand possible codes.

"But," Culver went on, "what people like your friend discovered was that if you leave one of these things set to AUTO SCAN FAST or AUTO SCAN SLOW, instead of LOCK, and then press the transmit button, it sends out *all* of the code signals, one at a time. At slow speed, it takes about ten minutes to go through all of the thousand possible codes. At fast speed, one minute. The only problem is, unless you're careful with your aim, the infrared beam can bounce off a window or a wall and set off all the other electric door openers in the area, which attracts a lot of attention. The smart burglars stopped using them real quick."

"Yeah, that's exactly what happened the first time I tried to use it." Molly-the-Hun nodded. "That is why I gave it away."

"Good thing you did," Culver commented as he carefully removed the battery from Tess Beasley's transmitter, wrapped the transmitter up in his dirty T-shirt, put it on the floor, and then smashed it into several dozen small pieces with the heel of his shoe.

"Hey, why'd you do that?" Molly Hunsacker furrowed her eyebrows in confusion as she watched Culver drop the transmitter pieces in the bedroom trash can that was about half-full with empty Budweiser bottles.

"Do you know what Kathy actually did when she triggered that relay switch?" Culver asked.

"No, what?"

"She activated a trigger for a bomb."

"Bomb? What bomb?" Molly Hunsacker and Kathy Harmon demanded almost in unison.

"This bomb right here in this computer," Culver said as he carefully pushed the computer innards back into its plasticized case. "Your friend Digger rigged it with what looks to be about a half pound of C-4. That first switch arms the ignition system and sets the trigger. The second one lights it off."

"You actually let me activate a real *bomb?*" Kathy Harmon demanded, her eyes widened in disbelief. "So that it was ready to go off, *right here in this room?*"

"That's right." Culver nodded his head, watching Molly-the-Hun's face to see if the minimal chance he'd taken was going to produce the desired effect.

"But somebody could have . . ." the ashen-faced burglar whispered.

"If somebody within maybe fifty yards of this house just happened to have a garage door opener set to the exact code of the second switch, and he was holding just right so that the signal managed to bounce in through that window, then yes, the bomb in this computer would have gone off and we'd be dead right now.

"As a matter of fact," he added calmly, "it still could. I don't have the tools to deactivate it, and I don't dare cut the wires because there could be a tamper-protect circuit."

"You son of a bitch," Molly Hunsacker said in a raspy whisper.

"Not me," Culver corrected. "Digger. Think about it. He's the one who rigged it, and he's the one who gave it to you. I just changed the code numbers, and set them far enough apart so that it would take about thirty seconds between arming and detonating the bomb with the transmitter set to AUTO SCAN FAST. I set the transmitter Kathy has to AUTO SCAN SLOW, so I had five minutes to shut the arming switch back to the 'off' position."

"You mean it's safe now?"

"More or less."

"But . . ."

"I reset both switches to different code numbers, with a higher number for the first arming switch," Culver smiled. "The chances of two of your nearby neighbors having garage door openers with those two specific codes, and using them in the right sequence, is pretty unlikely. We shouldn't have to worry about it."

"But what happens if someone has one of those devices set to scan quick, or whatever the hell you call it?" Molly

Hunsacker demanded, looking as if she was about ready to run from the room.

"If that first arming switch ever snaps close again, and you're close enough to hear it, then you've got about thirty seconds, more or less, either to get into the computer and turn the arming switch off manually or simply haul ass," Culver explained patiently. "But I wouldn't worry about it too much, because if somebody around here really did have one of these transmitters set to AUTO SCAN, that computer of yours would have probably detonated a long time ago."

Molly-the-Hun closed her eyes in a prayerful manner.

"As I said," Culver smiled, "it was a good thing you threw yours away."

Molly Hunsacker was silent for a long time. Then she looked directly at Culver.

"So what is it you want?"

"The names and addresses of everybody you know who's been working with Digger during the past three months."

"That's all? Nothing else?"

"That's plenty."

"And you'll write a letter for me? Tell the judge I cooperated?"

"If that's what you want."

Molly Hunsacker walked over to the old desk, pulled a pad of paper out of one of the drawers, sat down on her bed, and started writing furiously while Culver continued to clean up his tools.

About five minutes later, she suddenly looked up.

"Wait a minute. That computer was connected to the telephone," she said. "Couldn't Digger have set it off by telephone?"

"Sure, any time," Culver said. "Both switches were connected to the modem. All he would have had to do was send out both signals in sequence—probably while you were sending messages back and forth, just so he'd be sure you were here."

"Yeah, right." Molly nodded her head in solemn understanding.

"In fact, that's probably how he was planning on getting rid you if you ever got in his way," Culver added as he put away his tools, and then pulled Russelli's cobweb-covered denim jacket out of his equipment bag to replace the patrol jacket that he had torn while wrestling with Molly. "Remote trigger. Just as he nailed Gauss and Quinzio. Probably how he got Tess, too, now that I think about it."

Molly Hunsacker's head came up at the mention of the first two names, but Culver didn't notice.

"When I rigged the window in her station wagon, so that she could let Sasha out without being near the car, I went out and bought her one of these transmitters from an electronics dealer friend of mine who had them on sale. I set the code to eight-four-zero," Culver said in a quiet, distant voice as he put on the oversize jacket. "No particular reason other than that was my call sign.

"Then somebody—maybe Digger, maybe one of his helpers—goes out and burgs the same store and steals the rest of those transmitters to rig his computers. I remember the guy telling me I got the last one because he got hit that weekend. I should have thought about that when I saw all those empty reels of wire with the store name on them under Radlick's house."

"You mean the bomb that killed Tess—the one that was meant for you—*she* set off herself?" Kathy Harmon whispered.

Culver nodded. "It's one good possibility," he said. "Digger probably thought it was funny, coding the detonation switch to my call sign. Way I figure it, Tess probably got out of the car, saw something, and went to release the dog with her transmitter."

Molly-the-Hun cleared her throat. "You said 'Gauss and Quinzio.' How do you know those names?"

"Quinzio, Gauss, Russelli, and Culver. Those are the names Digger told you to spray on Kathy's living room wall, right?" Culver asked as he reached for the computer, started to turn, and then suddenly found himself being confronted by the bared teeth of a savagely growling black shepherd who was just barely being restrained by Kathy Harmon.

"Bear, what's the matter with you?" she yelled as Molly Hunsacker quickly backed up against the bedroom wall, leaving Culver alone in the middle of the room.

"It's okay, Bear," Culver whispered as he stared down at his exposed hands, saw the torn sleeve on Russelli's denim jacket, and only then remembered the small piece of torn blue fabric that Kathy Harmon's niece had removed from the dog's left incisor.

Little piece of cloth.

Probably ice-cold nerves and reflexes to match. Sorry Bear, better luck next time.

Russelli.

Being as careful as he could not to make any sudden move that might cause the fiercely snarling animal to break loose from Kathy Harmon's restraining arms, Culver slowly put the equipment bags and the computer down, and then carefully removed the denim jacket and dropped it over on the floor to his right.

Then, still moving as slowly and carefully as he could, he walked around to his left, watching as Bear switched his gaze back and forth between him and the jacket, still growling, but softer and less threatening now.

Finally, Culver managed to work his way around to where he was standing beside the black shepherd, who was now concentrating almost entirely on the stained and dirty jacket.

"It's okay, Bear. No bad guys, just me," Culver whispered as he knelt down and allowed the dog to sniff at his leg, and then at the back of his hand. Moments later, he and Bear were nuzzling each other with what appeared to be mutual relief.

"What was *that* all about?" Molly Hunsacker demanded

as Culver finally got back up and retrieved his equipment bags and the computer.

"Nothing, just a little confusion," Culver said as he removed his torn patrol jacket from one of the bags and put it back on, leaving Russelli's cobwebby jacket lying on the floor as he walked over to Molly's damaged front door, Kathy Harmon and a still-uneasy Bear following close behind.

"You are taking my computer with you, in your car?" Molly-the-Hun asked, her deep, gravelly voice filled with disbelief.

"It's safe enough. The metal panels in the car will shield it from most stray signals until we get it out to the range. Why, you want to keep it around here?"

"Hell no!" Molly Hunsacker shuddered, and then seemed to remember something. "But what am I supposed to do now?"

"If I were you, I think I'd be living in another state by tomorrow morning," Culver said. "Preferably one on the West Coast."

Molly Hunsacker blinked her eyes in confusion. "You mean you're letting me go? Just like that?"

"Sure, why not?" Culver shrugged indifferently as he walked out the door. "I already told you, you're not under arrest."

"But . . . but *why?*"

The genuine bewilderment in Molly-the-Hun's voice caused Culver to stop and then look back over his shoulder at the infamous Fairfax County res-burglar.

"You remember those four names that Digger told you to write on that wall?" he asked.

"Yeah, sure." Molly nodded. "What about them?"

"I'm Culver."

Chapter Forty

Elliott Parkinson's voice was filled with rage.

"Where the hell have you been?" the associate director of Operations demanded, almost screaming into the phone that had been giving him nothing but busy signals for the past forty-five minutes.

The voice at the other end of the line muttered something that was half-apologetic and half-bitter.

"I don't give a damn about your problems," Parkinson exploded. "You report in when I *tell* you to report in. And when I tell you to do something yourself, I don't expect you to send some goddamned flunky! Is that understood?"

This time, the voice at the other end was properly apologetic, and the pitch of Parkinson's voice dropped accordingly, although the fury that had driven those shouted words still churned in his gut.

"All right, Craven," Parkinson almost whispered. "Now tell me exactly what you're going to do about Henry Culver."

At precisely 2:45 on that cold and dismal winter afternoon, Henry Culver was huddling in a remote phone booth in the back parking lot of a run-down convenience store, thumbing through a torn, ragged telephone book to find the number for the Oakton District Fire Station that was only a mile away, but in a much-too-exposed location. He found it and quickly punched in the numbers.

"Station Thirty-four," the voice answered.

"This is Detective Henry Culver of the Fairfax County Police Department," Culver said, working to keep his voice calm and steady. "I'm doing a follow-up investigation on the

L'Que burglary in Area Eight-Eleven. One of your para-medic units transported Colonel L'Que's son . . ."

"Oh yeah, sure. Mindy and I handled that call."

"Do you remember where you took him?"

"Sure. Fair Oaks Hospital," the paramedic said. "Had to really burn rubber on that one. The kid was starting to drop off the charts before we hit the highway. Say, how's he doing anyway?"

"From what I hear, a whole lot better than anybody ex-pected," Culver said, already starting to thumb through the phone book again. "Gotta go. Thanks, bye."

Five minutes later, after making one more phone call—to the Fair Oaks Hospital—and then another to the Fairfax Po-lice Storage Yard, Culver was back in the mud-splattered Jeep.

"Well?" she said.

"He'll be there."

"Thank God," she whispered.

"Now you've got a choice to make, and you've got to make it right now," Culver said as he accelerated the Jeep back onto the two-lane rural highway. "We can go pick up Lisa, and then I can take you home and leave you there. But if I do that, there's a good chance that somebody's going to decide to either bring you in as some kind of hostage, or put you out of the way permanently."

"You mean they might try to kill us?"

"That's right."

"But why, for God's sake? We haven't done anything," Kathy Harmon whispered, her face turning pale as she tight-ened her arms around the black shepherd. "Why us?"

"All I know is that you're involved. I don't know why or how," Culver said as he went back to the tactic of making random turns.. "I can drop you off at the heliport, turn you over to the Homicide detail. You'll be fine as long as you stay with them."

"Stay at the police station?"

"That's right."

"For how long?"

"I don't know that either. Probably hours. Maybe days."

No one was making any rapid lane changes—no green minivans, no blue pickups, no cruisers. Nothing.

"And if I stay with you?"

The inflections in her voice had changed, Culver realized as he tried to concentrate on his driving. Anger had been replaced by curiosity, but the visceral fear was still there.

Good, he thought. *You wanted to know what it's like. Now you know.*

"I'm not planning on losing," he said calmly as he made another right turn onto Highway 29 heading toward the center of Fairfax County. "But there aren't any guarantees. The only thing I promise you is that if you stay with this, it's going to get real interesting."

"So whadda ya think?" the retired New York street-cop-turned-property-officer demanded as he rolled the intact driver's side window of Molly Hunsacker's van partway up, and then back down.

They were in the vehicle section of the Fairfax County Police Evidence & Property Storage Yard—a huge, thick-walled concrete warehouse that currently held thirty-eight impounded vehicles of assorted make, age, and condition, two of which were of particular interest to Culver.

"New glass," Culver said, staring through the almost-virgin safety glass at the pattern of the bullet holes that riddled the blood-soaked back of the driver's seat, "after the shooting."

"Right," the white-haired property officer nodded cheerfully.

"What caught your attention?" Culver asked.

"Crawling around in there making the property inventory," the property officer smiled. "Started looking under the seats and figured there was a hell of a lot of glass fragments down there for one little broken side window . . . and besides, the pattern of those holes didn't look right for a shotgun—

not that I'm some hotshot forensic scientist or anything," he added with a wide, self-satisfied grin.

"You'll do until one comes along," Culver said thoughtfully, distracted by his memories of a similar warehouse in Washington, DC, and a new panel truck.

DE GUELLE'S GLASS—WE DELIVER.

Yeah, you sure as hell do.

"Uh-huh, that's what I thought, too," the property nodded. "And since that asshole Gauss figures he's too goddamned important to talk to us ignorant ex-cops, I decided that maybe somebody around here ought to start rummaging around, see if they can find any more pieces to this friggin' puzzle."

"Did you?"

"Maybe. Com'ere and take a look." The property officer gestured with his head as he led Culver and Kathy Harmon over to the office portion of the warehouse, where he had several items of evidence laid out on one of the three-by-six tables.

"What do you think of these?" the property officer asked, holding a pair of plastic evidence bags out to Culver.

"Mobil credit cards?" Culver frowned, holding the transparent bags up to the light.

"Uh-huh. Normally, no big deal, right? I wouldn't have thought much about it either, except that I've logged in six of those little hummers on homicide cases during the past couple of months."

"Six?"

"Yeah, so I'm figuring, what are the odds on six homicide victims all having Mobil credit cards and nothing else. Especially homicide victims who happen to be burglars. And then I start rummaging around in those two vans out there, and guess what I can't find."

"Mobil credit card receipts?"

"You got it." The property officer nodded approvingly. "Might make a good New York City beat cop out of you yet."

"I don't think I'm going to be any kind of a cop much longer," Culver muttered, staring at the embossed names of Molly Hunsacker and Bobby Morgan on the two thin plastic cards.

"Oh yeah, that reminds me, Craven came by here a little while ago. Said if I saw you, I was to get on the horn right away on account of he's got some sort of fucking warrant for your arrest. You know anything about that?"

"There seems to be a little confusion about who the bad guys are on this deal," Culver said. "Apparently Craven's got Russelli and me fitted for a couple of black hats."

"Christ, no wonder they made him a lieutenant. Guy who thinks like that'd be dangerous out on the streets," the property officer muttered. "Anyway, I ain't seen you. And besides, I kinda figured you might not have much time to screw around with stuff that might not mean anything, so I did a little calling around, to see what the scoop is on these cards."

"And?"

"They're all legit, but the background's kinda interesting. Seems like all six of these cards started out being billed to one of two PO boxes at the Merrifield Post Office before the company finally got change of address cards that match all of the victims' current addresses."

"Fascinating," Henry Culver nodded.

"Yeah, well wait until you hear the best part. According to the Mobil billing department, not one of these cards has ever been used to buy a tank of gas."

"Who were you talking to?" Kathy Harmon asked as Culver came out of the phone booth and got back into the Jeep Cherokee.

"R. C. Cohen—a friend of mine," Culver said as he started up the Jeep and headed out into the snow-lined street. "He's going to go take a look at those cards, see if he can figure out what's going on."

"You trust him?"

Culver thought about that for a moment.

"Yeah, I do," he finally said. "Or at least as much as I trust anybody right about now."

They waited there, partially concealed by the surrounding trees, for almost fifteen minutes before the Bronco pulled into the driveway next to them.

For a few moments, Lieutenant Colonel Charles L'Que and Henry Culver stared at each other through their driver's side windows.

"Are you certain? Absolutely certain?" L'Que finally asked.

Culver shook his head. "No, I'm not absolutely certain about anything anymore. I just think that it might be very important for us to know, one way or the other."

"You are a police officer, and yet you have a technical knowledge about such things?"

"I wasn't always a police officer. I used to work for them a few years ago."

"I see," L'Que said quietly. And then, after a long moment: "You understand, of course, that there may be serious repercussions over all of this?"

"Yes, I do. And I'm also aware that it's your home and I don't have a warrant, and it's probably none of my business anyway. In other words, you don't have to let me in there."

L'Que nodded his head. "Yes, Mr. Culver, that I *do* understand."

They parked both vehicles in L'Que's garage, closed the doors, and then entered the house quietly through the kitchen door—L'Que first, then Kathy Harmon and Bear, with Culver bringing up the rear. Culver watched the French military officer step into his living room, visibly alert and ready, and for a brief moment, felt something tug at the collection of images deep in his memory. But then he immediately pushed that whole problem aside because he had work to do.

Motioning for Kathy Harmon and the dog to move up next to him and to remain silent, he reached behind the

TV/stereo system and pulled the six electrical plugs out of the yellow circuit protector. Then, after carefully pulling the console boxes away from the wall, he took his equipment bag from Kathy Harmon, removed a pair of medium- and fine-tipped screwdrivers and a multimeter, handed her a three-cell flashlight, and then went to work.

Sometime later, Kathy Harmon asked L'Que in a quiet whisper if she could use his phone, and received his nodded permission. She came back into the living room five minutes later to tell Culver that her neighbor would keep Lisa there at her house until they could pick her up, but Culver was far too involved in what he was doing to do anything more than nod.

Forty-five minutes later, he finally looked up, blinked his tired eyes, nodded his head, and then motioned toward the nearby den.

"Well," L'Que demanded as he shut the door to his spacious den and then turned to face Culver and Kathy Harmon.

"How did you know it wasn't your TV?" Culver asked.

L'Que shrugged. "My son has always been careless. In helping us move it in, he gouged the back panel of the cabinet against the porch railing. That mark is no longer there."

"But the serial number on the plate matches your records?"

"Yes, it does. I found that interesting."

"Something else you may find interesting. So far, I've managed to locate eight mikes, two memory units, two signal processors, and two transmitters that seem to make up a primary system and a backup. It was rigged to draw power from the wall plugs, so everything should be off now."

"Are you certain of that?"

"No, I'm not. Right now, there's no power running to either of the processors or the transmitters. But," Culver added with careful emphasis, "I can't be sure I found everything, and there's always the possibility of a concealed battery backup, although I couldn't see anything that *looked* like a battery."

L'Que muttered something that Culver couldn't catch, but it didn't matter because the meaning was obvious.

"Why would they do it?" Culver asked.

"In a short while, a very carefully protected man will arrive at my home to provide testimony for the Select Intelligence Committee of your Congress. The evidence this man will produce will be very damaging to certain members of your Central Intelligence Agency," L'Que said.

"Why here? Why not somewhere in DC?"

"This is not intended to be an official visit."

"One of those meetings that never happened, regardless of the consequences?"

"Yes, precisely."

Culver thought about that for a moment.

"So I guess they wanted a recording of this meeting."

"So it would seem."

"Did they know for sure it was going to be held here?"

L'Que shook his head. "No, they could not. There were several other possible sites. The decision was made at the last minute, for reasons of security."

"Then you'd better change your location for those very same reasons."

"That might be . . . very difficult at this point," L'Que said. "Are you sure that would be necessary? You said the transmitters no longer function."

"I said I *think* they no longer function," Culver corrected. "But that's kind of a secondary problem right now, because I found something else," he added, finding himself staring at a photograph on L'Que's desk that for some reason looked chillingly familiar.

"Yes?"

"There's an antenna in the CD player that traces back to a separate unit that I couldn't identify. It may be another processor, and if it is, it may be picking up signals from your telephones. Another, more likely possibility is that it's there to receive a coded signal which would set off the detonators in the bottom of your speakers. Each of which, by the way, is filled with about a kilogram of an explosive compound."

L'Que didn't even blink. Instead he just smiled—a cold, hard, and deadly smile that Culver didn't like at all.

"Two kilos?" he said calmly, as though he were inquiring about the amount of oil in the engine of his Bronco.

Culver nodded. "Probably C-4. I pulled the detonators, but there could be another set hidden underneath. I didn't want to move anything."

"So there is no doubt," L'Que whispered.

"What?"

"Never mind, it's not important," L'Que said in a cold, hard voice that suggested exactly the opposite.

"One more thing, Colonel," Culver said after a few moments.

"Yes?"

"As I said, I can't be sure that the system is completely off. Other than pulling and removing all of the detonators that I could see, I've left everything in place, just as it was, so that you can turn the entire system back on if you so choose."

"Just put the plugs back into the wall, yes?"

"Yes. If you don't plug the system back in, they will certainly know that something is wrong. But if you do restore the power, it's also possible that you may transmit a signal indicating that someone has tampered with the system, although they may be aware of that by now anyway. I can always disable the receiving antenna, too, if you wish, but there may be others."

L'Que nodded his head silently.

"What I'm trying to say, Colonel," Culver said, staring straight into L'Que's eyes, "is that you and your wife should not return to this house. And if you still have that pistol, you might keep it handy."

"You think they are so mad as to try to do such a thing?"

"Colonel, if I'm right about all of this, at least five people that I know about have been killed, including a Fairfax County police officer and an attorney. Several other people, including your son, have been severely injured—all because of this man Digger. We also have reason to believe that this individual has targeted four other Fairfax County officers—myself included—and that he's already made several attempts to kill or injure all four of us."

"My God," Kathy Harmon whispered.

"And if some people in the Agency are really involved in all of this," Culver went on, his eyes still drawn to the disturbing photograph on L'Que's desk, "I think they would do just about anything to keep people like you and me from making it public. Anything at all."

"Yes, of course." L'Que nodded calmly. "And these people you mentioned—the ones who are following you, and who may be involved with this Digger—what did you call them?"

"Normally, they'd be called a MOSS team. Several tracking vehicles—usually sedans or small trucks—and at least one concealed antenna van. But this one's a little different because they've added an extra player."

"A rock, perhaps?"

Henry Culver froze.

And then, in that instant, he knew exactly where he had seen the face in that photograph on L'Que's desk. It had been in the view field of his long-lensed camera eighteen years ago, in Wahran, Algeria; just before . . .

"My first son," Lieutenant Colonel Charles L'Que whispered, watching the shock of recognition appear in Henry Culver's eyes. "A likeness, you think?"

Culver could only nod silently as he continued to stare at the framed photograph, knowing now why L'Que's face had also seemed so familiar.

L'Que had been the controller, the one who had been about to receive important information from the young courier—his son. The images appeared once again out of his memories. The youthful face, flushed with excitement, coming into focus, and then suddenly disappearing—ripped away from Culver's viewfinder by a streaking bullet that had left only a gouge in the wall . . . and a bright red pattern of splattered blood.

"Until today, when you came to my house, I knew only your name, not what you looked like," L'Que said. "But Arthur Traynor told me about you . . . explained why you resigned. Please understand, I do not hold you or Arthur responsible for the death of my older son."

Culver nodded his head slowly, remembering how the dark figure had stepped up out of a crouch with the pistol held loosely in his hand, there in the house, and wondering what L'Que would have done in that moment of decision if he'd known the true identity—and the past history—of the intruder who had forgotten to put his badge back on his jacket.

"You have some understanding of forensics, in addition to your photographic skills, Mr. Culver," L'Que went on in a deadly quiet voice. "Tell me, is it ever possible to take fingerprints off a mossy rock?"

Culver shook his head slowly, remembering it all now; the look of surprise and disbelief on both faces—father and son.

"No, it's not."

"So that would make it an excellent weapon of choice, would it not? You understand what I am saying, of course?"

Culver hesitated, and then nodded his head. "You're setting them up. The people who murdered your son."

"The man who squeezed the trigger, and the man who gave the order. Yes, as you say, I am 'setting them up,' " L'Que said, staring directly into Culver's eyes. "Does that concern you greatly?"

Culver paused only a brief moment. "No, it doesn't."

Lieutenant Colonel Charles L'Que smiled—that same cold, hard, and deadly smile.

"Good. So perhaps you will allow me to offer a suggestion."

They made the transfer in the darkness of the garage, moving everything from Kathy Harmon's Cherokee to L'Que's new Bronco. Then, as Culver and Kathy Harmon returned to the living room and watched from the window, a solemn-faced Colonel L'Que backed the mud-splattered and bullet-pocked tan Jeep down the tree-protected expanse of his long driveway with what appeared to be a small, terrified figure huddled down low in the passenger seat.

Five minutes later, Culver cautiously backed L'Que's Bronco down the same driveway and then accelerated down the slush-filled road in the opposite direction, with Kathy Harmon curled up in a fetal position on the new floor mats behind the front seats.

They were less than three miles from L'Que's house when Henry Culver suddenly pulled off the road and stopped next to a telephone booth.

"Why are you stopping?" Kathy Harmon called out nervously from her concealed position.

"I've got to try one more time, just in case."

Moments later, Henry Culver fed a quarter into the slot, punched in a number from memory, and waited for the first ring at the other end.

It wasn't likely that Russelli was still at his house if they'd been looking for him for over an hour, Culver knew, but there was always a chance that Sharon Russelli or one of the kids might know something.

The distant phone rang a second and third time.

Come on, somebody be there.

He let it ring six more times while he was trying to figure out what he was going to do next, and then was just about to hang up when the line clicked and a hesitant voice answered.

"Hello?"

"Hello," Culver almost yelled, "this is . . ."

"Henry!"

"Sharon?" He could barely recognize her voice.

"Please, can you come over here, right away?"

"What's wrong?" Culver's voice caught in his throat.

"I don't know," Sharon Russelli said, sounding as if she was ready to break into tears at any moment. "I just got home, and I can't find the girls, and there's no note, and John . . ."

"Is he there?" Culver interrupted quickly.

"No, he's . . . not here," Sharon Russelli whispered, "but . . ."

"Sharon, what's the matter?"

"I know he's done some strange things before," she whispered, "but never anything like this."

"Like what?" Culver implored, trying to keep his voice calm and even.

"I . . . I think he cut a hole in the middle of our living room floor."

"Sharon, listen to me," Culver rasped, his voice almost frozen in horror, "get out of your house, right now!"

Chapter Forty-one

Saturday, 1645 hours

When Culver slid the Bronco to a tire-screeching stop in the middle of John Russelli's driveway, Patrol Sergeant Jack Hattabaugh and Sharon Russelli were standing outside on the driveway next to a pair of Fairfax County police vehicles— one a blue-and-gray patrol cruiser, and the other an unmarked detective unit. Even from a distance, he could see that she was trembling, but at least she was still alive.

He closed his eyes for a moment, breathing a grateful sigh of relief.

He wasn't there. Thank God for that.

Then he turned and looked at Kathy Harmon.

"I'm not sure what's going to happen here."

"I have a friend who's a criminal attorney," she said, taking his hand. "I can give her a call right now."

Culver squeezed her hand affectionately, and then shook

his head. "Let's try thinking positive for a change. They're either going to take me in or let me go; and either way, there's not a whole lot that I can do about it."

Leaving them in the Bronco, Culver stepped down onto the driveway and found himself wrapped up in the arms of Sharon Russelli. He stroked her head as he felt her shudder against his chest. "Hey, come on, it's going to be all right."

"But I can't find the girls . . . and Tess . . ." she whispered, her voice cracking with emotion.

Culver remained silent, not trusting his voice or his emotions.

"They've been asking me questions about you and John, like they think you did something," she continued to whisper. "And then I . . . heard somebody on the car radio say something about arresting both of you for burglary and murder, and God I don't understand anything . . ."

"I know," Culver said quietly, holding tight the woman he had once dated and, since then, had always loved. "Everything's kinda screwy right now, but we'll get it all figured out."

"But they said . . ."

"Hey, come on," Culver continued to whisper softly against Sharon Russelli's ear, "John and I may be a little nuts at times, but we're not burglars or murderers or psychopaths. You know that."

"But . . ."

"Listen, why don't you go over to the car and sit there with Kathy and Bear, and let us take care of things here, okay?"

He waited until Russelli's shaken wife had joined Kathy Harmon and Bear in the Bronco, and then he turned and walked slowly up to his ex-supervisor who had his hands folded casually across the front of his wide leather gun belt.

Away from the gun. Thanks, Hattabaugh.

"Hi, Sarge."

"For the life of me, Henry, I don't know what I'm ever gonna do with you," the veteran street cop commented in his characteristic gruff voice.

"It's been one hell of a week," Culver agreed.

"I understand you and that lady go back a long way," Hattabaugh said pointedly. "Anything there that might have something to do with you and Russelli?"

Culver blinked, hesitated a moment, and then shook his head. "If there is, I don't know anything about it," he said, meeting Hattabaugh's questioning eyes squarely.

"Okay, I'll take your word for it. But I'll tell you, I'd feel a whole lot better about all this crap if I could find some angle that made sense."

"You and me both. Is that Carpenter's cruiser?"

"Yeah, he's in the house." Hattabaugh gestured with his head as he calmly surveying the criminalist turned street cop that he never had managed to figure out.

"Anybody else?"

Hattabaugh shook his head. "Craven was here for a couple minutes, but he got an emergency call and left. I sent everybody else back out on the street. Told 'em Brad and I could handle things around here, keep an eye on the place in case you showed up."

"You guys could get yourselves into a big pile of shit over this."

"You constantly drive me nuts, Henry, but you haven't managed to disappoint me yet."

"I'll try to keep it that way," Culver promised as they walked into John Russelli's living room. Homicide Detective Bradford Carpenter was standing in the far corner with a shotgun cradled in his folded arms.

Looking casual and relaxed, Culver thought, but he knew better because he'd watched Carpenter stand just that way out on the firing line and then take out twenty-five clay pigeons in a row.

"Hello, Henry," the somber detective said in a neutral voice.

Culver nodded a silent greeting as he walked over to the middle of John Russelli's living room and stared down into the crude hole that had been cut through the carpet and floorboards. "You been down there?" he finally asked.

"Not yet. Figured we'd wait until you got here."

"Yeah, thanks," Culver said drily as he squatted down and stared into the dark hole, wondering if he really had enough nerve to go down into another crawl space. But then he shook that thought off immediately.

Yeah, sure I do. He went in after me.

He tried not to think about the images that he'd finally managed to bring under control. The images . . . and the horrible possibility of what might have happened to Russelli's daughters.

Hattabaugh handed him a flashlight, and he was on his hands and knees, searching around with the narrow beam for some sign of the inevitable wires, when he suddenly realized what he was seeing.

Or rather, what he was *not* seeing.

The ground beneath the crudely cut hole was visibly soft and smooth. The cut-out piece of plywood floorboard was lying where it had dropped, having made a good-sized dent in the soft dirt, and there was a pair of brass hinges lying next to the board that hadn't been made into a trapdoor yet. But it was the things that *weren't* there that had caught Culver's attention.

No footprints and no scrape marks. How the hell . . . ?

Then he looked closely at the curved flap of carpet that dangled down into the hole, and he suddenly knew how.

"Look at this," Culver said, rubbing his fingers along the edge of the carpet. "See how the hole in the carpet is just a little bit bigger than the hole through the plywood?"

"Yeah, so . . . hey, wait a minute, that can't be right," Hattabaugh exclaimed.

Culver nodded. "Exactly. Whoever did this went in through the top, but probably wanted to make it look like a crawl space entry, like the trapdoor in Radlick's closet."

"Russelli?" Carpenter asked.

"I don't know, Carp. I honest to God don't know what to

think anymore," Culver said as he stood up and walked toward the sliding glass door that led out into the backyard.

"Hey, where're you going?" Carpenter demanded, suddenly alert and suspicious.

"Outside. I want to check something."

Stepping out onto the concrete patio—and followed immediately by Carpenter and Hattabaugh—Culver looked around in John Russelli's backyard, tapping the heavy flashlight against the side of his leg as he eyed the monstrous blue plywood castle and the icy concrete walkway that led along side the house.

Okay, Stewart, so I get a pair of baby-sitters instead of a jail cell. That's fair, he nodded to himself as he cautiously started to follow the slippery concrete walkway. *Maybe Russelli really is a nutcase after all, and I don't know what I'm looking for anyway, so . . .*

Oh shit.

The icy slush had covered most of it, but the bright reddish brown stains were still visible. Drag marks that led to the dog door flap that Russelli had cut in the side of his house. And an opened plastic container of chocolate chip cookies lying in the snow.

Oh no.

Culver got down on his hands and knees in the slush and tried to pull the door flap open enough so that he could see inside, but his bruised ribs still hurt too bad to twist around like that. So, instead, he braced his legs against the wall, pulled the thin aluminum doorframe loose with a savage growl, and then used the leverage of his shoes against a sprinkler head to jam his two arms and his head into the hole.

For almost ten seconds, Henry Culver just lay there on the icy concrete, mute and immobile, until Jack Hattabaugh couldn't stand it any longer.

"Henry?"

"Pull me out." Culver's muffled voice was barely audible.

Hattabaugh and Carpenter were down on the slippery wet concrete instantly, yanking at Culver's legs and belt until they finally managed to get his shoulders loose from the tight-fitting doorframe. Only then did they see the bloody cloth bundle that he held in his arms.

"What . . . ?" Hattabaugh started to ask, but then Culver opened the wrapped bundle up and they all saw it.

"Ocha," Culver said in a soft, whispery voice as he came up to his knees and then stared down at the brown bloody form. "Russelli's dog."

"Did he have another one?" Carpenter asked quietly, and then they all looked up to see the small lifeless body of Nori the dachshund hanging from one of the rear parapets of Russelli's huge blue castle.

In the tightly secured confines of Elliott Parkinson's sixth floor office, and for the first time that J. Winston Weathersby, his special assistant, could remember in the past six months, the CIA Operations chief finally smiled.

"They found him," he whispered as he hung up the phone, making a conscious effort to conceal the relief that threatened to overpower his tightly controlled mask of professional confidence and control. "Everything is in place now."

"What does that mean?" Weathersby asked cautiously

"It means that we've won," Parkinson said with a look of calm assurance on his face.

"Are you certain of that," the director of the Central Intelligence Agency demanded.

"Yes."

"What about track-backs?"

"The end phase is a closed loop," Parkinson said reassuringly. "By the time it's over, all loose ends will have been clipped, and all outside links severed. There will be no possibility of a track-back to the Agency."

"None?"

"Absolutely none."

"How can you be sure?" the director pressed, nervous and impatient now because he sensed that it might be too late to change sides.

"Because dead men don't testify before congressional committees," Parkinson said calmly. "And also because this time, I'm going to handle the end phase myself."

"He wants to talk with you," Hattabaugh said, handing Culver the phone.

"This is Culver."

"Russelli got a letter today from Paul Radlick. It was mailed to the station." Stewart said without preamble.

After several moments of dead silence at the other end of the line, Stewart said: "You still there?"

"Yeah, I'm here."

"It was postmarked Thursday," Stewart went on. "You want to know what it says?"

"Sure, why not," Culver said, not really giving a damn that they'd opened his partner's mail as part of their investigation. He just wanted to hit back at something. He'd already destroyed Hattabaugh's flashlight by pounding it into the concrete, and that hadn't helped at all.

That bastard, he thought. *That goddamned, pale-eyed, cold-hearted bastard!*

" 'My client wants his computer back,' " Stewart recited. " 'Important that I talk with you immediately. Paul.' "

Stewart paused for a moment. "I assume he's talking about Digger. Does any of that mean anything to you?"

"No."

"You and Russelli searched his place," the Homicide supervisor reminded.

"Al, if there was anything that had even *looked* like a computer in that goddamned apartment, I would have *seen* it, and I would have taken it, and I would have documented the seizure in my report," Culver said heatedly.

Stewart sighed. "All right, I believe you, but that doesn't resolve the basic issue."

"Yeah, tell me about it."

"One more thing. Jim Waldrip from the coroner's lab's been trying to get hold of you."

"Okay, I know about that. I'll give him a call." And then, after a moment: "I take it I'm not under arrest yet?"

"Carpenter wants to give you some more rope, in spite of his better judgment," Stewart said. "And Hattabaugh's backing you up one hundred percent."

"What's Craven going to say about that?"

"I don't really care what that sniveling little shithead thinks," Stewart growled. "What's the deal on those plastic wads?"

"I caught the end of Russelli's sawed-off on a nail when I was under Radlick's house," Culver explained. "That had to have torn up all those metal burrs in the end of the barrel, so I don't see how any plastic wadding or shot-cups fired through that barrel afterward could possibly match wadding fired before I went down in that hole."

Stewart was silent for several seconds.

"We want to believe in you, Henry. I really do. But it doesn't look good right now. I'll give it to you straight. You're right out on the edge, and it's a long way down. Keep that in mind."

"I know," Culver said. "Appreciate it, Al. I'll talk to you later."

He hung up the phone and then dialed the coroner's office.

"Hi, Ginny, this is Henry Culver," he said quickly. "Could you hook me in to Jim? Yeah, thanks."

"Waldrip."

"I hear you've been trying to track me down."

"Henry Culver, just the man I wanted to talk to. Hold on a moment while I shut my door." Culver heard the soft click of a door lock being engaged, then the forensic pathologist was back on the phone.

"Are you in a place where you can talk?"

"Yeah, sort of."

"Okay, I understand. Listen, I don't know what the hell's going on around your shop, but I just had two of your detectives and an FBI agent poking through our lab about an hour ago asking a whole bunch of very pointed questions."

"About me?"

"Uh-huh."

"They tell you what was going on?"

"No, but I've been in this business for almost thirty years now, so I can usually read between the lines of bullshit. In this case, I don't like what I'm reading."

"Me neither. Would it help if I told you it's all bogus?"

"Yes, as a matter of fact it would."

"Tell you what, if I'm feeding you a line, ask the judge to sentence me to morgue cleanup for the next thirty years. How's that?"

"Good enough for me," Jim Waldrip replied. "You want to know whose hand you dropped off today?"

"Sure, why not. Can't make my day much worse than it already is."

"I wouldn't bet on that," Waldrip said. "I still don't know his name, but you guys have him listed in your print files as John Doe Thirty-three."

Culver almost dropped the phone.

"What did you say?"

"I take it that means something to you?"

"He's dead? You're sure?"

"Most of the body parts I get in here are from dead people, Henry. That's usually how it works. And if he *isn't* dead after getting his hand chewed off like that, I'd say he's in a *real* world of hurt."

"Are you sure?"

"You mean about the chewing-off part? Oh yeah, you could see . . ."

"No, I mean are you're sure about the ID?"

"I stopped at fifteen matching points on each of the five fingers, Henry. I guess I could have gone for thirty, but it would have taken me an extra five minutes."

"Any idea about how long?"

"Not really. Been awful cold around here the last couple of weeks, so it's kinda hard to say. I'd say at least twenty-four hours at a minimum, maybe a week at the outside. But the way that hand was chewed, you'd better get a move on if you want to find much more of the body. Lot of hungry critters out there looking for something to eat this time of the year."

Shit, Russelli, you really did make a deal with him, didn't you? And then you cut him out of it.

"You going to tell me what all this is about someday?" Waldrip asked when Culver didn't say anything for several long moments.

"You'll be one of the first to know, Doc," Culver promised. "Talk to you later." Then he hung up the phone and looked over at Hattabaugh and Carpenter.

"I think we've got a problem."

Moments after the Bronco and the two police vehicles took off in two separate directions from John Russelli's house, one of the lab technicians working for Dr. Jim Waldrip looked up from his stereo microscope.

"Hey, Jim, was that Henry Culver you were just talking to?"

"Yeah, what about it?"

"Take a look at what I've got here."

Jim Waldrip looked under the scope for a few seconds, and then brought his head up, his tired eyes blinking in confusion.

"That artery's clean cut."

"Right," the lab technician nodded. "Don't know if it makes any difference . . ." he started to say, but Waldrip was already reaching for the phone on his desk.

Chapter Forty-two

Saturday, 1730 hours

Henry Culver turned onto New Landing, and then drove Colonel Charles L'Que's Bronco down the icy, two-lane road as fast as he dared with Bradford Carpenter's detective unit following close behind. Then, just before the turnoff to Kathy Harmon's house, he suddenly tapped at his brakes, and then made a sharp right-hand turn up a long narrow gravel road.

"Wait, this isn't my driveway!" Kathy Harmon yelled as the Bronco bounced and slid and roared up the rough incline.

"I know," Culver said, "but I went this way to your house last night. Figure if I take the same path, I've got a better chance of finding the body, especially with Bear along to help. You can stay in the car, and then we'll call your neighbor and pick up Lisa."

"Okay." Kathy Harmon nodded.

"Which reminds me, you think the people who live up here are going to get upset if we park another car in their driveway?"

"Don't worry about him. He's kind of a freaky little guy anyway. I hardly ever see him. Which is probably a good thing because those pale blue eyes of his really give me the creeps."

Henry Culver jammed on his brakes so hard that the normally stable four-wheel drive vehicle almost went off the side of the road. He started to say something, and then he and Kathy Harmon were knocked forward into the steering wheel and front dash when Bradford Carpenter's detective unit slammed into the back end of the Bronco's solid trailer hitch.

Out of control, the unmarked detective vehicle slid backward and sideways in the mud until the left rear wheel finally dropped into the runoff ditch and brought the vehicle to a sudden stop about thirty feet down the driveway, effectively blocking the road.

"*Jesus Christ, Henry!*" Carpenter yelled out through his open window, but Culver had already shaken off the impact and had grabbed Kathy Harmon by the shoulders.

"What did you say?"

"I said his blue eyes give me the creeps," Kathy Harmon whispered. "What's the matter with that?"

"No, you said *pale* blue. Which is it, regular blue or light blue?"

"They're a real light blue color, almost white."

"Kathy, this neighbor of yours," Culver said, trying to force himself to remain calm, "is he about thirty-five years old, five-eight, maybe 150 pounds, light brown hair, pale complexion?"

Kathy Harmon nodded her head. "That sounds pretty close, but how'd you know that? I thought you said there wasn't anybody home here last night?"

"There wasn't," Culver growled as he twisted around to reach for the door handle.

Bradford Carpenter had worked his way out of his severely damaged vehicle and was walking unsteadily up the driveway when Henry Culver burst out of the Bronco and came running and slipping downhill toward the disabled unit.

"*Carp, do you still have that mug shot of Digger?*" Culver called out over his shoulder as he pulled open the driver's side door of the marked vehicle.

"Yeah, sure, in my briefcase," Carpenter said, turning around and watching in confusion as Henry Culver rummaged around in the front seat of the detective unit and then finally reemerged with a small three-by-five photograph in his hand.

Brushing past Carpenter again, Culver staggered uphill to the Bronco, pulled open the front passenger side door, and then shoved the mug photo into Kathy Harmon's hands.

"Is that him?" he gasped, almost out of breath and starting to shiver from the cold in his torn light patrol jacket.

"Who, my neighbor? Yes, that's him. What is he, some kind of criminal?" Kathy Harmon asked, staring at the Fairfax County Police Department arrest data displayed under the front and profile shots of the familiar face.

"This is the guy I've been telling you about. John Doe Thirty-three, a.k.a. Digger."

"My *neighbor?*"

Culver shook his head in disgust because he'd never even *thought* about such a possibility. "Christ, no wonder he was using you. You're right in his goddamned backyard."

"But . . ." Kathy Harmon started to say as she stepped out of the Bronco, but then she was almost knocked to the ground as Bear came over the front seat, shouldered her out of the way, leaped down to the ground, and then immediately began sniffing around in the nearby bushes.

"Bear, come back here!" Kathy Harmon yelled, running toward her dog as Culver turned around to find Carpenter staring at him from about twenty feet away.

"Carp!" he yelled to the still mildly stunned and now thoroughly confused officer, "get on the radio to Stewart and Hattabaugh. Tell them we've found Digger's house. Hurry!"

Bradford Carpenter blinked in surprise, turned his head to stare at the old wooden house less than fifty yards away up the road for a brief moment, and then turned and ran for his vehicle. Culver started after him, and then he heard Kathy Harmon scream.

"Bear!"

Culver looked back up the hill, saw the black shepherd charge up the slushy driveway with Kathy Harmon scrambling forward in a futile effort to catch up, and then instinctively drew his .357 as he turned back toward Carpenter's damaged cruiser.

"Carp!"

"Radio's out!" the Homicide detective shouted, his head

coming up over the roof of his vehicle. "Crash must have knocked something loose!"

"Oh Christ," Culver whispered, turning back around to see Kathy Harmon stumbling up to the top of the driveway in pursuit of her dog. "Forget the radio and grab the shotgun!" he yelled, and then started running up the long, slushy driveway after her.

When he and Carpenter finally reached the top of the driveway, neither Kathy Harmon nor the dog were anywhere to be seen.

"I thought you said he was dead?" the overweight detective gasped, working to catch his breath.

"Yeah, that's what Jim Waldrip from the coroner's office said," Culver said through gasping breaths, bent over with his hands on his knees, his chest heaving as he tried to keep his eyes on the house, the shed that was separated from the house by about fifty feet, and the two cars—the Honda Accord and the old pickup that hadn't moved since he'd last been here because the snow and slush around the tires hadn't been disturbed. "But *somebody's* been sending messages through his computer network, and shotgunning burglars, and setting off bombs."

Jesus, what a spooky goddamn place, he thought as he finally started to get his breathing back under control, and then stared up at the old two-story wooden structure. *No wonder your mind was all screwed up, you crazy bastard.*

"You really think Russelli's involved in all of this?" Carpenter asked, continuing to stare at Digger's house.

"I don't know. It doesn't make any sense—not with those kids of his missing, and all that shit with his dogs. That's not John Russelli. Or at least not the John Russelli I know."

"Then we've got to make a decision about something right now," Carpenter said firmly.

"What's that?"

"What you and I do if he pops up with that sawed-off?"

Culver hesitated for a long moment. "I'll tell you what," he finally said, turning his head to stare directly in Bradford

Carpenter's eyes, "as far as I'm concerned, if we see him out here, and he aims that thing at either one of us, then I don't know the guy anymore."

Carpenter nodded. "Fair enough."

Then Culver remembered why they'd run up the hill in the first place. "Hey, which way did those two go?"

Carpenter motioned off to his left. "Their tracks went off in the woods over there, but there's two other sets of prints that come around from the back of the house to the front porch. Looks like a couple of heavyweights wearing work boots," the detective added. "Russelli wears boots like that."

"Yeah, I know," Culver said, staring uneasily over at the house for a long moment, and then looking around at the forested front yard. It was only then that he realized that Carpenter had stepped back slightly so that his shotgun could cover all the angles.

Including me.

Culver blinked in surprise for a moment, and then he shrugged inwardly.

Yeah, and I don't blame you one bit, Carp. One of those sets of footprints could be Russelli's; and if I was in your position, I'm not sure I'd trust me either.

"Okay, let's . . ." he started to say, and then they both saw and heard Kathy Harmon, yelling and waving her arms over by the shed.

Culver ran down the driveway toward the shed with Carpenter close behind. When they got there, they found Kathy Harmon standing in front of an eighteen-inch-diameter hole that had been crudely dug into the steeply sloped hillside. The digging had exposed the rough edge of a corrugated aluminum pipe that was about two feet in diameter, and Culver could see several large dog prints in the semifrozen mud.

"I saw him," Kathy Harmon gasped. "His head was sticking out through a hole here, and Bear saw him and started digging, making the hole bigger, and then he went in there after him."

"Saw who?"

"Spanky. He must have been digging all over around here. Look, you can see all the holes. This whole place must be one big tunnel system." Kathy Harmon pointed out at least a half dozen gopherlike holes scattered across the wide hilly landscape that surrounded the house and driveway.

Digger. Culver nodded to himself as he turned his attention back to the metal-lined hole that had been exposed by Bear's furious digging. *So that's why you liked that name. Couldn't stand to be out in the light where people could see you, so you had to go underground. You poor sick bastard.*

"Shit, now what the hell do we do?" Carpenter growled.

"One option is for one of us to stay here and watch the house, and this hole," Culver suggested, "while the other guy goes to Kathy's house and uses her phone to get us some backup."

"Or we could both go," Carpenter said as he looked uneasily over toward Kathy Harmon's distant house, remembering Stewart's direct order not to let Culver out of his sight.

"Fine by me," Culver agreed, not the least bit interested in exploring Digger's underground warren of tunnels without some serious backup.

"But we can't leave until Bear and Spanky come back out," Kathy Harmon protested.

"Kathy, we may have at least one homicidal maniac running around loose out here," Culver said impatiently. "The evidence is probably in that house, and if it is, we're going to need some help. We can't just stand around this hole all day and wait for a goddamned dog!"

"I'm not leaving here without him," she said, her eyes flashing dangerously.

"Well then, go get him for Christ's sake!" Culver exploded.

"All right, I will!" Kathy Harmon yelled, shoving Culver into Carpenter, dropping down to her knees in the slushy cold mud, and then scrambling forward into the narrow hole before either of the two investigators could regain their footing.

"Kathy!" Culver dived to his hands and knees and yelled down into the echoing tunnel opening, and then heard only the rapidly receding sounds of her shoes scraping against the corrugated metal surface.

"*Shit!*" he screamed in frustration, slamming his empty fist into the wet ground. Then he looked back up at Carpenter.

"I've got to go in after her," he said with a stricken look on his face. "We can't leave her in there by herself."

Carpenter nodded. "The car won't start. I'm going to have to take the Bronco, find a telephone." But then he looked back down the road and cursed. "Shit, there isn't enough room to get through down there. Goddamn runoff ditches are like a couple of moats."

"Her house is right over there, straight through the trees," Culver said, scrambling to his feet and pointing off into the woods with a muddy and half-frozen hand. "You can just see the roofline by that big pine."

"Okay." Carpenter nodded. "You want this?" He held out the heavy twelve-gage shotgun.

"No thanks, already tried that once," Culver said as he got back down on his hands and knees in the cold slush and peered into the tunnel opening. He vaguely understood that Carpenter had offered the weapon as a symbol of trust, but he wasn't interested in that sort of thing right now because he had other things on his mind.

"I can use a flashlight, though," Culver called out over his shoulder. "Can you get me that equipment bag in the back of the Bronco?"

Christ, it was bad enough under Radlick's house, but this is his goddamned playground, he thought as he stared into the narrow darkness of the tunnel, waiting for Carpenter to return with his bag.

"Watch yourself down there, Henry," Carpenter cautioned as he handed Culver the heavy tote bag that was filled with a wide assortment of electronic gear in addition to a heavy four-cell flashlight.

"Don't worry," Culver said as he pulled more of the dirt away from the narrow hole, pulled the .357 out of his shoulder holster and set it in the open equipment bag, removed the flashlight, and then got down flat on his stomach and started to work himself into the corrugated metal tunnel, "I intend to."

Wider in the shoulders than Kathy Harmon, Culver had to pull and twist and shove and grunt to work himself through the cold, narrow, confining tunnel as he tried to follow the echoing sounds of the determined young woman. He could hear her in the distance, yelling and cursing and scraping against the corrugated metal in her single-minded effort to catch up with her dog.

Because the terror of Paul Radlick's crawl space was still fresh in his mind, Culver used his equipment bag as a focal point, concentrating on pushing it forward a few inches at a time in order to block out the claustrophobic fears that kept screaming that he was going to get lost, or get stuck, or that the air was beginning to turn foul.

Plenty of air, and you're not going to get stuck because it's all the same diameter, and it doesn't matter if you do get lost because there can't be that *much pipe down here.*

Yeah, but . . .

Stop whining, for Christ's sake. You're just pissed because she cares more about that damned dog than she does you.

That last thought caused Culver to blink his eyes, and shake his head, and wonder where the hell *that* had come from. But before he could dwell on anything involving a relationship with Kathy Harmon, the glary beam of his flashlight revealed another pair of branching black holes.

He'd already run into three "Y"s in Digger's underground warren, and he was hesitating now at the fourth, trying to decide which of the scraping sounds in the narrow tubes sounded less like an echo, when he heard Kathy Harmon cry out, "Oh my god . . . BEAR!"

Twisting himself into the right-hand tunnel, Culver thrust his shoulders against the tightly confining metal, heaved with the toes of his rubber-soled shoes, and pulled at the slippery corrugated surface with the fingertips of one hand, while trying to hold onto the flashlight and push the heavy bag forward with the other, until all of a sudden he came to a right angle turn that put him at the entrance to what—in comparison—seemed to be a huge, lighted twelve-by-thirty-foot underground room.

Lunging forward, headfirst, with a final push of his feet, Culver dropped about three feet to the floor of the lighted underground room that seemed to be filled with—*what? Computer furniture? Electronics? More tunnels?*—cushioning the equipment bag with one arm, and then scrambling for the zipper opening and twisting around with the .357 in his right hand when he heard a sudden scraping sound to his left.

"Henry!"

"Christ, I ought to strangle you," Culver gasped as he staggered to his feet and then found himself caught up in the strong hugging arms of Kathy Harmon.

"I thought you were . . ."

"Yeah, I know. Me too," Culver said shakily, trying to control his breathing as he held her tight against his heaving chest for a long moment. But then he remembered why he had gone into the tunnel in the first place, and started looking around the low-ceilinged room.

"Where'd those damn animals of yours go?" he demanded, still breathing heavily as his eyes took in the room, noting the presence of five more corrugated tube openings, each framed with an open, heavy-gage wire grid door that stood about three feet off the ground—*probably to keep curious animals out,* Culver thought—and three rough-cut wooden doors leading off to . . . somewhere.

His immediate impression was that the room looked like some combination between a sewer pipe junction and a crude version of an underground military command center.

At least half of the room was filled with computer furniture, wall-mounted TV monitors, shelves of electronic equipment. On the far wall, there was a huge bulletin board with about thirty Polaroid pictures tacked to the cork surface.

Christ, what is this place?

"Spanky jumped into that tunnel over there," Kathy Harmon whispered, pointing with her hand at one of the open grill tunnels on the opposite wall, "and Bear went in after him. They were too fast, I couldn't stop them.

Damn you, Bear!" she screamed suddenly, and a distant answering bark echoed back into the small room.

"That make you feel better?" Culver asked, wincing from the impact on his eardrums.

"No."

"Then don't do it again. You're liable to attract the wrong kind of attention."

"But . . ."

"Look, let's just let them run around in there for a while, get it out of their systems. That'll give us a chance to look around and see what we've got down here."

And give me a chance to get my head straight, and start thinking, Culver told himself.

He walked cautiously over to the computer table, noting the presence of a huge controller board with dozens of knobs, dials, and switches, and two computers—one an older desktop model and the other one of the new color portables. Then he turned to look at the Polaroid photos on the bulletin board, and froze.

"What are those . . . oh my God," Kathy Harmon whispered.

"Souvenirs," Culver said, almost able to feel feeling his crime scene hardened mind shift into its indifferent, protective mode as he examined each of the photographs. Most of them were close-up shots of animals—dogs and cats—their faces caught in a rictus of terror. The last seven, however, were of people.

Culver recognized the Kostermanns immediately, and Paul and Doreen Radlick, but he was still trying to identify the face of the man wrapped tightly in what appeared to be long strips of white nylon strapping tape when Kathy Harmon grabbed at his arm.

"But why . . . the animals?" she whispered, her face ashen with horror, disbelief, and disgust.

"We don't know. He seemed to have a thing about other people's pets," Culver said, reaching out and removing the photo of the unidentified man, turning it over and reading the name that was crudely printed on the back.

Rudder?

Culver blinked his eyes as more of the pieces dropped into place.

Rudder and Forecastle? Parts of an old wooden sailing ship . . . and unifying code names for some kind of operation?

A complex operation, starting to come apart.

Jesus, Culver thought, remembering the nervous expression on young Forecastle's face in that small, concealed Library of Congress meeting room. *No wonder you were pushing so hard. You were afraid he was after you, too.*

"Okay," Culver said as he put the horrible picture of Alberto Paz back up on the bulletin board and then turned to the table bearing the complex control board and the computers, "let's see if we can figure out what he's been doing down here."

Ten minutes later, Culver sat in front of the wall-length table with the .357 on the Formica top and his equipment bag lying on the dirt floor next to his left leg, surrounded by maps, gory Polaroids, lists of names and codes, radio frequency settings, and racks of electronic transmitters, receivers, telephones, and color monitors.

After making one last visual check, to make sure he had the sequences right, he reached up over his head and snapped on a single wide switch.

Instantly, a mild electric hum filled the room as the desktop and portable computer monitors glowed into life with a pair of simultaneous sharp beeps, causing Culver to smile with a sense of pride and accomplishment at having figured out the control board. ·

Nice, very nice.

He brushed his hands over the smoothly functioning controls, noting the extensive use of heavy-duty bearings and seals and connectors. It was only then that he noticed that one of the photo albums from the Kostermann trial was lying on the table top under several computer manuals.

Probably Radlick's copy.

Some of the images started to surface again, enhanced by the earthy, musty smell of the underground room, and he had to fight to force them back down.

Guy had a nice feel for equipment, Culver thought, numbed by the realization of how thoroughly he was beginning to understand Digger . . . and how much alike they had been in so many ways. *Might have had some interesting conversations. Too bad he was such a goddamned pervert.*

Confident now, because he was also starting to understand what Digger had been trying to do, Culver reached up and snapped on a second similar switch, and then nodded his head with satisfaction as the twelve small overhead video camera monitors clicked into life simultaneously, displaying a wide diversity of black-and-white scenes that were mostly outdoors.

He was still trying to figure out how the microphone attached to the control board functioned when he saw Kathy Harmon's hand reach over his shoulder toward the thick photo album.

"What's this?" Kathy Harmon asked, starting to pull the album out from under a pile of computer manuals when Culver put a restraining hand on her arm.

"Don't," he warned. "Unless you want to risk losing your breakfast down here, don't even *think* about looking at those pictures."

"That bad?" she whispered, slowly drawing her hand back.

"No, worse. Much worse."

"My God, what . . . was he?"

"I don't know, we never did figure that out," Culver shrugged as he turned his attention to the monitor screen for the desktop computer that was flashing a C> sign at the upper left hand corner. Intent on finding out what was in Digger's computer, he typed in DIR, hit the enter key, and then watched a message flash up on the screen:

INSERT CARD OR ENTER PASSWORD

"What card?" Kathy Harmon asked, but Culver was already reaching into the breast pocket of his patrol jacket for the plastic bag that he'd checked out from the Fairfax County Police Evidence & Property Storage Yard—the bag containing the Mobil credit card that bore the name of Molly Hunsacker.

There was a stand-alone device with a cable attachment to the desktop computer and a slot that looked the right size and shape to receive a plastic credit card, but Culver hesitated because he had no idea what information was recorded in the magnetic strip on Molly-the-Hun's card. And he wasn't about to try to find out the easy way, because he'd seen enough of Digger's traps by now to know that there had to be a protective circuit in the works somewhere.

Instead, he reached for the handset of the telephone on the other side of the computer, smiled when he received a dial tone, and then dialed a long-memorized number that was answered on the second ring.

"Hello?"

Culver recognized the cautious voice of Sci-Tech Operative R.C. Cohen immediately.

"You find anything?" Culver asked.

"Henry? Where the hell are you?"

"I found the guy's playground," Culver replied, and then went on to describe the layout of Digger's communications center, and his suspicions about Molly Hunsacker's Mobil card.

"Put that card back in your pocket and keep it there," Cohen advised. "Whoever programmed those things knows what he's doing. He's got a lot of code packed into those magnetized strips. Most of it's pretty standard—automated bank teller stuff—but there are a couple of lines that might be a command sequence for a pair of relay switches. I'd need to see the programming in that computer to be sure, but I think you've got a mouse trap."

"What about the computer itself?" Culver asked, "any ideas on the access code?"

"I think so."

"What do you mean, you *think*. Come on, R.C."

"Your friend apparently knows quite a bit about automated teller systems, but not so much about bank computers," the tech operative explained. "For example, he apparently didn't know that the bank computer maintains a rotary memory of all passwords used to access the system. Keeps the last five thousand entries for reference."

"Yeah, so?"

"As best I can tell, the access password for the programming computer—presumably the one you're using—used to be 'PIPELINE,' but just recently, it was changed to 'FOOTPRINT.' "

"Footprint? One word?"

"Uh-huh. But with two 'T's in the middle. Nice way to throw off a dictionary search."

"I assume that means you've been wandering around in the bank's data files?"

"Of course. And you want to guess what I found?"

"A whole bunch of money with my name on it?"

"Among others. Too bad you didn't know the access code, Henry. You'd have made a nice suspect."

"Maybe I used my own Mobil card to make the deposits," Culver suggested.

" 'Fraid not. All those deposits for you and Russelli were actually transfers of funds, made through the programming computer, not a teller's window."

"Shouldn't somebody at that bank be getting suspicious by now, with all that unauthorized traffic?"

"Not when it involves perfectly good money." The Sci-Tech operative chuckled, and then turned serious. "Listen, Henry, this isn't a fake deal. From what I can see, a lot of people have been putting a whole lot of very real money into the system using those cards. All your programmer's been doing is relocating the money into different accounts, yours included. As long as everything balances out, there's no reason for the bank to ever look."

"You mind explaining all that to somebody who cares?"

"For a price, sure, but . . . uh-oh, hold it, I've got company. Let me call you back. Gimme a number."

Culver quickly read off the number on the telephone, and then hung up after the line went dead.

"Now what?" Kathy Harmon asked.

"Why don't you get back into that tunnel for a minute," Culver suggested as he adjusted his chair so that he was sitting squarely in front of the flashing screen. "Just in case."

He waited until Kathy Harmon had pulled herself back into the protective corrugated metal tubing, and then he typed in the word FOOTTPRINT, hit the enter key, and watched the screen come alive.

PIPELINE MENU:

A: BANK ACCOUNTS
B: BURGLARS
C: COPS
D: CULVER
E: FORECASTLE
F: GAUSS
G: HÄMMERCHOV
H: L'QUE
I: QUINZIO
J: RUDDER
K: RUSSELLI

L: SEA GLASS
M: SITES
N: TOPCASTLE
O: TRAPS
P: TUNNEL MAPS
Q: CHANGE ACCESS CODE

Forecastle, Rudder, and . . . Topcastle? What's a topcastle? The main control deck of an old wooden sailing ship. The head guy. Parkinson?

"Is it okay?" Kathy Harmon asked.

"Yeah, sure, come on out," Culver said, thinking *What the hell's sea glass,* as he hit the "L" key and watched the first lines of text appear on the screen. Then he hit the "N" key, and his eyes flashed first on the designation: 'Associate Director—Operations' . . . and then on the color photo image of Elliott Parkinson in the right-hand corner of the screen.

Okay, now I'm starting to understand. Henry Culver nodded to himself, lost in the fascination of finally understanding the elements of Digger's viciously clever plan when Kathy Harmon's voice caught his attention.

"Somebody's coming!"

"Where?" Culver demanded, swinging his head around as he grabbed for the Smith & Wesson.

"On monitor number seven. Look."

The video camera sending a signal to the monitor identified with a large numeral seven was focused on the access road to Digger's house, which gave Culver an excellent view of the sedan that was slowly moving up the driveway. As he watched, the sedan came to a slow stop behind Carpenter's damaged cruiser.

After searching hurriedly around the control board, Culver found the right selector switch and the control knobs, and then quickly zoomed the camera lens in on the windshield—and the familiar face in the front passenger seat. The face that he'd seen standing next to Russelli and Forecastle outside that warehouse . . . and finally identified only moments ago on Digger's computer monitor.

Hi, Parkinson. Thought you might show up around here, you bastard. And who's that behind you? Your little buddy Forecastle. Culver smiled.

"Who are they?" Kathy Harmon asked.

"Remember those guys we saw at the warehouse?"

"Oh."

"The one in the front passenger seat is a CIA type who goes by the code name of Topcastle. We want to stay the hell away from him if at all possible," Culver said. "But I don't think he and his friends are going to be too anxious to get their suits dirty crawling around through these tunnels, so let's see what else we can find."

Looking up at the monitor screens, Culver quickly determined that two of the cameras were mounted somewhere in a house—*presumably the one up top,* he told himself—and the other ten were set to cover specific fields of view in and around the yard.

"Is there an air conditioner in this place? It's really starting to get warm down here," Kathy Harmon whispered as she took off her jacket.

"Haven't found one so far, but I'll keep looking. Let's see what we get with the first camera," Culver said, moving the selector switch to "1" and then reaching for the control knobs.

He had panned across approximately half of what appeared to be a large dusty den when the overhead monitor suddenly scanned past a large blurry face.

Blinking in confusion at what he *thought* he'd seen, Culver stopped the pan, searched the control board again, found the focus adjustment, scanned back and then looked up.

Oh Jesus, no.

The cold, hard, bloodied face of Detective Sergeant John Russelli stared up at the moving camera.

Henry Culver was so shocked to see Russelli's face that he never heard one of the wooden wall doors mounted in the back wall start to swing open.

"Goddamn it," Culver snarled as he spun around in the chair and reached for the computer keyboard again, brought up the PIPELINE menu, hit the "Q" key, entered in a seven-letter word twice, and then hit the "A" key.

"What are you doing?" Kathy Harmon asked nervously.

"I'm going to even things up a little bit," Culver muttered, his fingers flying across the keys as he brought up submenu after submenu in the Bank Accounts directory, searching for the one program that would do what he wanted. "Digger used this computer to move the money around, so he probably had some way of taking it out. See how they like it when all those accounts read zero."

"NO!"

"What . . . ?" Culver started to turn around, and then the explosive roar of a twelve-gage shotgun sent him tumbling out of the chair and onto the hard dirt floor that seemed to melt away, and then he was falling and falling . . .

Chapter Forty-three

Saturday, 1830 hours

Somewhere in the back of his head, Culver thought he could hear people screaming, cage doors rattling, and a dog barking and snarling, but he couldn't be sure because the noises kept drifting in and out before he could get his blurred mind to focus on any one source.

Something else was demanding his attention—something that seemed to be white and hot—but he didn't know what that was either, so he ignored it. And eventually, it went away too, leaving him to drift alone in the clamorous darkness for some indeterminate time . . . until somewhere, a voice yelled out.

"Shut up!"

Which seemed to stop the screaming, but had absolutely no effect on the rattling and barking and snarling. And then, suddenly, the other thing that had been demanding his attention returned, and this time it definitely *was* white and hot and burning.

"Culver?" the yelling voice queried.

Henry Culver groaned.

"Come on, Culver, wake up. I need to talk to you."

He felt a jarring impact against his foot, and heard another voice screaming *"Leave him alone!"*

A loud slapping sound and a cry of pain set the dog off into a frenzy of barking, snarling and cage door rattling as something heavy fell against Culver's chest—which caused *him* to scream, because it felt like somebody had turned the white-hot burner all the way up to fry.

In the time it took for the agonizing pain to subside to something bearable, Culver thought he heard the sound of cloth being torn. Then a pair of gentle hands were brushing away the glass fragments, and unbuttoning his shirt, and pressing something cool and clean against his right arm and shoulder as he fought against the growing nausea, and tried to get his trembling limbs and his breathing back under control.

Then he heard the voice growl: "Get away from him, right now!"

Henry Culver blinked his eyes open and stared up at the man whom he now realized had caused them all so much grief and pain.

"Hi, Gauss," Culver rasped, trying very hard now not to move because the entire right side of his body seemed to be on the verge of bursting into flames, and any movement at all . . .

"Hello, Henry," the balding, heavyset criminalist said, squatting down next to him and smiling pleasantly. "I hate to bother you right now, but I've got a bit of a problem."

"You've got a lot of problems, Gauss," Culver mumbled.

"Start with, you're a lousy shot and a traitor all rolled into one."

"Now, now, let's not be bitter," Theodore Gauss chided as he maliciously jabbed the barrel of the pump shotgun at Henry Culver's torn shoulder, causing Culver to gasp in agony.

"You bastard," Kathy Harmon hissed through bloodied lips, but stayed backed up against the dirt wall behind Culver's head by the threat of the deadly shotgun. But there was one other individual in the small underground room who wasn't the least bit intimidated by Gauss or his shotgun.

"Leave him alone, you fat bag of shit!" a younger, feminine voice screamed from the opposite side of the room.

Culver started to laugh, and then grimaced in pain as he recognized the furious voice of one of John Russelli's daughters. Michelle Russelli was so much like her aggressive father (while her identical twin sister Martine was so much more like their gentle, easygoing mother) that Culver had always been able to tell the twins apart simply by their body language.

Not to mention her language, period. He smiled to himself, relieved to discover that she was alive. *That's the way, Michelle, you tell him.*

"Looks to me like you're in serious need of a doctor, Henry," Gauss said, ignoring all of the ruckus in the background. "Maybe we can make ourselves a deal."

"The deal's simple," Culver whispered, swallowing back the nausea. "You're under arrest."

"What?" Gauss looked like he was going to burst out laughing.

"You have the right to remain . . . ughhhh!" Culver's head recoiled away from the sharp impact of the shotgun butt.

"Uncle Henry!" Martine Russelli screamed from the other side of the room while her enraged sister cursed wildly as she tried to tear the restraining handcuffs loose from the tunnel grate.

This time it took almost a minute for the pain to subside

enough so that Henry Culver could focus his blurred eyes on the chubby face that wasn't grinning anymore.

"Okay, Gauss, fine by me," Culver whispered, staring up at the Fairfax County Police Department's crime lab director through blurry eyes. "Screw your rights. You're still under arrest."

Gauss started to say something, but Michelle Russelli was still screaming violent threats at the top of her lungs, and he had to go over to the other side of the room and threaten to hit her sister with the shotgun before she finally quieted down. Bear, however, continued to bark and snarl and bare his teeth at the harried lab director from behind the tunnel grating.

"Shut up!" Gauss yelled again, which had absolutely no effect whatsoever on the raging dog. For a moment, it looked as though Gauss was going to blast the shepherd through the grating with the shotgun. But then he appeared to remember something, and he withdrew the barrel of the shotgun from the tunnel grating and walked back over to the computer console area where Culver and Kathy Harmon were sprawled on the floor.

"Jesus, what a zoo," he said, shaking his head as he knelt back down beside Culver.

"Be smart, Gauss," Culver whispered. "It's all over. Cut your losses now and give it up."

"Henry, you don't seem to understand the situation. I'm in control here. If you or your girlfriend over there try to do *anything,* anything at all, then I'm going to shoot one of those girls with their father's shotgun," he said, motioning with his head at Michelle and Martine Russelli, both of whom—Culver could see now—were handcuffed to one of the tunnel grates on the far wall.

Next to them, Culver could also see one of the other wire grid grates—this one securely bolted shut—clanging and rattling with every lunging impact of the raging black shepherd.

Come on, Bear, rip that damn thing off the wall.

But much to Culver's dismay, the thick wire grates appeared to have been built to withstand all of the momentum that a furious ninety-pound German shepherd could generate within the confines of a two-foot-diameter corrugated metal tunnel.

"Gauss," Culver said weakly, slowly turning his head so that he could see his tormentor, "I don't know what kind of deal you think you've got going with Russelli, but I'm telling you straight, if you so much as *bruise* one of those kids, he's going to find you . . . and when he does, he's going to take you apart like a Christmas turkey. And besides, that's not his shotgun."

"Don't worry about Russelli. He knows *exactly* what he's going to have to do if he ever wants to see his daughters alive again. He and Digger have a very clear understanding of each other."

"Digger's dead," Culver whispered.

"Yes, of course he is, but Russelli doesn't know that. He thinks I'm Digger."

Culver closed his eyes for a moment. "Gauss, you're the wrong kind of guy to be running a high-wire act like this."

"Oh, I don't know. That depends on how you look at it," the forensic scientist smiled. "Take Russelli's shotgun, for example. You see that piece of plastic wadding on the floor next to your arm? Which, I might add, is not looking very good at all. You really shouldn't be losing so much blood, Henry."

"I can see the wadding. So what?"

"I have a feeling that when the CSI teams finally get down here and start sorting thing out, they're going to come up with the interesting conclusion that you got shot by your partner. Fact is, they're going to discover that the striations on that little plastic shot-cup match up perfectly with those little burrs in the barrel end of Russelli's sawed-off."

"Let me guess. You stole Russelli's shotgun out of the trunk of his car, and then test-fired a bunch of rounds through it so that you'd pick up those striations on the shot-cups. Then you reloaded all those cups back into new rounds so that you or your friends could use them in regular shotguns to kill off your competition and make it look like Russelli did it.

"And just to make things look good," Culver finished, "you probably dumped a few of the original casings with firing pin impressions from Russelli's shotgun at some of the scenes."

Then something else occurred to Culver.

"Russelli's jacket. You took that too when you got at his shotgun, didn't you? Whoever you sent in to burgle her house . . ." Culver nodded his head in the direction of Kathy Harmon ". . . let the dog tear a piece off of it and then put it back in Russelli's trunk."

Gauss nodded approvingly. "Very nice, Henry. Isn't this fun? You get to lie there and figure out how all of the pieces of the puzzle fit together, while I get to sit here and watch you bleed to death."

"So what happened to Digger?" Culver asked, trying to ignore Gauss's comments as he felt his jaw starting to swell from the impact of the shotgun butt. "Wasn't he a little pissed off when he found out you stole his computer and his whole burglary system?"

"Yes, I suppose he was. But he wasn't going to need it anymore, and I didn't know the warrant we had didn't cover his car when I popped the trunk, so I couldn't very well log a computer into evidence that wasn't the product of a legal search, now could I?"

"Sounds reasonable," Culver said, realizing that he was starting to feel cold and light-headed.

He's right. Losing too much blood. Watch it. Moving slowly, he slid his left hand in under his shirt and pressed down on the torn strips of sheeting that were now soaked with blood, gritting his teeth and groaning from the resulting pain.

"Exactly, but the thing that none of your brilliant investigators realized," Gauss went on sarcastically, "was that John Doe Thirty-three really wasn't all that smart. I mean the stupid little bastard left all the details of his burglary system tucked away in the hard drive of his computer, and that little trick he put in to erase everything if somebody else got into the system was a waste of effort because he left it in the batch files where anybody with any brains could find it.

"And you know what's *really* funny? He even got caught in one of his own stupid little traps because it never occurred to him that someone like me could reprogram the safety switches. You should have seen him, Henry, flopping around like an insect on a pin. I even have it on tape. Maybe I'll play it for you if you're nice and cooperative."

"You having fun telling me all this?" Culver whispered, continuing to press the soggy sheeting into his wounds, and having to blink away the hazy clouds that were threatening to send him drifting back into the darkness.

"Yes, I am. But what I'm really actually doing is explaining to you why we need to come to an arrangement."

"Oh yeah, and why's that?"

"Can you see those TV monitors up there?"

Culver turned his head slowly, and then had to blink his eyes several times, but the twelve screens finally came into focus.

John Russelli's face was still being shown on monitor number one, but of more interest to Culver now, screens three through six were showing a great deal of activity out in Digger's front yard. There were several sedans out on the driveway now, and a number of professional-looking men standing around in small groups, partially concealed behind the large stands of trees that surrounded the house.

Topcastle, Forecastle and Company. Wonderful.

And who else?

Traynor, R.C., and . . . oh Christ, even Craven, crutches and all. Beginning to look like a convention down there, or up there, or wherever the hell . . .

He could see Craven, Traynor, and Parkinson—who had a pack set radio in his hand—clearly now, apparently arguing over something.

And then R.C. Cohen came up and started yelling and gesturing at the house, and one of the three-piece-suiters tried to push him away, and it took Traynor and two of Parkinson's bodyguards to separate them.

Come on Traynor, stop screwing around with those bastards. I'm starting to lose it down here.

Then Culver's foggy gaze shifted to monitor number seven and he realized with a start that this video camera was directed at Kathy Harmon's house.

He was still trying to digest this bit of information, vaguely aware that Gauss was asking him something, when he realized that there was a vehicle parked in her driveway—a vehicle that he recognized at once—the all-too-distinctive blue pickup that had slowly driven past him with its lights out at that Georgetown gas station. And there was something else in the corner of the screen too—something long and thin and dark.

Culver blinked and the blurry images became a sprawled dark-skinned arm, and the long dark barrel of a Remington pump shotgun half-hidden in the snow.

Oh Jesus, Carp . . .

"Culver, I'm talking to you," Gauss repeated, nudging him with the barrel of the shotgun.

No backup now.

"Yeah, yeah, I see them."

"Look at monitor number five, Henry."

Henry Culver tried to turn his head and refocus his eyes on the blurry screen, but Kathy Harmon's horrified voice told him all he needed to know.

"Lisa!"

Culver blinked and the black-and-white video picture of the young girl with the tear-streaked face, who was sitting in the front seat of the distant sedan between two solemn-faced men, came into focus.

"You bastard," Culver whispered weakly.

"Not me, them." Gauss chuckled. "They seem to think that they can use the child as some sort of bargaining chip with you or Digger or Sea Glass here. Which is rather absurd, all things considered, because *I'm* certainly not interested in her welfare, but . . ."

At that moment, Kathy Harmon lunged for Gauss, but he saw her coming and dropped her to the floor, unconscious, with a swift butt stroke of the shotgun.

Culver heard her grunt and fall, but the pain was so bad that it was all he could do to remain conscious.

"Stupid bitch. Okay, Henry, now pay attention to monitor number one. You're going to like this."

Gauss did something with the control board, and the picture on the first monitor zoomed back to show John Russelli sitting on a couch—his wrists encased in a pair of handcuffs—as he glared up at the camera with a savage expression on his blood-smeared face, and then widened out further to show a gray-haired, heavyset man standing beside a window with an automatic rifle in his hands.

"That man standing there next to Russelli is known as Hämmarchov," Gauss said. "One of Digger's hired hands. From what I've been able to determine, he's a very dangerous fellow who seems to be amused by vicious dogs and obstinate detectives."

"Why pick on the dogs?" Culver mumbled.

"You mean that shepherd and those two mutts of Russelli's? Come on, Henry, you disappoint me. Everybody knows that Digger hates pets. What better way to demonstrate that he's the one doing all of this? Personally, I think it was rather ingenious of me to think to use them as red herrings. And then too," Gauss added, "I suspect that Hämmarchov actually enjoys that sort of thing anyway.

"He's an interesting man, Henry," Gauss went on when Culver didn't respond. "Vicious, controlled, and for some strange reason which probably involves a great deal of money, extremely loyal to Digger. You see, at the moment, he firmly believes that Digger is still alive and directing the entire operation from his underground command center, which, of course he's not, because I've already dealt with him. In fact, his body is down there in one of the tunnels. And that, you see, is the problem."

"I don't follow," Culver rasped.

"I'm in radio communication with those people out there. It seems that they used to control Digger, and apparently would like to continue the arrangement. In fact they're very insistent on that point. I've advised them that Hämmarchov is guarding the house, which has been keeping them back so far. But they really want to see me—or to be more accurate, they want to see Digger—very badly, and I don't think they're going to wait much longer."

"Wait to do what?"

"Assault the house," Gauss said calmly. "They would like to take Digger alive, but I gather that they'd be perfectly happy to find him dead. Mostly they just don't want him talking with anybody on the outside—especially a Homicide investigator like Stewart, which, I suppose, is a perfectly understandable concern."

Culver blinked at that, and Gauss smiled.

"Oh that's right, nobody explained all of that to you, did they? Well, the way I have it figured, those people out there have been using Digger to burglarize homes of certain well-placed people, such as foreign dignitaries and embassy personnel, and then using a variety of techniques to gather intelligence data through implanted transmitters and the like. Devious little tricks for devious little minds."

"Gauss, those people out there are CIA. You're not going to stand a chance," Culver whispered, but the lab director ignored him.

"Of course, they don't realize that I've been Digger for quite some time now—certainly long enough to know far more than I should—so I really don't think that they're going to be overly concerned about my welfare, do you?"

Culver shook his head slowly. "No, probably not."

"The central issue, of course, is that I have to escape, so that I can enjoy all of the retirement money that you, Russelli, and Digger have so thoughtfully provided," Gauss said cheerfully. "Digger also provided a nice escape tunnel, so that part's going to be easy. In fact, I have it all arranged so that once everything settles down, Craven and Stewart and Carpenter will be absolutely convinced that you and Russelli killed Digger, took over his burglary ring, and then quarreled over the arrangements. You'll deny it, of course, but all of the evidence, the bank accounts . . ."

"You?"

Gauss smiled. "While I was setting things up for myself, I arranged for you and Russelli to have your own retirement accounts, too. Modest sums, but substantial enough to whet the appetite of a suspicious mind like Stewart's. Ultimately, the circumstantial evidence against you and Russelli should turn out to be overwhelming.

"But then you had to go and make things complicated by trying to erase the accounts," Gauss went on calmly. "I had to stop you, of course—that's why I shot at the computer. Not my fault if you were still in the way, now was it?"

Culver mumbled something inaudible.

"Actually, I probably *should* have killed you right there. But as it turns out, it's a good thing I didn't because you apparently managed to change the access code to Digger's program, so now I won't be able to get at my money until you tell me what you changed it to."

"Gauss," Culver whispered weakly, "you keep talking like you're going to disappear and leave us here to take the rap. Did it ever occur to you that somebody in this room—me for example—just might tell Stewart all about your little game?"

"Oh yes, of course, that's the best part. With all of the lunatic raving that everyone here"—he looked around the small room—"is *bound* to do, I'm sure that I'd end up being a prime suspect, except for one minor little detail."

"Yeah, and what's that?"

"I'm going to be dead."

"Dead?" Culver repeated, not certain that he'd heard right.

Gauss nodded. "Quite dead, in fact. And as it happens, you're the one who's going to do the honors, so to speak."

"Keep talking, Gauss," Culver smiled as he felt the haze start to drift across his eyes, "I'm starting to like this."

"It's going to be a spectacular event, Henry. No body, of

course, but I can modestly say that even *you* would be impressed with the degree of circumstantial evidence, assuming that they'd allow you anywhere near the scene, which they certainly won't. Not after the way you mishandled the Kostermann evidence."

Culver mumbled something, but Gauss wasn't paying any attention. He was too wrapped up in describing his own death scene.

"I've even managed to set aside seven pints of my own blood, which certainly ought to be convincing, not to mention . . . Henry?"

Gauss looked down closely and discovered that Henry Culver's mouth had dropped open and his eyes had closed.

"Henry!" Gauss yelled, slapping Culver hard across the face.

"You shithead!" Michelle Russelli screamed, and then Kathy Harmon started to move around and Gauss was forced to bring the shotgun back up again to keep her at bay.

"What?" Culver mumbled, blinking his eyes open.

"Come on, Henry, pay attention. You can't die on me yet, until you tell me the new password. And you will tell me, because if you don't, those girls over there are going to have a very rough time," Gauss muttered as he hauled Culver back up into a sitting position in the desk chair, ignoring his anguished groans.

"Forgot it," Culver whispered, holding on to the chair tightly with his good arm as he tried not to faint.

"Listen to me, Culver. If those people try to take that house with Hämmarchov inside, there's going to be a lot of shooting. If that happens, John Russelli is almost certainly going to die because Digger gave Hämmarchov specific orders to use him as a shield. Do you understand what I'm saying?"

Culver nodded wordlessly.

"So, unless you want these girls to watch their father get his blood and brains splattered all over the floor up there, you are going to get on this microphone and talk to those people out there, tell them where Digger's body is, while I . . ."

"You faked the Kostermann scene, too, didn't you?" Culver whispered, starting to weave in the chair and forcing Gauss to get in closer to hold him upright. He was scanning the control board now, trying to make sense of the control buttons for the microphone.

Gauss smiled. "Of course I did, Henry. And it was a lot of work, too. It took me almost two days to reconstruct the footprints with those shoes you and Russelli found, and then make new prints and retake all those photographs with Quinzio's tags. Then I had to make a new cast, and then razor-cut all the edges of the new negatives so they'd match up with the old ones. It was a lot of work, Henry. A tremendous amount of work."

"So somebody really did cheat that crazy bastard after all." Henry Culver laughed weakly, and then started to fall forward onto the control board, catching himself with his left hand and thumbing the microphone switch marked number one as he forced Gauss to shift his weight again . . .

"RUSSELLI!" Culver yelled into the now-live microphone, *"THE KIDS ARE DOWN HERE UNDER THE HOUSE, IN THE TUNNELS!"*

And then Culver was snarling and lunging forward with his one functional arm, going for the lab director's flabby throat as his wobbly legs tried to drive Gauss back into the far wall, but then he dropped to the floor in agony, hearing Martine Russelli scream: *"POP, HELP!"*

Culver was still trying to get back up on his feet when Gauss swung the shotgun barrel at Martine Russelli's head, missed—discharging the weapon into the low ceiling with a loud, concussive roar that temporarily deafened everyone in the room. Then he screamed and dropped the shotgun when Michelle Russelli lunged forward and slammed a savage heel kick into his groin.

Clutching at his crushed genitals with his left hand, Gauss started to reach down for the shotgun, stopped when he realized that Kathy Harmon had thrown herself across the weapon, and then staggered forward and caught Michelle Russelli with a jarring right fist to the face.

The rapid muffled sounds of shots being fired were audible through the pipes that vented the small room, but nobody in the underground chamber heard them.

Stunned and bleeding from the mouth as her head snapped back against the wood-braced wall, Michelle Russelli blinked in shock. Then, screaming with rage, she lunged forward to the length of the restraining handcuff and drove her fingers straight into the crime lab director's eye.

Kathy Harmon had the shotgun clutched to her chest and was scrambling for the far corner of the room. Culver was crawling now on one hand and two knees, still trying to get to Gauss—who in turn had stumbled away from the frenzied teenager who was still screaming and cursing and trying to get at him with her feet, a fist, or her fingernails.

At that moment, the small underground room was suddenly rocked by a series of concussive explosions that drove Henry Culver, Kathy Harmon, Theodore Gauss, and the Russelli twins to the floor.

Chapter Forty-four

Saturday, 1845 hours

At first, Henry Culver thought that the low ceiling of the small underground room was going to cave in.

The force of the explosion, which seemed to have come from some of the tunnel openings, had sent clouds of dust and dirt flying around the small room, and had also wrenched loose several of the rough-cut beams and planks that supported the earthen ceiling.

Chunks of dirt and small rocks were falling through the gaps in the planks now, and the clamor of barking and screaming had started up again. Only this time, Culver realized as he crawled over to the table and grabbed for the .357 that had fallen back behind the computer table—when he and the desktop computer had been hit by Gauss's shotgun blast—Bear's furious barking was now muted with fear.

Henry Culver pulled himself up into the high-backed chair with a loud groan, and then looked up to see what could only be described as an unbelievable nightmare.

The two Russelli girls were still handcuffed to the tunnel gratings, but both of them were down on their knees now, their faces blackened with dirt and blouses streaked with blood as Kathy Harmon crawled toward them, her own clothes torn and bloody.

The sight of the three injured young women wrenched at Culver's shell-shocked mind, but it was the sight of Theodore Gauss that caused Henry Culver to sit there in the high-backed chair with the .357 laying useless in his lap as he stared in groggy disbelief at the sight before his eyes.

Gauss was on his knees now also, shaking his head wide-eyed and screaming "NO! NO! NO!" as he tried to pull himself loose from the gristly stump of an arm that was wrapped tight around his neck, the festering severed wrist tied off with a pair of blood-soaked shoestrings.

But he couldn't get loose, because in spite of the horrible, self-inflicted injury, the arm that was squeezing tight around his throat now was still incredibly strong.

"Henry!" Gauss gasped, his eyes bulging with fear.

But then the other arm—the one with a hand—came around and pressed the terribly sharp knife blade tight against his neck, and Gauss finally stopped screaming. Instead, he just stared helplessly at Culver, pleading with him to do something, as Henry Culver's eyes locked with those of the pale blue–eyed freak who had suddenly appeared like an apparition of death—filthy, ragged, hollow-eyed and reeking a foul odor—to claim his due.

Digger.

Without really being aware of what he was doing, Culver brought his left arm up and centered the sights of the .357

Magnum, which had suddenly become impossibly heavy, right between the two pale eyes.

"Don't," Culver warned in a raspy, tired voice.

"But he cheated me!" the pale thin man who had spent the better part of his warped childhood building and playing in these tight, confining tunnels protested as he forced the knife in tighter against the lab director's flabby neck. "You heard him, he even admitted it!"

Culver shook his head slowly. "I don't care," he said. "Don't do it."

"He *deserves* to die!"

"You cut him, and *you're* the one who's going to die, right here, right now," Culver warned, slowly thumbing the hammer of the .357 back into the full-cocked position.

There were distant, muffled crashing sounds coming in through the vent pipes now, but nobody was paying them any attention. All eyes were on Digger—who stared at Culver for a few, long, appraising moments, and then he shook his head slowly and smiled.

"You won't shoot me. You can't."

"What makes you think that?" Culver asked, not really caring. He just wanted to keep Digger talking, to give himself time to regain his strength.

"Your friend Radlick. He kept telling me that you couldn't be the one, because you never cheated on anything. I didn't believe him, but he was right, wasn't he? You had to play it fair. That's why I'll win—because people like you are so stupidly predictable," he grinned, his pale eyes glistening madly as he glanced over at Kathy Harmon. "You couldn't even resist a meaningless little piece of sea glass."

Culver didn't say anything.

"You see, I *know* what you're thinking," Digger went on in his whispery, demented voice as he looked down at the terrified Gauss. "You want to arrest him, bring him in so he can go to trial. But that's so incredibly stupid because he'll just claim he was insane, and the judge and the jury will believe him. I know that, because the judge believed me, and I'm not insane."

Oh yes you are, Digger. You are absolutely, irretrievably out of your mind.

"It doesn't matter," Culver said, having to work harder now just to hold the .357 Magnum steady. "You can't be the judge and jury. It doesn't work that way."

Digger blinked. "Is that what you want, a judge and a jury?"

"Is that what *you* want," he demanded of Gauss, pressing the knife against his neck once again.

"Yes," Gauss nodded frantically. "Please."

"Which one?"

"What?"

"Which one do you want?" Digger repeated. "A judge . . . ?" He pressed the knife in deeper. ". . . Or a jury?"

"A jury," Gauss whimpered. "Please, a jury."

"Gauss, don't play his game," Culver warned.

"Of twelve? You want a jury of twelve?" Digger demanded.

"Gauss . . ."

"Yes, yes!"

"Okay," Digger said in a soft voice, "I've got one all picked out for you." Pulling Gauss up to his feet, and staying in close so that Culver wouldn't have a clear shot, Digger dragged him over to one of the wooden doors near the spot where Kathy Harmon was trying to comfort the Russelli girls.

"Get away from them!" Culver snarled, rising up out of the chair. But before he could do anything other than gasp from the sudden, shearing pain that tore through the entire right side of his chest, Digger turned, shoved Gauss through the wooden door, slammed and bolted it shut, and then dived to the floor.

Black rectangle. What was that?

Oh no . . .

Henry Culver was reacting to the pain, and to the stunning realization that Digger had one of the deadly transmitters stuck in his back pants pocket, when Bear started to go wild—smashing into the grate with his now bloody jaws, and trying to turn around in the narrow, confining tunnel—and then Digger was back up again by the computer table with the bloody stump of his forearm wrapped around Kathy Harmon's neck, and his other hand was coming up . . .

Only this time, in addition to the knife, he also held the black plastic transmitter in his one remaining hand.

"Stay back, there's more explosives in those other tunnels," he warned Culver, pointing at the two remaining tunnel grates that still restrained the Russelli girls and the nearly berserk black shepherd.

"Okay, I'm back," Culver said, pushing the chair backward with his feet until he was back against the far wall next to the two girls.

"Put the gun down."

Culver released the hammer of the .357, and dropped it onto his lap.

"On the floor," Digger demanded, but Culver shook his head.

"I'm not giving up the gun. It doesn't matter what you say or do, but I'm not giving it up."

The demented killer smiled. "This is Sea Glass, Culver. You really don't want me to kill her, do you?"

"No, I don't," Culver said, keeping his eyes fixed on the transmitter in Digger's hand. "That's why I'm keeping the gun. You harm her, you die."

He was trying to make sure he had it right. To use the transmitter, to set everything off, Digger would have to drop the knife and change his grip—maybe two seconds at the most.

"Michelle, can you hear me?"

"Yes," the teenage girl responded, her voice shaky but still defiant.

"Listen to me. If I yell 'Now,' you open that grating next to you, as fast as you can, and let the dog loose. But not unless I say so. Do you understand?"

"Yes." This time he could hear the anticipation in her voice.

Digger blinked uncertainly as he considered the obvious implications.

"That's right," Culver said, "you can kill her before the dog can get to you. But if you do, he'll tear you into shreds."

Digger twisted his thin lips into a wide, maniacal smile.

"Okay, Culver, you made a nice move. Now watch this," he giggled as he put the transmitter down on the table, slipped the knife into his back pocket, reached down to the keyboard of the portable computer that Gauss hadn't managed to hit with his shotgun blast, and keyed in a series of commands.

Culver caught a brief glimpse of two large bodies thrashing around on the overhead video monitor number one, then all twelve monitors flickered and simultaneously switched to display dark, hazy sections of a long tunnel. Monitor number twelve now showed Theodore Gauss huddled down against the wooden door.

"There's your jury, Gauss," Digger whispered into the microphone as he reached down and pressed one of the computer keys. On the alarm panel mounted over the twelve small monitor screens, twelve sets of lights began flashing back and forth between red and green in what appeared to be a random pattern.

"What are you doing?" Culver demanded as he stared uncomprehending at the flashing lights.

"I installed a special kind of burglar alarm in my main tunnel," Digger said, still holding Kathy Harmon tight against his chest as he watched the monitors. "Twelve very effective traps." He wiggled the stump of his bloody, severed wrist as a demonstration.

"Each trap has a safety switch that can be turned on or off. But now," Digger went on, smiling evilly as he stared up at the flashing alarm board, "they're all set at random. There's no way for him to tell if the safety switch is on or off, until he tries to go through."

"Gauss!" Culver yelled hoarsely in the direction of the microphone, "Stay there, don't move!"

"That's right, Gauss, listen to him," Digger laughed into the microphone, "stay right where you are. In about five minutes, I'm going to blow all of the tunnels. Then you'll stay there until you rot."

Digger was still laughing madly when the fuzzy video image of Gauss suddenly came to his feet, hesitated at the concealed safety switch, and then dived forward through the first wooden doorframe in the tunnel. Nothing happened and he collapsed on the dirt floor just in front of the second doorway.

"Juror number one votes not guilty, Gauss!" Digger laughed with glee. "Only eleven more to go."

Culver, Kathy Harmon, and the two Russelli girls all watched in horror as Gauss staggered up to his feet again, slowly reached up for the second concealed safety switch, moved it hesitantly to the opposite position, and then lunged through the second trap.

Video monitor number ten showed a distant view of the terrified forensic scientist huddled on the floor of the narrow tunnel and trembling. Digger adjusted a knob on his control board and suddenly Gauss's whimpering and labored breathing could be heard through one of the overhead speakers.

"Another not guilty, Gauss," Digger called out. "Come on, go for it! Only ten more. You're going to beat the rap!"

"Gauss!" Culver yelled again, "Stay there! You can't beat the odds! There's no way!"

But even as Culver was yelling, Gauss scrambled to his feet and lunged forward again, only this time his hazy video image seemed to hang there in midair, and the underground room was suddenly filled with the horrible sound of high-pitched screaming.

"Turn it off, goddamnit!" Culver yelled, but Digger ignored him, staring up at the video screen and laughing at the sight of Theodore Gauss—the cheater—impaled by three of the six long sharp spikes that had been driven outward from the wall by the force of the heavy truck leaf springs.

At that moment, Culver spun around in the chair, shoved the .357 deep into the tunnel opening behind the Russelli girls, yelled "NOW!" as he came up out of the chair, took three lunging steps forward, and then launched himself toward the computer table.

Digger had allowed himself to get caught up in the dying agony of Theodore Gauss, but the sound of the Smith & Wesson clanging against the corrugated metal and Culver's yell alerted him, and he turned his head just in time to see Culver coming at him.

Howling with rage, Digger yanked Kathy Harmon away from the table, and threw himself back against the wall, realizing only then that Culver hadn't been going for him at all.

Culver had the transmitter in his hand and was heading back toward the tunnel door where he had thrown the .357; but one of the buckshot pellets in his torn shoulder suddenly jammed against a nerve and he gasped and stumbled to the floor. At that moment, Digger—seeing Michelle Russelli struggling to pull open the latch of the cage door restraining Bear—slammed Kathy Harmon into the teenage girl, smacking her head hard against the heavy wire grate, and then held on to Kathy Harmon and fended off the two Russelli girls as he thrust his wrist stump into the open tunnel behind them, trying to reach the deadly handgun.

Realizing he was too late, Culver jammed the transmitter deep into the left pocket of his patrol jacket pocket, and then rolled to the floor, grabbing for the shotgun that Kathy Harmon had left on the floor, jacked the slide one-handed, and then realized why Gauss hadn't shot the dog.

Empty. Only had the two rounds. Shit!

Culver was starting to bring the shotgun around anyway, intending to use it as a club, when he heard Digger scream.

"NO, NO, GET IT OFF ME!"

Culver blinked through the waves of pain and saw Digger stagger backward and then thrash hysterically around on the floor, trying to hold on to Kathy Harmon with his one hand and at the same time knock loose the weasellike ferret that had buried its sharp fangs into his severed wrist and refused to let go as it twisted its head back and forth in savage fury.

"SPANKY!" Kathy Harmon yelled, and then smashed the

back of her head into Digger's face as she struggled frantically to get loose and protect her pet. Momentarily losing his grip, he reached for the knife in his back pocket.

Diving forward, Culver swung the shotgun one-handed and knocked the knife out of Digger's hand just as he was bringing it around to slash at Kathy Harmon's neck, and then tumbled backward in a blinding flash of pain as Digger's foot slammed into his side.

Culver was reaching for the shotgun again, thinking that he had to kill him now because he wouldn't be conscious much longer. Digger was pulling Kathy Harmon back toward one of the metal tunnel openings with his one good arm, leaving a trail of blood on the compacted dirt floor. Spanky had scrambled for a hiding place under the computer table with another small chunk of Digger in his teeth. Bear was becoming more frenzied by the moment. And Martine Russelli had taken over for her stronger but now unconscious sister and was trying to pound the cage lever open with her one free hand, when they all heard the sudden, distant, high-pitched screeching sound above their heads.

"What's that?" Digger whispered, blinking through the blood streaming down into his eye from his split eyebrow. It took every ounce of strength he had left to hold Kathy Harmon in place as a shield against the twelve-gage shotgun that an equally exhausted and nearly unconscious Henry Culver had aimed in the general direction of his head.

Culver looked up at the crumbling ceiling for a moment, and then he smiled through bloody lips.

"I think you've got a problem," he rasped weakly.

"What? What're you talking about?" Digger demanded in a strained voice, pushing his matted hair out of his face and then trying to wipe the blood out of his eye against Kathy Harmon's hair.

"Russelli," Culver said, gesturing with his head up at the ceiling and then at the two teenage girls. "Sounds to me like he's heading down this way to get his kids back."

Digger blinked again and looked up at the ceiling.

"Something you need to know about Russelli," Culver went on, determined to fight off the nausea and the pain for just a few more minutes. "Last time I saw him—about five minute ago, on one of those monitors—he was up in your house somewhere, handcuffed to a chair, and some Neanderthal named Hämmarchov was watching him."

Digger blinked his pale eyes again in sudden hope, but then it immediately died out as the obvious implications became clear.

Culver nodded. "That's right. Unless Hämmarchov likes to play with power saws, I'd say that he's out of the ball game. And knowing Russelli, he's going to get to these kids if he has to take your whole goddamned house apart, board by board.

"Oh, and when he gets here," Culver went on, "don't bother hiding behind her, or threatening to use her as a hostage, because Russelli isn't going to give a shit about anything except tearing your head off and pounding it flat with that goddamned computer."

Digger's frantic eyes flickered toward Martine and Michelle Russelli, and Culver shook his head.

"Uh-uh, you move one inch in their direction, and I'm going to open that cage door, let the dog tear your fucking throat out."

"I'll break her neck," the feverish burglar warned. "You can't stop me."

"Maybe, maybe not. But you go for those kids and I'm going to do it anyway."

"But . . . but . . . ?" Digger stammered, holding Kathy Harmon tighter and looking as though he was about ready to start crying before Culver interrupted.

"You want to know what you can do, right?" he rasped, fighting off the urge to vomit.

Getting shocky, watch it. Too close now.

"Yes, please."

Digger's voice was starting to shift, becoming childlike, and Culver forced himself to hurry because he wasn't sure he could deal with the personality he knew about, and he didn't even want to *think* about any of the others.

"There's a man out on your driveway right now, goes by the name of Topcastle or Parkinson or whatever. Last time I saw him, he was smiling. Those names mean anything to you?"

Digger nodded his head slowly.

"Yeah, I thought so. Anyway, he wants to talk to you, so maybe I'll make you a deal."

"What kind of deal?" Digger whispered suspiciously.

"I let you go, you let her go."

Digger's eyes blinked in disbelief.

"You'd let me go?"

"You blew up some of the exit tunnels, but there still at least one way out left—the tunnel that goes out to the shed—right?"

Digger nodded cautiously, easing his grip on Kathy Harmon's neck.

Culver braced the shotgun against his legs, reached across into his pants pocket, and pulled out two sets of keys.

"Martine," he said as he tossed one set of keys over to Russelli's still-conscious but exhausted daughter. "There's a handcuff key on that ring. Unhook you and your sister."

"Wait a minute," Digger started to protest, but Culver wasn't paying any attention.

"Listen to me, asshole. You killed the Kostermanns, and you killed Paul and Doreen Radlick, and you killed Tess with a trap that was meant for me, and now I'm letting you go, so shut the fuck up," he rasped, tossing the other set of keys over next to Digger's functional arm. "Those are to a Bronco. It's parked out there next to the shed. It's all yours. You manage to talk your way past Parkinson and his goons, then I don't give a shit. Russelli and I'll hunt you down later."

"I need a hostage."

"No hostage," Culver shook his head. "You can have your computer, the Polaroids, and the album. That's it. One-handed, that's about all you'll be able to get out of here anyway."

"If I go into that tunnel without a hostage, you'll turn the dog loose," Digger whispered.

Culver nodded his head. "Yeah, I was wondering if you'd think about that."

"Okay," he said after a few moments, "Martine, come over here."

He waited until the shaken girl came over beside him. "There's a transmitter in my jacket pocket, right side. I can't get at it . . . yes, that's it. Okay, now you walk around over to that tunnel opening on the far left—yes, that's the one. That's right, stay away from him. Okay, now get inside and put it about thirty feet or so inside the tunnel."

For a moment, Digger glanced over at Martine as though he was considering going for the tunnel and a hostage, but Culver shook his head.

"You don't even want to *think* about trying to take one of them with you," he advised, gesturing with his eyes up at the ceiling where the power-sawing noises were getting louder. "And beside, I'd just kick the dog loose."

Culver waited until Martine crawled back out of the tunnel.

"Okay, hon," he said, "go pick up that portable computer, the small one. That's right. Be careful, there's some cables in the back. Okay, now put it over there in the middle of the floor. Good. Now go pull all those photographs off the board. Try not to look at them. And the album too, but don't look in it either, it'd just make you sick. Okay, now put them in the tunnel and then go over there by your sister and get my gun, bring it over to me, and help me up into this chair."

"Thank you, Martine," Culver whispered as the teenage girl set the .357 revolver in his lap, seeing for the first time that there was more of her father in Martine Russelli than he had ever realized.

Hang in there, hon, it's almost over.

"Now go see if you can get your sister behind that table over there."

He waited until Martine Russelli had dragged her now-conscious but still-groggy sister over behind the computer table. Then he settled back into the chair, waited for the room to stop moving around, wrapped his fingers around the familiar—and now very comforting—grip of the Smith & Wesson, and began to roll himself over to the computer table.

Once he was there, he turned and looked over at Digger, who had been following every movement with his pale, deadly eyes, and was now staring at the shotgun that Culver had left in the middle of the floor.

"Forget about the shotgun," Culver said. "It's empty."

He ignored the flash of surprise and rage that passed across Digger's face.

"Here's the deal," Culver rasped. "You get a head start, your computer, *and* your transmitter back. That gives you the option of blowing the tunnels behind you so the dog or I can't follow."

"But if I've got the computer, you can't reprogram the switches in the main tunnel. You'd be trapped," Digger reasoned suspiciously. "You aren't going to do that."

"Russelli's going to be down here in a few minutes," Culver shook his head. "That gives us a way out. And if you're not gone by the time we get up there, tough shit."

"I still don't trust you," Digger whispered.

"I don't blame you," Culver nodded. "So let's see if there's anybody out there you *can* trust."

Chapter Forty-five

Saturday, 1915 hours

After fumbling around with the control board for a few moments, Culver got the video monitors back on their original settings, noting as he did so that it was getting so dark outside that it was difficult to see much of anything on the small black-and-white screens.

Going back to the control board again, he found a series of switches marked "OUTSIDE LIGHTS" and flicked them all to the ON position, and watched the images on monitors two through twelve brighten perceptibly.

He also noted that monitor number one showed the gray-bearded man Gauss had identified as Hämmarchov lying in a chair and facing the camera, his eyes open, his face bloody, and his head twisted at a very unlikely angle.

Nice going, Russelli, he thought calmly, listening to the savage tearing and prying and cutting sounds above his head for a moment before he started searching the other monitors.

On number six, he found exactly who and what he was after.

Well I'll be damned.

Looking down at the control board again, Culver found the frequency setting for what he assumed was the outside antenna attached to the radio communications system. Quickly switching the dial to the Fairfax County Police Department's main patrol frequency, he leaned forward and spoke into the microphone.

"Hey, Hattabaugh, what took you guys so long?"

Patrol Sergeant Jack Hattabaugh, who was crouched down in a barricade position behind his police cruiser, jerked away from the radio in his hand like it was a snake.

"Henry?"

"Hi, Sarge."

"Henry, where the hell are you?"

"Tunnel system under the house. Not sure where."

"Did you turn on those damn lights?"

"Yeah, that was me."

"You want to tell me what the hell's going on around here, and why you've got half the FBI out hunting your ass?"

"Not FBI," Culver whispered weakly, trying to conserve his strength. "Those guys report out of Langley. Guy with the red beard and the skinny one with glasses are the white hats. I used to work with them."

"*You* were CIA?"

"Uh-huh."

"Christ almighty, Henry . . ."

"Tell you about it later," he mumbled. "Gotta let Stewart know . . . Russelli's clean. Didn't kill anybody."

"We know," Hattabaugh said. "The FBI Lab team really went ape-shit when they started looking at that plastic wadding. Far as they're concerned, somebody set you and Russelli up. From what I hear, they're looking real hard for Gauss right now."

"Tell 'em not to bother, he's down here in the tunnel. Digger killed him."

"Jesus," Hattabaugh whispered. "Is Russelli down there too?"

"No, he's up in the house. Think he just took out one of Digger's bodyguards. Sounds like he's taking apart the house trying to get down here, find his kids. Tell him . . . watch out for booby traps in the main tunnel."

"Hang in there, buddy, we're coming in after you."

"No, don't!" Culver mumbled hurriedly, finding it increasingly difficult to speak clearly. "Can't come down here. Screw things up. Got Digger boxed in, standoff situation."

"Henry, listen to me. Shoot the bastard."

"Can't. He's got a hostage. Need to talk to the guy with the red beard. Hurry . . ."

Culver watched the monitors as Hattabaugh quickly ran over to the small group of men who were crouched down behind Elliott Parkinson's three sedans.

Parkinson, Craven, Stewart, L'Que, Traynor, and R.C., and a bunch of Parkinson's goons, Culver thought. *And everybody looks pissed except Parkinson, so he probably thinks he's got it all under control, goddamn him.*

"Something you need to understand," Culver rasped, turning to stare at Digger. "Looks like the CIA's in charge out there, so your buddy Parkinson can probably get you past the cops. But you use that transmitter to blow the tunnels, try to seal us in here, one of those cops out there is liable to say to hell with federal jurisdiction and put a bullet through your head anyway. You hear what I'm saying?"

Digger nodded his head slowly.

"Okay," Culver said. "It's all there. You want it or not? All you've got to do is let her go."

"What's the new password?"

"Cheater," Culver said, having to work hard to keep his eyes open now.

Digger's pale eyes blinked, and then he smiled as he put the knife down out of Kathy Harmon's reach, used an outstretched foot to pull the portable computer in close, turned it on, pressed several keys, stared at the flickering screen, and then smiled again.

"It's all there, right?" Culver said, wanting Russelli and Digger to hurry now because his hands were starting to tremble again, and he didn't know how much longer he could hold out.

Digger nodded. "Yes, it's all there." Then he used the hilt of his knife to smash the screen and keyboard of the portable computer—the one that he'd stolen from Alberto Paz just before Gauss stole it from him.

"What are you doing?" Culver demanded.

"I changed the codes again, so I don't need it now. You can have it."

Culver started to say something, but then he was interrupted by the voice on the overhead speaker.

"Henry?"

"Hi, Traynor, I thought you went AWOL on me."

Henry Culver watched several of the men stare at the radio with varying degrees of shock. Only Lt. Col. Charles L'Que seemed to be disinterested in the radio. He was standing next to one of the trees with his eyes fixed on Elliott Parkinson. From what Culver could see, it seemed likely that the surrounding bodyguards were the only thing keeping L'Que from going after the visibly nervous but still smiling associate director.

"Where are you, Henry?"

"Tunnels under the house . . ." Culver started to say when Craven grabbed the radio out of Traynor's hand.

"Culver, is that you?" he demanded.

"That's right," Culver answered, and then discovered that he had to hold himself up to keep from falling out of the chair.

Gotta get this going.

He realized that Craven was giving him some sort of order, but he'd missed the first part and it really didn't matter anyway. Not now.

"Craven," he said when the flustered lieutenant stopped to take a breath, "I don't know what you've got to do with the CIA, but I understand you tore up that ankle *real* bad, so that probably puts you in the same retirement category as Russelli now, right?"

"Culver, you . . ."

"SHUT UP!" Culver yelled as loud as he could, and then let his voice drop back down to a raspy whisper. "Craven, listen to me. I've got Digger down here, and I've lost a lot of blood, and he's got Russelli's kids blocked off and another hostage, and Russelli's trying to take the house apart over our heads to get to them. So would you kindly shut up and give the radio back to Traynor."

Craven was still staring at the pack set radio when Stewart peeled it out of his hand and brought it up to his mouth.

"Henry, this is Al. What's this crap about letting Digger run?"

"Have to, only way I can get his hostage loose. He says he'll meet with that asshole in the three-piece suit standing next to you, but nobody else. Gotta keep it cool because he's got a transmitter and he'll blow the tunnels if anybody gives him any shit. Gotta keep everybody else back—and watch out," Culver suddenly remembered, "those guy's have a shooter on the north side in a blue pickup."

Culver watched Elliott Parkinson's face break out into a broad smile, but he forced himself to ignore that and concentrate on what he had to do to keep Kathy Harmon alive.

"All right, Henry." Stewart nodded after a few moments. "Go ahead and let him go. We've got a few questions about jurisdiction to be worked out around here, but we'll deal with that later," he added in a voice tight with barely restrained anger.

"But the guy in the pickup . . ." Culver started in when Stewart interrupted.

"Forget the guy in the pickup. Colonel L'Que already took care of that little detail for us," Stewart said as Elliott Parkinson's smile suddenly disappeared.

Culver looked up at the bank of monitors and saw that the familiar blue pickup was still parked next to Kathy Harmon's house, only now there appeared to be three tightly spaced bullet holes in the driver's side windshield, and instead of a thick, dark-skinned arm, a portion of a Jeep Cherokee was now visible in the foreground.

"What about Carp?"

"We've got him en route to Fair Oaks. He'll be okay."

Thank God, Culver smiled. Then he hesitated.

"Hey, Al?"

"Yes?"

"Can you see if L'Que has another set of keys for his Bronco."

Homicide Sergeant Al Stewart turned to the French military officer for a moment and then came back on the air.

"He does."

"Okay, ask him if he'll move the Bronco over by that shed at the other end of the driveway. That's where Digger'll be coming out. Oh, and one more thing," he added, barely able to talk now, "tell L'Que, if Digger runs that thing into any rocks around here, I'll buy him a new one."

"A new . . . ?" Stewart started to say, but then another much louder voice broke in.

"Culver, you are not to release him! Do you understand? That man is my prisoner!"

Lieutenant Morris Markham Craven had hobbled over on his crutches to grab a radio mike out from one of the police cruisers.

"Traynor," Culver whispered into the microphone again, having to hold his head up to steady himself, "you and Carpenter were right, I make a lousy cop. You still want me back?"

Culver watched the video monitor as Arthur Traynor took the pack set radio from Stewart and held it up to the side of his face.

"Certainly," Traynor replied. "When would you like to be reinstated?"

"Culver, I'm giving you a direct order!"

"How about right now?"

"Fine. Would you like me to inform your lieutenant that you've resigned?"

"Why don't you just tell him that he's interfering with a federal investigation, and that if he keeps it up, I'm going to file charges with his boss when I get out of here."

"Message understood. Welcome home, Henry."

Culver blinked his eyes, trying to keep it all straight in his head. But then he finally gave up, not wanting to think about it anymore.

Come on, just do it. Get it over with.

"Okay, Traynor," he whispered, "I'm going to send him out. You sure everybody's under control out there?"

"Everything is fine at this end, Henry. Are you certain about yours?"

"Yeah, I'm sure."

"All right then, we'll be waiting."

Culver turned off the microphone and then rolled the chair out to where he had a clear view of Digger.

"You heard it all," Culver said. "Everything's balanced. It's strictly up to you and Parkinson now."

He could see from the expression in Digger's eyes that he was still hesitant and distrustful, so he went on:

"I figure you've got maybe two or three minutes before Russelli digs his way down to this room," he said calmly. "Once that happens, God help you, because you're on your own—I can't stop him."

Stop him? Shit, I can't even stand up.

"I don't . . ."

"Come on, Digger, you're supposed to be so goddamned

smart. Figure it out. You're a federal case, so the cops can't touch you. And Parkinson can't do anything to you either because the cops are watching. You've got one shot out of here. You want it, you'd better take it *now.*"

Moments later, John Doe Thirty-three was pulling himself into the tunnel, leaving his smashed portable computer on the floor, and Kathy Harmon was scrambling over behind Culver.

He waited about five seconds, until he was sure that Digger was moving, then he hissed, "Quick, somebody shut that tunnel grate, bring me that computer, get Bear in here, *and find me a screwdriver, fast!*"

Culver rolled the chair over to the computer table as quickly as he could while the three young women secured the grate, released Bear—who immediately lunged for the closed grate where Digger had disappeared—and then found the screwdriver.

He'll have another antenna up there somewhere to pick up the signal. Only way he could protect this place. But he'll have to be outside that tunnel to reach it, Culver thought as he fumbled with the case of the shattered desktop computer.

"Martine, watch monitor number eleven," he whispered. "It's aimed at the tunnel exit by the Bronco. Tell me as soon as he comes out. Kathy, Michelle, help me with this."

He had found the arming and detonation switches, and the connecting antenna, in the desktop computer and disabled the entire system in a matter of seconds. He wanted to do both of them himself, to be absolutely sure; but the portable was more complex, and he was too weak from the loss of blood, and they were fast, terrified, and sure-handed, so he directed them through every step, trying to hurry.

"Uncle Henry, there he is, he's coming out!" Martine Russelli yelled.

"Okay, there's the detonation switch, the red one, disconnect it now!" Culver directed with a trembling hand.

"I can't it won't come loose," Michelle Russelli gasped, her face reddened by her efforts.

"Use the screwdriver and rip it loose!" Culver ordered, and then watched numbly as the veins in Michelle Russelli's arm bulged . . . and then the plastic part snapped loose and Culver breathed a sigh of relief as he turned his attention to the screen.

Using the control knobs, Culver zoomed the camera in on Digger, watching closely as he staggered toward the driver's side door of the Bronco—where Elliott Parkinson and the youthful Forecastle were waiting for him—with the album clutched tightly in his one functional arm.

Standing off to the side, apart from all of the others, Lt. Col. Charles L'Que watched the entire scene with a look on his solemn face that Culver couldn't even begin to interpret.

"It's okay, Colonel," Culver whispered. "Trust me."

Then he watched as Digger handed Parkinson the transmitter, pointed back at the house, and then scrambled into the front passenger seat of the Bronco.

Okay, Topcastle, so what are you going to do now?

Culver continued to watch as the still-smiling three-piece-suited bureaucrat got into the driver's seat, shut the door, waited until his youthful assistant worked his way into the back seat, auto-locked the doors and windows, and then started up the vehicle.

"My God, they're just letting him drive away," Kathy Harmon whispered at his shoulder, but Culver ignored her, focusing his complete attention on the driver's side of the Bronco—the side that no one else in the front of Digger's yard could see.

Then, moments later, a manicured hand stuck the transmitter out the driver's side window and aimed it toward the house.

Kathy Harmon and the two girls jumped when the single intact arming relay switch in the computer they had been taking apart closed with a loud "SNAP!" but Culver's attention was still focused on the Bronco, and he never moved a muscle.

He heard a crashing sound of splintering wood, falling

rocks, and the grunting sound of a heavy body landing on the ground behind him, and John Russelli's raging voice as his daughters screamed "POP!" and ran to him. But Culver kept his eyes on the screen, even when his furiously protective longtime partner and childhood friend staggered up beside him with both of his daughters clutched tightly in his dirt-covered arms and snarled up at the monitor:

"Goddamn it, Henry, you let the bastard get away!"

"No I didn't," Culver said weakly as the video image of John Doe Thirty-three suddenly spun around in the front seat and stared into the back storage compartment of the Bronco, searching for the source of the all-too-familiar "SNAP!" sound of an arming relay switch. Then he saw Molly Hunsacker's portable computer.

As Culver continued to watch in silent fascination, Digger shoved the youthful Forecastle aside, scrambled across the back seat and grabbed for the computer, seemingly trying to pry the case open with his one hand.

Then, apparently remembering the time factors, he started to throw the small computer out the window, discovered that the doors and windows on his side were locked, twisted back around and lunged toward Elliott Parkinson, a.k.a. Topcastle, who was still pointing the transmitter—the one set to AUTO SCAN FAST that Bobby Morgan had once used to open Colonel L'Que's garage door, and then left there for the military officer to find and give to Henry Culver—in the direction of Digger's house, waiting impatiently for something to happen . . . and found himself tangled once again in Forecastle's frantically waving arms.

But by then it was much too late, and the Bronco disappeared in a roaring ball of fire that sent debris flying in all directions—Traynor, Craven, Stewart, and all of the others except the now-smiling Lt. Col. Charles L'Que diving to the ground—as Henry Culver slowly removed the transmitter he'd grabbed away from Digger out of the deep left side pocket of his thin nylon patrol jacket and set it on the table.

"I cheated."